The letters in *rearguard* sparkled before rearranging themselves into something different, which was now firmly displayed in the job field.

D1622813

"Huh...?" Louisa appeared to be at a loss for words.

Date: 3/9/20

GRA TOWA
Tôwa,
The world's strongest rearguard. Labyrinth

REARGUARD

The WORLD'S STRONGEST REARGUARD | Labyrinth Country's Novice Seeker

"Wha...?"

I steadied my hand as I inserted the key into the hole in the girl's chest. It felt like it clicked into place when I pushed it all the way in—and then, the girl began to tremble slightly.

The WORLD'S STRONGEST REARGUARD
Labyrinth Country's Novice Seeker

1

Tôwa

Illustration by
Huuka Kazabana

Translation by Jordan Taylor
Cover art by Huuka Kazabana

This book is a work of fiction. Names, characters, places, and incidents are the product of the author's imagination or are used fictitiously. Any resemblance to actual events, locales, or persons, living or dead, is coincidental.

SEKAI SAIKYO NO KOEI -MEIKYUKOKU NO SHINJIN TANSAKUSHA- Volume 1
©Tôwa, Huuka Kazabana 2017
First published in Japan in 2017 by KADOKAWA CORPORATION, Tokyo.
English translation rights arranged with KADOKAWA CORPORATION, Tokyo, through
TUTTLE-MORI AGENCY, INC., Tokyo.

Yen On
150 West 30th Street, 19th Floor
New York, NY 10001

Visit us at yenpress.com
facebook.com/yenpress
twitter.com/yenpress
yenpress.tumblr.com
instagram.com/yenpress

First Yen On Edition: October 2019

Yen On is an imprint of Yen Press, LLC.
The Yen On name and logo are trademarks of Yen Press, LLC.

The publisher is not responsible for websites (or their content) that are not owned by the publisher.

Library of Congress Cataloging-in-Publication Data
Names: Tôwa, author. | Kazabana, Huuka, illustrator. | Taylor, Jordan (Translator), translator.
Title: The world's strongest rearguard: labyrinth country's novice seeker / Tôwa ; illustration by
    Huuka Kazabana ; translation by Jordan Taylor.
Other titles: Sekai saikyo no koei: meikyukoku no shinjin tansakusha. English
Description: First Yen On edition. | New York, NY : Yen ON, 2019– |
Identifiers: LCCN 2019030466 | ISBN 9781975331542 (v. 1 ; trade paperback)
Subjects: CYAC: Fantasy. | Future life—Fiction.
Classification: LCC PZ7.1.T676 Wo 2019 | DDC [Fic]—dc23
LC record available at https://lccn.loc.gov/2019030466

ISBNs: 978-1-9753-3154-2 (paperback)
       978-1-9753-3155-9 (ebook)

10 9 8 7 6 5 4 3 2 1

LSC-C

Printed in the United States of America

CONTENTS

In Line for Reincarnation

All of a sudden, I realized I was in a long, dimly lit tunnel, standing in a line with an assortment of people: men and women, young and old. I'd been trying to get some sleep on the overnight bus en route to my company's ski trip. I didn't remember getting off the bus, so suddenly being in an unfamiliar place seemed, well, not so great.

Somewhere in the line people were saying things like, "Seriously?" and "Just reincarnate me already!" A woman farther up was handling the questions and guiding everyone. She seemed used to the work and kept things moving like some sort of assembly line in a manufacturing plant.

Does that mean the bus was in an accident...? Everyone here... died?

Was heaven at the end of this line? I was relieved to learn there really was some sort of afterlife, that it wasn't just nothingness. I hadn't considered that I might die, and there was still so much I wanted to do.

But this tunnel might just as easily lead to hell, so I guess I shouldn't get too comfortable yet.

There was also a chance I was just dreaming; maybe I was getting ahead of myself by considering all these serious possibilities. I didn't see my coworker who was on the trip with me, either. He'd said he was getting married soon, so if he did indeed survive, then I guess those so-called death flags weren't all that effective. I was glad, but if the bus happened to crash in the snowy mountains, then it'd be really rough waiting for rescue to come. *Hope he doesn't get frostbite or anything.*

There had to be someone here from my company who'd been going on the trip like me. I tried to get out of line to look, but my feet wouldn't move. I could only keep moving forward. There was no way for me to see if I recognized anyone.

Is that...is that Igarashi? Did she die, too...?

You could call her my sworn nemesis. She was my manager. I thought I could see her a little ways ahead in the line. It had to be her; that woman had the same long, shiny hair with brown highlights.

At twenty-five, she was four years younger than me, but she already had this uppity businesswoman air to her. There were quite a few of my male coworkers who were totally taken by her strong character, but she was my immediate superior. Emphasis on the *superior* part.

However, it seemed like not even she could get out of this situation. She was just filing obediently forward like me, but I still felt that overwhelming presence of hers. Being behind her didn't make it any less overwhelming.

There was a girl in front of me who seemed like a high schooler.

She had reached the person who was managing the queue while I was thinking, and she took something from her. The guide then pointed toward the light ahead, and the girl walked forward. I'd seen that girl when I was getting on the bus. Her hair was so black, it practically disappeared before my very eyes. She seemed like the traditional Japanese beauty, but she had a friend with her who was a bit more girlie, and— Actually, now probably wasn't the time to think about that.

Before me stood a woman whose clothes looked like they came right out of a fantasy game. Her seemingly natural purple hair was just long enough to brush her shoulders. She dressed relatively casually: a shirt with half-length sleeves and one of those skirt things that wasn't really a skirt. A skort? But longer. Anyway, it definitely wasn't the kind of thing you'd see in Japan. Her hat looked similar to a beret, but it had some detailed crest on it. Her whole ensemble gave me a magic user vibe.

The girl was handing something to the people in line and sending them on ahead. She looked calm and had kind eyes, but her voice was clear and energetic. She left me with a good impression.

"Next, please. Here, take this," she said. "Go straight ahead, and the first thing you'll need to do is go to the Guild and choose your job. You may not take any detours."

"Guild? Hold on, what exactly is up that way?" I asked.

"Ahead is the Labyrinth Country, where your souls have been collected for reincarnation. I'm afraid you cannot choose to be reincarnated somewhere else," she replied. There were so many other questions I wanted to ask, but it didn't seem like I'd be getting much more of an explanation. She did explain one other thing, however. "You'll be starting your new life as a Seeker in the Labyrinth Country. I also live in the town ahead when I'm not guiding the reincarnates, so we may meet there someday."

So there wasn't a god or angels ahead. She made it sound like I did have some sort of special power, but I guess I'd have to wait to learn about that. I took the sheet she offered—it wasn't really paper, more like a sturdy card made of leather—and headed toward the light in front of me.

CHAPTER 1

The Start of My Life as a Seeker

Part I: The Labyrinth Country

The Labyrinth Country was where Seekers, the people who explored the labyrinths, and those who supported them lived. Basically, everything revolved around the labyrinths. There were quite a few entrances scattered around town, with each labyrinth ranked according to the difficulty of the monsters inside.

Apparently, there were about thirty of us new reincarnates this time. An accident of this scale would probably be big news. Thankfully, I didn't have a wife or kids who would miss me. There were a few people who I knew would grieve, and I felt bad that they'd have to handle my funeral and stuff, but there wasn't really anything I could do about it. I had to focus on how I was going to live in this world.

The other reincarnates and I appeared in the town in various places after emerging from the tunnel, but as we all gathered at the Guild as we were told, I was able to talk to them and learn a few things. When we were being reincarnated, the girl in the tunnel didn't give us any choice about becoming one of these Seekers, but none of us had any desire to resist. None of us thought about trying to escape instead of going to the Guild. The reason being that it sounded like there wasn't much you could do in this Labyrinth Country if you didn't first become a Seeker. It didn't sound too bad to me anyway, though I had no basis for feeling so optimistic.

When I came out of the tunnel, I found myself in an open square near the Guild. I didn't get lost on my way, but I wasn't the first there, either. The Guild building was large and conspicuous. A few reincarnates had already finished registering as Seekers and were about to head off on their first adventure.

"Hey, you're new, right? If you're going solo, you should stick to the one-star beginner labyrinths. You'll be a goner in no time if you go into anything with two or more stars," one of the Guild veterans cautioned.

"A g-goner? You can't be serious...," replied the newbie, a man in prime physical condition who looked to be in his thirties. The warning sounded genuine, so it didn't seem like newbies got such bad treatment.

"You don't wanna get shot down by a goblin, do ya? They're pretty hostile creatures. Goblins'll just come right up and attack us, so we just fight back, no questions asked. It's all over if you take a hit from one of their arrows. They're covered in shit and filthy as all hell. Even poisoned arrows would be overkill on a novice like yourself," continued the veteran.

"Urgh... R-right. Then I'll go to the beginner labyrinth..."

"Good choice. You know, I've already gotten my daily pay, so I could show you around. Don't worry, we'll split what we make."

"Oh, thank you!"

I didn't know how much of the exchange was out of pure goodwill or if there were Seekers who made a living by showing around the newbies.

I hoped the new guy would be all right, then I suddenly had an idea. Wouldn't it be cool if I got the other new reincarnates—my former coworkers—to join a party with me? That said, apparently there were quite a few who thought it'd be a good idea to join more experienced Seekers. A bunch of parties were inviting the newbies to come along. The girl who'd been in front of me in line was among those still unaffiliated with a party. At first, I thought her friend was in the same boat, but it turned out she'd actually been invited into one already. I stood there wondering what kind of person would abandon their friend like that, but the black-haired girl didn't seem bothered. In fact, it was almost as if she'd expected as much.

I wanted to join a party soon and make some friends. Maybe then I'd feel a bit better. I wanted to invite the black-haired girl, tell her we could work together since we came from the same world, but I didn't get the chance.

"Ms. Suzuna Shiromiya, thank you for registering. You requested Shrine Maiden as your job, yes? Congratulations, you have been accepted. We have determined you meet all the requirements," said the Guild registrar.

"Th-thank you so much..."

Suzuna… I wonder what characters she uses to write her name.

The registrar wrote Suzuna's desired job on the card she'd been carrying from earlier. Apparently, you could opt for a specific job class if you happened to meet the requirements.

Suddenly, a dashing young Swordswoman about Suzuna's age approached the newly minted Shrine Maiden. She wore a silver breastplate over a blue padded doublet. Her golden hair was pulled back behind her, her almond-shaped eyes sharp and clear. She was the kind of girl who'd turn heads even from a distance. The people milling around who were about to depart on an adventure also ceased their chatter to focus on her every move.

"…Do you have a moment?" she asked Suzuna.

"Oh, y-yes… What is it? I only just got here…"

"I know that. Only new reincarnates come here to register."

Suzuna seemed nervous as the girl started talking to her. The gold-haired Swordswoman's voice was soft, but it carried far through the hush that'd fallen over the Guild.

"I'm looking for a rearguard… There's a few downsides to having me as a vanguard, and I have a tough time getting beginners to join me…b-but, if you join my party, I'm sure you'll level up quickly…," said the gold-haired girl. The armor and longsword strapped to her hip for easy access made her appear fairly experienced despite her casual attire. And yet, for some reason, she didn't have anyone to form a party with and was trying desperately to convince Suzuna to join hers.

"Elitia's still trying to get people to join her. How many days straight is this now?"

"Doesn't matter how strong she is, she's not gonna find anyone as long as she's got *that*."

Some men were making fun of the girl, whose name was apparently Elitia. She ignored them but cast her gaze downward and clenched her fists. It seemed she was known around the Guild. I would've imagined a gorgeous, formidable Swordswoman like her would have plenty of companions, but it appeared there was a reason why that wasn't the case. I glanced at Suzuna, wondering what she would do. She did seem to notice the trash-talking, but she reached out to the downcast Elitia and took her clenched fist in her hand.

"It would be my pleasure. I'm still just a novice, but I'll do the best I can as a rearguard," said Suzuna.

"Oh... R-really? Y-you're sure...?"

"I actually wanted to join my friend, but she went with someone else... You've really lifted my spirits. Even if you have 'a few downsides,' I'd really like to join your party."

"...Thank you. My name is Elitia Centrale. And you are?"

"I'm Shiromiya... No, Suzuna Shiromiya."

The two seemed to click and left the Guild together. There were still some people who were looking at them condescendingly, so whatever the "that" Elitia had was, it must have been pretty serious.

It piqued my curiosity, but my first priority was choosing a job. I looked toward the registration counter to see another man, a reincarnate like me, having a disagreement with the registrar.

"I am incredibly sorry, but it appears you aren't fit to be a Holy

Knight as you requested. It does seem you would be well suited as a Warrior, Thief, or Martial Artist, however..."

"But I want something more heroic! C'mon, just change my job already!" shouted the man, his loud voice a match for his rugged body as he chewed out the registrar.

It didn't last long, though—the registrar must have taken it as a threat, because several armed soldier types approached and grabbed the man.

"Whoa, wh-what the hell?! Let go of me! I just thought she could help me out—!"

"Unfortunately, your actions have been deemed a threat to the Labyrinth Country. Your *karma* has risen, and you will be subjected to mandatory prison labor until it returns to zero."

"Wha—?! S-stoppp! Let me go! I'm sorry! I'll apologize right n— Aaaggghh!"

I didn't need reminding that this guy was reincarnated at the same time as me, so I took this as a good lesson of what not to do and warned myself to keep order in the Guild building. It did sound like he'd be released from prison once this karma stuff had gotten back to zero, so this didn't seem like the kind of thing you could never come back from. Probably.

Anyway, I just wanted to get my job sorted out without any major issues and make the necessary preparations to take it easy. I probably wouldn't be able to secure a comfortable life in this world until I'd found a way to make a living.

Part II: The Guild Registrar and My Former Boss

"Hello, sir. I see you have a registration card. You will not be allowed to enter the labyrinth until you've completed your registration as a Seeker," the registrar informed me. She was the same person who'd registered Suzuna as a Shrine Maiden earlier.

"Ah, right... Sorry about that. I was just distracted by the commotion."

The registrar looked otherworldly with greenish hair, glasses, and a small mole under one eye. She was an incredibly attractive young woman. And...her boobs were massive. They filled her registrar's uniform to the point that I just couldn't manage to keep my eyes off them.

"Ah... Now, now, sir. I understand the attire of a different world may be more revealing than what you're used to, but depending on your relationship with the person, staring might result in increased karma. Please adjust your gaze accordingly."

"...I-I'm so sorry."

"Ha-ha... How polite of you, sir, apologizing right from the beginning. Now, please relax. I won't bite," the registrar said reassuringly. Her kindness really struck me.

I found pretty much any hairstyle attractive, but as I was particularly drawn to hair that was pulled up, I was aware that this honest and kind registrar lady was pretty much my exact type.

"I apologize for not introducing myself sooner. My name is Louisa Farmel. I am responsible for your registration process and will be available to answer any questions you may have as a novice Seeker. I can assign you a different registrar, or are you happy to continue with the current arrangement?"

"Y-yes… Looks like I'm still a bit nervous. Yes, please continue."

Back before I got reincarnated, I had to work with a lot of outside companies for my job. I found things went more smoothly if you responded to the other person with the same level of familiarity. Business relationships required collaboration, and being overly formal could hinder that, but—

"Ow…"

"S-sir? Oh, your memories must be quite mixed-up since you've only just been reincarnated. I'm sorry for talking to you so much at once. Would you like me to summon a Healer for you?"

"Oh, no. I'm fine. I just have a bit of a headache." Truthfully, I had just remembered something particularly unpleasant.

Last spring, I had been transferred from the Web Content Creation Department to the Media Strategy Department. Not only was I in a completely different department, my entire career path had changed, too. I'd been told I would still be making websites, but that wasn't really the case. Since I'd been working in media for a while, I ended up becoming assistant manager. And of course, the department manager for the newly formed "Second Media Strategy Department" was Igarashi. She was only twenty-four years old at the time, the youngest department manager in company history. That made her a pretty big deal.

She was an incredible beauty; I couldn't even think of words to describe her. She was so beautiful that she stood out in a crowd like she was some A-list celebrity, and she had a fashion sense to rival any pinup fashionista, so I'd originally fostered some weird hopes for how things would turn out. Anyway, after meeting her and spending about half a day with her, I realized she wasn't a young, sexy manager. She was a brutal, manipulative higher-up.

Even after I'd been transferred, I was still helping my former department. No one seemed to take that into consideration, however, so between that and the assistant manager gig, I ended up doing two employees' worth of work. Of course, my salary didn't go up, either.

At first, I thought I could do my work as assistant manager and help with any leftover tasks in my former department if I had some time. That didn't go so well. I don't know if Igarashi was just asking for too much or what, but my work as assistant manager just kept snowballing as if she was trying to prevent me from running away. I mean, sure, someone needed to gather data and prep for meetings, but with meetings all day every day, I was constantly running on all four cylinders. It felt like Igarashi was testing my limits. As a result, I had to focus on only my assistant manager duties during the day, and any work for the other department had to be pushed to overtime.

I'm not a particularly ambitious kind of guy. I was pretty happy doing routine tasks daily, so I couldn't get behind Igarashi's mind-set of doing something new all the time. But she seemed to think that as assistant manager, I must've shared her ambitions. One day, she said to me:

"Someone as talented as you, Atobe, will be able to do so much and get so far as my assistant."

There's a huge difference between taking that as her burdening me with unreasonable demands or just her own sky-high expectations. Personally, I couldn't bring myself to tell her I was already overwhelmed by work and to stop asking me to do the impossible.

Meanwhile, in the other department, people joked that the manager had a thing for me, but I didn't have time to think about that. I mean, she probably did, but only in the sense that as her assistant manager I was readily available.

Since I was so incredibly busy, I didn't have time to study or work on the things I needed to in order to advance in my career. I never told her as much, but she said to me:

"Atobe, if you never get promoted, then you can stay and help me as my assistant."

I doubt she meant it in a bad way, but I couldn't help thinking she actually did. It all came rushing back to me in an instant when I thought about my miserable life as a corporate slave.

Since arriving in this new world, I no longer had to be pinned under the thumb of some manager I didn't like. I'd been freed from my corporate shackles. The realization lifted an enormous weight off my very spirit.

"Good, I see you're feeling better," said Louisa.

"Yes, thanks to you. Okay, so how do I go about registering?"

"Please have a seat. On your Seeker's license, there should be an empty job field. In that field, please write the name of a job you feel you are suited for or that you would like to try out."

"Got it. So I won't be selecting from a set list of jobs."

"Correct. That's because reincarnates come with such a wide

variety of experiences. Some opt for jobs that we might not understand ourselves. Since we haven't received their permission to make their jobs public, I cannot provide you with information regarding others' choices."

That means Suzuna's Shrine Maiden job was public, which is why Elitia and I heard about it. In that moment, I realized the competition between Seekers began now, at registration. And even though I hadn't gone into the labyrinths yet, I'd gotten some form of explanation as to why I needed to. Basically, since the labyrinths clearly supported all these Seekers and the corresponding infrastructure, becoming a Seeker came with some sort of appropriate compensation.

If I could choose an important job, that'd give me a running start. The issue was my lack of any specialized experience. In my previous life, I'd been in management for a marketing firm, so I could make business plans, presentation materials, even do a bit of desktop publishing–type stuff. But otherwise, I didn't have any skills. The only other thing I could think of was my middling English skills, something that had helped me get the job in the first place.

Louisa didn't rush me along and instead assisted other reincarnates. As this was a decision that would determine my life here, she seemed to be giving me plenty of time to consider it, but I really just wanted to pick something as soon as possible and start trying out this whole seeking thing. Most of the other reincarnates had already completed this step and were moving on in the process.

"Hey, Atobe. What job did you pick?" came a voice.

"Huh… Ack, Ms. Igarashi!"

"H-hey… What d'you mean, *ack*? I just thought I'd say hi, since I actually found someone I recognize."

I turned around to see a headstrong woman with wavy brown hair—Kyouka Igarashi. I'd had advanced warning since I'd seen her while in the line for reincarnation, but I couldn't help letting out a yelp when she came up to me. She was on the same ski trip we got with our employee discount. Not that we were going together; we just happened to be on the company trip. Anyway, it was probably safe to assume she'd been in the bus accident, too.

"What are you staring at? …Are you so in shock from getting reincarnated that you forgot who I am?"

"Uh, no, that's not it… I was just thinking, *Wow, that's Ms. Igarashi.*"

"Hmm? Guess you're not that shaken up after all."

Even though we'd arrived in the Labyrinth Country, we were still wearing the same clothes as before. Igarashi's outfit looked familiar. It was something fashionable enough to be in a magazine but still well suited for the office. She had on a warm-colored knit sweater, the kind with the knitting lines running up and down. She looked pretty much the same as she would at work except for the thick tights for warmth. Her figure was still well proportioned, as always, but acknowledging that would have been an affront to her demonic, sharp-tongued nature.

Anyway, my evil boss looked no different from usual. I was pretty pathetic and couldn't keep a cold sweat from appearing on my brow, and I felt nervous even though she'd barely said anything to me.

"Looks like you didn't hear me the first time, so I'll ask again. Atobe, what job did you pick? I assume it wasn't web designer."

"W-well, no, I doubt that would be of much use in an alternate world. I'm actually still thinking about what to choose."

"Quit dillydallying; just hurry up and pick. Once you do, I'll consider letting you form a party with me."

Her phrasing could've used some work, but she probably meant I could join her party. Not that I was all that jazzed about it.

"Geez, why'd this have to happen…all of us dying at once?" Igarashi grumbled.

"I've been wondering if the bus was in an accident and we were all reincarnated, except for the people who are still alive."

"In that case, our entire department might not be totally gone. I hope the people left can manage without us… Well, I guess this really isn't the place to worry about that. Anyway, if the bus driver happens to be here, too, I'll have to give him a piece of my mind."

"This is truly an awful situation. Take care of yourself," I replied in the hopes we'd wrap this up so I could get out of there, but she glowered at me. Personally, I wasn't that crazy about getting the silent treatment from a woman. It really sucked, to be honest.

"You ought to take care, too, Atobe. This world's labyrinths are full of monsters. You have to pick the proper job class."

"Y-yeah. I'll pick something," I said, trying to give a safe answer, but Igarashi just seemed to get more annoyed.

"No, not just 'something.' If you'd just tell me you'll pick a job I can depend on..."

"Uh... What were you saying just now?"

"...N-nothing. I g-guess I'll just see you around. Don't ruin my day by getting yourself killed."

"Uh, yeah...I'll figure something out... Oh, Ms. Igarashi!"

"I'm not your manager here, you don't have to call me *Ms.* But I guess it'd feel weird if you just called me by my given name...so you can go with that. Anyway, what do you need?"

"Uh, um...if you don't mind, could you tell me what job you chose?"

Knowing her, she wasn't exactly the kind to reveal her hand to me. I wouldn't have been too surprised if she'd gotten angry at me for asking.

"Are you asking to get some ideas?" Her reaction was much gentler than I had expected. There was a high probability of stepping on a land mine now, though, so I needed to choose my words very carefully.

"Y-yes. I'm really not sure what I should pick."

"Hmph, anyone could tell that just by looking at you. You shouldn't pick the same as me, though. It'd be better if you picked something that shared responsibilities. We'd have problems if you picked some sort of fighter job."

"Oh, but I thought a party made up of all fighters would be pretty strong..."

"Are you saying I'm wrong?"

"Uh…no, not at all," I stammered, all nerves. I wasn't very good with women, so it felt like I was walking on eggshells. The two of us just didn't really get along anyway.

Hmm…Igarashi said something about sharing responsibilities. If she's thinking she wants to join a party with me…

"Well, I decided to go with Valkyrie as my job. I can use swords and spears and apparently some spirit magic."

"W-wow… That sounds amazing."

"It just popped into my head, so I tried writing it down. I thought it'd be hard for me to stay alive if I didn't pick something with a variety of skills. Does that help you decide?"

"Yes, thanks a lot. I'll try choosing something that can share responsibilities in a party and handle a variety of different situations."

"…That's it?"

"W-well, I mean, Valkyrie sounds like it's for women, so I'll have to think of something else…"

Igarashi had her arms crossed the entire time I was talking, her finger tapping impatiently. My mind was racing, but I just couldn't think of the right thing to say.

"Right, so I will do everything I can to stay alive, and I hope you stay well and we meet again and…," I said.

"*Sigh…* Why can't you see where this conversation is going?"

"Uh… Did you just—?" I started to ask, but Igarashi glared at me. That look rendered me completely powerless. I wish I was the kind of guy who could keep his cool under a beautiful woman's gaze.

"Never mind. I hope we meet again, too. I'm gonna go over there and try to find a party to join."

"Y-yeah. I'll try to find something, too. Take care, Igarashi." I was more concerned for her safety than I was about her control over me in our previous world now that we were both new reincarnates. And I couldn't keep worrying about other people all the time.

Igarashi suddenly hurried back to me as I got lost in thought. It seemed like she'd forgotten to say something, but since she looked angry, I prepared myself for the worst.

"...Just remember—next time we meet, it'll be too late for you to say you regret this."

"Huh...? I-Igarashi—!" I called, but she zipped out of the Guild without so much as a glance back. She said she was going to find a party to join, but I wondered if she'd actually decided to find one on her way to the labyrinth.

If she tries to enter the labyrinth on her own... No, I'm worried, but if I offer to go along with her... Well, it's Igarashi. She'll be fine anyway.

It was hard to break out of the roles of superior and subordinate even outside of the shackles of corporate work. I'd thought I'd been liberated from it all, but things were the same as before. It looked like I was back to square one.

If only I could just throw off those chains. Igarashi was a Valkyrie now, and I knew she was strong-willed. If possible, I'd want to form a party with her.

Part III: Job Selection

"Was that your manager from your previous world? That must be tough," said Louisa with a bright smile. I'm sure she treated every Seeker who came to the Guild with such kindness, but it made me feel better.

Ever since I was a kid, I'd never been popular with girls. I hadn't had many opportunities to meet women outside of committees or work, either. It made me happy if a woman was just nice to me, which even I thought was pretty simple-minded.

"Now that you've come to the Labyrinth Country, your status as a Seeker is determined only by your achievements. That's why I want to help you pick a job you won't regret."

All I needed were achievements. If I could accomplish that much, then maybe Igarashi would come to see me in a better light.

No, that wasn't a good goal. I should aim as high as I possibly could. In my old world, the only way I could've ever gotten to the top would have been if I quit my job and started my own business, became my own boss. That didn't seem to be the case here.

"Louisa, what kinds of achievements do I need to be considered?"

"Well...first, you'll need to climb higher in the Seeker ranking. New Seekers aren't even put in the rankings yet, but as you do more, the rank on your license will change." Louisa pointed to my license. She traced the characters shown in the top left, and the displayed information changed.

So can this be used like some sort of miniature tablet? If so, I should be able to get the hang of it quickly.

"This page shows a record of your work in the labyrinth. There's nothing in here at the moment, but your actions will be evaluated once you leave the labyrinth, and your new rank will be calculated. Please make sure that you don't enter the labyrinth and then leave immediately, or flee right after a single monster attack. The lowest ranks have to sleep in the barn or even the dungeon."

"…Well, I guess I'll at least aim for the barn."

"Your magic and vitality only recover a tiny bit in the barn, so your situation will likely just worsen. If you find yourself in such circumstances, please come to me with a request for assistance. You can't keep doing it over and over, but I can arrange accommodation for you."

It'd be wonderful if she meant she'd take me in, but I doubted I'd get that lucky.

"…Oh, will you need something immediately? It is difficult for me to arrange something on such short notice, so as an emergency arrangement, I could find something in my—"

"N-no, that's fine. I might not even mess up in the labyrinth yet," I said, turning her down in a bit of a panic. Maybe I should have let her go on. *No, if I let Louisa help me before I've done anything to end up the lowest in the ranking, there's a chance she'll doubt me in the future.*

"Louisa, can I ask you one last question? It seems a lot of people look for newcomers who are rearguards, like what that Elitia person mentioned. Is that correct?"

"Yes, rearguards are in high demand. They typically have lower physical strength and defense; they tend to have the lowest survival rates after five years, so the number of people in rearguard jobs has hit an all-time low. Vanguards are able to use better protective equipment, but rearguards tend to be lightly equipped. That means that a monster a vanguard can stand against could potentially kill a rearguard in one hit. It's a difference that's even more pronounced in newcomers who have weaker physical abilities," explained Louisa.

So that meant rearguards had a high chance of perishing in an accident while they were just starting out as Seekers and more likely to make newbie mistakes. But that's when your companions in vanguard or midguard roles weren't doing their job and an attack got past them to the rear.

"It's necessary to be part of a party if you want to try the high-rank labyrinths. For whatever reason, Elitia left her former party, and she tried to train up her own rearguard. However, I don't know any more about her situation beyond that, and I don't want to speculate."

"...I see."

So vanguards weren't enough on their own to take on too much, and rearguards were definitely not capable of acting solo. One way for me to make an ideal party would be if I became a rearguard, made it hard for me to die, and added lots of companions. But even among rearguards, what sort of job was I even suited for? I wasn't particularly religious, so a Priest wouldn't work. I also didn't have any skills like archery, which were suited to being in a rearguard position.

Eh, anything'll do, I guess. I just wanted to be a rearguard. If I wrote *rearguard*, then it'd automatically assign me to a job I was suited for.

"It looks like you've made your decision. Please use your finger to write on your license," said Louisa.

I steeled myself and wrote *rearguard* in the job field.

The next moment, the letters in *rearguard* sparkled before rearranging themselves into something different, which was now firmly displayed in the job field.

"Huh...?"

I felt relieved it was over, but Louisa appeared to be at a loss for words. I thought I'd heard an "Eh?" but that could've just been my imagination.

"Um, Louisa, the shape of the letters changed... I wrote *rearguard*, so shouldn't I have been put in some rearguard job?"

"Well, n-no, not necessarily... Whatever you wrote should have changed to something like Wizard, or Priest, or Marksman. But this..." She flipped my license toward her, took a monocle out of her pocket, and examined the letters as if she were appraising a piece of jewelry.

After a moment, she leaned far over the counter to speak directly into my ear. It seemed like she didn't want the people around to hear.

"I have never seen symbols like these before," she whispered.

"Um, you are…Arihito Atobe. What exactly did you write, Mr. Atobe?"

"Uh…um, as I said, I wrote *rearguard*." I managed to keep calm despite her whispered voice on my ear.

Louisa stepped back, compared the license against me once more, then apparently came to a decision.

"Congratulations, Mr. Atobe. You've been accepted into your desired profession," she said.

"W-wait a second. What exactly is the job I ended up with…?" I asked, slightly flustered.

For the second time, Louisa took care to lean across the counter to keep others from overhearing. This time I noticed her full breasts riding on the countertop, but I couldn't stare without risking my karma going up.

"W-well…your job is literally rearguard. But I don't think people will believe it even if you tell them, and some may even make fun of you. I am partly responsible, since I was the one providing you with advice, so I feel compelled to provide you some extra support. Please use these Mercenary Tickets so that you can better understand the strengths of your job," said Louisa, and she stuck her hand into her pouch-like sleeve and brought out a few slips of what looked like paper, then passed them to me while hiding them under her sleeve. "If you use these tickets, you'll be able to hire one mercenary for one expedition into a labyrinth. I say mercenary, but since these are only bronze-level tickets, you won't be able to hire any humans."

"By not human, you mean like…animals or something?"

"No. There are some animals that have been trained, but they only work with Animal Tamers. For special purpose hiring, there is the demi-human type monsters. The most dependable in my opinion are the lizardmen. Their base abilities for being a vanguard are excellent, so they tend to have fighter-type jobs."

It didn't seem like this whole being a rearguard thing was a total loss. With these bronze Mercenary Tickets, I'd be able to hire someone, even if once per ticket, but I could go into a beginner labyrinth. I could use this opportunity to learn about being a rearguard, find my strengths and weaknesses, and maybe figure out how I was going to survive here.

"I know I've just taken on this job, but do I have any skills or that sort of thing?"

"Yes, even rearguard jobs should be able to select two skills in the beginning. Since I've never seen your job before, though, I can't be absolutely certain...but if you turn the page of your license, you'll come to your skill set. Please select from the skills that are shown there. I cannot provide you with any advice in that selection process. Skills are a Seeker's lifeline, so in general, we don't show others what we have available."

"Okay...so it's only something I should share with companions who I trust enough."

"Exactly. If it's someone you trust to watch your back...or rather, watch your front, then you should let them know. Parties are about teamwork. You can't get strong if you don't work with other Seekers," she said, then clasped her hands together in front of her chest and closed her eyes. "...It is part of my duty as caseworker, but I will pray for your safe passage. May the Secret Gods smile upon you."

Yet again, our interactions just left me with more questions than answers. What were these "Secret Gods" she was talking about? Were they something the people in the Labyrinth Country worshipped? I decided it was fine to learn things little by little rather than asking about it all at once. Right now, I needed to focus on learning what exactly my job was.

Louisa took my license from me and drew a map to the Mercenary Office on it. I thanked her, then got up to leave. After standing from my seat, I moved by a wall where I wouldn't stand out and turned my license to the skills page.

```
◆Available Skills◆
Defense Support 1: Reduces injury to party
                   members in front by 10
                   points.
 Attack Support 1: Adds 10 injury points to
                   attacks made by party
                   members in front.
Recovery Support 1: Restores 5 vitality points
                   every 30 seconds for party
                   members in front.
        Rear View: Uses 5 magic points to
                   expand your vision to
                   cover your rear for a set
                   period of time.
Remaining Skill Points: 2
```

...How much is ten injury points?

I assumed injury points were like damage, but I couldn't find a way to make the license display damage. I guess I just had to feel how much ten points was. I had no idea how many vitality points I had, though.

If ten points was equal to someone flicking me in the forehead, then adding that wasn't exactly useful. I didn't want to have to do it, but I decided I just needed to hire a lizardman, have them take some damage from a weak enemy, and I'd try to gauge how much damage it was.

Seems like "Rear View" is a skill that lets the low vitality rearguard keep an eye on their own rear... Sounds useful, but I think to start, I'm gonna take "Defense Support 1," then maybe "Recovery Support 1" for healing once I've tested out Defense Support... Actually, maybe I'll hold off on healing.

There wasn't even any damage to heal yet, so it might have been a bit soon to be taking Recovery Support 1. I stood there unable to decide for a little while before putting one point into Defense Support 1. I wanted to also try out Attack Support 1, but I wanted to use my remaining skill point carefully.

I didn't notice any glaring changes as a result. The people around me probably had no way to know that I'd just taken a skill. I wouldn't know if I'd made a good choice or not until I put a party together. I double-checked I had the bronze Mercenary Tickets Louisa had given me, quietly readied myself, then left.

Part IV: Hiring a Mercenary

The Labyrinth Country appeared to be a fortified city encircled by an incredibly long wall. I had no idea how many entrances to the labyrinths there were inside the walls, but it didn't matter what direction you went, there was a wall there eventually and no way to get past it. Starting in the north, the Labyrinth Country was divided clockwise into eight districts, and the other reincarnates and I were in the eighth district. There were a few one-star beginner labyrinths in this area. I was headed for the nearest one called the Field of Dawn.

Louisa had drawn a map to a mercenary hiring office on my license, so I stopped by on my way to the labyrinth. It was near some facilities like the Monster Dissection Center and the Slave Market. When I tried to enter the Mercenary Office, a red-headed woman wearing an eyepatch came out to meet me.

"Hey, you're a novice, aren'tcha? You've got some backbone comin' here as a brand-new reincarnate," she barked at me.

"Is it that dangerous around here?" I asked.

"Nah, not really. But there's the occasional reincarnate who takes one glimpse at the Monster Dissection Center and gets so scared that he turns tail," the eyepatch lady scoffed. She came off as a sort of Amazon, carrying a sword and clad in tight-fitting leather armor that exposed her well-sculpted midriff.

"Hmm...I see you recognize the value of strong muscles. You may yet have some promise. The last thing a Seeker has to rely on is their own brawn. You'd do well to remember that."

"Ha-ha... Well, I'm not a vanguard, but I'm sure I could do with some physical training. Sitting at a desk all day has left me pretty flabby."

"Certainly, in your current state, even the small monsters that appear on the easy levels of the beginner labyrinths would be a threat to you. I'll give you one piece of advice. Avoid getting hit until you're at least level three. You could die in one hit if you're not careful."

The way she so casually used the word *die* sent a chill down my spine. I flipped through my license and found the page displaying my job and level. Below that there was a red and a blue bar. Farther below that were ten circles in a row. The red must be vitality, the blue could be magic, and the black circles must be my experience points.

"Didn't they explain this to you at the Guild? Who's your caseworker?" asked the woman.

"Uh, no, it's my fault for not asking... My caseworker's name is Louisa."

"Oh, well then. Louisa's a veteran, she's been doing it for five years. She's a dependable one. There's some useless caseworkers out there."

"Louisa's the one who gave me these bronze Mercenary Tickets. She said it was just for extraordinary circumstances, though, and she can't keep helping me too much." I showed the woman my tickets. She handed me the boards she was holding. It seemed a bit like a binder. There were sheets of paper with lines of characters written on them sandwiched between the boards.

"Sorry for not introducing myself sooner. My name's Leila. I'm the assistant manager here at the Mercenary Office. The people at the Guild buy quite a few Mercenary Tickets, so I see them for work a lot."

"So that's how you know Louisa."

"Yeah. As a matter of fact, she was originally a Seeker before she retired and decided to take on a support role. You could say something like that about the demi-humans here, too... Well, anyway. What kind of mercenary do you need?"

"I'd like a lizardman, preferably a vanguard. I see some on this list here." Leila's expression turned apologetic. I got the impression they'd all been hired by that point.

"Unfortunately, all the male lizardmen who have strong physical builds are out on jobs at the moment. We've got a female lizardman, but her equipment's different, and I can't really say she's suited to be a vanguard."

"Is she a fighter type?"

"She's got a job called Rogue. It's not really a vanguard or a rearguard, more like a midguard job. They can use some weapons, but they're not as good as a specialized fighter. They also don't have the same dexterity as a Thief, but they can use a bow. It's kind of an all-around sort of job. Rogues are pretty rare among lizardmen, but it's usually safer to gather newbies with specialized skills, so this one isn't very popular."

Which is why she was the only one left. Since I didn't have many tickets, it'd probably be better to choose a male lizardman who was very clearly oriented toward fighting.

"Can this Rogue lizardman use a shield?" I asked.

"Yep. She comes with a leather buckler. It's not the greatest piece of equipment, but it should be plenty if you're only going to the first floor of the Field of Dawn. But be careful, both the person's physical abilities and the shield's performance change how much they can take."

If I have her take a low-risk attack, taking into consideration her physical abilities, I should be able to test Defense Support 1. Then I wouldn't have to waste time waiting for my turn.

"There are some other mercenaries you could employ, but if there's too big of a gap in level between you two, they might not listen to your orders. They won't just leave your party, though. Knowing that, this young lizardman is probably good for you. She's level three; she'll do what you tell her."

"Thank you. In that case, I'd like to hire that lizardman, please."

"All right. I'll bring her out, you wait here," said Leila.

There were other people who'd come to the Mercenary Office to hire mercenaries, but there were other workers assisting them. It was sheer luck that I was able to get help directly from the assistant manager.

A few moments later, Leila returned with something…completely different from what I imagined a lizardman would look like.

…Is this just someone dressed up as a lizard?

When you say lizardman, I assumed…well, a man that was also a lizard. Like, a human-shaped lizard creature. I think most people would agree with me. But what Leila brought out was definitely a "person," no matter how hard you tried to argue otherwise. It looked like a human woman who'd put on the head of a lizard costume and then clothes made of lizard skin.

"Yeah, everyone's surprised their first time. Demi-humans are transformed humans who've been defeated by monsters in a labyrinth. Other than that, resurrection generally isn't possible in the Labyrinth Country. If they're able to undo the demi-human transformation, they go back to the form they had in their previous life," explained Leila.

"...But they're considered lizardmen?"

"There's no law against using demi-humans as subordinates. It'd be good if they could communicate, but generally they just follow other people's orders. Once in battle, though, they fight independently, based on their instincts."

I did not see this coming. They say they're not human, but that's just a legal definition. Actually looking at her, though...

"The lizard mask and whatnot are equipment special to demi-humans; we don't take them off. There's a lot of people who might not realize it by looking at them, but just because they're working as your subordinate doesn't mean they won't defend themselves. We get the occasional person who ends up killed by the demi-human they'd been employing when they tried to do something to them. We ask you to agree to this oath to prevent that."

She had called it a mask, but it was more like a big hood since it didn't cover the lizardman's full face. The lizard-skin leather she wore clung tightly to her figure, and for some reason there was a slit in it that extended from between her breasts to her abdomen. What she wore on her hands and feet also didn't cover all her skin. The more I looked at her, the more I had to say it was a bit sensual, but…looking at the simple yet cutesy eyes on the lizard mask killed any strange ideas I had.

I signed the document and promised not to put the demi-human into any unnecessary danger. Once that was done, the display on my license automatically brought up the party page.

```
◆Current Party◆
1: Arihito    ※◆$□  Level 1
2: Theresia  Rogue  Level 3  Mercenary
```

Still can't read what my job says… Guess it might be rearguard *written in some other language. And this lizardman actually has a pretty normal girl's name…Theresia, sounds kinda European.*

"Leila, will switching these numbers around change our battle formation?"

"No, that page is just for checking your party members. There's another page for battle formation where you can set each of your member's positions. Mercenaries should automatically maintain their position in the formation, but real, flesh-and-blood humans need practice."

All right then… Oh, everyone's in the front right now. Let's change that…

```
◆Battle Formation◆
1: Arihito    Rearguard
2: Theresia  Vanguard/Midguard
```

I didn't designate her solely as vanguard to make sure she

didn't get too far ahead of me. First, I wanted to try using Defense Support 1 with her standing just in front of me so I could see the effect up close.

I guess I could now consider this lizardman, er, Theresia in her lizard outfit, as my companion. She just stood there staring silently in my direction...except that her eyes were covered, so I didn't actually know where she was looking.

"Um...my name's Arihito. Nice to meet you, Theresia."

"......"

I held out my hand, and slowly, very slowly, Theresia brought hers up as well. Her grip was fairly strong and gave me the sense that she was someone reliable.

"By the way, mercenaries will prioritize their own safety if they find themselves in serious danger, like if the battle formation breaks up," added Leila. "Then they'll return to the Mercenary Office. Some people even do that on purpose just 'cause they don't want to bother bringing the mercenaries back themselves. Best not do that, though, or your karma'll go up."

"Okay, understood. I'll bring Theresia back safely after we're finished exploring."

"Hmph, you seem like a pretty decent guy... Oh, also, I saw a young woman head into the labyrinth on her own earlier. She a friend of yours? You oughta keep an eye out for her. No matter what your job is, it's dangerous to go it alone at level one."

I wonder if that was Igarashi...? It can't be, though, she said she was going to join another party. Eh, it doesn't matter anyway; we're all up against the same things, so I'd want to help out anyone who seemed in danger.

First things first: I needed to figure out exactly how strong my party was. I set off with Theresia following close behind. The only part of her face not covered by the mask was her obviously human mouth, but even that didn't give an indication of any sort of emotions at all. Right now, she was my only companion. I hoped that the two of us would manage to get through this without incident as I headed off toward my first dungeon.

Part V: The Weapons Salesman

There wasn't just one labyrinth that had a difficulty of one star, but apparently, it was customary for the newbie Seekers to go to the Field of Dawn first. Not far from the Mercenary Office was a huge set of stairs, which looked like it could be the entrance to the labyrinth. The crowd gathered around it was so immense that I'd have assumed it was some sort of tourist attraction if I didn't know any better.

"You a novice?" a young man asked me. "If you don't have a weapon yet, you should go to one of the stalls over there and pick one out. Your first one's free, too."

"Oh, really? Thanks a lot."

"You must have a rough job if you went and hired a mercenary. Eh, every job's got a way forward. Good luck," said the boy. He seemed to be much more experienced but still sort of came off as a newcomer. Either way, he was going into this beginner labyrinth, so he'd probably only arrived here shortly before I did.

I didn't see Igarashi nearby, but I did spot Suzuna and Elitia. Elitia had taken Suzuna to the weapons stall and was giving her an explanation.

"Hey, mister, what's your job? I can help you pick out the right weapon for you," came a voice from another stall. I didn't realize it right away since she was wearing a turban over her bobbed hair, but the stall worker looked like another Japanese person like me. I could tell just by the fact that she called me *mister* that she was fairly young, even younger than Suzuna. She seemed like a cheery young girl.

"It's surprising, isn't it, that there's so many Japanese people here. There are people from other countries, too, of course. It's great how we can talk to anyone since we have a license," said the girl.

"Uh, yeah…it is. Did you start selling weapons after you were reincarnated?" I asked.

"Yep. My family actually ran a sports equipment shop back home, so I wanted to be a Merchant."

Ah, that made sense. Some Seekers managed to find a place for themselves in the city. My job wasn't something that could really be used for sales. The easiest way to apply it and make a living would probably be defeating monsters.

"So weapons are usually divided into close range and long range, and then there's some that would be considered mid range. What type would you prefer?"

"Let's see…I guess I could just go with the classic, a sword."

"A sword? Hmm, you… Oh, you seem to be able to use any weapon. That's incredible. Is your job Weapons Master?"

"Nah, nothing that exciting. But if I can use anything, maybe I should go with something different."

It sounded like I didn't have any set weapons for my job, since rearguard covered such a broad scope. I would mostly be providing support from behind, so perhaps I should get used to using a bow or some other type of long-range weapon. I looked around the stall and my eyes fell on a slingshot.

"I think I'll go for that slingshot."

"Is that what you'll be using? It won't be very effective if you don't have the applicable skills."

"Really? Well, if I can use it without skills, then I'll just need to practice."

The slingshot was made from what seemed to be pretty sturdy wood. It came with a small pouch, which contained twenty bullets made of some sort of metal—I couldn't tell what kind. When I picked it up, it fit in my hand almost like it'd been stuck there, and I just knew how to use it. I guess that's what was meant by being able to use a certain weapon with your job. I guess you'd be able to tell what weapons you couldn't use just by picking them up.

"If you don't mind, I'll just need to calculate the cost of additional ammo."

"Of course. I get the feeling I'll need a lot if it turns out I can use this. I'll come back once I've made the money to buy more."

"Oh…I forgot to give you this. You can put the things you find in the labyrinth in this leather sack. If you gather materials from weak monsters, you should be able to purchase ammo."

I wondered if it'd be hard to decide what to bring back if I happened to defeat a larger monster. I'd have to think of the most efficient way to bring materials back from the labyrinth in the future.

"Then best of luck to you, Mr...."

"Oh, I haven't introduced myself. I'm Atobe Arihito, and you are?"

"My name's Shinonogi Madoka... It's been so long since I've said it in that order, surname then given name."

Apparently, it was normal for Japanese people who'd come to the Labyrinth Country to switch their name order to given name first and surname second. Saying it in the typical Japanese order was probably quite rare.

"Well, until we meet again, Ms. Shinonogi."

"Oh, just Madoka is fine. Everyone in this town uses your given name, right?"

"O-okay... It just feels weird to call you Madoka since you're so much younger than me."

"U-um...you can call me whatever you like. But cutesy nicknames are kind of embarrassing, and *Ms.* just feels so stuffy. S-so I guess then..."

In Japan, the name with which you addressed someone was one way to show your consideration for them. At this rate, it'd probably be nighttime by the time I got out of the labyrinth, but I wanted to be able to say hi to Madoka if I ever ran into her again.

"Phew... Sorry to make you wait, Theresia. Shall we go?" Theresia appeared to nod ever so slightly. We were heading toward the entrance to the labyrinth when a grizzled veteran-looking man who seemed like a guide of some sort called out to us.

"Hey, another novice, huh? You're only the seventh I've seen today. I heard we had more than thirty new reincarnates coming in, but it looks like most of you were a little spineless. A Seeker's gotta seek, y'know."

"Is there any way to make a living in this town without seeking? Or is it best to just continue as a Seeker?" I asked.

"Do it for as long as ya can. There are some folks like me, though, who've gone over to the support side of things but still do some seeking, too."

The man's hair and beard were almost entirely white, but his body still seemed sound, and he had an ax slung by his side. He definitely looked like he used to make a living as a Seeker.

"Goin' in and out of those labyrinths time after time will wear a person down. There're some like me who have a side gig going into the beginner labyrinths and rescuing any novices who are out of commission. Oh, I haven't even told you my name yet. I'm Ribault."

"I'm Arihito. Nice to meet you."

"Arihito... Mind if I just call you Ali? Or maybe Reheater?"

"I-I'd rather if you didn't. I know it's not the easiest name to say, but I'd really appreciate if you just called me Arihito. I actually had a question I was hoping I could ask you..."

"Hmm? No way I'm gonna be your guardian. If someone with a high level beats the monster, the low-level members of the party won't just get the same experience. You won't get any experience points if you don't contribute to the fight."

That wasn't actually what I had wanted to ask, but I did learn something new. It sounded like grinding a low-level person with a high-level person's assistance took a lot of effort.

"Thanks for letting me know. But I wanted to ask, about how much is 'ten injury points'?"

"What? Ah-ha-ha, you think this is some kinda game? There's no way to express the injuries you get from a monster's attack with numbers… I mean, you can make a rough guess if you look at your vitality on your license and factor in your defense. You might be able to get an idea of how much you can take."

So with other jobs, their skills don't describe the damage they do using numbers…which makes it something unique to the rear-guard *job.*

"For starters, you can go to the first level here and find one of the small-fry monsters in there called a Cotton Ball. You don't wanna be too worn down after just one hit. Those monsters are the only ones in all the labyrinths that won't kill a beginner outright even if they're not defending. There're no points or nothing, we Seekers have to just figure out our enemy's strength based on our real-life pain. You've always got to be careful that you're not taken down with the first hit."

"Thanks a bunch, you've been very helpful."

"You're a gutsy fella. And you've got a mercenary with you. Arihito, I think as long as you're careful, you'll be one of the ones who can walk themselves out of the labyrinth on their own feet.

Even if there's some other Seekers around, if you think there's trouble, give me a shout, and I'll come over. I do regular patrols, but I don't catch everything."

"Got it. I'll submit a request for your support if I end up in a fix and feel like I'm about to die," I replied, and Ribault roared with laughter as he patted me on the back. He smiled as he saw me off. It sounded like there were others just like him who I could rely on for support.

"Ribault, earlier, there was a party with a couple of beginners in it that went into the labyrinth. Should I be worried...?"

"Oh, them... A *Named Monster* appeared, and they ran off, leaving the beginners behind. No point in worrying about them if they joined the party of their own accord, though."

Was it some of the people I just saw at the Guild...? And is a Named Monster a really strong one? If they get abandoned, they're probably gonna die...

Obviously, I wanted Igarashi and Suzuna to live, and I even hoped that all the people who reincarnated with me would be all right. I couldn't be too reckless in the labyrinth, but I did just get another goal.

Part VI: Defense Support

Theresia and I walked down the long, gently sloping stairs, and suddenly the stairs were coated in grass and before our eyes was a field filled with light despite the fact that we should have been underground. This was the labyrinth known as the Field of Dawn. It far exceeded even my wildest expectations.

It wasn't just a completely flat field of grass as far as the eye could see; there were a few trees sprouting up here and there. I glanced at my license and saw a map of the area displayed. This first level of the labyrinth was so vast you wouldn't be able to cross to the other side even if you spent all day walking. It would be hard to believe that numerous expansive places like this were dotted around under the city, so it'd probably be safer to assume that we had been transported to a labyrinth that was somewhere else as we came down the stairs.

"Cotton Ball…that's what we need," I said. "If it's a weak monster, it should be somewhere around here…"

Theresia didn't respond but instead set out in the same direction I was headed. We surveyed our surroundings as we walked, and suddenly, Theresia stopped and drew her short sword and buckler.

◆Monster Encountered◆
COTTON BALL
Level 1
On Guard
Dropped Loot: ???

Out from behind a tuft of grass appeared a fluffy creature that almost looked like a cute stuffed animal. According to my license, the creature was apparently "on guard." The Cotton Ball turned a slight tinge of red. I wondered if maybe it was angry, or—

"...!"

The Cotton Ball bounced, then suddenly flew violently at Theresia. Theresia readied her buckler and used it to catch the Cotton Ball's tackle. There was an incredible thump like a small explosion, loud enough to rupture eardrums, which made me wonder how the buckler hadn't been crushed with the single blow.

This thing's no joke... It's the weakest monster but has this strong of an attack?!

Theresia was able to take most of the blow. I glanced at the red bar below her name on my license and saw that it'd been reduced only by about one twentieth of its total. But her vitality—her life force—was being whittled away, so I had no intention of taking it easy.

Theresia was unsteady from taking the attack, but she bravely struck out with her sword. The Cotton Ball wasn't going down in one hit, though. Her attack flung it backward, and the moment it landed, it went to counterattack at a dizzying speed.

Now...I need to activate my rearguard skill!

I knew I needed to protect Theresia as she stood in front of me and readied her shield. I had naturally known how to use my skill when I'd put the skill point into it.

◆Current Status◆
> Arihito activated Defense Support 1 ⟶ Target:
                                            Theresia

The first attack had been strong enough to crush bone if you were unlucky enough get hit directly, but...the second attack was different. The moment before the Cotton Ball crashed into Theresia, it went flying back like something had flung it. I wasn't able to see it too well since I was behind Theresia, but it was like there was an invisible barrier in front of her. Theresia stood still for a moment as if she didn't understand what had happened, either.

"Theresia, you attack it after I shoot!"

"……"

I jumped out from behind Theresia with a bullet ready in my sling, aimed at the Cotton Ball, and let it fly. I couldn't waste a single shot, and that was a direct hit. I was shocked I was able to handle myself in a fight; my body actually seemed to know what it was doing even though it was the first shot I'd ever taken.

"—!"

As I would have expected, Theresia didn't have anything to say about the critical hit she was about to deal. She closed in on the motionless Cotton Ball and brought her sword down on it.

```
◆Current Status◆
> Arihito's attack hit Cotton Ball
> Theresia's attack hit Cotton Ball
> 1 Cotton Ball defeated
```

"…W-we did it…?" I asked in disbelief.

Theresia turned to me and nodded. I approached the dead Cotton Ball, which looked like some kind of small, rat-like animal covered in long fur. But upon closer inspection, it had an evil-looking face. Even if it was violent, I would feel pretty guilty killing a cute animal that could be a pet, so I was happy that it did actually look like a monster.

"I'm sorry, Theresia. I should have used my skill in the beginning...," I said, assuming she wouldn't answer, but she shook her head slightly. It seemed like she could only respond with a yes or no. I guess as her employer I really just needed her to be obedient.

If you had the necessary skills, you could just remove whatever useful materials there were on the Cotton Ball and take those back, but I didn't, so I picked up its whole body and put it in my leather sack. I wondered if the Dissection Center could give me enough money for more ammo if I took this to them... No, it was just lodged in the Cotton Ball, so it'd be better to take it out and reuse it. *I've got to be thrifty until I've reached my earning goals.*

"Theresia, are you injured? We could go outside for a bit so you can recover..." She shook her head to imply she was still okay.

Then I realized—the second attack on Theresia hadn't reduced her vitality at all thanks to my skill, which had reduced the attack's damage.

The Cotton Ball did less than ten damage when it attacked Theresia. Whether it was one point or just barely under ten, my skill practically nullified it. I'm starting to think Support Defense 1 is pretty useful...

I needed to test my skills a little bit more. I wanted to try it out on a stronger enemy, but I couldn't ask Theresia to do that for me. But it was good to just know we could defeat a Cotton Ball without taking any damage even if they came at us as ridiculously fast as before. It would depend on how much I could get when I turned in the Cotton Ball, but we would have the option of hunting here.

"Okay, shall we try hunting a few more?" I asked Theresia,

who nodded in response. The two of us headed toward a large tree just up ahead.

"—EEEEEK!"

"AAAHHH! I-it's a Named Monsterrr!"

Just then, we heard a woman screaming—Igarashi. The other scream belonged to that more experienced Seeker who'd been in the Guild, the one full of confidence who'd said he'd show the newbies around.

"Shit…Theresia, let's go!" I said, then started running in the direction the voices came from.

There was a big tree in the way, but once I'd gotten past it, I saw a bunch of Seekers fleeing as if they were being chased by something. Igarashi was running pretty quickly, but there was a new male Seeker who was lagging behind. Behind him was something that looked like a normal Cotton Ball but was somewhat different. It was completely red. It was chasing after the Seekers, who were running with all their might, trying to snap at their heels.

Part VII: A Rearguard's True Strength

Even the attack from a normal Cotton Ball was enough to put a level 1 in mortal peril, but this red one was much bigger and much faster than the one Theresia and I had just defeated. It wasn't quite twice as fast as a normal one, maybe about 30 percent faster.

That last guy isn't gonna outrun it... But just what can I do against a Named Monster...?!

◆Current Status◆
> ★REDFACE activated BOOMERANG DIVE ⟶ Target: BALDWICK'S party

It was a monster with its own special name: Redface. It activated its skill, and I witnessed something that was hard to believe.

"AAAAHHHH——!"

In the blink of an eye, the entire party that was desperately trying to flee was mowed down by Redface. The creature flung itself at terrifying speed and, like a boomerang, arched across the field and crushed the fleeing party. The attack was merciless; it hit every single member and crushed their bodies.

I couldn't believe a Named Monster could be this powerful even though it was appearing in the beginner labyrinth... Even if I had multiple lives, it wouldn't be enough. Were the people who'd run into Redface just that unlucky? Was I that unlucky?

"Gah...agh...I—I don't wanna die... Screw this...!" gasped one of the men in the party.

◆Current Status◆
> BALDWICK used RETURN SCROLL
> BALDWICK'S party fled the labyrinth

Baldwick's party ran away...but Igarashi was still there. That meant she wasn't actually part of his party. She just happened to be in the same place.

"—Don't think I'll go down without a fight!" cried Igarashi.

◆Current Status◆
> Kʏᴏᴜᴋᴀ activated Mɪʀᴀɢᴇ Sᴛᴇᴘ ⟶ Kʏᴏᴜᴋᴀ evaded
  Bᴏᴏᴍᴇʀᴀɴɢ Dɪᴠᴇ

Igarashi...she dodged using one of her Valkyrie skills!

That's the kind of nerve I'd expect from her, the kind that let her use a skill she'd just learned when she was in the thick of it. But how often could she activate her skills with only level-1 magic? The stronger the skill, the more magic it'd take.

"Igarashi, run! We'll keep it back—"

"Atobe...! Hurry, you need to get out of here! As if I'll lose to this thing!"

I'd never seen her so emotional before, but I aimed for Redface just after it used its powerful skill and let loose a bullet from my sling.

◆Current Status◆
> Aʀɪʜɪᴛᴏ's attack hit ★Rᴇᴅғᴀᴄᴇ
No damage

Wha—?!

Even though I'd put everything I had into that shot, it just bounced off Redface with a ping, and it turned its target toward my party. It bounded once and ramped up its speed. If it went like this and Theresia took the hit, we might be able to survive one hit, but I had no way to attack this thing. If we couldn't damage it, we couldn't beat it.

Theresia would be able to go back...but I don't know what'll happen if she takes more damage than she can handle before she retreats...Leila said she'd died once already, but what happens if she dies again...?

"—Your fight's with me, rat monster!" Igarashi suddenly shouted.

◆Current Status◆
> Kʏᴏᴜᴋᴀ activated Tʜᴜɴᴅᴇʀʙᴏʟᴛ ⟶ Hit ★RᴇᴅFᴀᴄᴇ

She had said Valkyries could use magic. The magic that Igarashi had selected from her abilities flashed out fast as a bolt of lightning, much as the name would imply, and struck Redface.

Why...is she trying to save me? I thought she just saw me as a subordinate to be conveniently used and thrown away...?

Redface shifted its target. It bounded backward, then turned to face Igarashi and prepared itself to throw another Boomerang Dive at her.

If she takes this hit, she'll die. This thing was so strong that not a single person in the party from before was doing all right, but Igarashi didn't have the energy left to activate a Mirage Step. She gripped her spear with a determined expression on her face and struck out at Redface.

"Hyaaa!"

Even if her spear attack didn't make it through Redface's defenses, maybe it could keep it from getting off its Boomerang Dive, but—

```
◆Current Status◆
> KYOUKA's attack hit ★REDFACE
No damage
> ★REDFACE's attack hit KYOUKA
```

Igarashi's spear snapped apart, and Redface launched at her, sending her flying to the grassy ground before she could even react.

"…What the hell…are you doing…?" I stammered, incredulous.

I felt something snap inside my mind. I had wanted to save anyone I'd found who was in trouble, but…with Redface's absurd strength and the party that just ran, and me, just standing here watching this pitiful fight… I felt rage—anger at myself boiled through my entire being.

"She did all that for me… And now she's gonna die…!"

I should have said *Yeah, let's work together* when she came up to talk to me earlier. I got so wrapped up in our relationship as manager and subordinate, I just decided that'd never change even though we'd been reincarnated. I had wanted to run away from her…and now it was all going to come to an end, and I didn't even know if she knew that about me. I wouldn't have been able to make my decision if I hadn't been backed into this corner.

Why would she try to protect someone like me…? I'm no different from before I got reincarnated. How could I be so pathetic, not changing at all even though I've been reborn!

I was too slow; I was just now realizing this because she'd protected me. But I wasn't going to let the same thing happen twice.

"Theresia, will you help me? We're gonna have to get through this together."

"……"

With Defense Support 1, she could maybe manage to survive Redface's attacks, and with Attack Support 1, which I had just put a skill point into, she might just be able to get through its defense. If we failed, Theresia and I would both die. I didn't think this enemy was going to be kind enough to wait for Ribault to come and save us. I wouldn't have been surprised if Theresia, as a mercenary, decided to put her life first and make a run for it, but she just gave the same small nod she'd been giving me all day.

And then—

◆Current Status◆
> Theresia activated Accel Dash

"—Theresia!"

The whole point of this was to buy me enough time to save Igarashi and run.

Even though Theresia wasn't necessarily a close-combat fighter, she instantly put herself in front of Redface. The monster was trying to make another run at Igarashi, who still seemed to have some life in her. It was one of Theresia's Rogue abilities I hadn't seen her use yet.

Trying to protect someone else, protect everyone, by throwing yourself in harm's way. I couldn't have predicted how the protected people would have felt if that happened to them.

If that's what we're doing...I should be the one doing the protecting!

It wasn't just the people directly in front of me I could protect. When my skills said *in front*, all party members in front of me were treated as vanguard. I understood that now that Theresia had put such a large distance between us. My Defense Support skill was like a wall that could protect my companions even if they were fighting across a large area.

"—Theresia, I'll back you up…!"

Redface pulled back from Theresia, who had suddenly moved in front of it, then braced itself for a moment so it could throw another of its powerful skill Boomerang Dive. That skill…it couldn't be on a completely different level from the Cotton Ball's tackle, could it?!

◆Current Status◆
> ★Redface activated Boomerang Dive ⟶ Target:
                                         Theresia
No damage

We defended! Theresia's defense plus my Defense Support worked!

Even though there was such a huge distance between me and Theresia, my Defense Support was still effective. And Theresia was unharmed. The damage she'd taken from a normal Cotton Ball must have been only one or maybe two points, so I could completely defend against something that was ten times or five times more powerful, like Boomerang Dive.

If Boomerang Dive is ten times as powerful, that means Theresia has at most only twenty vitality points. Ten isn't something to be taken lightly; in this world, it seems like it's actually a large amount…which means…

Redface had been launched backward through the air by my Defense Support, leaving it wide open. I could guess what would happen to it if we hit it with my Attack Support 1.

"Now, Theresia! I'll *back you up!*"

"—!"

◆Current Status◆
> THERESIA's attack hit ★REDFACE
No damage
10 support damage

Her normal attack didn't get through…but the ten injury points did!

But it wasn't over in one hit. Redface flinched away from Theresia, but she launched attack after attack at it.

◆Current Status◆
> THERESIA's attack hit ★REDFACE
No damage
10 support damage
> THERESIA's attack hit ★REDFACE
No damage
10 support damage
> 1 ★REDFACE defeated
> ARIHITO leveled up

I almost wanted to pump my fists in the air at the sight of Theresia's slashes landing on Redface, followed by the invisible

Attack Support 1 damage. We had defeated a monster that had crushed a more experienced party in one attack. The urge to shout in triumph bubbled up inside me, but this wasn't yet the time.

"Theresia, I'll take care of Igarashi, you go get Ribault from outside!" I ordered, and Theresia dashed out of the labyrinth.

Igarashi was collapsed on the ground in terrible condition. She'd taken one of the blows to her arm, which was now red and swollen; it was likely broken.

"Uh...gh..."

She was in pain. She had fought for us, and looking at her, I couldn't stop memories from our previous life running through my head.

"You're such a big help to me, Atobe. I can't rely on anyone else for this kind of thing."

...If only you'd just worded things a little differently. Actually, I was pretty stupid, too.

Unreasonable demands and high expectations, there's just a fine line between those two. I didn't know her intentions; it was too naive to think that way...

I sort of assumed I'd get more skill points when I leveled up. I flipped through the pages to my skills and saw that I'd gotten two more points I could put into them. I put one into Recovery Support 1. But I had to somehow get the unconscious Igarashi to agree to be in my party so I could use it.

"Igarashi, it's me, Atobe. Help is on the way, but I can do some first aid. Could you join my party so I could do that?" At first, there was no response. I almost gave up since she wasn't in any condition to be asked, but a moment later, her eyes opened just a tiny bit, and she nodded weakly.

"...If you do...anything weird...I'll sue...," she stammered. She had risked her life to protect us, but she still had her pride, which showed her spirit hadn't yet been broken.

After she was in my party, though, I could see her vitality bar, which had been reduced by over 70 percent, and I only had using my new ability to heal her on my mind.

...So I can just make myself her rearguard... Will this work?

I nervously lifted Igarashi's limp upper body and sat behind her so she was sort of in front of me.

"......"

She didn't say anything, but she did seem somewhat opposed to the arrangement. That was to be expected, I guess, since I was basically hugging her from behind. I wondered if I could lay her on her side then I lay behind her, so I would sort of be a "rearguard" then. I wasn't sure I'd have another opportunity to test it, but I just continued to hold her for what felt like the longest thirty seconds in my life until she recovered the five vitality points.

Part VIII: End of My First Adventure

Based on what I'd learned from the two fights today and looking at the red vitality bar on my license, I decided that Recovery Support 1 was a fairly useful skill for us novices. It took thirty seconds from when I activated Recovery Support 1 to when its effects could be seen in Igarashi's recovery.

◆Current Status◆
> Arihito activated Recovery Support 1 ⟶ Kyouka's vitality was restored

Yeah...that proves it.

Igarashi's vitality bar, which had been reduced by about 70 percent, suddenly jumped up to 50 percent. Her painful-sounding ragged breathing seemed to come a little more easily, and the swelling in her arm almost completely disappeared, leaving just some redness behind.

If a level-1 Seeker had about ten vitality points, then healing five every thirty seconds was incredibly useful. Obviously, it was pointless if an enemy dealt more than ten points in one hit, so the fact that Redface's attacks were just weak enough to not do that might be the only silver lining here.

Igarashi remained unconscious, though, perhaps from the shock or continued pain. I seemed to be able to heal vitality but not that... Perhaps I needed some different method that healed statuses or something.

I laid her on the ground for a moment and placed the body of Redface in my leather sack to take back as loot. Before we'd defeated it, it had looked like a super fluffy rat-like creature, but its face really did look evil. It was quite a bit bigger than a normal Cotton Ball, so it filled my leather sack, which probably could have fit four normal ones.

"Hey, you okay?! We'll take you to a Healer!"

It was Ribault and some others who Theresia had fetched. His companions lifted Igarashi onto a stretcher and carried her away. I walked along with them as Ribault interrogated me.

"What the hell happened? Did you guys run into a Cotton Ball herd?" he asked.

"Baldwick and his party will have more information," I replied. "A Named Monster appeared, and they used a Return Scroll to flee."

"Tsk… Named Monsters are stubborn. They remember their first enemy and appear out of nowhere if that person enters the labyrinth. They should've known that, but I guess they just needed the cash too bad. Looks like you lot were able to get away, though," continued Ribault.

I decided it would be pretty hard to just say we beat it. If it weren't for my special job, we wouldn't have been able to beat Redface. If word got out, I'd probably get too much attention, and who knew what that would lead to.

I'll just report the Redface incident to Louisa. Maybe she can hold off on making it public that it was defeated. It's unfortunate for Baldwick's party, too, but I'll just need them to keep the whole thing quiet. My skills just aren't ready yet.

My rearguard skills had one major disadvantage: I couldn't support myself in any way, so depending on the battle formation, I could get killed pretty easily. I'd need to get some skills to avoid that, such as some way to handle attacks that came from the side or a way to force enemies to focus their attacks on the vanguard. But if I could work on strategies where the vanguard fought and

I supported from the rear, I should be able to handle the beginner labyrinths with little difficulty. Well, as long as no enemies appeared whose attacks weren't made ineffective by my skills.

Today, the ten points was really effective, but it'd quickly become useless if the monsters' vitality was higher or their damage was in a different class. The skill was called Defense Support 1, so I'd be willing to bet there was a Defense Support 2. *I just hope I can get stronger.*

As we were about to exit the labyrinth, we happened to pass by Elitia and Suzuna. They weren't near us, so they didn't know we'd been in the fight with Redface, but they sensed the grave air around us and came running over. Maybe she did her hair like that when she was fighting, but now Elitia's golden hair was in two braids on either side of her head. I decided this wasn't the time to poke fun at her and call her the Twin Tailed Knight.

"What happened here...?" she asked.

"A Named Monster appeared. It was really dangerous, but we managed somehow," I replied.

"...Managed... You don't mean the red Cotton Ball, do you? That only appears once a month and has been able to defeat even a level-three party. It's so fast, it's impossible to run away from—how did you...?" Elitia seemed to know about Redface and thought it a miracle we had survived so started to bombard me with questions, but she suddenly looked like she realized something and shut her mouth. "...I'm sorry, I should just be happy that you survived, but here I am asking all these questions. It's amazing—you've just been reincarnated, but you were quick-witted enough to manage."

"No, we were mostly just lucky. You don't need to worry about me, but you should be careful if you plan to keep hunting in this area. I don't think the red one will pop up again, though, so you shouldn't worry about that," I said. I was trying to be careful not to give too much information, but I didn't want to let Suzuna get scared at the possibility of Redface appearing again since she was also just a newbie like me. There was a chance they'd realize we'd defeated it, but actually, that didn't seem to be the case.

"Named Monsters viciously pursue the first opponent they see, no matter what. We could meet another Named Monster, but that red Cotton Ball won't be coming for us. Thank you for your concern, though," said Elitia, thanking a novice like me even though she was clearly a much higher level. Her humble and kind attitude left a good impression on me.

"You…you probably don't have much time to chat, you should look after your party member… My name's Elitia. And you are?"

"I'm Arihito. I know it's probably difficult to say, but I would appreciate it if you could call me Arihito and not shorten it. And you must be Suzuna, right?"

"Y-yes…you and the lady who they carried on ahead were reincarnated at the same time as me…"

"Yep. But she's okay. She's unconscious, but her vitality is recovering."

"Did you use a potion? They're so rare, but it's good you had one…," said Elitia as she looked directly in my eyes. I had a feeling I knew what she was wondering: my job.

"…No, that's impossible. If there were such an amazing rearguard…," murmured Elitia.

"If there's something you'd like to ask, I'll answer," I said.

"N-no, it's nothing…a rearguard who can handle both healing and defense…Arihito, you'll go very far if that's the kind of job you have," said Elitia.

She had wanted to find an excellent rearguard. If we talked about my job here, she'd probably ask me to join her. I got the impression that her job was more geared toward solo work, and there was some sort of risk to the rearguard. I would need to know that beforehand. As long as Suzuna was traveling with Elitia, there'd be a day she'd have to face that. It didn't seem like a problem at the moment, but I was concerned to leave the situation as it was.

If we could somehow eliminate that risk and fix the difference between our levels, she could potentially be an excellent vanguard. But right now, it's just a possibility…

First, I needed to worry about Igarashi. I'd talk about it more with Elitia and Suzuna if I met them again.

"All right, well I'm going to head off," I said.

"O-okay…I'm glad I was able to speak with another Japanese reincarnate. Perhaps we could talk again if we happen to meet sometime…?" asked Suzuna.

Everyone seemed lonely since they'd just reincarnated. Suzuna bowed her head to me a number of times before walking away with Elitia. I got the impression they'd been doing some test runs, so they'd probably leave the labyrinth after seeking for a bit more.

I turned to Theresia, who'd been waiting for me and was about to suggest we go, but…something seemed different about her.

"…Theresia?" I asked.

"……"

She didn't say anything; she just stared in my direction. Whatever it was didn't seem like a problem, so I started walking and she fell in behind me. I had a sudden thought so stopped and turned around to face Theresia.

"…So I'll be using a Mercenary Ticket tomorrow, too. Would you like to come along with me again?" I asked.

Theresia didn't answer for a moment. I guessed mercenaries didn't have the right to choose who employed them. After a moment, she nodded her head to say she would come with me the next day, too.

"Great, then it's decided. We'll say good-bye at the Mercenary Office today, but thanks for helping tomorrow, too, Theresia."

This time Theresia didn't reply at all. I grinned and we ran off to catch up with Ribault and his party, who had left us pretty far behind by now, then made our way out of the labyrinth.

```
◆Expedition Results◆
> Raided FIELD OF DAWN 1F: 5 points
> ARIHITO grew to level 2: 10 points
> Defeated 1 COTTON BALL: 5 points
> Defeated 1 bounty ★REDFACE: 200 points
> THERESIA's Trust Level increased: 50 points
> KYOUKA's Trust Level increased: 10 points
Seeker Contribution: 280 points
```

CHAPTER 2

Forming a Party

Part I: Trust Level

After leaving the labyrinth, I swung by the Mercenary Office on the way to the Guild to drop off Theresia. Leila, the assistant manager, came out to meet us.

"It's only been a couple of hours, but you've come back after fighting together. That's brave. Theresia, make sure to drop off your equipment with the craftsman. It'll need cleaning and maintenance."

Theresia nodded in response but didn't move. She just stood there staring at me.

"...Hmm? Normally you go without me having to say anything. Theresia, is there something you want to say?" asked Leila.

"......"

"Not that we could understand anything since you can't talk. Wish I had some sort of telepathy skill," muttered Leila.

Today we worked together, helped each other fight, and defeated a strong enemy. Theresia protected me, and I definitely felt reluctant to part ways with her so easily. As long as I had tickets, though, I could hire her again. I only had two left right now, but there had to be a way to get more.

"Leila, I was hoping to hire Theresia tomorrow as well, but...I only have two more tickets, so I was wondering if I could purchase more somehow."

"Well, you can't reserve a mercenary. Every Seeker gets the same fair chance to hire one, so as a rule, you can only hire a mercenary when you come to the office. You can buy more tickets from the Guild, but only ten per month. It's to prevent Seekers from relying too much on mercenaries and losing their own ambition, but even so there are those who become dependent."

Which means...even though I've made a connection with Theresia, I can't think of her as a permanent member of my party.

Theresia was staring at me the whole time, but partway through our conversation, she suddenly turned and went back into the Mercenary Office. Leila seemed amused; the corners of her mouth turned up into a smile.

"Hmph. It's pretty rare, but for some reason that lizardman has taken a real liking to you," said Leila.

"Uh... You think so?"

"Only jobs like Monster Tamers can naturally get demi-humans to like them. To be honest, even we don't know much about the minds of the demi-humans. Every once in a while, one will take a particular liking to a person who doesn't know telepathy or isn't a Monster Tamer."

I did have one clue that Theresia had started to take a liking to me: My license said her `Trust Level increased`. I wondered if that was because I'd supported her with Defense Support 1 and Attack Support 1, or maybe because we were in a party together. I decided to bring up Trust Levels to Louisa when I asked her about contribution levels.

"Even if you're not a Monster Tamer, if a demi-human likes you enough, it is possible to make them a permanent member of your party. You'd have to pay to cover the cost, but you could have Theresia's ownership transferred to you. The cost is set at a hundred Mercenary Ticket's worth."

A hundred tickets...enough money to hire Theresia a hundred times. I actually don't think that's too expensive if it means I can have her as a permanent companion.

But if I could only buy ten tickets per month, I'd have to wait at least ten months to do it, and I wouldn't be able to hire her during that time. I decided to ask Louisa about that, too. Maybe there was some way I could get around it.

"Also, if you purchase a mercenary, then you're responsible for their care, clothing, food, shelter, the whole lot. There's no way to get that kind of money if you're just starting out as a Seeker. You should get more experience under your belt and hire Theresia again if you want. There's no need to rush things. In my experience, it's almost unheard of for a mercenary to like someone else enough for them to purchase the mercenary before you could," continued Leila.

Almost. If it's difficult to raise this Trust Level or if it depends on how well you get along, then what Leila says is probably true.

Even so, I wanted to gather one hundred bronze Mercenary Tickets as quickly as possible. Parties were made up of vanguards, midguards, and rearguards. I could ask Theresia to cover either vanguard or midguard, then I could probably even easily convince another rearguard to join. Over time, I could invite someone who could take over vanguard and eventually make the perfect party.

It was more than that, though. After a single outing together, we ended up cooperating so well that I couldn't even consider forming a party without her.

"Okay. I'll gather one hundred tickets as soon as possible," I said.

"All right. The office opens at eight in the morning, so you should get here early tomorrow."

Leila bowed her head, and I left the Mercenary Office. I saw the Monster Dissection Center, but since Redface had a bounty on it, I wanted to show it to Louisa first. It'd probably be fine to just take the materials as proof, but I didn't want to risk it.

Ribault and his party were coming out of the Guild as I approached. They were probably going back to the labyrinth entrance after having taken Igarashi to a Healer.

"Hey, Arihito. We've left that lady Seeker in a Healer's care. They'll probably transfer her to a patient room, so you should check in with them," said Ribault when he saw me.

"Thank you, Ribault. You've been a huge help."

"Ah, don't worry about it—we're just doing our job. Sorry for not using a Return Scroll earlier. We could've teleported over, but they're so expensive and end up reducing your contribution level. You lose a hundred points if you don't go out on your own feet."

"That seems like a lot... So then Baldwick and his party who used a scroll..."

"It'll depend on what they did before they ran into the Named Monster, but they'll probably be in the negative and fall in rank. They didn't have much choice, though. At least this way they live to fight another day. Hopefully they'll learn from this, stop pretending to be guides, and just do some good old-fashioned seeking."

If Redface hadn't shown up, there'd probably be a few beginners who'd benefit from the guidance, but if the guide wasn't a particularly strong Seeker, the risks were too high. Looks like I learned something from their mistake as well.

"Arihito, you coming to the Field of Dawn tomorrow, too? Or are you going to one of the other one-star labyrinths?" asked Ribault.

"I hadn't really decided yet, but I do think I should try out the same labyrinth again."

"Yeah? Well, if you can, you should invite that lady Seeker to join your party. I dunno if it's 'cause she's not specialized in vanguard or rearguard, or if it's her personality, but it seemed like she couldn't find a party... It's too dangerous to go it alone at level one."

It was generally accepted as Seekers that it was better for novices to gather people with highly specialized jobs. Valkyries probably became really strong at higher levels, but it was like a Rogue in that, at low levels, they were seen as a jack-of-all-trades and master of none.

Would Igarashi even come with me if I invited her? If I asked now, she'd probably just think I was doing it out of pity.

But at this point...what I feel about Igarashi is less that I can't handle her and more that I'm grateful that she protected me.

She'd been forced into a terrible situation, but she stood her ground and took on Redface. If someone wasn't watching her to make sure she didn't do something else that reckless... Ribault was right, she couldn't be left on her own.

"What's the scowl for? Oh, did the two of you not get along in your previous life or somethin'? Lots of people open up after reincarnating. It can go surprisingly well; maybe you should give it a shot."

"I sure hope so. I just don't want to come off as hostile."

"Ha-ha-ha... At least you're self-aware. In any case, mull it over a bit, even if you think this is all just pointless chatter from an old man. But I doubt there's a soul who could keep on hating someone who saved their life. Well, good luck. See you later." You couldn't really deny the fact that I'd protected Igarashi.

He wished me good luck, but...can I even convince her?

"Mr. Atobe! ...Oh, thank goodness. You're unharmed and not poisoned."

While I was thinking, Louisa came running up to me looking like she was on the verge of tears. She must have worried after seeing Igarashi getting carried off unconscious.

"Yep, as you can see, I am perfectly fine. It's all thanks to the tickets you gave me."

"Oh, n-no, that's not... I just pushed my responsibilities off on the Mercenary Office...," said Louisa, her face flushed red as she spoke, but she had just been running.

I was about to shock her with some more news, but I wanted her to know what happened. There was a chance that I'd need her help to keep some secrets in the future, too.

"Louisa, could I speak with you for moment?"

"Y-yes... Is it something particularly secret?" she asked, leaning in so she could hear as I spoke in a low voice so that the others around us couldn't hear.

"I defeated this monster called Redface. Would you mind looking these over for me?"

Louisa did seem incredibly surprised. She pulled away from me, her eyes wide, lower lip trembling. I showed her the leather sack containing the result of the hunt. She didn't seem to quite understand for a moment but then became very conscious of who was around us.

"U-understood. Well then, why don't we go into one of the rooms inside...?" she said, trying to hold on to her composure as best as possible, but her voice wavered slightly. I carried the sack as I followed behind, slightly curious what exactly I'd get for it.

Part II: The Adventure's Reward

Louisa guided me past the large reception room to a private chamber. There seemed to be different rooms of various sizes depending on how large the corresponding party was. Louisa led me into a small one that had only a square table and four chairs. She suggested I take a seat and left the room for a moment, but I decided to look around and saw some scales and other pieces of equipment that looked like they were meant to be used for loot.

I probably shouldn't just pull out Redface since I've already surprised her...but I just stuffed it in the bag without thinking much; I don't know how well it's kept.

I started to worry but had been told to carry my loot in this sack, and there wasn't any point in thinking about it now. I finally decided to take a seat, and a short while later, Louisa knocked politely on the door before coming in with some drink glasses on a tray.

"Here, have some tea. Do you like herbal?"

"Yeah, I'm not too picky about what I drink, so this is fine. Thank you."

My favorite drink of all was probably just sparkling water. It was better at waking me up when I was working overtime than a cup of coffee, and it didn't destroy your liver if you drank a ton. But anyway, I should just forget about my days as a corporate slave.

The herbal tea had a refreshing aroma and was chilled to a perfect temperature. I was honestly pretty impressed because I'd assumed based on this society's level of advancement that they'd only have lukewarm drinks.

"Right, I don't want to rush you, but could I first check your Seeking Record on your license?"

"Of course. A lot happened. Here it is." I was interested to see what her reaction would be but also a bit nervous. *I'm pretty sure every human being gets nervous right before an evaluation.*

Louisa looked at the page of my license I showed, and her hand flew to her mouth in shock. She almost said something, but she managed to hold it back.

"Oh... *Cough, cough.*"

"A-are you okay?"

"N-no need to worry... Two—two hundred eighty... How could you get these numbers...? Oh, you really did defeat a creature with a bounty on it!"

She had changed from an official Guild caseworker to her normal self. Her cheeks were burning red, and she looked at me like I was some sort of celebrity.

"That's amazing... Absolutely incredible, Mr. Atobe! The highest contribution level I'd ever received when I worked as a Seeker was one hundred and five, and I didn't get to level two until a month after I started!"

"R-really? So I guess defeating Redface was a good thing after all."

"I believe it was. The amount of experience you gain from a monster with a bounty on it is far more than that from a non-bounty monster of the same type. By the way, it's estimated that it takes hunting approximately fifty Cotton Balls to go from level one to two."

Which meant the experience I got from Redface was about

fifty times more than a normal Cotton Ball. That was probably right, since it was strong enough to defeat a level-3 party.

"...N-now then, could you please place the item you took from Redface as proof that you defeated it on the plate here?"

"Sure. Um, I just put the whole thing in my sack... Is it all right to just take it out here?"

"Y-yes, that's quite fine. I've worked as a caseworker for five years now, so I've seen plenty of monsters... Ah!"

I pulled myself together and reached into the leather sack to remove Redface's body and placed it on the plate. It was pretty unpleasant to touch, so I decided I wanted to invest in some gloves when I got my bounty.

"Here it is... Wh-whoa, Louisa, are you all right?"

"...You really did defeat it... Wow... To think someone with your potential came to me, and I completely misjudged you..." She had her hand over her mouth, her cheeks burning red. I'd never had a woman look at me like that. I was worried she might realize I didn't really know how to interact with women.

"Uh, um, like it says on my license, I was with the mercenary Theresia, plus Kyouka, who was brought in earlier, so the three of us defeated it together."

"No... I don't mean to be blunt, but if you were fighting with your two companions normally against Redface, you wouldn't have received such a high contribution level. I firmly believe that it was all you and the ability of your unknown job. Amazing...you really are amazing..."

"L-Louisa, look, I'm just a normal guy. You keep saying I'm

amazing, but I'm not sure it's true. I don't think you give yourself enough credit, either." I probably should've used the opportunity to sell myself instead of denying it, but alas, that just wasn't my personality.

"...Oh. I—I do apologize for getting so worked up all of a sudden. It's just, this is the first time I've ever been the caseworker for someone with such potential. Reaching two hundred eighty contribution points is, without a doubt, the best out of all your fellow reincarnates. Congratulations!"

The best. I hadn't heard those words used to describe me in so long. It sounded pretty good. I couldn't help getting a bit excited, but I needed to make sure I didn't get too full of myself that people would get annoyed. Besides, it'd come back to bite me if this info got out. *Better consult with Louisa about that, too.*

"Th-thank you... Also, Louisa, I had something I was hoping you could help me with."

"Of course, what can I do for you?"

"If possible, I'd like to keep other people from finding out it was me who defeated Redface. It was already targeting another party when we just happened to show up, so we were forced to stop and fight it. But normally, a party of our level wouldn't have stood a chance against a monster like that."

Louisa understood what I was getting at and why I didn't want everyone to know. She stroked her green hair, which was up in a bun, an attentive expression on her face as she listened.

"Yes...you're right. Many people out there would try to take advantage of you if they learned of your abilities. Of course, as your caseworker, I have no intention of letting that happen. I want to put you in a position where you'll be able to continue seeking without any needless restrictions."

"Thank you, Louisa. I really appreciate your understanding."

"Very well. I won't make it public that you were the one to defeat Redface. I will, however, have to put a notice on the bulletin board at a later date that Redface was in fact defeated."

Good thing the Guild was so flexible. This took care of one of my concerns, and I felt like a weight had been lifted from my shoulders.

"Redface has injured many a Seeker to a point where they will never recover, so the bounty reflects the risk of injury. However, since it was only a one-star bounty, the award is not very high. You will receive twenty gold coins."

"Twenty gold coins…how much is that worth?"

"Currency comes in copper, silver, and gold coins, each worth ten times the one before it. That means that twenty gold coins is equal to two thousand copper coins. For reference, a lunch from a dining hall in District Eight costs three copper coins."

So I managed to make enough to cover lunch for nearly two years with about an hour's work. But would this amount of award be enough? If armor and whatnot was expensive, I wouldn't have much left once I'd gotten all my necessary equipment.

"How would you like to receive the payment? I can deposit it directly into your bank account or I can give it to you in cash. Every Seeker is given a bank account when they register with the Guild."

"Okay, could I have one hundred copper in cash and the rest placed in my account?"

"Yes. I will need to make a print of Redface's foot as proof it was defeated, but you can then decide what to do with its materials after that. The Guild can purchase them, but it tends to be at a lower price than at a dissection center."

"So I even receive the materials? Oh, I'll have to take this to a dissection center right away then, since I only just put it in this sack."

"That's not necessary. Items placed in this sack won't degrade after one day. You can purchase higher-quality bags, which hold more or have longer preservation periods. They also come in a variety of styles, such as a backpack."

I was learning about more and more things that I wanted to buy, but I wanted to get them in a way that fit in with my plans. If Redface's remains lasted for a day, then I should have no problems stopping by a dissection center before going into the labyrinth tomorrow morning.

There were still two more things I wanted to ask Louisa. First was about this Trust Level, and second was about my ranking after calculating my contribution points.

"Louisa, I had a question about this 'Trust Level' it mentions here…"

"The Guild also evaluates Seekers on whether or not they are building harmonious relationships. For example, if you go on an expedition together without any strife, your points may increase…"

She apparently hadn't taken a good look at the numbers shown on my license, but suddenly her eyes were glued as she looked down at it. She slowly raised her head to look at me, and her face was again flushed red. Apparently, Louisa was the kind of person who wore her heart on her sleeve.

"F-fifty...? How exactly could you become so close in such a short period? And with a mercenary no less, whose Trust Level rarely increases...?"

"H-huh? So are those fifty points how much my Trust Level increased?"

"N-not quite... Trust is by nature not something you can reduce to numbers, but your license automatically makes rough estimates and turns it into numbers based on the situations between members of the party. Unless there's something extreme, the contribution points from increased Trust Levels are usually five or below."

So it wasn't just my imagination that Theresia's attitude had changed. Apparently, our relationship had improved beyond a normal degree just like Leila had said.

I have to improve my relationship with a vanguard and mid-guard so I can use my rearguard skills properly...which means, while I'm supporting them, they might start liking me far more than would be expected... Oh man.

I wanted to think that if men joined the party, we'd become closer friends. But trust isn't the same as affection. Probably. Definitely. I might get suddenly closer to the women in the party, Theresia and now Igarashi, but...I wasn't actually looking forward to that. I wanted to gain their trust a normal way.

"…I wonder what this means, I almost want to join your party for one day to see. The more I learn about you, Mr. Atobe, the more questions I have…," said Louisa with a smile as she removed her monocle.

If she came along with me, I'd have to protect her from behind with Defense Support, and her Trust Level for me might go up… but that felt manipulative; I'd have to remember my place…

"Mr. Atobe? What happened? You look so cheerful all of a sudden."

"Oh, uh, no. I mean, I don't really understand the Trust Level much, either. I think it's best if you just don't worry too much about it. The last question I wanted to ask you was…did I manage to avoid having to sleep in the barn or jail?"

"Yes, of course. Your rank is now thirty-seven thousand five hundred and twenty-nine. Only looking at District Eight, you are ranked one thousand and twenty-four out of approximately three thousand, so you are in the upper half of District Eight. You will be provided a suite at an inn in District Eight. I'll give you the room information in a moment."

Suite…sounds like a large hotel room to me, but this is a different world, so I wonder what it'll be like.

"Oh, speaking of which, you fought alongside Kyouka Igarashi, the Seeker who was taken to the Healer shortly before you arrived, correct?"

"Y-yes. We just ran into each other, though…"

"Ms. Igarashi was able to defeat one Cotton Ball, but her attacks were ineffective against Redface. She was defeated and required rescue. Her current contribution points are at zero, meaning she will have to stay in the barn after she's been discharged from the Healer."

Igarashi? In a barn?

"I should be the one to tell her, right?" I said. "We knew each other from our previous world."

"If it's not too much trouble. Her caseworker was quite new, and he took this as a reflection of his abilities…and decided he couldn't continue in this line of work."

It'd probably be hard to tell a prideful woman like Igarashi that she had to sleep in the barn. And to top it all off, I'd been given a suite. She might even demand we switch rooms, but I decided I'd be firm. I wanted to protect what would become my stronghold.

"You seem concerned for her, Mr. Atobe," said Louisa, breaking off my train of thought. "I understand how you feel."

"Oh, well, actually… I mean, I am worried, but that's not—"

"Your suite does have two beds. If you're worried she's still weak, perhaps you could invite her to stay with you? I doubt there would be any issues given how you're such a gentleman."

Louisa had offered to provide me with accommodation if things got too difficult because of a low ranking. Why didn't she think to do the same for Igarashi? But that wasn't the point. Even if it meant she could avoid having to sleep in a barn, I didn't have the courage to invite her into my suite.

Part III: Valkyrie

I left the Guild and headed toward the Healer's, which was nearby. Reception told me where Igarashi's room was. Her vitality must've been restored by then, since she was apparently sleeping in the first-aid room. A nurse exiting the room saw me and asked how I knew Igarashi. I said she was an acquaintance. The nurse checked my license, then let me in to see her.

"She's sleeping at the moment, but I expect she'll wake soon. She is likely still in shock from the battle, so please be mindful when you speak with her."

"Understood. Is it all right if I go inside now?"

"Yes, that's fine. If you need anything, just call one of us Healers."

She was a Healer, not a nurse. I was a bit curious since I hadn't yet seen a healing job's abilities in practice, but I decided to leave that for when I took damage and needed it myself. Although as rearguard, I was theoretically in a position that prevented me from taking damage.

I knocked on the door, but there was no answer. The Healer had said it was okay to go in, so I opened the door to the bright room, which had thin curtains drawn over the windows, and saw Igarashi sleeping in a bed with unbleached sheets.

"...Pardon me," I said quietly and sat in a wooden chair next to the bed.

Igarashi's face was somewhat pale, but she was sleeping peacefully.

What should I tell her first when she wakes up? Should I try not to injure her pride? Or should I tell her she shouldn't go off and do reckless things without even making a party?

"...Mm..."

Before I could organize my thoughts, Igarashi stirred slightly and opened her eyes a little.

"Good, you're awake. Everything's going to be okay, boss."

"......"

I was worried that she still wasn't entirely conscious, but Igarashi looked in my direction and gave a pained smile when she saw me.

"...I know we're in another world, but waking up to you at my bedside feels like a bad sign," she replied.

"Sorry about that. But I really am glad you're okay. I wasn't sure what would happen..."

"I thought I was going to die, too, but I guess not. It looked like that monster slowed down a bit after I hit it with my Thunderbolt, so I don't think I got the full force of the blow. Still, my arm hurt so much I thought it was broken."

I couldn't decide for a moment if I should tell her the Healer fixed her arm. She'd probably grill me about what I did while she was unconscious if she thought of when I used Recovery Support. While I was busy hemming and hawing, Igarashi looked down pensively and spoke.

"...You...you took care of me then, didn't you?"

"Uh...um, well...," I stammered.

"Yeah...that red thing must've already been defeated. It was gone. Monsters don't just jump out then run away, which means you and your companion must have beaten it, but..."

The Igarashi I knew would never believe I'd beaten Redface. This was about where she'd laugh off the idea...but something seemed different about her now. At first, she'd been like she always was, acting like I just got on her nerves, but now her tone was gentle. It was almost like she was trying to be considerate.

"...Feel free to laugh if I'm totally off the mark, but if you hadn't been there, I probably would have died. That's a fact, isn't it?"

"I...I guess that's true. But I was just lucky. There's no reason to think things will go as well the next time a strong enemy appears."

"There you go again... Shouldn't you be a little more confident in yourself when you've achieved something?"

"...I guess so."

She'd gone back to her normal self. Maybe it would be too painful for me to be in a party with her. Even so, the normal Igarashi would've taken one look at my pained expression and gotten even more annoyed, but instead, her hostility suddenly disappeared, and she looked away.

"...Sorry. I'm the one who's useless here," she continued. "I picked a job just because it seemed cool but then couldn't find a party... I thought I could do something on my own, but it turns out I can't do anything."

"Th-that's not true. All jobs are strong at higher levels. I think you can make a solid party no matter what the members' jobs are. So...don't let it get you down. You're just starting out anyway."

"...Atobe..."

"Uh... S-sorry. It's not my place, I just..."

I was suddenly embarrassed for getting so worked up. I'd never talked to Igarashi like this, so emotionally. Our company's attitude was that employees who were easily flustered were harder to work with.

"...Wh-what I mean is...I think Valkyrie is a good job. It seems like something that'd get really powerful in the future, it gets good equipment, and it's cool."

"...Are you seriously that eager to please? I knew you were busy, but I just threw more work at you and said good luck, not taking any responsibility myself... You always helped me, but I just called you useful. I knew it, but I was just arrogant and using you. Why do you still worry about me...?"

I didn't know if she realized now why I had such a hard time getting along with her. Maybe she realized since I didn't want to be in a party with her even though we had been coworkers before.

"...It's not that I worry about you. You didn't run away back there. I hit that monster with my slingshot, and it went after us, but you still used your magic on it. I'm grateful for that...and I thought it was pretty cool." Flustered, Igarashi fidgeted and averted her gaze.

"Wh-what about that was cool anyway? ...I was reckless and made an even bigger mess for you to clean up..."

"Yeah, you were reckless. But what you did lit a fire in me. Luck did play a part in me defeating that thing, but now I have confidence that I could beat it if I ever ran into something like that again."

"Is the job you chose really that powerful?"

"I'll be able to harness its power if the conditions are right. That's why I want to start gathering party members..." That alone appeared to convince Igarashi of my intentions.

"...With such an amazing job, you ought to be able to get some really strong people to join, right?" she asked.

"Probably. But I think it would be better to have members who are closer in level. It'd be great if they could consider what skills to take based on my skills."

"So you would be the leader? You would be the one bringing in people?"

"W-well... I know you may think that I don't have it in me. But I want to be able to do the things I feel like doing in this world, and I think me being the leader will set the groundwork for that."

I felt like we were in a business meeting. I wondered how she would take my leadership proposal.

"And if...if you think I'm not an effective leader, that you can't rely on me, you are free to leave. But, Igarashi, would you join my party?"

Igarashi lay there staring at me for a moment, her expression unchanged as she looked away once more. I guess her pride would keep her from working under a former subordinate. Not much use there. I thought it would just be easier to back down now, but what followed changed my mind.

Igarashi glanced up at the ceiling, then back at me. If things were normal, this would be where she would glare at me, but everything was different now.

"…You saved my life. You encouraged me. What the hell kind of person am I if I don't listen to you now?"

"Uh, um… I assume I can take that as a yes?"

"I'll sign something if I need to. I doubt you can trust my word."

"N-no…that's not it. Anyway, Miss—"

"Don't call me *miss*. I'm not your boss anymore."

"O-okay, then… Igarashi. Going forward, I'd like to clarify the benefits of joining my party—"

"Ha-ha… You don't need to worry about that. It's got plenty of benefits already. The fact that I'm still alive is the greatest benefit of all."

I was struck again that she could smile like that and couldn't help smiling myself, but that seemed to make Igarashi a little self-conscious. Thinking about it, she'd never had the opportunity at the company to just show me who she truly was. I think this was the first time I ever saw the real Kyouka Igarashi. I no longer viewed her as my demon boss; I just wanted our relationship as party members to go well. I'd finally managed to think that earnestly.

"Right…first, I want to do something about our clothes," said Igarashi. "This stands out too much, and I'm afraid it'll attract attention from the wrong sort of people."

"Ha-ha-ha… You're right about that. Afterward, we can go to a weapons shop," I replied.

She had on a sweater, pencil skirt, and boots. It didn't quite feel right to just hand her a spear and call her a Valkyrie.

"Oh yeah, I'm sure my rank went down since I was defeated...," said Igarashi as she checked her license. Her hands began to shake when she saw her contribution points were bottomed out, so her rank must be quite low. It did seem possible, though, for contribution points to go in the negative, so surely she couldn't be ranked last.

"I'm two thousand nine hundred and eighty-seven out of three thousand and thirty-nine... G-guess that means I'm sleeping in the barn tonight, eh?"

"...Igarashi, I do have one suggestion. Please hear me out without getting angry."

"Um, okay... What exactly is it? You look so serious."

"Uh, um... Would you mind staying in my lodging temporarily? I won't do anything strange of course, it'll just be an emergency measure until your rank increases."

Igarashi didn't say anything, not even a *Huh?*—she just stared up at me, studying my face before answering.

"...I can't restore my vitality if I'm in the barn, so...i-if it's not too much of an imposition..."

"R-right, it's settled, then. Okay, so shall we hurry up and go?"

"Uh...g-go where?"

"My lodging. Apparently, it's a suite, so I get the impression that it'll be fairly large."

"A suite? Is your rank really that high...?" said Igarashi as she looked at me enviously.

A short while ago, I could have never imagined her being envious of me. To be honest, it made me a little happy. I guess I'm easily pleased.

I looked at the map on my license, and we decided to briefly stop at the lodging to rest before heading out to dinner.

Part IV: The Necessities

Once we'd gone through the process to have Igarashi discharged from the hospital, we headed toward my lodging but stopped on the way in a clothing store at her request. She browsed the racks and put the items that matched what she was looking for in a basket. I thought I should look for something for myself as well, but she started talking to me before I could.

"They did say they'd provide us with a change of clothes if we wanted, but what they had available just wouldn't have worked for a modern person like me."

The Guild did offer new Seekers some cotton or hemp clothing in the way of T-shirts, pants, underwear, and whatnot, but they didn't provide shoes. You needed to earn money to purchase them yourself. Also, apparently, the female Seekers couldn't get bras if they didn't earn money, which was pretty rough for them. However, you could trade in the body of one Cotton Ball for five copper coins, so you could get a full set of clothes after hunting just five Cotton Balls.

"I guess they need large amounts of that fluffy Cotton Ball fur to make clothing. I'm not sure how I feel about wearing things made with materials from monsters who attack us, but I guess I'll get used to it," said Igarashi.

"And it means there's a constant demand for Cotton Balls. I was wondering why the price you could exchange one for was set," I said.

This country had only the Seekers and the people necessary to support them. The labyrinth was one location from which the materials necessary to maintain their lives were produced. That didn't mean that the only food available was the meat from monsters, though. There were some people in the town who ate a bread-like food.

"Anyway, thanks for helping me out with so much, even lending me money," said Igarashi.

"It's for necessities. I'm sorry I didn't realize, I'm sure a lady wouldn't be comfortable wearing the same clothes tomorrow," I replied.

"Can't really say anything once it comes down to it. We've only been here for about half a day…," said Igarashi with a glance at me like there was something on her mind.

"Oh, no, you don't smell sweaty or anything, don't worry," I stammered.

"Urk…um. Even if that's the case, you shouldn't say anything about it."

"S-sorry, I'm not really good at interacting with women…," I said, but she would probably argue that I saw her basically every day, so it wasn't a good excuse. Unexpectedly, though, she just huffed, not necessarily because I upset her.

"Well then, you'll start to get more experience once you've got a party put together. And I'll try not to get too annoyed, like now."

"Ha-ha...sorry," I replied with a nervous laugh.

"You don't need to apologize so much. I'm not really that angry... Heh-heh."

Louisa had also mentioned I was quick to apologize. I guess it's something I should be careful of.

Igarashi smiled happily even though she was gently chiding me.

"You know, we would've never had the chance to talk like this if we hadn't been reincarnated," she said.

"Ha-ha, you're definitely right about that. I don't think I've even spoken to you about anything other than work."

"Because if you weren't careful about what personal information you gave, it'd come back to bite you as rumors and gossip. You remember that one time I stayed late with you to work? I got a warning from a higher-up about that."

I had no idea that kind of thing happened. Well, actually, I did know about one rumor in particular...the one that Igarashi had only been promoted so quickly because this "higher-up" she mentioned—the company's CEO—had taken a personal liking to her. I didn't really believe it, but I also didn't think it was entirely impossible. I didn't really know what the truth was. I was a little curious, but I figured asking would make her hate me.

"...You're probably aware, Atobe, that the reason I was promoted was because it was arranged by the CEO," she suddenly said.

"Uh… R-really…?" I stammered.

"Oh, you misunderstand me… We weren't intimate or anything like that. He just had his eye on me and was trying to turn me into his pawn. After I was promoted, he'd constantly remind me of how he was the one who gave me the opportunity."

"…I'm sure he had his eye on you because you're so beautiful. Apparently, the CEO's gotten himself into trouble for his relationships with women ever since he was young."

Men in positions of authority, even married men, tended to get wrapped up in other women. It's something you see fairly often once you're out in the real world.

I suddenly realized I must have said something wrong. Igarashi's face turned bright red, and she was staring at me.

"…Is that really what you think of me?" she asked.

"N-no, I never really knew anything about your relationship with the CEO—"

"Th-that's not what I meant… Y-you called me beautiful… Well, whatever. Anyway, the point is that people were wrong when they assumed there was anything going on between me and him. Even I hated the fact that that's the reason I was promoted, and all his e-mails to me were pushy. I probably would've quit before long if nothing changed."

"…So maybe that's part of why you couldn't concentrate on work and pushed it all on me?"

"…Yeah, there's that, and other things. My parents suddenly told me I had to marry this guy they knew. Actually, they were against me going to college in the first place."

I was finding out that Igarashi's mountain of issues was far larger than I had ever imagined... Does being a young woman really bring so many troubles?

"Sorry if I misunderstood, but when you say your parents were making you marry some guy, do you mean you would be inheriting something...?"

"My dad did run a company, but I wouldn't say I was expected to inherit it," she said as she looked off in the distance, probably remembering her family. "My dad's company hadn't been doing very well recently. A long time ago at a party or something, the son of one of my dad's clients saw me and had a thing for me... It's been going on ever since I was in high school. All despite the fact that we basically only met once."

So her dad wanted her to marry some guy to improve his relationship with a client... She was going to be used as fodder for a political marriage.

"Well, that doesn't mean it was okay for me to push so much work on you... I really am sorry. Whenever I thought about how I might have to quit, I couldn't really find it in me to do any work..."

I couldn't even say that she should have talked to me about what was happening. If we hadn't been reincarnated, she probably would have been forced to marry this guy her parents had chosen for their own convenience.

"I did like my job, and I was glad that I was promoted. But if I hadn't had you to rely on, I wouldn't have been able to do my job as manager. I didn't have enough real-world experience, so it made me feel safe to have you there since you had so much more.

I leaned on you...but really, someone like you should've been the person to advance."

"No, I'm...I'm actually more suited to work behind the scenes."

"...People like you are suited to be leaders in this world. You rarely get angry, you listen to what other people have to say...and..."

"And...?" Igarashi had said something, but I didn't hear it clearly. She looked me in the eyes, then tried to laugh it off like it was nothing.

"What was your family like, Atobe?"

"Both my parents died when I was young. When you say family, I think about the workers in child welfare and my friends." A lot of people tended to pity me when this topic came up, so I tried not to talk about it. But now that we'd both been reincarnated, it wasn't something I could hide any longer.

"...I am so sorry. You worked so hard to get where you were, and I had no idea and just used you because you were good at what you did."

"Well, I'd just thought you were using me because I was convenient, but that's behind us now. It's water under the bridge. What's important now is that you listen to my directions as a member of my party."

"...As long as...as long as it's only orders that have to do with the party..."

"N-no, I mean...I won't, like, sexually harass you or anything. Do you really think I'm that terrible a person?" I asked, but Igarashi put her hand over her mouth and giggled at her joke, the first laugh I'd seen from her in a long time. It was a gentle ladylike gesture. She'd probably deny it, but I'd be willing to bet her refined behavior was another reason she'd been given a management position so young.

"All right, are you finished shopping? Your basket looks pretty full."

"Oh, sorry. It might be too expensive..." It looked like she'd picked out too many things and couldn't decide. I didn't mind helping out if that was the case.

"If I don't have enough now, I can always go to the bank and withdraw more," I told her.

"Oh, you still have more? But you've already lent me fifty."

"Yeah, I still have more. You can pay me back whenever you get a chance. Would you like to borrow another fifty?"

"...Um, I think thirty should be fine. I'm not sure when I can get it back to you if I take more."

If we were going to be working together as a party to go into the labyrinth, we'd be earning together, so I could argue that we could both carry the cost of purchasing resources, but maybe it'd be easier for people to shop if we put 50 percent of all earnings into a party fund and the rest was divided among the party members based on their contribution points.

I got the remaining funds necessary and watched Igarashi go off to pay for the clothes when I realized I hadn't bought anything for myself. Armor and things for the labyrinth were one thing, but I decided I should probably at least get a change of clothes to sleep in.

Part V: The Definition of *Rearguard*

After buying our clothes, we headed toward the lodging area of District Eight where all the Seekers were gathered. My lodging was a three-story building with eight rooms on each floor, located atop a hill. I was on the top floor—Nornil Heights, room 304. That's where we'd be staying.

An older lady, one in fairly good shape, showed us the room. Apparently, she and a number of employees cleaned and managed the building, which always had someone staying in it. She offered to give us a wake-up call, so I asked her to wake us at six thirty in the morning so that we could get to the Mercenary Office by eight.

"Please be careful not to lose the room key as there is only one. We would need to change the lock if we remake the key, so you would have to cover the cost of eight silver pieces. If you like, you can leave the key with me when you're out."

"Okay, we'll make sure it doesn't go missing," I said.

Eight silver pieces was eighty copper pieces. It wasn't exactly cheap, so we'd have to be very careful.

"Sorry, Igarashi, it looks like we can't have two keys."

"Hmm, you would make a key for each person even if they're living together?" she asked.

"Well, it makes sense for convenience's sake. It's possible that you and I won't come home at the same time always," I replied. I hadn't actually ever given someone else the spare key to my apartment back in my past world. I assumed it would be more convenient to have two, but that wasn't based on real experience.

"…Hmm. I don't think it'll be a problem right now. Sure, it's possible we might come and go separately, but we also might not have any arguments about it," she said.

"I suppose so…," I said. I felt like I was saying we'd never fight, but I wondered if our relationship had actually improved that much. Igarashi seemed to read my thoughts and grinned as she replied.

"I'll be up for the challenge if you ever want to fight," she said.

"No, I'm not that crazy. How about we try to keep things calm."

"Hmm, yeah…that'd be best. I want us to get along as well as we can."

Seriously…she's really gotten more relaxed in our interactions… I wonder if it's because we had that heart-to-heart at the clothing store?

My license had said her Trust Level in me increased, but I only got ten contribution points from it. That didn't actually indicate how much closer Igarashi and I had grown…supposedly.

"Should we go get something to eat after dropping off our things? The dining hall is open late, but I heard getting tangled up with the high-level Seekers who get drunk later in the night can be rough," she said.

"I don't think there's all that much crime around here since it means your karma will go up. Still, it's best to be careful."

"This karma stuff's pretty nifty, isn't it? You don't even need to call the cops or anything. The Guild guards just show up all on their own."

We opened the door as we talked and were first surprised to see there was a living room. Continuing past the living room was the bedroom, where there really were two beds.

"Wow, look at those high ceilings. And the room is so big... Atobe, exactly how high did your rank go that you ended up staying in a room like this? Is it because you beat that red thing?"

"Yeah. You fought it, too, so you have a right to stay here as well. Don't hesitate to make yourself comfortable."

"Y-you say that, but...," she said as she pulled back, still holding her bag with her shopping. I'd assumed she'd be happy since this was a pretty normal room and she'd sort of accepted staying with me as just a matter of fact, so I was surprised at her reaction.

...*Oh, that's right. Her parents were really strict, so she's probably never been to a hotel like this.*

"...Igarashi?"

"Eek?!"

"S-sorry to startle you. Um, there's two baskets for storing things, so you can use this one. We'll pick beds later."

"O-okay, got it. Fine with me— Eek!" Igarashi was about to stumble over absolutely nothing. That and her cute little yelp of surprise drew me to the conclusion that this twenty-five-year-old woman didn't have much experience with men. Not that I was in any position to talk, even if I could sympathize. For some reason I felt I could be more patient with a woman who was more nervous than I was—something that really rang in this situation.

…Hang on. I wonder if I'm headed for some big change in my new reincarnated life?

"…What are you grinning about? Y-you got a problem or something?" barked Igarashi.

"No, nothing, it's nothing. You put your things down, right? Let's head out. I'm paying, so you don't have to bring your wallet."

"…Always so tactful, even if it's a bit annoying. Are you used to this kind of thing?"

"No, absolutely not, as much as I'd like to claim I am. I just wanted to try to be a gentleman."

"Hmm, really? I always assumed you were popular with the ladies."

I had never even once had a woman say something like that to me, though I'd read in a men's magazine it was a sign she liked you if she did. Or was it on the Internet? Regardless, I couldn't get carried away. She wouldn't hesitate to give me a piece of her mind if she thought I was happy to be sharing a room with her, so I did my best to get control of my facial expressions so she wouldn't think I was still smiling.

We could eat in the lodging building, but that was fairly expensive, so someone suggested we walk down the hill to a tavern for dinner. The sun was soon going to fall behind the horizon, and the tavern was filled with Seekers who'd come back from their day's adventure.

"I have no idea what kind of meat this is, but it's not terrible," said Igarashi as she ate.

"Do you have any strong food preferences?"

"Not really, but I'm not a fan of fermented fish or blue cheese. Or stinky tofu."

Sounded like she didn't like anything with a really strong smell. She wouldn't be into stuff like durian, either. Not like I'd ever had it myself.

"Are the people who come to this area around the same rank as you?" asked Igarashi.

"I think so. It seems the highest-ranking people in District Eight live in a different area."

"The Labyrinth Country's divided into eight districts, and everyone's competing within each one. I bet District One is completely different from here, don't you think?"

"If we keep rising in rank, we'll find out someday. As long as we're moving up, we'll reach another district."

That's why I wanted to gather more party members, level up, and get strong equipment.

"Oh, by the way, who was that person in the lizard getup that was with you earlier?"

"That was Theresia, a lizardman. The Guild receptionist had some concerns since we didn't know the nature of my job, so she gave me some Mercenary Tickets. I used one to hire Theresia. I'd eventually like to make her a permanent party member."

"She seemed really strong, so I'd feel better if she was always around. I have to level up so that I don't drag you guys down."

"I'll help out. Tomorrow when we go seeking, I'll tell you how we defeated the red thing. Skills are a Seeker's lifeline, though, so I'd appreciate it if you didn't tell anyone else unless it's necessary."

"That sounds amazing... I can't wait. You know, when that red thing appeared, I thought I'd never want to go into the labyrinth ever again."

I'm sure anyone would be traumatized if Redface suddenly attacked them.

"Apparently, Redface's real target was that party with Baldwick. You were just in the wrong place at the wrong time," I told her.

"Yeah...actually, they came up to me just after I'd killed that one Cotton Ball on my own. They said they would protect me and I'd earn money faster. I was turning them down when it appeared."

They were going up to novices and trying to put them in a position where they owed them. Just thinking about what Baldwick and his party might have done after that made me sick.

"You were using a spear, right? I thought Cotton Balls moved so fast, but you were able to beat one by yourself," I said.

"I was in the naginata club in school. I chose a weapon that's a similar shape...but the red thing broke it. I'll need to replace it..."

"We'll buy something tomorrow at the stores in front of the labyrinth. We need armor to put over our clothes, too."

"Oh, right. Armor. I hadn't put that much thought into it, since the clothes were so expensive, and I'd broken my weapon."

"We'll work hard to make sure we earn a steady income. We'll get busy starting tomorrow."

Wrapping up that conversation meant the end of our after-dinner meeting. I started to think we should go home for the day and take it easy, but that's when I overheard a voice from somewhere in the tavern.

"Hey, did you hear? The Death Sword's come to District Eight."

"You're saying the Death Sword left the White Night Brigade and ran out here?"

"Yep. Guess she's teamed up with a novice and is trying to raise them until they're actually worth something."

At first, I didn't think anything of their conversation. It didn't seem to have anything to do with us. But when they mentioned a novice, the only people I could think of were the two girls I'd met that morning.

If they're talking about Elitia and Suzuna, then...Elitia is this Death Sword person?

"It's a good opportunity, don't you think? A high-level Seeker dragging around some deadweight, if things go well...," continued one of the people.

"Hey, don't go blabbing in public. We'll discuss this later," said a man with a scar across his cheek. Maybe he was the party leader.

"Atobe, what's wrong? You look upset," said Igarashi.

"It's nothing major. It just sounded like those men were talking about a girl who was reincarnated at the same time as us... But it's not a problem right now. Let's talk about it tomorrow."

"All right...if you say so."

The entire Nornil Heights building had shared baths separated by gender. The lower-ranking Seekers had to use public bathhouses, so it was convenient for us that the building had them inside. I went to take a bath after Igarashi had left, but I was back to the room before she was. I rolled into bed thinking about the conversation I'd overheard at the tavern. My eyelids started feeling heavier and heavier.

I'm dead tired and nice and sleepy...but I want to stay awake a little longer...

I closed my eyes and started to drift off. Right before I'd slipped into sleep, I heard the sound of the door opening.

"Atobe, the baths in this place are amazing! I didn't think they'd have shampoo and conditioner since it's a different world, but it turns out they do— Oh... A-are you asleep? Sorry, I'll be quiet..."

...That's great, Igarashi.

At least, the thought crossed my mind, but I was too tired to answer. I'd also been pleasantly surprised about the shampoo and conditioner and wanted to share that with her, but I was past my limit.

"...See you tomorrow, Atobe," said Igarashi gently as I slid into a deep sleep. It'd been a long time since I'd slept in a room with anyone else.

I continued to sleep in the darkened room. At one point, I woke up a little but didn't open my eyes and tried to go back to sleep.

"H-hey... Um, Atobe..."

"...Mm... Oh, good morning, Igarashi." I opened my eyes as

she gently shook me, and I saw her standing over me in her paja-mas. I was surprised to realize she didn't look any less beautiful without makeup on.

She stood by my bedside staring at me in the dim light as if she was trying to say something. When she'd had on her sweater before, I had a hard time finding a safe place to look, but even in her pajamas, I couldn't keep my eyes from stopping at her chest. My karma would go up, but I just didn't have the energy to look away. I wanted to look…but I shouldn't.

"…Are you not able to sleep? Is it because you're not using your normal pillow or something?" I asked.

"N-no, that's not it… How do I say this…? I don't want to make you feel weird or anything, but could you sleep with your back to me…?"

"With my back to you… Oh. Did I roll over? I didn't mean to face that way."

"It's not your fault, you can't help it. It's just, when you're fac-ing this way…I sort of…feel strange…"

I didn't really understand, but if it bothered her when I slept facing her, then I should just face the other way. But I might roll over again.

…Wait. *She feels weird when I'm facing her back… So even when we're sleeping in different beds, we're still in position like a vanguard and rearguard…?*

There was no way—or so I thought, but there wasn't any other plausible explanation for what she was saying and her embarrass-ment.

Does that mean my Recovery Support 1 is always active, even while I'm sleeping...?

I remembered my license showing me that Igarashi's Trust Level in me had increased. Just by sleeping facing her, Recovery Support 1 was working every thirty seconds...

"R-right, I understand. I'll be sure not to face that way, don't worry."

"...O-okay. Thank you, really. Sorry for waking you up for this," she apologized timidly before returning to her own bed. I waited until her breathing slowed and she sounded like she was sleeping before I got up.

If I sleep normally, I'll roll over at some point... But if I sleep on the couch, then I definitely can't be considered a rearguard. I hope. I don't even have any proof it's because of Recovery Support, but just in case...

If we moved the bed into the other room the next day, then we'd both be able to sleep peacefully after that. The couch turned out to be not as uncomfortable as I'd expected, so I decided I could just sleep there.

Then morning came. My eyes opened before the old lady came to wake us.

"...Hmm?"

I hadn't used a blanket at night since I wasn't cold, and yet someone had put one on me while I slept. Did Igarashi wake up and cover me? I looked around and saw a note on the table: *Don't worry about me next time and sleep in your bed.*

I guess just turning my back to her really did boost her Trust Level in me. I wondered what would happen if it went too high, but nothing was recorded on your license when you were outside of the labyrinth, so I had no way to confirm. I decided to try sleeping normally in bed tonight. If Igarashi woke up again, we'd move one of the beds to the other room.

Part VI: Rare Materials

Igarashi was sure to wake up soon, so I decided to stay in the living room so she could get changed in the bedroom.

"Atobe, you're not sore from sleeping there, are you?"

"Huh? Oh, uh, no, it's fine. This couch's like sleeping on a cloud compared to one of our office chairs," I replied, a little shaken when she asked while she got changed. Since we'd be living together, I really needed to get used to it soon, but I'd only spent one evening with this new version of her. I couldn't shake the feeling that I should be about to head off to the office, which made me nervous. It all felt a bit unreal.

"S-sorry, Atobe... There's still so much stuff I need to apologize for. Like saying such weird things in the middle of the night..."

"No, don't worry about it. It's hard to relax when you're suddenly sleeping in the same room as someone else."

"...You're far too kind. It's okay to be angry at me a bit, you know."

"Ha-ha...it's just not in my nature to get angry really."

Igarashi finished changing as we talked and came out of the bedroom, clearly tense. I had been so used to seeing her in her other clothes that this seemed sort of fresh... She was fitting more and more into this fantasy world.

"...You could maybe say something, at least," she said.

"Oh, uh, um. It really suits you. I was just impressed because it seems so natural."

"If it really suited me, you wouldn't exaggerate so much. I feel like a little farm girl. It's nothing like a Seeker at all. I just don't think I like it."

"I think it'll look the part once you put armor over it. I wanted to buy a breastplate or something for myself too if possible."

"Well, I only have three copper pieces left. I don't really have the money for armor..."

"That's fine, I'll pay. We're a team, right? It's not like a project at work. Our earnings belong to the whole team."

I got the impression she had never really borrowed money since her parents were so strict, but that's the kind of person you can trust with the money you lend to them.

"...I guess it's fine for you to lend me money, but don't coddle me. I want to work with you like a partner, as an independent Seeker in my own right... I don't want to be handled with kid gloves."

"I know. But part of being a leader is having your team rely on you."

"W-well, that's why you should get angry and tell me not to waste money. I'd feel more comfortable with that."

She didn't feel comfortable when people spoiled her and so wanted me to be strict and confrontational, but I just didn't think I had it in me.

"A change of clothes isn't a waste of money. I can't be angry at that."

"...Atobe, has anyone ever told you you're a bit like a big brother?"

Back in the home, even the older kids treated me like I was their big brother, and now I was starting to realize why.

After having some breakfast, I dropped by the Guild to let Louisa know what our plans were for the day and then headed off to the Mercenary Office.

"Good morning, Leila."

"Heh, you're early. Keeping promises is a good skill for a Seeker to have," said Leila when I greeted her. She was wearing the same leather armor and eyepatch as the day before. It made her seem really imposing, but she was actually quite friendly—the perfect example of the saying you can't judge a book by its cover.

"Hello, I'm Kyouka. I'll be seeking with Atobe starting today. It's nice to meet you."

"Hmm, you're the newbie I saw yesterday. I saw you head off to the labyrinth on your own, so I was a bit worried. Glad you were able to find a good companion."

"Yes, I just want to do my best not to hold him back." Igarashi finished off her businesslike introduction so smoothly I wouldn't have been surprised if she exchanged business cards with Leila. Leila seemed to like her.

"By the looks of things, Kyouka isn't exactly a vanguard, either... You want to go with a lizardman suited for vanguard instead of Theresia?" asked Leila.

"No, I'd like to hire Theresia today. She and I tried out a few different things yesterday, and we worked really well together."

"All right. I'll be back with Theresia in a minute."

This would use another bronze Mercenary Ticket. I had just bought seven more, so I was at my ten-ticket-per-month limit already when you counted the three Louisa had given me. I'd also asked Louisa about how I could get more bronze Mercenary Tickets, and apparently the limit was lifted if you got over a certain amount of contribution points. You needed to get a total of a thousand contribution points, at which time you'd become a two-star Seeker. That's when the purchase limit for bronze Mercenary Tickets would no longer be applied. Each ticket was three silver pieces, so I'd need three hundred gold to purchase a hundred.

"She's way cuter than a lizardman... Oh... Um, her body is covered in..." Igarashi was unnerved by the scales on Theresia's hands and feet, special characteristics that indicated she was actually a demi-human and not just someone in a lizard costume.

"She might come off strong, but she's dependable and talented. Looking forward to working with you today, Theresia," I said, and she responded with a nod, this time a little faster than the day before. Maybe she was less cautious since we'd already worked together once.

"Seems like Theresia was waiting for you to come and pick her up. I think you should go for a long seek today. It'd work out better for you anyway," said Leila.

"Yeah, we're planning on spending more time today," I replied.

"Atobe, what'll we do for lunch? We'll be in the labyrinth around lunchtime, so we should probably take something to eat," suggested Igarashi.

"You can buy food at the stalls by the labyrinth's entrance. It's a good idea to get something if you don't have someone in your party with the skills necessary to cook in the wild."

"Thank you for the information, Leila," I said.

"No problem. Take care." We took our leave and headed toward the Dissection Center. Theresia walked silently behind me, the same as yesterday, carrying her short sword and buckler, which had been repaired after she'd used it to defend against monsters.

When we arrived at the Dissection Center, there was a blond man in the process of tanning some leather from monster skins.

"Excuse me, we were hoping to have some monsters dissected...," I started.

"Ah, welcome to Rikerton's Monster Dissection Center. I am Rikerton, the owner of this establishment. Over there is my daughter, Melissa, who's responsible for dissecting the big game," said the blond man. The girl Melissa was wearing what looked a bit like overalls and seemed to be focused on dissecting the monster in front of her with her massive knife. Her eyes were sharp and clear as she worked, a telltale sign of a master craftsman.

"You've got a lot of monsters hanging here," I said.

"Yep, there're skins and things waiting to be moved after the monster's been dissected. We aim to handle all monsters within seven days so that they don't rot, and the neighbors don't complain of the smell," explained Rikerton.

So it sounded like the same technique as my leather sack had. Every once in a while, I was still encountering things that made me feel like this medieval city built from stone was more technologically advanced than our previous modern world. Although I suppose that shouldn't be too surprising since this world had magic.

At first, Igarashi seemed uncomfortable in the strange store, but after a short while, she seemed to relax and started looking at the hung-up skins. There were some that looked similar to mink fur, which could make high-quality clothing if worked properly. There was also a large box stuffed full of Cotton Ball fur.

"Could I get your name, sir?" asked Rikerton.

"My name's Arihito and this is Kyouka—"

"Ah, well, well, there's nothing better for a relationship than to join a party with your wife. When my wife and I were younger, we'd travel into the labyrinth together. Covered in the blood and flesh of defeated monsters, we'd have the most passionate, carnal… Oops, shouldn't say that in front of my daughter."

"A-actually, she's not my wife…," I stammered.

"Y-you don't need to deny it. He's just being polite, it's more embarrassing for you to overreact." Igarashi probably had a more mature way of looking at it, but it'd be so much harder to explain things if rumors spread.

Then there was this Rikerton guy. Maybe it was because he spent all day chopping up monsters, but he didn't seem quite normal, as rude as that was to think. It was like he was always smiling, but it never quite reached his eyes. Anyway, I suppose as a tradesman the most important thing was his skill, so if he was good, I'd like to keep working with him.

"…Dissection's done," Melissa suddenly piped up.

"Thank you, Melissa. Take care of these customers' materials next. Once you've finished with that, you can take a break."

"Okay," replied Melissa. Unlike Rikerton, her hair was almost silver in color, though she appeared to be only in her late teens. She was covered in blood splatter, but her face was fairly attractive. Add on the fact that she was mostly expressionless, and she looked like some sort of porcelain doll.

"Forgive her, she's a child of few words, but her dissection skills are even better than mine, so there's no need to worry."

"She's very talented for someone her age. It's impressive," I said.

I was a bit interested in their story, but right now we needed to take care of our business. I pulled the one Cotton Ball out of my sack as well as Redface. Igarashi had one Cotton Ball in her sack, too. Rikerton adjusted his glasses in surprise the moment he saw Redface, and even Melissa opened her eyes wide at the sight.

"You can get rare materials from a Named Monster. We can modify your equipment with the materials here or you can take them to a weapons shop," said Melissa.

"If possible, we would prefer to modify here, but we will allow you to make the final decision of course. If you allow us to work with Redface, we will offer a higher purchase rate, so we will exchange the Cotton Balls for two silver pieces. We can simply dissect Redface and give you the materials, or we can purchase Redface whole from you for eight gold. If you would like to only dissect Redface then return the materials, we will ask for a fee of ten copper," said Rikerton.

Materials from a Named Monster could be traded at high rates, and if the Guild had a bounty on it, the prize was also large. If we ever ran into another one, we should try to defeat it even if it was a strong opponent.

"Atobe, what should we do?"

"Hmm..." I thought for a moment. Should we ask them to process the materials or sell the whole thing to them? I wanted to make the party as powerful as possible so that we could defeat strong enemies, so we should go for processing the materials.

"What kind of materials can be made from Redface?" I asked.

"When Redface is near death, it releases spouts of fire from its body and starts Blaze Diving wildly. If we process it, we will be able to harness that power," answered Rikerton.

It uses such a dangerous skill when it's about to die... Good thing we had the ten support damage so we were able to finish it off before it could use that skill.

"We can remove the blaze stones inside Redface's fur and body, which you can then apply to your weapons. If you do, you'll be able to use a blaze-type skill without consuming any magic power," continued Rikerton.

"I see, so we can change a weapon from having no attribute into having a blaze attribute," I said.

"Exactly. If we're lucky, one Redface body will produce the materials to make three or more weapons. If you wish to leave both the dissection and processing of materials to us, we will apply the cost of remaining materials to cover our fee for dissection and processing, and then give you any excess there may be."

"Could we make defensive equipment with the remaining materials?"

"You can apply the fur to a shield, which will increase its fire resistance. You could also make some smaller items such as a scarf. You can expect a small item to also increase the wearer's fire resistance, but that will use up all the materials other than the meat."

We were lucky that Redface was bigger than a normal Cotton Ball because that meant we'd be able to make more equipment. We'd be able to strengthen some of the equipment of every party member. I decided we would improve the fire resistance of Theresia's buckler and give Igarashi a scarf. Then we could improve my slingshot.

"Atobe, have you decided what we'll do?" asked Igarashi.

"Yeah. Do you ever wear scarves?"

"Sometimes... Are you going to have one made for me?"

"A larger surface area would definitely provide more resistance, but we're heading to buy armor after this. I'd like for the vanguard and midguard to have fire resistance," I said. I didn't know if we'd run into any monsters today that could use blaze skills, but there wasn't any harm in taking the resistance. I wanted to be prepared so that our party could defend against attacks like that.

"All right, leave it to the Rikerton Dissection Center and Workshop. It will take some time, so you might like to attend to any other errands you may have," said Rikerton as he drew up the paperwork and Melissa took Redface's body into the back of the shop. I wasn't sure if it was because of the rare materials, but her eyes seemed to have more life in them than before.

Next was the weapons shop. I wanted to try and find Madoka the Merchant. Hopefully, she was still by the labyrinth's entrance.

Part VII: New Weapons

Ribault and his party were stationed in front of the stairs leading to the Field of Dawn like previous day. Nearby was a girl seeing off an all-male party. I recognized her as the girlie friend of Suzuna's who'd been on the bus, even though she'd changed her clothes and was wearing a hooded sweater and a skirt today.

"Good luck, everybodyyy!" she called to the group.

"Yeah! We're gonna earn a ton of money for you, Misaki!" replied one of the men.

Her hair was dyed a warm brown, cut to a medium length and permed into gentle waves. She was quite cute despite being so young; no one would really be surprised if you had told them she was a magazine model.

"It looks like she's using them as her gofers... She must have them wrapped around her finger," said Igarashi.

"If so, looks like she knows how to make it in life. But if a Seeker doesn't go into the labyrinths, then neither their level nor their contribution points go up, so it's high risk," I replied as the girl named Misaki walked our way. She spotted us and smiled happily.

"Oh goodie! There's Japanese people here! I feel sooo much better now. I've gotten mixed up with aaall sorts of people since coming to this new world. There's even monsters!" This Misaki girl had a habit of drawing out some of her words. I always felt sleepy listening to people who talked like that. I didn't exactly hate it, but it was kind of saccharine.

"Oh, you don't need to worry about thoose guys," she added. "I just joined up with them since I'd been wondering what this whole party thing's like in this world. They looked cool, but even if they're high level, it's juuust the two of them. I felt like they'd expect me to put in a lot of the work, so I'm gonna peace out."

"Peace...? Oh, you mean you're going to leave their party?" I asked.

"Yeah. I think an all-girl party would be waaay better," she replied.

"So you should've gone along with your friend, then," said Igarashi, her eyes as piercing as usual. Misaki looked a little thrown for a moment but then just laughed and brushed it off.

"Ah-ha-haaa, maaaybe. I just started following those guys around on a whim. They kept saying it'd be dangerous, though.

Oh, there's Suzu! Suzu, wait for meee!" Misaki noticed Suzuna and Elitia about to enter the Field of Dawn today as well. She had some sort of conversation with them, and then the three of them headed into the labyrinth together.

Geez... She's going right to the same place as the party she just left. Guess this girl really does everything on a whim.

While I stood there thinking, Igarashi and Theresia were both staring at me for some reason.

"You're not thinking it might be a good idea to invite her to join us depending on what her job is, are you?" asked Igarashi.

"No, that's not it. She seems like a bit of a troublemaker, so I was just worried. I hope I'm just overthinking things."

"Hmm...I thought all men loved a cute schoolgirl."

"Uh, well I guess there probably are a lot of people like that, but I'm not one of them." I actually hadn't put much thought into it, so I just said what popped into my mind. Ever since I'd become an adult, seeing schoolgirls in uniform just made me feel nostalgic.

"Besides, I've been thinking that I don't want to search for any particular person to join the party. I'd rather just naturally meet people and decide 'yeah, I want this person with me' and invite them from there."

"...So...was that the same with me...?" started Igarashi.

"......" Theresia stared wordlessly at me.

"Oh, oops, sorry to keep you waiting. Igarashi, it looks like Theresia's eager to get the ball rolling already, so let's go buy some weapons."

"Y-yeah, the ball. Gotta keep that ball rolling," said Igarashi.

I headed toward Madoka's stall to buy weapons. She waved at us when she saw us coming.

"Good morning, mister! Oh, and you're the miss I sold the spear to yesterday... You look like you're doing well now, but you seemed injured earlier..."

"Yes, I'm doing all right thanks to the spear you helped me pick out. Unfortunately...it broke."

"Oh no... It didn't even work on the first-floor monsters? I'm so sorry. I can't believe I sold you such a poor-quality item."

"No, it's not the weapon's fault. I ran into a Named Monster. The spear you sold me worked perfectly against normal Cotton Balls."

"A Named Monster? I've heard running into one of those can be just awful for a level-one person... I'm so glad you two are all right!" She had good reason to be worried for us, but tears started welling up in her eyes, which made Igarashi tear up, too.

I waited a moment for the two to collect themselves. They smiled in embarrassment once they had, their eyes still red, but we were able to get back to business.

"Thank you for worrying about us. We're planning to be very careful while we seek from here on out. I was hoping we could buy some new weapons to help us with that...," I said.

"Of course. In District Eight, I have one main shop as well as two branches. At this one, I have equipment for beginners as well as for one step above," said Madoka.

"You wouldn't have anything a step above a slingshot, like a super slingshot, would you? ...No, looks like you don't. I guess it's a good thing I asked to have it strengthened then."

"I'm sorry. We don't sell any strong slingshots in District Eight, though you could have one made for you if you bring the materials to a craftsman," suggested Madoka.

I had left my slingshot at Rikerton's so they could modify it. Seemed like that was the right decision. If they didn't sell any stronger weapons, then our best choice was to improve the ones we had.

"Okay, Igarashi, would you like to choose a new weapon first?"

"Sure... I bought a wooden spear yesterday."

"Madoka, do you have anything stronger than that? It doesn't have to be a spear, probably any type of long weapon would work."

"Let's see... How about these? We have lances, spears, and javelins made of bronze. I also have a trident, though that's a bit of a different style," she replied.

Igarashi looked at each option individually and ended up selecting the lance, quite possibly because it was sold in a set with a shield.

"You can attack with a lance while still guarding yourself. Many people use it when they're placed in the vanguard position," continued Madoka.

"All right, sounds like the lance is a good choice for now. It's handled a bit differently from a naginata, but I should be able to use it since I'm a Valkyrie... You think this would work, Atobe?"

"S-sure. It kind of bugs me that I, the man, will be stuck behind you the entire time...but that's where a rearguard's strength lies."

"The lance it is then. I can always change to another position if we get other party members who are more suited for vanguard."

"There are many people who use spears or javelins as both vanguards and midguards," added Madoka. "Please feel free to come back if you'd like something like that."

There wasn't anything better than Theresia's short sword available, but we had left her buckler to be modified, even though it was one of the Mercenary Office's pieces of equipment, so we bought one to replace it.

Next up was to find some armor for Igarashi that wasn't so heavy that she couldn't use it, so we bought her a bronze breastplate. Madoka also had the right size in stock of some leather armor, so we bought some greaves that looked suitably Valkyrie-like. Igarashi's new equipment came to a total of 250 copper pieces and Theresia's buckler was 50. I wasn't sure what I should buy for myself, but I ended up buying some banded armor with leather greaves and gauntlets.

"Heh... Atobe, you seem more heroic somehow. How do I look?"

"Actually, I think it suits you perfectly. Valkyrie is definitely the right job for you."

"...You're not even gonna try switching up your compliments? Oh well, as long as it doesn't look bad." She didn't seem overly delighted, but she did look a little happy. The compliment was genuine, though—I wasn't just trying to be polite.

The only thing was that the bronze breastplate emphasized the size of her chest...but I could tell that making women's armor must be incredibly difficult just by looking at the artistically crafted curves.

"Theresia can't change from her lizard equipment, right? ...I wonder if it's attached to her skin," said Igarashi.

"I don't think it's possible for me to remove it yet."

Theresia had once lost her life inside the labyrinth and been resurrected as a demi-human. According to Leila, it would be safe to assume that undoing that change into a demi-human wouldn't be possible for a one-star Seeker like me.

"Miss, mister, your new equipment looks great on you! I will pray for your safety on your next expedition. I'll do my best to get good equipment for you, too!" said Madoka.

"Thank you. Can you also make equipment if we bring you the materials?" I asked.

"Yep, our stores act as intermediaries with various craftsmen. Please feel free to bring me any ores you find in the labyrinth."

Monster materials, ores...there were so many things I wanted to find in the labyrinth. I also wanted to buy a larger bag since the leather sack I had didn't have much carrying capacity, but that problem was solved when we went back to Rikerton's.

We picked up the modified slingshot—now a blazeshot—a red buckler, and red scarf. Meanwhile, Melissa brought out a large knapsack.

"Hey! Those were some incredible materials you brought to us. Even Melissa's happy as a clam. This is just a small token of appreciation. May your hunts be fruitful, and should you run into another Named Monster, I hope you'll consider visiting our store again," said Rikerton.

"Oh, thank you so much! I was just thinking about how I

wanted a new bag," I said. Rikerton had probably noticed how small my leather sack was. This knapsack had more than double the capacity.

"...Not bad. Come again," said Melissa, the corners of her mouth turned up in a tiny smile before she went into the back of the shop. I didn't know if she just enjoyed dissecting or was excited to be able to handle a rare monster, but that was the first time I'd seen any sort of smile from her.

"It's been so long since my daughter's talked about wanting to go into the labyrinth. On top of that, there's talk of a Named Monster that appeared on the second floor of the Field of Dawn and hasn't been defeated yet, so it's got a nice bounty. Melissa's waiting excitedly for that to come in, too."

I filed that information away, since it meant that if we managed to make it to the second floor today, we could potentially run into another Named Monster, and checked out my modified slingshot.

Part VIII: New Battle Formation

Once we'd prepared our equipment for seeking, we each picked out some portable provisions being sold in the square and were finally ready for our second adventure into the labyrinth.

"Ah, see you've been hard at work getting ready. Glad to see you've decided to team up with Arihito, miss," said Ribault.

"Oh, please, don't call me *miss*… I'm younger than Atobe."

"Ha-ha-ha, sorry, sorry. Anyway, you take care now. I think you three might just be able to make it to the bottom of the Field of Dawn today. There's only three floors."

"Thank you. We want to go as far as we can," I said, then we headed down into the labyrinth as Ribault saw us off.

The wide expanse before our eyes, the sudden brightness—it was the same as the day before. I guess time didn't change in the labyrinth. At least the Field of Dawn seemed to be permanently stuck in the morning.

```
◆Current Party◆
1: Arihito    ※◆$□      Level 2
2: Kyouka     Valkyrie  Level 1
3: Theresia   Rogue     Level 3  Mercenary
```

I could arrange the party's battle formation using my license. I still didn't think there was any need to make a distinction between vanguard and midguard, so I decided it'd be fine to make them both vanguards.

"Today I'll have both of you be vanguards," I told them.

"Okay. I want to hurry up and try out my new weapon," said Igarashi.

"……"

If we ever found someone specialized in defensive equipment, like a heavy infantryman, I could have them act as our tank. Finding new party members was looking like it'd be an important issue to deal with.

"Let's walk for a little bit, then try our new battle formation out on a Cotton Ball," I suggested.

"All right. You know, I feel so much better having companions around…," replied Igarashi.

We hadn't even walked for three minutes when Theresia drew her short sword. I wasn't sure if it was a Rogue skill or something, but she seemed to have a wider range in which she could detect enemies compared to me or Igarashi.

◆Monster Encountered◆
COTTON BALL
Level 1
On Guard
Dropped Loot: ???

Hmm… What's this? Is the actual body of a defeated Cotton Ball not considered loot? Is it carrying something else then…?

"—Here it comes!" called Igarashi.

I looked up and realized it was going for an attack, but I wouldn't be able to take a shot with my slingshot if my vanguards didn't leave open my line of fire. It'd probably be easiest to try to stop a monster with a long-ranged attack before it even closed in, but first, there was something I needed to test. That was whether my skills affected only the person I indicated or if they affected every party member in front of me.

"Igarashi, I'll back you up!" I shouted the moment the Cotton Ball flew toward Igarashi.

"Ngh!"

First, I'd activate Defense Support targeting Igarashi.

◆Current Status◆
> Arihito activated Defense Support 1 ⟶ Target:
                                                    Kyouka

The Cotton Ball's violent tackle was completely prevented by the barrier, which protected Igarashi. She'd had her shield up ready to block but saw her enemy thrown backward and decided to take advantage of the opportunity by readying her lance and thrusting at the Cotton Ball.

"—Hyaaa!"

◆Current Status◆
> Kyouka's attack hit Cotton Ball
10 support damage
> 1 Cotton Ball defeated

So the skill activates even if I don't say I'm supporting them out loud. I guess being in the back really is all it needs.

Igarashi's lance attack got through the Cotton Ball's defenses, too, but the support damage struck the Cotton Ball with an invisible force and sent it flying. I wasn't sure I'd ever get used to seeing the strange sight. I wondered how Igarashi would respond.

"Igarashi, that was a great attack. I suppose I should expect as much from someone who used to be in the naginata club... Uh, i-is something wrong?"

Igarashi turned slowly back around, her expression jubilant—or maybe *ecstatic* was more accurate.

"...Just now, when the monster's attack got repelled, that was you supporting me and then helping with my attack, right?"

"Y-yes. My job lets me support the vanguard. It's different from a Wizard or a Priest, though."

Igarashi planted her lance in the ground, carried her shield under one arm, and patted her cheek with her free hand before sighing.

"...Did it feel good?" I asked.

"Yeah...it felt amazing..."

The way I phrased that could be open to misinterpretation... but I suppose it would feel nice to be supported. I mean, it would be exhilarating to feel invincible like that.

My skills were the type of support that could make a Valkyrie feel so ecstatic. I suppose that might be why Theresia thought of me as a good person, too.

"Seriously, yesterday I put everything I had into attacking that Cotton Ball, and it took five hits before I finally finished it off. But this time I just went *pow!* and it went *bam!* and, oh, it was so satisfying," explained Igarashi.

"I think you're saying you relieve stress with violence."

"Hey, I'm not that bad. I could practically star in some Sunday-morning cartoon."

That was the first time I'd ever seen her have so much fun. I hadn't thought my skills would make her so happy, so it made me happy, too, that she told me. Maybe this Sunday-morning cartoon she was talking about was a magical-girl anime or had super-heroes or cyborgs.

"Hey, Atobe. Let's do another one. Each Cotton Ball is five copper pieces anyway."

"All right, let's find our next target. Theresia's range for detecting enemies is larger, so you fall back from her a little, Igarashi. I'd also like to supply support fire, so could you leave a space open for me to shoot through?"

"Yep, understood. Don't shoot me in the back, though. It looks like it'd hurt."

I absolutely did not want to accidentally shoot them in the back. I wondered if my rearguard job had some skill that prevented me from hitting my allies in the back... I really wanted to get to level 3 as soon as possible.

Speaking of, I still had one skill point remaining. Perhaps I should double-check what skills I could get at level 2. I wanted to only take the necessary skills and save the remaining skill points, though. Three support skills should be plenty for now.

I noticed something as I bent down to pick up the Cotton Ball's body and put it in my sack—there was some sort of stone stuck to its head.

"This looks like it might be that dropped loot," I said.

"Did you find some treasure? Oh, that's a pretty stone; it's all sparkly," said Igarashi.

Was this some sort of ore? It was a round green stone, and it did seem somewhat metallic. Individual Cotton Balls seemed to produce these stones from their head...but was it a part of their skeleton? Or something they secreted, which formed into a stone? I felt like I was looking at one of the mysteries of monsters.

After our encounter with the Cotton Ball, I checked the Dropped Loot part of my license and discovered what the green stone was. Apparently, it was called "wind agate." Perhaps Cotton Balls were monsters with a wind attribute since they moved like gusts in a gale.

"…Hmm?"

The next thing we ran into was a Cotton Ball with some sort of fist-sized thing floating near it.

"Uh, Atobe… I-isn't that a giant bee—? Aaahhh!"

"—Igarashi, I'll back you up! Defend against its attack, then dodge to the side!"

The airborne monster went for Igarashi while the Cotton Ball attacked Theresia. I prayed my skill would work as I watched over what transpired.

◆Current Status◆
> Arihito activated Defense Support 1 ⟶ Target:
                                                    Kyouka,
                                                    Theresia

Nice…I can apply support to everyone in the vanguard!

The bee-like thing and the Cotton Ball's tackle were repelled with a *ping* by the Defense Support. Igarashi leaped to the side like I'd asked, her shield still up, and I fired a blazeshot.

C'mon, hit!

◆Current Status◆

> Arihito used Blazeshot ⟶ Hit Poison Spear Bee
> Poison Spear Bee was Burnt

"—KIIIII!"

I didn't know how much damage it took from it, but I was able to hit it after its movement seemed slower when it was repelled by the Defense Support.

"Hyaaa—!"

"—!"

Igarashi jabbed her spear at the burning bee; Theresia closed in on the Cotton Ball and swung her short sword down on it.

◆Current Status◆

> Kyouka's attack hit Poison Spear Bee
10 support damage
> Theresia's attack hit Cotton Ball
10 support damage
> 1 Cotton Ball, 1 Poison Spear Bee defeated

"Whew... What a shock. Bees are dangerous because of their venom. And one that big..." Igarashi hesitantly approached the fallen bee to examine it. "Atobe, the wings burned when you hit it with your slingshot. It moved more slowly then, so I was able to hit it with my lance. Did you do that on purpose?"

"Nope. It'd be pretty cool if I had, but it was just a regular coincidence."

"Ah, I see. Well, good thing you're using a blaze weapon."

Since it was a weapon made with the resources gained from Redface, who had appeared in these very same fields, I wondered if it would be useful on other monsters in the same area. Anyway, it seemed like the start of today's seeking was going according to plan.

"Should we head toward the second floor? We'll need to be careful of monsters on the way obviously," I said.

"Sure, I'm not at all tired yet. Plus, I want to level up soon, so I hope they keep coming."

By the time we arrived at the entrance to the second floor, we were truly aware of the size of this labyrinth and had managed to defeat fifteen Cotton Balls and six Poison Spear Bees. We could only just fit all the Cotton Balls even if we tried to use each of our bags as efficiently as possible. Cotton Balls were light, but they took up a lot of space. Soon we'd have to think about taking only the most valuable monsters back with us. Either that or find a companion who could remove just the materials from them.

CHAPTER 3

Our First Challenge

Part I: A Party of Two Girls

We ran into another party hunting Cotton Balls on the first floor who told us the entrance to the second floor didn't have stairs like the labyrinth's. Instead, if you continued across the fields, you would eventually come to two large trees standing near each other. We could get to the second floor by walking between them. Since it was called a labyrinth, I had the impression that passing through the floors would trigger a change in the floors themselves, but I guess that wasn't the case in the Field of Dawn at least.

We eventually found the trees we were looking for. The air between them seemed somehow hazy, like some sort of gate down to the next floor.

"Should we eat something before we go down to the second floor? I think it's better to sit down and have a proper meal instead of snacking here and there," said Igarashi.

"Yeah, you're right. Okay, let's keep going after we've had something to eat."

There had been a store selling dried foods that seemed like they would stay good for the day at least. The first thing the shop worker suggested a Seeker buy was a mix of nuts and dried fruit, which was formed into bars with wheat or some other flour and baked. They were like crackers or biscuits and seemed fairly nutritious. They were quite hard, so apparently, it was common to bring broth in a water bottle or thermos to soak them in and soften them up, but I just tore back the paper it was wrapped in and bit into one. It wasn't actually so hard that I felt my teeth might break against it, and since the inside was a little soft, it wasn't too difficult to chew.

"...Oh man, I'm really thirsty now," I said. "I'm starting to think it's more important to keep an eye on the amount of water you have instead of food when you're in the labyrinth."

"Yeah, it's not like you can just drink water from a spring if you happen to find it, so I imagine long adventures into the labyrinth can be quite taxing. But apparently, if you have magic, and you advance far enough into the labyrinth, you can return wherever you like along the way, or you can leave and return at the same place," said Igarashi.

"I bet people with those kinds of skills are really popular and hard to find to join your party."

Theresia was plenty hungry as well, so I had her choose something she liked from the store. She picked out jerky. The shop worker warned us that alone didn't have all the nutrition she would need, so they said we should make sure she also ate something like nuts and some dried fruit.

"…Mm…"

She's completely mute except when she's eating… Oh, never mind, that's just the sound of her swallowing.

"…So there's some reason why Theresia's a mercenary, right?" asked Igarashi. "I mean, she never even says anything…"

"Demi-humans aren't able to express themselves with words. That doesn't mean she's going to be like this forever, though. I think if I can find some way to remove the lizard gear…"

"That's one reason you want to make her a permanent member of the party, right?"

"It is one reason. The main thing is that she was so dependable when we were seeking yesterday." I knew that if Theresia hadn't been there with me, Redface would have destroyed us all. A rearguard can't do anything without a vanguard. If I can't use my support skills, then I can't use the real strength of my rearguard job, so I needed to make sure my relationship with my companions was always strong.

"Igarashi, we've been hunting for about an hour. Are you tired?"

"Nope, not at all. Sometimes when you're behind me, my body feels kinda warm and any fatigue just disappears. Is that another one of your skills?"

"Uh, yeah, sort of. Do you have any other weird sensations like that?" Igarashi had just taken a bite of her food and couldn't answer right away. Her cheeks flushed red as she focused on chewing.

"Mm… S-sorry, you asked me right when I took a bite."

"N-no, that's my fault. I'm just bothering you while you eat."

"Other weird sensations… Um, how do I explain this… It sort of feels like I'm being *protected* or something."

"Oh, I see. I guess it's good if that's what it feels like." I was, in fact, protecting her from behind, so I guess the feeling itself wasn't wrong.

"These portable rations are so bland. Maybe I'll try making some packed lunches for us."

"Yeah, that'd be nice. Does that mean you can cook, Igarashi?"

"About half the girls in our department would pack their lunch. I thought it'd be nice to eat with everyone, and I didn't have time to go buy something. Plus, the company cafeteria was always so crowded, so I started making my own food out of necessity."

Thinking about it, I remembered seeing the female staff eating their homemade lunches in a meeting room quite a few times.

"Could I go to the market once we're done seeking today? I feel like there I'll be able to find different ingredients I can use to make lunch."

"Yeah, of course. All right, so we've got our plans for after seeking… Theresia, are you full?"

I heard her gulp down her last bit of jerky, but she just looked at me. Had she been full, she would have nodded, so that meant she was still hungry.

"We have some more jerky or some of what Igarashi is eating. Which do you prefer?"

"……"

Theresia pointed at the meat but then moved her finger slowly to point at the food bars. I felt like there was some emotion behind that movement, and it made me unexpectedly happy.

"You like the meat better, don't you?" I asked and looked at her, and she gave a slight nod. I wondered why she hesitated... Was it because I had only eaten the food bar and she was concerned about finishing off the last of the jerky?

I gave her the jerky, and she tore off a small piece with her teeth, then looked at me for some reason while she chewed.

"Theresia, you seem...happy?" I said.

"......"

"...W-well, at the very least, you seem to like jerky."

The portable food was so hard and just clumped up in your mouth, so you had to sit there chewing forever. But it filled our stomachs and gave us the nutrition we needed, though having some homemade lunches every once in a while, like Igarashi suggested, would be nice.

We entered the second floor of the labyrinth to even more trees than on the first floor. It looked like it was progressing from a field to a savannah... Although I couldn't say I really knew what a savannah was.

"Which direction do we head now? Since we said our goal was to make it to the third floor," asked Igarashi.

"Apparently, there's another gate like this one if we keep heading northeast." If I hadn't received the information from Ribault, we could have ended up just wandering in a random direction and tiring ourselves out.

"Oh, right. Atobe, I'm only level one, but I've got two skills. I was wondering if you could give me some advice on how to use them."

"Right, the ones you showed me yesterday—Mirage Step and Thunderbolt?"

"Huh? …You can see if I've used a skill or not?"

"If you look at your license, it's shown on the page called Current Status." I flipped through the pages of my license. After sliding my finger along the surface a few times, I found the page I was looking for.

◆Current Status◆
> Arihito and Kyouka are talking
> Theresia is using Scout Range Extension 1

It even shows basic actions, huh? Good thing Theresia has a skill that's always active without using magic.

"Oh, that's interesting. Ah…a thing came up saying my vitality was restored. Is that what's making my body feel all warm and tingly?"

"Yeah, s-sorry. I think it's a skill that's always active… It's probably hard for you to relax with that, so I'll try to find a way to deactivate it."

"…Oh! Yesterday, when I was hit by the red thing, I was in so much pain, but after a bit, it didn't feel quite so bad…"

"Y-yeah…I used this skill. We have both vitality and magic, and my skill recovers vitality."

I remembered using the skill while basically hugging her from behind. I didn't have much choice, though, since I needed to make sure I was placed behind her in order for it to work. My Recovery Support seemed to be always active and effective even if my companion was about fifteen feet away. We'd need to find an easy enemy so that I could test to see if there was a distance limit to its effect.

—It was then that we heard another party in battle a little way away. Theresia's Scout Range Extension had alerted her. I looked into the distance and realized who it was: Elitia and Suzuna.

Misaki isn't with them...and the thing they're fighting...what is it, like a humanoid pig or boar...?

"GRAAAAW!!"

"Eeeek—"

"Suzuna, fall back! Don't go any farther!" ordered Elitia.

◆Monsters Encountered◆

FANGED ORC

Level 2

In Combat

Dropped Loot: ???

POISON SPEAR BEE

Level 1

On Guard

Dropped Loot: ???

POISON SPEAR BEE

Level 1

On Guard

Dropped Loot: ???

Elitia's golden hair billowed in the wind, the young girl clad in silver armor standing fearlessly against the creature much bigger than her as it roared in rage and swung its fist.

"—Begone!"

The force with which she spoke seemed out of character, but it probably came from her long experience in battle and showed that even she wouldn't be letting her guard down in a fight.

◆Current Status◆
> Elitia used Slash Ripper ⟶ Hit Fanged Orc
> 1 Fanged Orc defeated

The orc didn't even have time to let out a death knell. When it closed in on her, all I could see was Elitia placing her hand on her sword. The next moment, blood spurted from the orc, and it collapsed to the ground.

She defeated the stronger enemy... But there's still—!

"Igarashi, Theresia! Lure those bees away!"

"...Got it!"

"...!"

◆Current Status◆
> Theresia activated Accel Dash

Theresia used her skill to rush into one bee's range, forcing it to target her, but the other bee was in a bad location. It didn't matter how skilled a Swordswoman you were, if randomly placed enemies like these bees suddenly attacked, and if they targeted

Suzuna, who was the rearguard, there was no way you could react quickly enough.

"—Arihito!" cried Suzuna when she saw us, but she was unable to move as she was trying to keep herself down.

I launched a slingshot bullet at the bee that was circling her in the air before it could go in for an attack.

C'mon!

◆Current Status◆
> Arihito used Blazeshot ⟶ Hit Poison Spear Bee
> Poison Spear Bee was Burnt

"—KIII!"

I hit it, but it was so far away that the bullet didn't have much force behind it. If we couldn't follow up with an attack, we wouldn't be able to defend against it!

"—!"

When the Poison Spear Bee that was in midair to the left of Theresia came down to attack her, she swung her short sword in an attempt to slice it as it attacked.

◆Current Status◆
> Arihito activated Defense Support 1 ⟶ Target:
                                          Theresia
> Poison Spear Bee's attack hit Theresia
No damage
> Theresia's attack hit Poison Spear Bee
10 support damage
> 1 Poison Spear Bee defeated

As long as we could defend completely against the bees' stingers with Defense Support, we'd have no risk of getting poisoned. But there was still the burning bee in midair on the right—!

A swordsman's weakness is an enemy high up in the sky where they can't hit. Which means we need—!

"—Igarashi!"

"Got it... Take this!" She was the only one of us besides me who could use long-distance attacks. As a Valkyrie, she could use both sword and magic.

◆Current Status◆
> Kyouka activated Thunderbolt ⟶ Hit Poison Spear Bee
> 1 Poison Spear Bee defeated

The bee was weakened by the fire but tried to stab Suzuna with its stinger. Igarashi's Thunderbolt struck the creature, sending it flying and leaving sparks in its wake as it fell to the ground.

Elitia sheathed her sword and walked up to Suzuna but was unable to speak, perhaps because she was aware of the mistake she'd made. The two waited until Igarashi, Theresia, and I came up to them. I offered my hand to Suzuna to help her up.

"Are you all right? Are you hurt at all?" I asked.

"N-no... I'm fine," she replied. "I knew it; I'm holding everyone back..."

"No, that's not true," added Elitia. "You've come all the way here with me. You've worked so hard, and you've even beaten Cotton Balls."

If only Elitia fought, then Suzuna's experience points wouldn't go up. It sounded like Elitia gave Suzuna opportunities to attack, but even that would come with risks.

"Do you mean you've been drawing the monsters' attacks and having Suzuna deal the final hit?" I asked.

"Yeah...but there were some other people hunting, so we weren't finding much," replied Elitia.

"So then you came to the second floor in search of better hunting grounds. The orc alone probably would have been fine, but it was pretty dangerous with the bees, right?"

"I...I can't spend too much time here. If I don't get Suzuna quickly to the same level eight as me, I won't be able to go back..."

"Go back? When you say go back...sorry if I misunderstand, but do you mean to the White Night Brigade?" Elitia's eyes widened just slightly. She looked like she wanted to ask how I knew about that but didn't say anything.

"...I won't be returning to the Brigade. They abandoned my companion. In the depths of that labyrinth...my good friend is waiting for me there. If she's on her own for too long, she'll become a soulless demi-human," said Elitia.

"Do you mean there's some sort of monster that captures Seekers? Can't you ask the Guild or other parties for help?"

"You'll understand soon," she replied. "Seekers will do anything they can to stay alive. That's not a bad thing... We don't seek because we want to die. We seek because we want fame or freedom."

It seemed that even Suzuna hadn't heard this much from Elitia before, but she was calm as she listened. She had been scared when the Poison Spear Bees were after her, but that wasn't all that was in her. I could see something in her eyes; there was something in the labyrinth she was searching for, too.

"...I'm sorry. When I saw that huge pig monster, my legs just buckled. And here I should've been using my bow and arrow to back you," said Suzuna.

I wasn't quite certain why, but Suzuna was equipped with a bow. Maybe it was because when you think of a Shrine Maiden, you think of a shrine, and when you think of a shrine, you think of those holy arrows that drive away evil. She was wearing a white top with a red skirt, and her black hair was tied back with a ribbon. We were in another world, but it looked like a pretty typical Japanese Shrine Maiden outfit.

"So what happened to that other person I saw you enter the labyrinth with?" I asked, and both Elitia's and Suzuna's faces clouded over. It must've been something bad.

"...She...she opened a treasure chest but failed...," started Suzuna.

"That girl, Misaki, apparently took the Gambler job. She said she's supposed to have really good luck, so she opened the chest a monster had dropped, and then she disappeared...," explained Elitia.

"A treasure chest... We've been hunting monsters all day but haven't seen even one. Are they really a thing?" asked Igarashi. Like she said, we'd found some dropped loot but hadn't seen anything that even remotely resembled a treasure chest.

"There's a limited number of treasure chests that can appear on a floor. The stronger the monster, the more likely it is to drop a chest, but you wouldn't be able to find one even if you killed hundreds of Cotton Balls or bees. So I really do think that Misaki was lucky...but disarming the traps is usually done by the Thief jobs. If only I'd explained properly...," said Elitia. She had plenty of experience but seemed to be having trouble leading a group of beginners.

"If she was transported by a trap, where was she sent?" I asked.

"It was most likely a Floor Warp trap, so she should be on this floor somewhere. If we don't find her soon..."

"Yeah. Atobe, what should we do? Should we look for her with them?"

"I'd like to if we can... Elitia, were there any other parties on this floor? If there were, we could ask them to help as well." Fetching Ribault would take too long. If only Misaki had a Return Scroll. It didn't matter if she would get minus contribution points; this was an emergency.

"...It might've been my imagination, but I thought I saw someone right after we got to this floor," said Elitia. "It was probably just another party that I noticed out of the corner of my eye, though."

"Or maybe some sort of surveillance person?" Igarashi wondered. "But why...?"

I suddenly remembered the conversation I'd overheard at the tavern last night during dinner. It was a party of three men. They'd known that Elitia had come to District Eight. It sounded like they were planning something.

"...Guess we might have trouble getting other parties to work with us. That said, if we split up, we'll have a hard time dealing with any groups of monsters we might run into. Elitia, please, let us join your party. Even just temporarily," I suggested.

She was a level-8 Seeker... That seemed like something so powerful we couldn't even imagine getting there. The reason she was so desperate to train up a rearguard was that her own party had abandoned her companion. She was trying to form a new party in order to save her. It was too dangerous, though, as they were now. Even though Suzuna had heard Elitia's story now, she didn't seem to have any desire to leave her party... Even if the risk of a counterattack were there the entire time, she tried to make the killing blow.

"...You can't claim everything is fine as it is," I continued. "If you try to have her take the experience from killing Poison Spear Bees, there's a chance that Suzuna will get hit with a counter-attack. The same is true of Cotton Balls, but the poison is just too dangerous. If possible, it would best for her to join a party with people of a similar level."

"Are you saying I'm not capable of being in a party with Suzuna?" asked Elitia.

"No, that's not what I mean. I want to help you find your friend, too, if at all possible. But if the question is about raising Suzuna's level, she should join our party, and you should work solo for a while until she's up to your level."

"...He's right. I don't care what the reason is, I'm not going to abandon someone who's trying to save their friend," added

Igarashi. "And I'm worried about Suzuna, too. We were reincarnated at the same time."

"...You guys...," whimpered Suzuna as she pulled out a handkerchief and dabbed at the tears brimming in her eyes. Elitia didn't seem to know how to react but, after a moment, looked me in the face again.

"I have noticed how exceptional a rearguard you are. If you were helping, I'm sure we could raise Suzuna's level safely...but I had arbitrarily decided that you wouldn't agree to help us," she said finally.

"Because I need to keep knowledge about my true abilities from becoming too widely known. But I want to let a few trusted companions know about them so we can form a party and I can use my skills to their highest potential. As a vanguard, one issue you have is that you're not suited to protecting your rearguard. Are there any other issues?"

"...If you put Suzuna in your party and allow me to be a 'guest,' then I can keep my distance while I fight," replied Elitia. "If we do that, there won't be any other issues. But if I tell you to run, you leave me and you run. That's my only request... I've given Suzuna a Return Scroll, so you can use that." She put out her hand, which I shook, and I flashed her a grin in response to her tense expression.

"I look forward to seeing your skills, Mr. Arihito. Please excuse my handshake while wearing my gauntlets, they take some time to remove."

"Oh, no problem... I look forward to working together."

"I will be walking around and fighting alone, but since you've agreed to work together, you are entirely in control. Even though I'm not in your party, I'll listen to your orders, and any loot or valuables I find will belong to you. Let me know if you don't have enough money for day-to-day expenses."

"We're all right for now. Besides, I'm not the type to rely on others."

Elitia smiled happily. I wondered if that was more what she was really like. It wasn't a good emotional state if she was constantly brooding, her nerves stretched thin. I was glad we ran into them, for both her and Suzuna's sake.

Elitia then shook hands with Igarashi and Theresia. Suzuna timidly approached me.

"U-um… It's a pleasure to make your acquaintance again, Mr. Arihito. Allow me to introduce myself properly. My name is Shiromiya Suzuna."

"I'm Atobe Arihito. This is Igarashi Kyouka and Theresia, a lizardman." I gave our names in the traditional Japanese order, surname then given name.

"Nice to meet you," said Igarashi. "Glad to have more people in our party."

"……" Theresia was silent as always.

Igarashi smiled kindly, and Suzuna seemed to relax a little and smiled back. Theresia had a certain presence to her that would probably take Suzuna time to get used to, but Suzuna still shook her hand and greeted her sincerely.

My license displayed Elitia as a "guest"—perhaps it meant that she had only joined the party temporarily.

```
◆Current Party◆
1: Arihito   ※◆$□          Level 2
2: Kyouka    Valkyrie       Level 1
3: Suzuna    Shrine Maiden  Level 1
4: Theresia  Rogue          Level 3  Mercenary
Guest 1: Elitia
```

Part II: The Tyrant

We had more members in our party, but of course, I was still stuck in the back. I imagined this was probably the sight I would be seeing most often in life: the girls' backs.

Elitia's coming along with us as a guest, but I can't set her location in the party formation. There are some risks associated with her skills, but I still want to support her if possible...

"We can't go this way without those Fanged Orcs noticing us... I'll take them out." Elitia had decided this all on her own and went over to defeat them. I knew she felt responsible for Misaki, but this way, we weren't getting any experience.

...Hmm? Actually, we're not getting nothing in the way of experience.

When I looked at the party information page, there were the vitality and magic bars but also black and yellow circles. The circles seemed to be each person's experience, and whenever Elitia defeated a monster, it seemed to go up a tiny bit. When a black circle filled up, it turned yellow. I guessed that your level would go up once all ten circles had turned yellow. For convenience's sake, I decided to call these round experience-point circles *bubbles*. When a monster was killed, about one-tenth of a bubble was filled, so a tiny amount of experience was coming in. The amount for me was even less, and Theresia was getting basically none. I didn't think being a mercenary meant she didn't ever gain experience, so I assumed it was going up a tiny bit.

"Arihito, I have some orc fangs. Would you mind taking them?" asked Elitia. "I only took the high-quality ones, but I have a lot. You can keep the money you can trade them for—you are the party leader after all."

"Sure, I'll take them. I'm going to run out of space to carry things soon, though."

"About how much is an orc fang worth?" asked Igarashi. It was the same thing I had been wondering. Elitia thought for a moment before answering.

"In District Eight, I think it's about three silver pieces. They're not used as materials in the higher districts, though, so nobody collects them. I don't think they're much cheaper than that in this district."

"That's not bad... Let's gather as many as we can. They don't even take up that much space, either," I said.

Ten high-quality orc fangs would be worth three gold. We needed money right now, so I was grateful for it. Gathering was secondary, though. First, we needed to find Misaki as quickly as possible. If she was moving around trying to find us, we should be able to see her even from afar.

But we heard her far before we saw her.

"—NOOOOOO! …Help! Help me! Somebodyyy!"

"Misaki! Ah…oh…," said Suzuna. She seemed to believe that was Misaki's voice, but when she turned in the direction of the scream, she saw some massive humanoid form looming in the distance and lost any other words.

An orc… A massive one…and it's got company!

We finally found Misaki. She was tied up and unable to move, lying on the grass like some sort of sacrifice to the massive orc. She wasn't screaming anymore. She might have passed out from sheer terror.

"S-something that huge…appears on the second floor of the beginners' dungeon…?" stammered Igarashi.

"…It's a Named Monster… A Named orc. There shouldn't be any Seekers who could draw that out. Someone must be trying to make us take care of their dirty work!" said Elitia.

Those guys in the tavern—this is what they were talking about!

A high-level Seeker dragging around deadweight, that's what the men in the tavern said. If Misaki hadn't been there, they would have aimed for Suzuna and made Elitia beat the Named Monster they had forced to come out. They would have her defeat a monster they couldn't at their level, then steal the treasure.

Most likely they had some method ready to put Elitia out of commission after she defeated the Named orc. They were probably here on this floor right now, hiding themselves and watching it all go down.

"—Everyone, stay where you are! I should be able to defeat the Named orc on my own!" cried Elitia.

"Elitia, wait!" I shouted.

At that moment, the group of normal orcs was moving to attack Misaki, who laid helpless and unmoving on the ground. She didn't have time to think about how to save her. All she knew was she needed to defeat those orcs.

"—I'll scatter your entrails across the field, foul orcs!" she cried.

◆Current Status◆
> ELITIA activated SONIC RAID
> ELITIA activated BLADE RONDE ⟶ Hit 6 FANGED ORCS
> 6 FANGED ORCS defeated

Sonic Raid was a skill far more powerful than Accel Dash that allowed her to move incredibly quickly.

Elitia closed in on the orcs in an instant and bared her blade. The skill she used was more powerful than Slash Ripper and allowed her to attack multiple close enemies. Her sword flashed in an arc, and like she had promised, pieces of the orcs' bodies flew across the grass.

But something happened when she was hit by the blood splashing back. She seemed to take on a menacing air.

◆Current Status◆
> ELITIA activated BERSERK

"...Haah... AAAAAAAAHH!"
I heard her let out a gut-wrenching roar.

This was the "problem" she had—a unique skill that activated when she was drenched in the blood of her enemies.

"Elitia—!" cried Suzuna.

"Atobe, we can't leave her! No matter how strong she is, she can't take that massive orc alone!"

"—Don't come near me!" shouted Elitia.

As far as I could see, this was the side effect of that Berserk skill. She was very agitated and aggressive. I guessed her strength was likely increased but that she may have lost the ability to distinguish friend from enemy.

Which is why she wouldn't join the party and told us to keep our distance...but...

She was trying to handle it all herself—the massive Named orc, the group of smaller orcs. She made it all her responsibility.

The problem was that while we may have some distance between us and her, there was still a chance that Misaki could be dragged into things. We couldn't stop Elitia now that she'd used Sonic Raid to move so far from us.

"I will save her... I'm...I'm not a murderer... I don't kill people!" cried Elitia. She killed the leading orcs, and though the remaining ones were afraid of her, the Named orc didn't seem concerned at all. It advanced toward her, its footsteps shaking the earth, and she faced it head-on.

I glanced at my license and knew I was too late even as I tried to shout a warning.

"Elitia! It's—!"

```
◆Monster Encountered◆
★JUGGERNAUT
Level 5
In Combat
Immune to physical attacks
Dropped Loot: ???
```

"—Hyaaaaaaaa!" screamed Elitia as she flew at the mountain-like orc.

But her sword failed to pierce its hide, instead sliding along the surface. The orc dodged.

"Ah—!"

The Named orc, Juggernaut, let out a terrifying roar, completely different from a normal orc. It was so much bigger and so much fiercer.

"*GGRRAAAAAAAAAAAA—!*"

```
◆Current Status◆
> ★JUGGERNAUT activated BRUTAL VOICE ⟶ ELITIA was
  temporarily STUNNED
> ★JUGGERNAUT captured ELITIA
```

"Aagh... Rrgh... Let go of me! ...Aaahh!"

It was a horrifying and demoralizing sight. Elitia had killed the Fanged Orcs like they were nothing, but now she was screaming to be released from the massive orc's grasp. The orcs on the ground rallied themselves and rush toward Misaki. I didn't want to let Igarashi, Theresia, or Suzuna die.

"...Arihito... Run! ...Aaagh!" shouted Elitia. If we left her, she'd be crushed. Juggernaut's hand might even be able to crush a human entirely.

She'd made us promise that if she told us to run, we'd use the Return Scroll that Suzuna had. We could have done that now; we should have done that now. There was no way we could win against a monster like that. But...if we ran, we'd be throwing away both Elitia's and Misaki's lives.

Just thinking that made an incredible anger well up inside of me. I couldn't let that happen. I couldn't forgive myself if I let that happen.

"Like hell we'll run...!" I shouted.

◆Current Status◆
> Arihito used Blazeshot ⟶ Hit ★Juggernaut
> ★Juggernaut was Burnt

"GWAAH!"

I aimed my blazeshot at Juggernaut's face in the hope that flame would get through its defenses even if physical attacks didn't...and I seemed to be right. The massive creature that wasn't even fazed by Elitia's sword was shaken by my shot and relaxed its grip.

"Agh...!"

◆Current Status◆
> ★Juggernaut attacked ⟶ Elitia evaded

Once she was released from Juggernaut's grip, Elitia was able to right herself before she hit the ground and evaded Juggernaut's attack, which came down from above. It was a good thing the stun effect went away immediately, but she still didn't seem able to use her nondominant hand.

This Named creature was level 5, but it seemed that wasn't a good indication of its real strength. Elitia was level 8, but it put her on the brink of death. I didn't want to accept it.

"Igarashi, Theresia, Suzuna. If things start looking grim, you need to leave me and run," I said.

"Tsk... As if I'd do a thing like that! I'm fighting until the end—!" retorted Igarashi.

"Please...listen to me. I promise I'll do anything you ask if you just make it back safe."

"...Even if things look hopeless, we won't run. So you have to let us stay, please," pleaded Suzuna.

"Suzuna...," Igarashi murmured. I didn't even feel like I could live in the face of that beast... She really was courageous even when it looked like the end.

"...Suzuna, get that Return Scroll ready so you can use it at any moment. Promise me," I said.

There was no way we could fight Juggernaut. Just going near it would mean instant death...but Elitia could evade its attacks. That meant we could make opportunities to attack.

Defense Support won't be very useful against something that huge, but maybe Attack Support...

"—Elitia! Join my party, just temporarily!" I shouted across the field, but Elitia didn't respond. She evaded Juggernaut's attacks once, twice, and looked for a chance to counterattack. Maybe it was an effect of Berserk, or maybe she was trying to force herself not to run.

No, that wasn't it. She was luring Juggernaut's attacks so that it didn't hit Misaki.

"You can't save Misaki like this! Please, listen to me!" I yelled as loudly as I possibly could, but Elitia didn't turn to look back. She was at her limit just dodging attacks.

"Elitia, please! Please listen to Arihito!" called Suzuna.

"—You...you don't want to die there, do you?!" screamed Igarashi.

Maybe our voices weren't reaching her—but right when we were about to give up...

◆Current Party◆

1:	Arihito	※◆$□	Level 2	
2:	Kyouka	Valkyrie	Level 1	
3:	Suzuna	Shrine Maiden	Level 1	
4:	Theresia	Rogue	Level 3	Mercenary
5:	Elitia	Cursed Blade	Level 8	

She joined... Maybe now we can do it...!

I could now use my support skills on her. *If it's close enough that I can shoot a blazeshot, the effects of my skills will reach her, too!*

"Elitia! Use a multihit attack! ...I'll back you up!"

Even if the Named orc was immune to physical attacks, if the damage for Attack Support was set permanently at ten points, then maybe, just maybe...

"—Hyaaa!"

Elitia used her remaining magic to activate Sonic Raid and disappeared, leaving Juggernaut's attack to cut through air. The next moment, she rained attacks down over Juggernaut's entire body.

```
◆Current Status◆
> ELITIA activated BLOSSOM BLADE
> Stage 1 hit ★JUGGERNAUT
No damage
10 support damage
> Stage 2 hit ★JUGGERNAUT
No damage
10 support damage
> Stage 3 hit ★JUGGERNAUT
No damage
10 support damage
```

She executed an incredibly fast series of attacks while was using Sonic Raid. It was beautiful in a way, a heroic and overwhelmingly powerful secret skill. The invisible follow-up attack from Attack Support 1 made it through the defenses of a creature even immune to physical attacks. Physical seemed to be different from unattributed, but either way, I had to gamble on this attack. It was all we had left.

Do it... Take it down...!

```
◆Current Status◆
> Stage 16 hit ★JUGGERNAUT
No damage
10 support damage
> 1 ★JUGGERNAUT defeated
```

Its massive body stopped moving, then wavered for a moment before collapsing with a thunderous crash against the ground, crushing the orcs who were attempting to run.

And then—

"*Huff*, haah…"

—Elitia appeared in front of the fallen Juggernaut, her sword thrust in the ground as she leaned on it, about to collapse herself. But I hadn't forgotten that we couldn't relax just yet.

"Theresia, Igarashi! Cover Elitia! There are other enemies nearby!" I ordered.

Theresia found them before anyone else. A little ways off were three men, each holding a long-ranged weapon and aiming at Elitia.

"Tsk…you should have left well enough alone! You'll regret this, brats!" cried Igarashi.

They must have assumed Elitia had defeated Juggernaut with her own strength. They were taking us lightly. But I had no intentions of leaving them alone now that we'd found them.

"—I'll back you guys up!"

""Okay!""

The arrows from the men's weapons, which looked like small bows, were blocked by Theresia's and Igarashi's shields. The next moment, Igarashi launched her Thunderbolt, and I shot my blaze-shot, hitting two of the men.

"Gyaah!"

"Aagh!"

"—Haah!"

Igarashi swung her lance around, and the two men tried to stop her attack but were blown away by the Attack Support damage and unable to move. Either they were overwhelmed by the physical shock of suddenly taking the ten damage, or they were still only second level.

The remaining man seemed more capable and like the boss of the group.

"Useless bastards... Raaah! D-damn you...!" he shouted.

Theresia closed in and slashed out at him, but he jumped back and avoided the attack, which was when I took aim and shot.

"—Take that!"

◆Current Status◆
> Arihito's attack hit Bergen

"Gah—!"

I hadn't actually aimed for any vital organs but apparently hit some weak spot, and Bergen crumpled to the ground where he stood. My slingshot definitely wasn't the most incredibly powerful thing, but perhaps I got a critical hit or whatever. When I got closer, it looked like the metal bullet had struck him in the jaw.

Igarashi looked at me, seemingly speechless. It was less that she was happy that we'd won and more that she was completely drained from exhausting every last reserve of energy she had.

I turned around and saw Suzuna watching us. She was still unable to participate in the battle, but things for her were just getting started. I nodded, and she ran to Misaki and Elitia.

◆Current Status◆
> Arihito activated Recovery Support 1 ⟶ Elitia's vitality was restored

The first recovery round activated after thirty seconds. I'd thought more time had passed, but I suppose time seems longer when you're so focused.

"...Igarashi, Theresia, I'm glad you're both safe. I'm sorry I forced your hand earlier."

"Same to you, Atobe... Ugh, I practically lost myself..."

"......"

We were all relieved to see that none of us had been injured, then turned toward Juggernaut's body and Elitia who had defeated it.

◆Current Status◆
> Elitia's Berserk has terminated with the end of combat

Part III: Magic Stones and the Black Box

Elitia's vitality had gone down by about 70 percent. Even though she herself had said how valuable potions were, either she didn't have one on her or she didn't have the energy to use it. She just continued standing there, leaning on her sword in the dirt.

"Elitia, are you oka—?" I started.

"Guh…"

When I tried to talk to her, her last remaining will seemed to snap, and she collapsed like a marionette whose strings were cut. I instinctively dashed up behind her to try and catch her.

"…Thanks… I'm pretty pathetic. I used the last of my strength." A sense of calm returned to her tone. Her harsh words and bloodlust of a moment before seemed to have vanished when Berserk had worn off.

"Thanks for showing us what a level-eight Seeker is capable of. I think this time you and the enemy were poorly matched, though."

"Named Monsters sometimes have resistances or immunities… but it was thought no Named Monsters with resistances appeared in this labyrinth… I guess it wasn't investigated enough…"

She had said there shouldn't be any Seekers here who would make a Named orc appear. I understood the reason for that now after that battle. It was just far too strong compared to the labyrinth's level of difficulty.

Recovery Support activated again, and some energy seemed to return to Elitia, who I was still propped up.

"I felt it before, too...but when you're my rearguard, the pain seems to go away a little..."

I imagined she might feel uneasy being healed by some mysterious power so I decided I should explain a little bit to her now.

"I have a skill that lets me recover a vanguard's vitality when I'm the rearguard. You'll probably recover more if we rest here for a moment. I guess potions are pretty indispensable, huh?"

"...The upper districts use too many. There's not enough supply. And it's more profitable for people who can make potions to sell them through Merchant organizations to the higher districts than to sell them here..."

If that's true, any reincarnates who chose a Pharmacist or similar job would just need to gather materials, and then they'd be living a life of luxury.

"Oh, right, Misaki... Good, it looks like she's fine," I said.

"...She just has terrible luck. I wasn't even sure I'd be able to protect her, so...I'm glad she's okay...," said Elitia. She didn't blame Misaki for being reckless. She was just genuinely happy we were able to save her. I could tell with a glance at her tear-filled eyes.

"Hold on, Misaki. We'll get you out soon...," she added.

"Theresia, cut the ropes with your short sword," said Igarashi.

"......"

Theresia used her blade to cut the ropes as Igarashi had instructed. Misaki was still unconscious, perhaps from fear at seeing Juggernaut so up close. Her wrists and ankles were covered in painful red welts after we removed the ropes.

"Shouldn't their karma increase if they tie up another Seeker like that?" asked Igarashi. "Those assholes were trying to get the loot from Juggernaut even if it meant resorting to criminal means."

"There are ways to get around the karma feature on your license," explained Elitia. "For example, if they were threatened by Misaki or she stole something important from them. There are a number of different methods, but easiest of all would most likely be if they stepped in the way when she was attacking a monster, so her attack hit them. If they then tied her up to get back at her, their karma would even out."

So that's how they do it... Like those scam artists who set up accidents so they can sue.

"That's only from a license point of view, though. If we report what they did to the Guild, there'll be a trial," continued Elitia.

"...So you'd get Misaki to testify against them. That could work. Will it be a problem that we fought them?" I asked.

"They went to attack us first, so it shouldn't be an issue," replied Elitia. "Fighting between Seekers is, of course, forbidden, but they did something stupid just to get the goods from Juggernaut."

Even the materials and bounty for Redface were valuable enough to be a massive amount for people adventuring in District Eight. I couldn't begin to imagine how valuable those materials would be, let alone if there was a bounty for it. I also had no idea how we'd get the Juggernaut's massive body out of here.

"How are massive monsters like this handled?" I asked.

"There are people called Carriers who specialize in transporting large monsters. They do jobs all over the various districts. It's a good idea to take out any valuable magic stones before they move it, though. Even better if you can get to the stone sack inside the body, but it can be dangerous if you accidentally cut the wrong organ…so right now you should check the nails, horns, and teeth for any stones."

"We have no idea what we're looking for. Sorry to ask, but could you come, too? Can you walk?"

Restoring her vitality seemed to be healing the most severe of her wounds, but she was still unsteady on her feet. She took off her gauntlets. The swelling in arm was starting to subside, and the red on her ribs where her armor had been shattered was fading.

"…Mind if I lean on you?" Elitia asked me.

"Of course. Takes a lot of work just to check something of this size," I replied.

We'd more than likely want to ask the Carriers to take all the defeated Fanged Orcs, too, though they'd probably take a cut. There were a couple dozen of them, so we'd surely get an incredible amount of materials.

"…Hmm? Is that one of those treasure chest things…?" I asked upon spotting a black box that had fallen near Juggernaut. It was significantly smaller than I had imagined a treasure chest would be. I'd probably be able to fit it in my knapsack if I made some room.

"Named Monsters are said to have a higher drop rate for chests, but I've never even seen one that color before… A chest's value varies depending on its color. They're the kind of thing everyone wishes they could get their hands on. Better not to just go and recklessly open it, though. We should get help from an expert. There's some Chest Crackers in the city. We can ask the Guild for a recommendation."

"All right, we'll get them to help us."

"Atobe, is there anything we can do?" Igarashi asked as she and Theresia approached.

"Yeah, could you check the nails on its left hand? There's a chance there are some magic stones." I was worried about having them search and leave the men we defeated, but they were strewn about and seemed in no condition to move anywhere.

"Mmph…"

"Wh-what's wrong?" Elitia had suddenly let out a small moan. It threw me because it sounded really erotic.

She looked at me. Her cheeks were flushed a little red. Maybe she was starting to get embarrassed by walking so close together? If that was the reason, it would be better if we walked apart.

"…It's nothing."

"Oh, o-okay… Whoa, those massive things on its forehead were horns… That's different from the Fanged Orcs. Those ones don't have horns."

"If you find an orc-type monster with horns, you can sometimes find magic stones if you cut off and split the horns. The horns themselves aren't that strong so aren't used as materials and have no value. They're basically like a nutshell."

So Cotton Balls sometimes had wind agate stuck to their

heads, but Juggernaut's dropped loot was inside the horns. We would have lost out on a lot of money if we hadn't known that, so I needed to thank Elitia.

Juggernaut had multiple horns sprouting from its forehead, and out of the ten in total, we found a magic stone in two of them. One was an alkaid crystal and the other was a life stone. Apparently, life stones were sometimes dropped by Named Monsters and could be worked into accessories, which increased the wearer's total vitality. Elitia had never seen an alkaid crystal, so she didn't know much about it.

"Are you sure I can take these, Elitia?"

"Like I said in the beginning, anything we find is yours. If we happen to find something that, once processed, only I can use, then I'll buy it back from you."

"Really? Well, thank you, then."

I wondered if the alkaid crystal was like the blaze stones and could be added to weapons. Or armor, or accessories... I'd show it to Rikerton. He'd be able to tell me what we could make from it.

"After we're done, we can leave the labyrinth and ask for help from the Carriers. There are people in front of the entrance who can contact them for us."

"Is it okay to leave it here and go out? Will other Seekers try to take it?" I asked.

"Our licenses record who defeated it, so nobody will touch the actual body. Magic stones and treasure chests aren't, though," replied Elitia. "That's why it's fine as long as we do what we're doing now and take those before we go."

That meant Bergen and his group were planning on snatching up the dropped loot and treasure chests, which wouldn't be considered criminal. I was glad I'd learned so much about how the license and karma worked in this trip.

"I hope Misaki will learn something from this experience and be more cautious... She looks like she's having a nightmare," said Igarashi, looking at me and Misaki as I carried the girl. I wondered if there was any other support healing thing, not Recovery Support, that could wake someone up from being unconscious... That'd be too convenient, though.

"...Ngh... Wh-what are you doing to me?! ...No, orcs, no..."

"O-ow! Man, those nails of hers—!" Misaki thrashed about in her nightmare, digging her nails into my shoulder. Suzuna gently stroked her shoulder, and she seemed to calm down.

"...Zzz... Zzz..."

As a Shrine Maiden, Suzuna had a skill called Purify, which boosted the party's psychological state. There were a lot of places it'd be useful when you took into consideration the horrifying things you could come across in the labyrinth. I also wanted to ask Elitia about her job. I found it hard to imagine she'd deliberately written *Cursed Blade* when she first started, which meant she'd changed jobs sometime afterward.

First things first, though. We needed to get the Carriers to take care of our haul. I was really curious what my contribution points would be after this battle. In total, we'd beaten fifteen Cotton Balls, eight Poison Spear Bees, and twenty-three Fanged Orcs. And Juggernaut. I suspected once you added in any level up and increase in Trust Level that it'd blow what I'd gotten the day before out of the water.

Part IV: Heading Back and Quick Progress

On our way to the second-floor entrance, we ran into a party who were close to being annihilated by some Cotton Balls and Poison Spear Bees, so we saved them. It turned out they were Misaki's previous party who had been rushing to come save her. They were genuinely relieved to see her safe. It seemed like they wanted her to come back to their party, but Misaki didn't. I tried to encourage them, but later, once Misaki had woken up (while I was still carrying her), we talked about the situation, and I realized that wasn't likely.

"They're reeeally nice, but there are sooo many parties out there, as many as there are stars in the sky. I'm just going with the flow and finding where I should be. I want it to feeeel right."

"Well, yeah, but you only joined their party yesterday, and they were so happy to see you," I insisted.

"Oh, don't say that. It pains me. See, I was thinking, you know before, I thought they could be like my worker bees and I'd be the queen bee. But I've thought about it more, and I need to get stronger—at least so bad guys don't kidnap me."

"In that case, Misaki, are you going to join—?" Igarashi started to ask.

"Hmm… About that—it's just I think I'd have a tough time. Um, what was your name again?"

"Oh, I haven't introduced myself. I'm Arihito."

Misaki's job was a Gambler. Apparently, she had a skill that increased the drop rate for treasure chests. If she was with us, then we'd surely have some good luck, but I had a feeling she wouldn't come along with us.

"I might've passed out real quick, but I still got the sense your party's crazy strong, Arihito. I mean, I just feel like it's kiiinda rash for someone as incompetent as me to be joining you guys."

"Hey, it's not like I've been completely unfazed by my battles in the labyrinth. But I also don't have any plans to stay in District Eight forever. I want to move up in rank."

"See, it's sooo amazing that you're trying to get out of District Eight. You know, if you don't work hard every day, your experience points will go down, so there's tons of people stuck at level one or two who never leave. That's why there's, like, three thousand people in this district."

Now that she mentioned it, she was right. I was able to defeat strong enemies because of my rearguard skills. It hadn't felt difficult to make money or climb the ranks. Even if a party ran into a Named Monster, they'd probably just run if they felt they weren't strong enough… There were probably a lot of parties that hesitated to face something like that. Their entire world would change if they could just defeat it, but there was an ingrained belief that it's normal to run because there's no way they could win.

"If the party leader reaches first place in the district, then they take a test to be able to move on to District Seven. But you can make a living here in District Eight, so there's a lot of people who don't try to take it," said Elitia. She spoke from experience. She must have met people like that in her travels so far.

"I want to work hard and make it my own way. Oh, but I'd love it if I could be in your party tomorrow, just to commemorate our time together, but…I'm sooo useless," said Misaki.

"You're not useless. Oh, by the way, you set off a trap on a treasure chest, right? What was in the chest?" I asked.

"Oh, there was a bag in it. Those scary men took it from me," she replied.

Now that she'd said that, we really should've gone back to get it. But it'd be too much trouble if the entire party went, so Elitia just shrugged and dashed off using Sonic Raid. Seemed a waste to use the skills of such a high-level Seeker on something like that, though.

I hated to trouble Ribault again, but after I told him about Bergen and his men, he went bravely into the labyrinth. Apparently, Bergen and his lot had been using their skills for hiding themselves to do various nefarious deeds and causing problems, but they'd not had any proof until now and couldn't chase them down. This, however, should provide the information necessary to take them in.

Igarashi turned to me after Ribault and his party disappeared down the stairs to the labyrinth.

"Those guys are like some sort of neighborhood watch. I might even go as far as to say they're like a citizen police force," she said.

"Yeah. I'm sure there's lots of people who are safe because of them," I replied.

They had more experience than us and were most likely a higher level, but there was a reason they stood outside the first labyrinth. They had found their calling of raising the next generation of Seekers. That's the impression I got from them.

I wonder if I could become first place like I was aiming for. If a beast like the Juggernaut appeared in the first labyrinth, it was going to be a very long road until I'd be able to seek in the hardest labyrinth in District One.

"Elitia, are most Seekers in District Five level eight?" I asked.

"No, I think they're mostly around level ten. There's a reason why my level is a little lower..." She glanced around at the party. Igarashi and Suzuna looked back at her with concern. "...Let's discuss this later. Having seen me in that state, I wouldn't want to freak you out by not explaining things. Sorry for tricking you, Suzuna."

"No...I'm just happy to know even a little bit of what you're going through. I felt from the beginning that there was something you were trying to bottle up." They'd only met the previous day, yet they were already good friends. Misaki also seemed to sense that and ran up behind the two and threw her arms around their shoulders.

"Ack— Wh-what was that for?!" cried Elitia in surprise.

"I just felt kinda jealous that you were closer to Suzu than me,

even though Suzu and I have known each other since we were just itty-bitty little kids."

"I thought you invited Suzuna... I mean, you came here together."

"No, see, we had a tradition of going skiing every year... So it's not like either one of us invited the other," replied Suzuna. She must've been correcting Elitia since it had to do with the accident that led to their reincarnation. She was trying to say that she thought neither of them really invited the other so neither was responsible for involving the other in the accident.

"...I didn't get the fuss about this whole labyrinth and seeking stuff. But I've had a change of heart, and now I'll give it my all, too... Which is whyyy you should treat me to some food!"

"Well, I'll take a good suggestion when I hear one... Atobe, how about we go to the market another day? Instead, let's go to the Guild to make our report, then go out for a bite to eat."

"All right. I'll take Theresia back to the Mercenary Office." However, Theresia didn't nod in response. Maybe she was trying to ask if we could not do that.

"Atobe, did you ask Leila how long Theresia's allowed to stay with us?"

"Wooow! I've been thinking this for a while now, but this lizard hat is sooo cuuute! Ooh, it feels so smooth and cool!" Misaki patted Theresia's lizard hat...well, her almost-full-face mask. I could only see her mouth, and though the expression didn't last long, she looked a little embarrassed. I kind of wanted to try touching it to see what Misaki meant by *smooth and cool*, but given that it would have likely been considered sexual harassment if a man like me did, I had to restrain myself.

When we returned to the Guild, Louisa came out to meet us, and she seemed to have some premonition that something had happened since she looked nervous.

"I see you worked with Ms. Elitia and Ms. Suzuna today. Ms. Igarashi also seems to have worked hard," she said.

"Thank you, but I was only with Atobe and his party near the very end," said Elitia.

"Me too… I just watched, I couldn't do anything. I'll try harder next time…," added Suzuna.

Louisa gave our party a brief, pensive glance but then gestured for me to come over. She lowered her voice so the others couldn't hear.

"First you were alone, but now I see you've added five girls to your party… Was that your intention, Mr. Atobe? To only recruit girls, I mean."

"N-no, that's not it at all. That girl, Misaki…I wouldn't really call a party member. We just happened to rescue her. I have a feeling she'll be doing her own thing after this. She's a bit of a free spirit."

"But you will be working with the other four from here on out. Elitia's level eight, so you will likely move on from District Eight very soon…"

"Even if that happens, I was hoping I could ask that you continue to be my caseworker. Though I imagine that would prove difficult after I change districts…"

"A-actually, I'm able to transfer anywhere in the Guild, so…if that is your request, I should be able remain your caseworker for the foreseeable future."

"That's fantastic. I've gotten so used to working with you, I'd be sad if I had to change caseworkers… Hmm?" Someone tapped my arm, so I turned and saw Elitia standing there.

"Arihito, it's the leader's responsibility to report the results of an expedition. Also, we'd like to get changed, so we're going back home for a bit."

"Oh, yeah. Sure, I'll take care of this."

"Kyouka's going to take Theresia back with her, so you don't have to worry about that. How about we all meet up at the tavern near your place afterward?"

Since we were allowed to keep a mercenary with us until eight PM, we still had plenty of time. We would probably be able to make it to the Mercenary Office in time if we left the tavern by seven thirty.

The others left, and Louisa asked me a question before leading me to the private room we had used the day before.

"Um, additionally, I'm sure there's no way this could be possible, but you didn't happen to run into another Named Monster again today…?"

"That's correct. We defeated Juggernaut on the second floor and asked the Carriers to take care of what we left behind.

Apparently, they'll come report to the Guild once they've finished, so— Louisa?!"

"Ohhh..."

Louisa had been so surprised to hear about Redface yesterday, and it seemed hearing the word *Juggernaut* today was just too much of a shock for her to handle. She fainted.

A younger coworker of Louisa's showed me to a different room in the Guild in Louisa's stead. It was furnished very differently, with leather-upholstered chairs and a dark ebony table, though I had no idea where they would find wood like that. A moment later, Louisa came in carrying a tray with the same herbal tea, then sat in the chair next to me instead of across the table. She cleared her throat with a cough before speaking.

"The last Named orc that appeared on the second floor of the Field of Dawn was defeated four months ago. That individual was called Yellow Fang. Its body was a bright yellow; it had a wonderful personality and was apparently very popular at dinner parties."

"Monsters have dinner parties?! Louisa, I think you're too shaken up—you're talking nonsense!"

"Huh? ...M-my apologies. I've been put in charge of organizing this month's Guild Party, and it's just so much work. What I meant to say is that while its color was different, it wasn't all that much larger than a normal Fanged Orc." Maybe the shock had mixed up her thoughts. What exactly did I do by confusing her so much with this Juggernaut thing?

"Louisa, first, please just calm down. This orc from four months ago isn't the same as Juggernaut, right?"

"Ah, right, of course. It's said that if you defeat two hundred orcs on the second floor of the Field of Dawn, you'll become the target of Yellow Fang's hatred, and it will appear. It's a level-three Named Monster, so it's much more powerful than Redface. When that one appeared, we lost seven Seekers before a group of sixteen was finally able to put it down."

"That many…? I can see that Named Monster was incredibly vicious. But it's not the same creature as the Juggernaut that we defeated, right?"

"You are correct. There are two types of Named Monsters, those who appear fairly easily and those who very rarely appear. Juggernaut is one of the rare Named Monsters among the Fanged Orcs. The last time it appeared was three years ago. There have been eleven Named orcs defeated since then, and all of them were Yellow Fangs."

There weren't enough defeated to assume accurate statistics, but if two out of thirteen Named Monsters that appeared were Juggernauts, its rate of appearance was about one in ten. And if it was one every three years…

"We thought it was Bergen and his party who made Juggernaut appear, but I doubt they'd be able to defeat two hundred orcs. They were fairly low level," I said.

"It was a different party. Since it was so much larger than Yellow Fang, they gathered twenty-four Seekers in four parties total, but unfortunately, they were almost completely destroyed. We have a record that says the only ones able to survive were in the party led by Bergen. There's a high probability they abandoned the other parties and ran. The Guild investigated the incident, but they testified that they managed to live through sheer luck. Since we had no other evidence, the investigation was shelved."

They couldn't even defeat Juggernaut with twenty-four Seekers, and then Bergen and his party ran away. They weren't able to return to the second floor of the Field of Dawn, and Juggernaut went undefeated. Once they heard Elitia had come to District Eight, they realized they could use the Juggernaut that was after them for their own profit and so hatched their plan. That was the situation we'd walked into.

"…So if a Named Monster appears and hasn't been defeated for a long time, people just prepare themselves to be sacrificed and gather lots of companions to take it on?" I asked.

"Yes. Of the twenty-one people Juggernaut defeated, three became demi-humans and are now available for hire at the Mercenary Office. The remaining eighteen…"

What happened when Seekers were killed by monsters? I wanted to understand, but it was such a harsh reality. *If they don't become demi-humans, they might never come back…*

"Named Monsters frequently cause significant damage to Seekers, so we often place a bounty on them. However, if we make that bounty public, many people will attempt to make a profit off it even if they have to use the party the Named Monster is targeting. That's also why we don't announce the value of the bounty given, so we don't encourage people to take a gamble and risk their lives. But when considering safety and peace of mind, we must announce the fact that Juggernaut has in fact been defeated…"

"The Guild has so much work cut out for them to maintain balance. That's unlikely to change soon, but it's just a good thing that we're safe. I think knowing what Named Monsters are on what floors from here on out will be important information, even if it's not easy to get."

"I appreciate your understanding. But…I really am so happy you're all right…" Louisa wiped at her eyes. She did seem truly relieved that we had survived. I got the feeling that the reason she fainted earlier had nothing to do with her being delicate and everything to do with the fact that she knew exactly how terrifying Juggernaut was.

Louisa seemed a little embarrassed by her now red eyes, but she took out her usual monocle. She was preparing to examine the record on my license.

"Right, may I please look at the Seeking Record on your license?"

"Please, go right ahead." I handed her my license.

```
◆Expedition Results◆
> Raided FIELD OF DAWN 2F: 10 points
> ARIHITO grew to level 3: 20 points
> KYOUKA grew to level 2: 10 points
> SUZUNA grew to level 2: 10 points
> Defeated 15 COTTON BALLS: 75 points
> Defeated 8 POISON SPEAR BEES: 64 points
> Defeated 23 FANGED ORCS: 230 points
> Defeated 1 bounty ★JUGGERNAUT: 800 points
> THERESIA's Trust Level increased: 50 points
```

```
> KYOUKA's Trust Level increased: 50 points
> SUZUNA's Trust Level increased: 10 points
> ELITIA's Trust Level increased: 50 points
> Rescued another party: 30 points
> Rescued MISAKI: 100 points
> Defeated 3 criminals: 90 points
> Returned with 1 BLACK TREASURE CHEST: 50 points
Seeker Contribution: 1,649 points
District Eight Contribution Ranking: 2
```

Three people leveled up, including me. Even though Elitia doled out the vast majority of the damage, Juggernaut gave such a massive amount of experience that everyone in the party still gained quite a bit.

"Wow…contribution points in the triple digits is impressive enough, but you've managed to reach four digits on only your second day." Louisa clutched her monocle to her chest and stared at the record, her face beet red.

I wasn't positive how Trust Levels counted toward contribution points, but it seemed like the max was fifty points per adventure into the labyrinth. Also, I figured out that each activation of Attack Support came to ten contribution points. Suzuna hadn't lost any vitality, so Recovery Support didn't give anything for her.

"One thousand six hundred and forty-nine…that is a truly amazing figure. And it comes in second as the most contribution points gained in one adventure ever. First place belongs to a party that made a large number of monsters appear in the labyrinth, so they were able to hunt an incredible amount of Cotton Balls, giving them one thousand six hundred and sixty contribution points. However, having defeated Juggernaut, you and your party are the only ones to have exceeded one thousand while defeating so few monsters."

"So does this mean I'll be able to become a two-star Seeker?"

"Yes. Congratulations! Would you like to purchase the necessary bronze Mercenary Tickets today? The bounty for Juggernaut is one hundred gold pieces, so I could give you the tickets now."

I had thought it would take much longer, but since we defeated Juggernaut, I was able to reach my goal far quicker than I could have ever imagined.

"I have eight tickets left, so could I please have ninety-two tickets? I believe that would make two hundred seventy-six silver pieces total."

"Of course. With this, you'll be able to make Theresia a permanent member of your party. Since she is a demi-human, I do hope you keep her in your party forever. Should you decide to remove her from your party, she will return to the Mercenary Office."

"Don't worry, she has a very clear role in the party...and it might be weird to say this since she and I only just met, but I want to turn her back into a human."

"...That won't be easy. But if anyone can do it... First, you'll need to advance to District Four. They say she would need to make several visits to the cathedral there. If you continue to excel as you have so far, I imagine you could accomplish such a feat in a few months' time."

The cathedral in District Four... That's gotta be important info.

Each district seemed to have different facilities necessary for the Labyrinth Country. It was called a *country*, so there obviously had to be some sort of governmental body overseeing the whole thing. *Maybe I should ask...*

"Louisa, sorry to only ask this now, but does the Labyrinth Country have a king?"

"No, the founding family was exiled from District One. The people with any actual authority is the head of the cathedral, as well as us, the Guild leaders."

"...Does that mean our seeking is what the Labyrinth Country wants? We were told we had no choice but to become Seekers."

"Yes. You have most likely realized by now, but all of the labyrinths within the Labyrinth Country are somewhere else in this world. Only the entrances were collected within the walls to teleport Seekers to the labyrinths...though I am not in a position to know why that is."

That meant there were a variety of different labyrinths, not just ones with fields. They might even require different skills or tools, so we needed to prepare in order to be able to adapt to the various environments.

"Thank you very much for all the information, Louisa. On another note, what's our new rank?"

"Each person's contribution points are calculated separately based on their function in the party. Mr. Atobe, you have become... Amazing, seventh place! In the single digits already. As for the others, Ms. Igarashi has moved up to four hundred and thirty-eight, Ms. Suzuna four hundred and thirty-five, and Ms. Elitia one hundred and fifteen out of twelve thousand in District

Five. Congratulations, your lodging has been upgraded to a royal suite! I will need to start preparations for it, though, so you won't be able to use it until tomorrow."

A royal suite...so basically, bigger than what I had now. That meant me, Igarashi, and Theresia could live comfortably there—actually, no. Igarashi's rank jumped up this time, too, so she wouldn't have to stay in the barn. She would have no need to stay at my place.

She said she'd make us lunches...but I guess she can still cook them even if she doesn't live with us. Last night was an exception. I can't expect things to stay the same.

"...Mr. Atobe? Would you prefer to stay in your current room? You look glum."

"Oh, no, it's not that. I'll go look at the new lodging tomorrow, and if it's nice, then I would definitely like to move."

"Understood. I'll submit a preliminary contract with the landlord. The next thing is opening your black treasure chest. Would you like me to suggest a good Chest Cracker for you?"

"Chest Cracker? Is that a specialist who can remove any traps on the chest?"

"Yes. People with the job Trap Master will always be able to open chests without fail. Of course, there are extremely rare exceptions, but that's just one of the dangers of working with treasure chests. You'll have to pay the Trap Master a service fee, but since there will be plenty of treasure inside, it's a small price to pay for acquiring the treasure safely."

So I was able to buy the Mercenary Tickets I needed, confirmed how high in the ranking I moved, and got a recommendation for a Chest Cracker. Louisa really helped me with so much and would even continue to be my caseworker in the future, so I wanted to show my appreciation somehow. She might not be able to come since it was such short notice, but I decided to invite her out with us.

"Thank you so much for all the help you've given me. Louisa, what time do you get off work today?"

"The Guild is open late, but I'm not on duty, so my shift will be over soon."

"Well…if you like, would you be interested in coming to have dinner with us? Sorry to ask on such short notice, but I really am grateful for all your help."

"Oh… Are you sure that's all right? If you don't mind, I would be happy to accompany you."

This time, I simply wanted to share our sense of accomplishment at having finished a great job with Louisa. We'd be going to a tavern, so the adults—everyone except Suzuna, Misaki, and Elitia—would likely have a bit to drink. I wondered what Igarashi was like drunk. Louisa, too. I couldn't even fathom anything like that happening.

Part V: Chitchat

Louisa asked me to wait for her in the square outside the Guild, so I was again waiting there, staring at my surroundings.

Juggernaut had been so massive that the Carriers had used

teleportation-type skills to move it to a dissection center. There was only one center in District Eight that could handle large monsters. Rikerton's shop wasn't able to do it. I felt bad that Melissa wouldn't have a chance to handle the rare materials, but since all the district's Dissectors were joining together to help, maybe she'd at least get a chance to help dissect. The massive tree trunk–like bones made high-quality building material, the nails and other parts were apparently used as material to make glass, and many of the other parts had uses.

We'd taken the Fanged Orcs' teeth as Elitia suggested, but apparently, someone with dissecting skills would have been better able to preserve their value when removing them than we were. *Well, there's no point sweating the small stuff if you don't have the skills to deal with it.* The only choice we had was to take the valuable parts back with us.

It was quite normal for other Seekers to take the materials we threw away, like the Cotton Ball bodies. There were a lot of things in the labyrinth that couldn't be carried back and so were just left. The general rule was that if something was left for an hour, then any possession rights were gone and it was free game. Anyone who took it wouldn't gain any karma.

"Sorry to keep you waiting, Mr. Atobe," said Louisa.

"Oh… You've changed out of your work uniform."

"Yes, we stand out quite a bit if we walk around in our uniforms… I can't really say this too loudly, but the registrar ladies tend to get catcalled, so we've been asked by the higher-ups to dress more plainly in public."

She had now let down her hair, which changed her image quite a lot. She was wearing sort of relaxed but mature clothing that I suppose you could call plain, but the material the clothes were made from was soft and really showed off her curves.

It's the same with those knit sweaters; it emphasizes certain parts, and my eyes just... It's probably a traditional design for this world, but why is there always a low neckline...?

"...? Is something the matter, Mr. Atobe?"

I thought she was going to say that my karma would go up, but she didn't. She had said it was based on your relationship with the person, so maybe we'd gotten to a point where I could look all I wanted... If I was wrong, though, I'd be in trouble, so it was safer to assume it was still taboo.

"I was just surprised; you look so different now. I was thinking it's amazing how different women look when they're on duty and off."

"Ha-ha... It's always the stoic-looking ones who change the most. I'm not too different when I drink, but I do enjoy it, so I might get a little chatty."

"Nothing wrong with that. I like to watch everyone have fun while I drink."

"You enjoy being a rearguard even at a party."

"You're not wrong. People always told me I was an old soul."

Louisa seemed to enjoy my joking and chatting. She wasn't holding back, either—we'd managed to get this comfortable with each other in only two days. Once we started walking, I noticed a man coming from the other direction. He looked like he was about to run into Louisa.

"…Whoa, watch out. He sure looked like he was in some sort of hurry," I said after reflexively grabbing Louisa's hand and pulling her out of the way. He might not have actually run into her, but I was worried he might.

"There's only three thousand people here, but it's always so busy around the Guild… Louisa?"

"Uh, um, I was just…just thinking I might accidentally drink too much tonight."

"Ah, well… Everything in moderation. It'll affect you tomorrow if you drink too much."

I had a feeling we weren't quite talking about the same thing, but Louisa seemed happy. After that, she walked closer to me than she had before. I had a feeling she was looking at me, but when I glanced at her, she just smiled like nothing happened.

The tavern was busy again today. I was thinking it would've been a good idea to get seats before it got too crowded, but when we went into the tavern, we saw Igarashi waiting for us.

"Atobe, our seats are this way," she called. "There was a big table open— Oh, you invited the lady from the Guild, too? Nice going."

"I'm sorry for the sudden imposition," said Louisa.

"We're the ones who should be apologizing. You're always such a huge help. You've been Atobe's caseworker since he first chose his job, right?"

"Yes, I'm starting to feel like it might be fate. I could never have imagined being assigned to someone so talented…"

"He's saved my neck so much… I used to be his manager, but now things have flipped. I'm basically like the subordinate now."

"Oh, is that so? Manager and subordinate… So you two knew each other before since you used to be coworkers…"

"Yeah, but ever since we got reincarnated, I feel like we just mesh better."

They're smiling and chatting, but I feel some strange tension… Or maybe I'm just imagining things?

"Atobe, you're the leader, so you should sit in the middle tonight." I suddenly realized a drinking party was a valuable opportunity to observe Igarashi.

She never really came to any of the company parties, save for every once in a while, and when she did, she always left early. I guess because her parents were so strict.

A lot of people claimed Igarashi didn't have to grace us with her presence since she was had the CEO's favor. It embarrassed me a little to think I used to generally agree with all that.

"…Were you just thinking about work? I think I've started to figure out what face you make when you do," said Igarashi.

"Oh, uh, it's nothing. Do you like to drink, Igarashi?"

"Yeah, I drink sometimes. I wouldn't say I'm too hard-core, though. Want to have a drinking competition and see?"

"I'm really not much of a heavyweight, either. I'm keeping it moderate tonight."

"Heh… Proper as always. And Louisa's even come out tonight and is sitting right next to you."

"And so are you. Today's about celebrating our party, though."

"Oh, really? Well then…would you like to sit next to Suzuna or Theresia?"

"Oooh, don't forget me!" Misaki piped up. "I'm so grateful to Arihito, and I'm always the one stuck pouring drinks at parties. I'll pour for him. I'm, like, sooo good at it, too!"

"No, you're out. Atobe said he doesn't like girlie girls."

"Awww, you're just jealous of me 'cause I'm younger!" Igarashi froze on the spot. Even Louisa seemed bothered—did that mean she was in her twenties, too?

"And young people make stupid mistakes. I thought you turned over a new leaf or something?" retorted Igarashi.

"Yep, I suuure did! Sooo, Arihito, how old are ya?"

"Um… I think he's a bit older than you," Igarashi shot back. "Aren't you being a little overly familiar?"

Who knew a career woman and a teenybopper would butt heads this much? It made me a little anxious to watch, but Misaki generally seemed to listen to me. *I should tell her later not to argue so much.*

Theresia and Suzuna were sitting quietly across from us, somehow peaceful. Theresia still had on her equipment since she couldn't unequip it, but Suzuna wasn't wearing the red-and-white outfit from before. She'd changed into something that was pretty close to the farm maiden style Igarashi talked about earlier. Her hair was up in a ponytail like always, and her pale white skin shone in the tavern's light.

"Arihito, do you prefer well-behaved girls? Like Suzu?" asked Misaki.

"I don't discriminate… Also, you're not allowed to talk about this topic anymore."

"Awww, come onnn. Oh, I bet you like older girls more, don't you?" Misaki was trying everything she could to get me to tell her my type. I actually didn't really have a specific type…but I did like those knit sweaters. *Gotta be careful not to let that one slip.*

All seven of us ate and drank to our hearts' content, and we'd still not used a whole gold piece. It felt like a very large amount of money.

We sat around the long rectangular table with Theresia, Suzuna, and Misaki on one side and Louisa, me, and Igarashi on the other. Everyone chowed down, and the liquor in my cup kept flowing. If it ever got to about half-empty, someone would pour in more, and then I'd drink some more. After a few cycles of this, I was feeling pretty buzzed.

"Heeey, Arihito, are you feeling good now that you've had plenty to drink?" asked Misaki as she stood from her seat and refilled my tankard. Suzuna followed suit.

"I mean, hey, the booze is nice. That's juice you're drinking, yeah? Since you're underage and all."

"Suzu used to make alcohol as part of her job at the shrine, but I'm not allowed to drink any?"

"M-Misaki... That's an old tradition. It's not like I actually drank anything I made." Igarashi seemed interested by what Suzuna said. She kept asking questions: *"You made alcohol at the shrine? Was it sweet rice wine, or something else? It didn't actually have that much alcohol in it, right?"*

"So when you say you worked at a shrine, do you mean you lived there?" asked Igarashi.

"Yes, my dad was a Shinto priest, and I helped out around the house."

That must be why she chose the Shrine Maiden job. Still, I guess it wasn't completely impossible a normal high school girl would think that sort of thing would be a good fit for her. Lot of girls worked part-time jobs as Shrine Maidens during the busy season.

"Here you are, Arihito... Oh..." Suzuna tried to refill my tankard, but she must have been a little nervous because the alcohol came pouring out and spilled. A little got on my pants, but it was no big deal.

"Ah, thanks. It's okay, I'll wipe it off."

"Oh no, I have a handkerchief. I'll just... I'm so sorry," said Suzuna, her face completely red as she tried to wipe the stain from my pants. Handkerchiefs were actually fairly valuable items in this world, so it was unfortunate to see it go to that use.

"...Oh, good. I poured it okay," she chirped after trying again, this time successfully. I'd thought it would take time for everyone to open up like this, but that didn't seem to be the case.

My tankard was half-empty again; I could probably do another refill or two.

"...Atobe, want some more?" asked Igarashi. "Though I bet your stomach's pretty sloshy at this point from all the drinks..."

"I'm all right. Actually, let me pour you a drink, boss."

"Boss? You mean Kyouka? Whoaaa, I wanna be Arihito's boss, then I can order him around aaaalll the time!" said Misaki.

"Order him around...? I didn't... Actually, I can't say I didn't..." Igarashi hung her head as she remembered her days as my evil manager. I wished Misaki would have the common sense not to say such ridiculous things.

"Don't worry about it, Igarashi. You've helped me a lot since we came here."

"...But you've helped me far more. You don't need to give me any credit." Igarashi picked up the jug of alcohol and refilled my tankard.

I suppose it would take a while before we were both able to feel completely comfortable around each other...but there was no need to rush it. We were still working as a team in this world, too.

As I brought my tankard to my mouth, Louisa poured some fruit wine in Igarashi's glass.

"You still haven't had anything but juice. How about you have your first drink here?" offered Louisa.

"Oh, yeah... Thanks. I was thinking I should have something to drink."

"Louisaaa, your glass is empty, toooo! Do we need more alcohol?" asked Misaki.

Theresia was also drinking some alcohol while she chewed away on some sort of meat. Her skin seemed a little flushed; even

the lizard mask looked like it'd turned red from the alcohol…
Maybe she had a low tolerance.

"Theresia, can you handle one last drink?" I asked as I stood
from my seat.

"……"

She nodded silently and pushed her glass forward. She'd done
so much for me from day one. I hoped she understood how grateful I was as I refilled her drink.

"Right, now that we've all refilled our drinks, cheers!" I said.

"Cheers!"

Everyone brought their tankards and glasses together with a
clink. I drank deeply from mine, thinking this would be my last
one of the night.

It'd been so long since I'd been able to have a few drinks with
this much fun. We still had a little time before we had to leave in
order to get Theresia officially added to the party. Until then, I
wanted to continue drinking and chatting away.

Part VI: The Light of the Moon

Louisa, Igarashi, Theresia—I wasn't yet certain how old Theresia was, but there actually wasn't an age limit for drinking in the
Labyrinth Country. Suzuna and Misaki could drink if they wanted
to. Elitia seemed to need more time to change or something since
she didn't arrive until later. Her golden hair was down, and she

was wearing the same dress with blue highlights that she typically wore under her armor. Once she arrived, we needed to give another toast, so we'd drunk quite a lot by then.

"Misaki, your face is turning red. You haven't been drinking alcohol, have you?" asked Elitia.

"Nope, Suzu wouldn't let me. How about you, Ellie?"

"E-Ellie…? No one's ever called me that before. Just 'Tia'…"

"Would it be all right if we called you Ellie?" asked Suzuna.

"…Yeah. Can I just keep calling you Suzuna? I like how it sounds anyway."

"Wooow, you two really are sooo close!" said Misaki. "You're both quiet types, so you guys go well together."

"H-hey… I can talk your ear off when I really feel like it!" retorted Elitia.

The three younger members of the party chattered away. Theresia sat next to them drinking at a slow but steady pace.

"Mm… Yummy. Being here with everyone today makes everything taste so much nicer," said Louisa.

"You suuure can drink, Louisa. Here, here, have another."

"Misaki, Louisa's already had four, you shouldn't push her…," Suzuna chided as Misaki poured Louisa another drink. She was trying to keep an eye on Misaki because she was afraid she'd get carried away. Elitia seemed overwhelmed by Louisa's mature sex appeal and avoided looking at her by lifting the bottle of alcohol and staring at it.

"Suzuna, it really strikes me how considerate of others you are, but sometimes the adults want to drink," said Igarashi. "And not just like when your dad has a beer with his dinner—sometimes we'd rather go to bars with our friends. Atobe, are you listening?"

"Yes, I'm listening, but soon the alcohol—"

"Ugh, you're still practically sober. I've never even seen you drunk. Last night you only had water... Do you not wanna drink with me?"

"No, no, that's not it. I have been drinking today, but it's getting late and soon—"

"Oh, that's quite all right. If you're talking about taking Theresia back to the Mercenary Office, there's plenty of time," said Louisa, flushed in the face as she was refilling my tankard before I could stop her. She slipped her arm around my back and came very close as she clinked her glass against mine—hard to believe, I know.

"L-Louisa, what's gotten into you all of a sudden?" I asked.

"Sorry, I think I'm a little bit tipsy. I have a bad habit of hugging my friends too much when I get like this..."

"Whoaaa... Aren't you getting a little frisky with Arihito?" asked Misaki.

"Uh..."

I knew that Louisa trusted me, but that was also why I felt like she was just too close. Even Misaki was blushing, and Suzuna looked like she couldn't decide if she should say anything.

Is she really the type who gets flirty when she's drunk? When she's this close, her breasts are practically— Oh man, and Igarashi's behind me, too!

"Uh, I'll be right back. I need to get up for a second...," I stammered.

"You don't have to hold back like that, y'know? You've done something so amazing, Atobe, you should relax a bit. You can even order us around a little, it's fine. Here, I'll pour you another drink. Drink up and eat up. Okay, open wide!" Igarashi stabbed the last piece of ham with a fork. She was starting to sound a bit preachy or like a mother. She made me eat the ham and finish my drink.

Things would have gotten complicated if we'd gone out for drinks together yesterday... I can't decide if it's better that we didn't or not.

I wasn't exactly a seasoned drinker, but I could tell you one thing about how Igarashi acted when she got drunk: She really let her guard down.

"Hic... Ahhh, so good. Y'know, Atobe, I always thought you had what it took to go far. You were so much better than everyone else at paperwork, not to mention looks. I just kept asking you to do things. I knew it was wrong. But you were the only employee I could count on."

"Y-yeah, I know. Um, excuse me! Could we please have some water and mixed fruit?" I asked a waitress.

"Of course. I'll be back in a moment," she replied before heading to the back of the tavern. The whole time we were waiting, Igarashi gabbed on about how much she could rely on me. Maybe she was trying to tell me she was sorry for how poorly she treated me.

If she'd just told me this back in our old life, then she and I... No, there's no way. Maybe that's one thing we gained by coming here. You never know what life's gonna throw at you.

"So, you know, at Valentine's Day, I got you a different

chocolate than the others, partly as a thanks for everything you do for me every day. But I put them all in the same packaging, so you didn't notice, did you? Hey, are you listening to me? Did you actually eat that chocolate?"

"Yes, I ate it. It was delicious. Now please calm down," I insisted.

"Hmph. You didn't actually eat it, did you? Probably thought you didn't need any chocolate from some manager you hated and threw it away. I cherished the chocolate you gave me in return on White Day. I took it home but told my family it was just chocolate given to me out of obligation from my workers, so my mom and little brother just went and ate it. Is that normal? Eating chocolate that I went out of my way to bring home, even if I did just get it out of obligation. I opened the fridge, and it was all gone."

This was the entirely wrong place to tell her she should have put it in her room. I wondered if Igarashi did really care in her own way about me as her employee. I just didn't realize it because I was so tired. Actually, it didn't mean anything if I didn't notice it.

"Wait, Arihito, Kyouka, are you reeeally saying nothing ever happened between you two? Then you guys are super-platonic," said Misaki.

"Do you think things would've gotten like this if there had been something? Isn't it obvious?" I retorted.

"Atobe, don't be so angry. Here, have some more meat. Everything's better with a little meat. You're only annoyed 'cause you haven't eaten enough."

I wasn't sure our little party counted as a drunken frenzy, but this was how things continued to go. On my other side, Louisa continued leaning against me, so there was nothing I could do to escape.

Elitia watched our exchanges the whole time until, at last, something seemed to dawn on her.

"...Isn't Valentine's Day when you exchange gifts between friends?" she asked. That's when we learned that Elitia was from northern Europe, which had different customs for Valentine's Day. Unlike Japan, not all countries got worked up about giving out *giri* chocolate (obligation chocolate, the kind you give to coworkers) or *honmei* chocolate (given to boyfriends or husbands).

By the time we were leaving the tavern, Igarashi and Louisa seemed to have hit it off. They said they were going back to my place to chat. So basically, they meant Louisa was going to be staying the night.

While Elitia was sober, she seemed to have been affected by the heat in the tavern and patted her cheeks when we came out.

"All right, I'm going to take Louisa and Kyouka home. Suzuna, Misaki, are you coming, too?" she asked.

"Definitely! ♪ Arihito, what's your suite like?"

"...I've never gone to a man's home this late before, but I guess if everyone else is going...," said Suzuna.

Well, they'll be going back to their own place afterward, right? Even without them, we're at four people once you count Theresia.

Even if I slept on the couch, we wouldn't have enough beds for each person to get their own.

"Louisa, you take good care of Atobe from here on out, okay?" Igarashi said.

"I'm rather excited to see your own progress as well, Ms. Kyouka. I hope I can be of some assistance to you all."

I guess those two could share a bed since they seemed to get along well now. I gave Elitia the key to the room, and they went off while I took Theresia back to the Mercenary Office. I asked an employee outside if I could speak with Leila, so they went and got her for me.

"Ah, you're back. Good thing you made it in time—otherwise, you're required to pay to hire them the next day," said Leila when she came out.

"Leila, after today's adventure, I was able to get the number of tickets that I need. Please let me make Theresia a permanent member of my party," I said as I handed her the bronze Mercenary Tickets. Her eyes were wide with surprise as she took the bundle of paper and flipped through it twice to double-check the amount.

"...One hundred. You really did get them all. I heard a massive orc got taken to a dissection center near the outer wall. Was that your doing?"

"It was, but I'd rather you keep your voice down. I'm hoping to keep this quiet, so please don't tell anyone." Leila let out a small sigh. She didn't seem surprised per se, but more like she was impressed.

"Pretty incredible for a newbie like yourself. I thought it'd take you a month at least. I never could've guessed you'd get the tickets the day after you promised you would."

"I'm sorry for all the trouble. A lot of things just happened to line up. Luck was a big factor, too. I'll be taking extra care going forward, both in general and in turning Theresia human again."

"Very well… I admire your will. It's my job to give demi-humans a home, but I've never stopped wanting to mend their souls. I just don't have what it takes… A strong and dependable Seeker like you is everything I could have hoped for."

"Theresia was my first companion here. Even though she can't talk, I feel like we can somehow understand each other. There are moments where I truly think I know what she's feeling. Although I can't be sure, since I can't speak to her…"

Theresia still said nothing, but she had been staring at me ever since I'd handed Leila the bronze Mercenary Tickets. She had emotions, that much I could tell. She just had no way of expressing them.

"Arihito, when I said that Theresia seemed to like you, I didn't just mean that she was becoming attached to you because you were working together. I can't prove that demi-humans have emotions, but I do believe each and every one of them has a heart. With that in mind, Theresia seems more comfortable with you today than she was yesterday…I'm sure of it."

"Thank you. I hope that's true, too."

It wasn't just that my license said her Trust Level in me had increased; it was that the time we spent together felt important. She was important to me, and I wanted us to keep depending on each other.

Leila approved the transaction, and we shook hands before Theresia and I headed off home. Partway, I noticed that Theresia was still walking quietly behind me. I didn't know if she had a Rogue skill that made her steps silent or if it was an effect of her lizard equipment.

"Theresia, you don't have to walk behind me. You can walk wherever you like."

"……"

After a moment's thought, Theresia walked next to me. I thought she'd walk by my side, but she moved a little ahead.

"…Does that mean that you want to walk in front of me like usual? As my vanguard?" I wasn't sure if she was trying to express something, but I wanted to ask. As usual, Theresia didn't reply.

Actually, that wasn't true. She nodded slightly, then a moment later, shook her head. I wondered what she meant, but then she came back to walk right next to me.

"Yeah, you can walk anywhere. During battle you'll go in front of me, even if it's just by a little. That way we can protect each other like we've been doing."

Theresia nodded, then stared at me and gently tugged on my sleeve.

"Are you trying to say we should hurry home?"

"……"

She didn't answer. Maybe she meant we didn't need to hurry. Well, if she wanted to walk together for a little, we could walk off some of the alcohol. That didn't sound like a bad idea. We slowly strolled through the town toward home where everyone was waiting. At some point, the moon appeared and joined the streetlamps in lighting our path.

Part VII: Seeker Traditions

When we got back to Nornil Heights, the old lady called to us from the property manager's office.

"Goodness, Mr. Atobe! Your room is rather lively tonight. I saw a group of women heading in there earlier. Oh, to be young again!"

"I'm sorry for all the ruckus. Three of them will probably be going home soon."

"Oh, really? Normally when a party is this friendly, after an expedition, they'll...you know," she continued, her chubby cheeks blushing. I guess there was some sort of tradition that Seekers took part in after they'd gone on an adventure?

Theresia and I were walking up the stairs to my room on the third floor when Theresia suddenly froze stock-still on a landing.

"What is it?" I asked.

"......"

She didn't say anything. She glanced up the stairs and then once more at me.

"Are you saying there's something that way and it's difficult to go there?"

I was just thinking that some of the other residents were

probably ahead when I realized. I had been hearing a sound since earlier that I'd assumed was a cat yowling or something, but I realized then it was something much more shocking.

I—I mean…I've had to stay in business hotels with really thin walls and had to listen to that, but here? Seriously…?

I also suddenly realized what the old woman was implying earlier. Men and women in a party going to bed together. Like, you know, how a married couple might. I guess it's not that surprising; people come back from an adventure in the labyrinth, maybe they had a great day and they're really excited and worked up, then night comes… It wasn't exactly a shock, but it did make me incredibly uncomfortable. Theresia was still as silent as ever, so I figured it was on me to break the tension.

"Well, they seem preoccupied. I can't believe they're making such a racket with the door open. I wish they would've at least given us a heads-up."

"……"

I started walking again and came out into the second-floor hallway. The door of a room a little farther down was open.

It's their own business, would it be wrong of me to shut it…? I hope the others don't have to listen to this.

"……"

"I'm sorry I brought you here with this going on. Normally, it's really quiet."

Theresia nodded slightly. This time she left me and went on ahead herself. Once we got up to the third floor, I could barely hear it anymore. Thankfully, the floors were thick or something.

One thing I did know was that demi-human lizard mask was basically part of Theresia until we could remove it. It was definitely turning pink with embarrassment. Not that I'd ever seen an embarrassed lizard before to know what it looked like. Theresia's equipment also didn't cover every inch of her skin, so I could see her blushing there, too. She was walking a little farther away from me than she had before. She kept glancing at me as we approached the room. I couldn't just leave this alone because I felt awkward. I needed to make her feel safe.

"Theresia, starting tomorrow you can get your own room, too. Just because I brought you to my room doesn't mean you have to, y'know, do anything."

Theresia looked at me. Her mouth peeping out from under the lizard mask was drawn in a tight line. It wasn't just the mask that was blushing—the entire lower half of her face was bright red as well.

"……"

"Really, I mean it. I just followed the necessary process to keep you as a companion. It's not like I bought you with those tickets or anything."

She kept quiet for a while before eventually nodding. Her face was still flushed red, though… Maybe this was what happened when she drank?

"Sorry to interrupt your important conversation, but…can I warn you about something?"

"Whoa, Elitia, you scared me! And Suzuna, too… Did you two go somewhere?"

"We were just getting some fresh air," Suzuna replied. "It sounded like there was a cat out there..."

"O-oh, yeah. Probably some cat yowling," I said.

The two of them had been on the third-floor balcony. Outside they could hear the sounds coming from the second floor, but thankfully, it didn't seem like they had realized what the sounds really were. Seriously, I'd never thought I'd be so worried about soundproofing in rooms after being reincarnated. I hoped the next place we moved to would be made with the best building materials available and showcase this world's greatest architectural capabilities.

"Elitia, what was it you wanted to warn me about?"

"There's a limit to how many people can stay in a single party's room. How high is your rank for this district now?"

"I'm at seventh place. Tomorrow I'm gonna take a look at a royal suite..."

"A royal suite has capacity for eight, so only eight people can live there. There's also a limit on the number of people in a party, which is also eight, and you can't rent capacity for more than eight people at any given time. The room Suzuna and I have can have two residents..."

"You originally rented a room in District Five, so what you have here in District Eight is just temporary. We were talking about how I would rent another suite room if my rank went up."

So basically, with my new royal suite we were already at the max size we could rent, meaning Suzuna and Elitia wouldn't need to continue renting their room.

"Generally, the smaller rooms also have lower-quality facilities, so I was hoping to talk with you about it and see if we could all live together. If the bed isn't very good, then we can't recover properly," continued Elitia.

I'd heard that your vitality and magic barely got restored at all if you stayed in a barn. That actually made sense because if your bed wasn't comfortable, you couldn't sleep well and would still be tired the next day. That said, I had started to assume that this was the end of me living with the others. I felt awkward seeing Igarashi now that it was going to keep going for this reason.

"Okay…how about we look at the room and then decide? Once we move on to District Seven, though, we'll have to start all over with small rooms again, right?" I asked.

"You can keep renting the same place for up to a week, so we could make the royal suite our base while we continue seeking. You have to purchase the property if you want to stay there permanently. It's really expensive, and only Seekers of three stars or higher are allowed to purchase houses," said Elitia.

I'd just become a two-star Seeker, but I didn't feel that three stars was that far away. *I should find out more about this.*

"How do you get three stars?"

"First you need to go to District Seven. Once you reach ten thousand contribution points, the Guild there will assign you a number of tasks, and you receive your third star if you are able to pass them all."

"All right, I'll keep that in mind. Are you two going home?" Suzuna and Elitia looked at each other and smiled awkwardly.

"Hmm? Oh…did you want to take a bath, too?" I had thought she didn't take baths because of the lizard gear, but I guess she still could if it was all a part of her body. It could be a problem if it wasn't washed properly.

Theresia looked like she wanted to say something, but as usual, she was silent as she looked around the room. Finally, she walked behind the couch I was sitting on.

"……"

"Uh, you can sit whenever you like, but it just makes me feel a bit awkward if you don't sit at all." I turned around to see her head was slightly atilt. Her lizard mask had put me off a bit when we first met, but now I found it a little charming.

"Oh, right, I leveled up today. Mind if I take a look at my new skills?"

"……"

Theresia seemed to understand that a Seeker's skills were their lifeline. She came around to the front of the couch to take a seat. I didn't really care if she looked and wanted her to take it easy, so I was happy.

Right, then… So can I get any new skills?

◆Acquired Skills◆

Defense Support 1: Reduces injury to party members in front of you by 10 points.

Attack Support 1: Adds 10 injury points to attacks made by party members in front of you.

Recovery Support 1: Recovers 5 vitality points every 30 seconds for party members in front of you.

◆Available Skills◆

Morale Support 1:	Increases morale of party members in front of you by 10 points.
Rear View:	Spends 5 magic points to expand your vision to cover your rear for a set period of time.
Hawk Eyes:	Improves ability to monitor the situation when in the back line.
Rear Stance:	Fixes your position to be behind the target.
Backdraft:	Automatically counters when attacked from behind.

Remaining Skill Points: 3

It looked like you got two skill points per level. I knew I couldn't waste them, but just looking at the skill descriptions got me all excited.

One of the skills available was one that somewhat covered the greatest concern I had, which was the risk that I might be attacked directly from behind. The name "Backdraft" made me think of a closed room with a fire burning inside. When a door or something was opened, oxygen flooded in and it caused an explosion, or something like that.

If I could only counter attacks from behind me, then that left my sides open. Well, I couldn't expect perfect defense at level 3. That was most likely a problem I'd always have to face as a rearguard. It's a strong job, but it's not perfect.

I found the other skills really interesting, too. I thought I could activate the skills that said *support* at any time, and they didn't use any magic, so they'd generally be a good choice. It was possible, though, that there was some downside to the support skills that I just wasn't aware of.

Theresia looked at me while I pondered which skill to take. I wanted to check her skills again, and I wanted to ask the others about theirs as well... I was looking forward to having a meeting either tonight or tomorrow.

Part VIII: Equipment Limitations

It was probably going to take a little while longer before the others came back from their baths. Misaki hadn't woken yet, so I didn't want to leave the room empty while she slept. I felt like the building was fairly safe, but I was worried about leaving her alone.

"Theresia, do you have a license? All Seekers are supposed to have one."

She shook her head. Mercenaries didn't carry licenses. Maybe they lost them when they died?

"......"

"Hmm? ...You want me to look at your back?"

Theresia nodded, her back turned to me though she still sat on the couch. The lizard mask came down to her neck with her black hair flowing out from under it. Theresia's hair looked really long from this direction. She slipped her hand behind her back and pulled her hair forward, revealing a part of her back I'd never seen before. Her back was covered in the lizard-skin leather armor that she always wore, but there was a hole in it on the back of her neck. Her skin there looked like it'd been branded with some symbol.

"Is this a symbol that represents the fact that you have to serve someone?"

Theresia put her hand behind her back again, this time taking my hand and making me touch the symbol on her neck. When I did, it glowed red, then changed to blue before the symbol itself changed, too.

"...Ng..."

Theresia let out a silent yelp. Once the symbol had finished changing, she finally let go of my hand.

That's right. Leila did say her ownership would be transferred to me... Is that what that was?

Even so, the lizard armor was still stuck fast to Theresia's body. Since she had a mask on, I couldn't be certain about her age, but I started to have a feeling that she was younger than I'd thought.

"......"

Theresia turned silently around. Her lips had been pulled tight but were now slightly open, perhaps because I touched the symbol. Even though I could only see the bottom part of her face, the skin was smooth like porcelain. I guess she didn't have any major scars or anything when she was killed. Nothing I could see right now, at least.

She looked at me for a moment, then glanced at my license and pointed toward it.

"My license? Do you want to use it?"

She nodded, so I handed it to her. She swiped her finger on it until she got to the party member page and then tapped on her own name. When she did, a page showing her own skills popped up.

◆Mercenary Skills Display: THERESIA◆

Lizard Skin 1:	Inherent demi-human skill. Increases defense and attribute resistance.
Accel Dash:	Momentarily increases speed.
Scout Range Extension 1:	Increases the range in which enemies can be detected.
Lookout 1:	Increases awareness of potential surprise attacks from behind.
Silent Step:	Quiets the sound of footsteps. Sound can be made intentionally.

◆Available Skills◆

Pickpocket 1:	Steals a specified item from target without their knowledge.
Escapology:	Escapes even when restrained.
Sleight of Hand 1:	Undoes simple locks and traps.

Remaining Skill Points: 1

She had the same six skill points that I did at level 3, and all but one had already been used up. Rogue was supposedly not a job specialized in any particular field, but she had specialist skills for removing traps like the Thief-type jobs. Still, Sleight of Hand seemed useful, and all her combat skills had been acquired by now. The Escapology skill might be handy if it could be used for attacks that bind people and not just normal ropes and things. I really didn't want to run into a tentacle monster, though. Pickpocket would be nice if it could be used against monsters, but karma would go up if she ever used it on a human. Given that, I might not let her even if the situation called for it. *Maybe I should just go for Sleight of Hand for now...* No, I didn't need to rush things.

"If possible, I want to improve areas that only you are capable of. Let's wait until you gain another level and you can learn some really great skills. We can always pick one of these three skills if need be."

"Oh, Arihito! Welcome back! Where'd everyone run off to?" asked Misaki, who had just woken up right when I was putting my license away. She casually undid her hair, which came cascading down as she headed over to us.

"They went to take a bath. What about you, Misaki? You could probably catch them if you hurry."

"Then that's what I'll do. Suzu loves baths, so she takes sooo long. Could I borrow some money from you for a change of clothes?"

"You don't have to return it. You've been through a lot today."

"Whaaa? Is this, like, a parting gift or something? And here I had my heart set on being a member of your party!"

"I thought you said you were gonna try out a few things."

"Uh… W-well. I couldn't leave once I found out how nice it was to sleep in a suite bed. Pleeeaase, please let me stay with you until I reach my goal!"

So it's come to this, huh? …I mean, I did say we'd take her along on one adventure anyway.

"Misaki, why'd you write Gambler for your job?"

"I just thought it'd be really fun if there was a job like that. Plus, I always get the highest fortunes when I go to a shrine, and I'm suuuper good at cards. Do you like to gamble, Arihito?"

"I've bought a lottery ticket once or twice. Have you ever won anything before?"

"Hee-hee, I once won a hundred thousand yen from a ticket my family bought. That's about it, though."

So maybe she thought she'd become a Gambler because she had a natural disposition toward it. I imagined if I went ahead and jumped into every challenge so haphazardly, I'd just lose everything. It was that luck of hers that reeled me in. If she were in our party when we defeated a Named Monster, then we'd have better drop rates. She wasn't in our party when we fought Juggernaut, though, so she didn't have anything to do with the black treasure chest.

"I've acquired one skill called Increased Drop Rate and another called Child of Luck. I'd deeefinitely be a help to your party, Arihito."

"I know, I know. We reincarnated at the same time, too. Looking forward to working with you."

"Yaaaay! Oh my gosh, I haaave to go tell Suzu and the others!" I'd taken her for more of a calculating, underhanded type girl, but really, she was surprisingly innocent.

"……"

"Theresia, you can join her if you go now." But Theresia didn't nod back. She did follow me down toward the baths, though, when I decided I'd go. Well, she didn't necessarily have to nod in reply to everything. She'd probably go take a bath if I took her to meet the others…though I was worried about her armor getting damp since she couldn't remove it.

Since I had the key, I needed to get back to the room quickly after taking my bath. I hurried down the stairs and went into the bathroom. I pulled my clothes off in the dressing room. There weren't any other residents there. This lodging building didn't close the baths, so I guess there were a lot of people who used it really late. They must boil the water when they opened the baths because it got colder and colder over time. It wasn't even hot by the time I got there, but that was entirely my fault.

I wondered what facilities the royal suite would have. Maybe no baths in District Eight were reheated over time, though shouldn't they be able to do something using magic? Well, I guess it was just nice of the manager to heat it at all.

I went into the actual bathroom and used a bucket to scoop water from the shared bath to pour on myself. That was one massive difference between here and Japanese-style baths. It didn't make it too difficult to have a bath, but it was inconvenient that they didn't have any faucets for washing yourself before getting in the shared bath. Apparently, there was also a set amount of hot water they kept in the tub, and they would change it out after a certain number of people had used it, so I couldn't use too much like this.

I'm just glad I can take a bath every day. I imagine Igarashi and the others would want to take a bath every day, too... It would've been so hard to start off in the barn.

Suzuna had also been concerned about being covered in sweat. It really affected morale if we weren't able to take care of the basics in life. That's probably why there was so much lodging available for the Seekers.

It was normal to wash your head first, so I poured water over myself and started rubbing the shampoo-like stuff in my hair that Igarashi had been so excited about. It smelled fruity and had a nice lather to it, but it was definitely different from what I was used to. It made my hair kind of dry.

It was then that someone touched my shoulder, making me jump a little from surprise.

"Huh? ...Wh-who is it?" I hadn't noticed anyone enter the bathroom, but there definitely was someone behind me. They tapped my shoulder again, so I had to turn around and slowly opened my eyes, though I was afraid of getting shampoo in them.

The first thing I saw was reptile scales. *Okay, no big deal, it's just a lizardman. I'm used to seeing scales from being around Theresia.*

Then I noticed this lizardman's feet were covered in leather. I moved my gaze slowly upward. The leather was open on the front near their hips, and I looked up farther— Actually, no. That's where I finally realized what was happening.

T-Theresia... Why is she in here...?!

"......"

"T-Theresia... Just to let you know, this is the men's bath. You can't come in here," I tried to explain once I'd calmed down enough to speak. I didn't know what Theresia was thinking, but she lifted her hand to her chest.

"N-no, your armor can't come off anyway, so you just keep it on. Anyway, you should go over to the women's bath, everyone's there. That way..." I tried desperately to reason with her, but she just stared at me. I prayed my explanation was getting through to her, but she didn't budge.

Then...she moved her hand to her throat and undid a metal fastener with a *ping* sound. The leather armor, her lizardman namesake, the lizard-like leather that fit perfectly to her body, which I thought couldn't be removed, something I was convinced was like a second skin...she took it off.

I couldn't comprehend what was happening in front of me. I had thought her full body armor was like her lizard mask and could never be taken off, but undo a little metal clasp, and it just came right off. There were some parts, though, on her wrists, shoulders, and ankles where the lizard equipment wouldn't come off, where there was some leather left behind. No, actually, that must have been a result of her Lizard Skin skill. Other than that, the pale white skin, which had only peeked from places in her armor, was now practically bare in front of me.

"…T-Theresia… You can t-take it off…? …N-no, uh, I mean—!"

"……"

She looked at me in what seemed to be bewilderment, like she was trying to ask what I was getting so worked up about.

I jumped up and rushed to the dressing room where I hung the RESERVED sign out so no one would come in. We were only allowed to use it for fifteen minutes, but hopefully no one would mind right now. I grabbed a towel and went back to the bath, then tried to get Theresia to wrap it around herself. Nothing I could do about what had already been seared into my brain… Her limbs were surprisingly graceful and strong. My mind just kept replaying the sight of her removing the leather armor, which wrapped around her body.

She was always wearing her equipment so the marks from it… No, don't think about it… I said those things earlier to make her feel safer, but was she even aware?!

"……"

Theresia tapped my shoulder again as I was regretting what I'd said. I had no idea why she was trying to cheer me up, but she didn't seem embarrassed in the slightest that I'd seen her naked. Was she really brave or just lacking emotions about it?

I'd thought she was showing embarrassment earlier, but now she was suddenly bold. Someone might take this unpredictability as proof that demi-humans didn't actually have any emotions. But you could also argue that it was because her Trust Level in me had gone up… She must have come to the bathroom because she felt comfortable with me. It had to be good intentions on her part.

"...Are you trying to say that you came to wash my back or something?"

Theresia nodded immediately, and suddenly, I felt less nervous, though it was my fault for giving her a reason to take her armor off. I bet she wouldn't have shown that she could take off her armor if I hadn't said *"Your armor can't come off."*

"...Uh, o-okay then... Something simple like that's just fine. Would you mind washing my back?"

"......"

Theresia nodded, then went behind me and started rinsing my hair. I just realized I was still covered in suds, but for some reason, her fingers got caught less in my dry hair than if I had done it myself. Next, she gently washed my back, and I told her to rinse herself off while I went into the bathtub, keeping my back to her so she couldn't see anything.

...Urgh, I feel like some sort of slave master for not returning the favor... B-but washing her back would definitely be going too far.

I was suddenly curious as to what she would do with the lizard mask, but it did seem like that didn't come off. Apparently, that was the only thing that she couldn't remove even if she wanted to.

Eventually Theresia finished washing herself and slowly glanced over her shoulder at me. She'd taken off the towel that had been wrapped around her, but she was still keeping herself covered.

"The water's a bit hot. You think you can stand it?"

"......"

She nodded in response, and I had to close my eyes again,

since she wouldn't be able to wear the towel as she was getting into the bath. Theresia slipped into the water with a small splash. I was feeling a little more comfortable, but I had to be careful about looking in her direction... Okay, I guess I really needed to say it.

"Theresia, thanks for washing my back, but next time you need to go to the women's bath."

"......"

"N-no, I'm gonna need you to nod to show you understand. I'm a man. You need to be a little more careful."

But Theresia still didn't nod. It was a good thing that she didn't just follow all my orders no matter what they were even though her ownership had been transferred to me, but I really couldn't have her coming along next time, too.

"Theresia, I get the feeling you're happy to do stuff for me, but we can't keep taking over the entire men's bathroom all the time..."

Also, the others would be suspicious of me once we were finished in here. Theresia was stubborn and gave no response.

"...Theresia?"

"......"

Her lizard mask turned red—although I already knew that could happen. She hadn't been in the hot water for very long, and yet she was completely scarlet.

"Wait... Oh man... Don't tell me...you're cold-blooded because you're a lizard...?"

"......"

"Ack... H-hang on! I'll cool you down!"

She looked like a human in lizard equipment, some of which came off, but she in reality, she had the characteristics of a lizard. If she overheated that quickly, it would probably be better for her to only take lukewarm baths. But rather than reflect on that right now, I needed to find a way to safely cool her down as soon as possible, since she was completely red and close to passing out.

Part IX: The Night Rearguard

I dragged Theresia out of the bath before she had become so overheated that she couldn't move. The last time I'd carried someone like this was when I went back to the foster care facilities to say hello and some of the younger kids took a liking to me and wanted to play. I'd never carried an adult like Theresia, though. Thankfully, she didn't feel too heavy. Part of it was definitely that she just was relatively light, but I also got the impression that my physical abilities had improved as I gained experience and leveled up. I'd known vitality would go up, but apparently, my strength did as well.

That can only happen since this body is my reincarnated one. Also, why I can use skills probably...

I tried to use them and was able to, so I'd adapted to this new world, but my support was some power similar to magic. If I ever ran out of magic, then I'd really know how it felt.

Heat seemed to be one of Theresia's weaknesses. Her vitality bar had actually gone down a tiny bit. In the future, she'd need to bathe in lukewarm water, or maybe even cool water would be better. It wasn't just being strict with her; this was a matter of life and death.

I decided it was a good thing I'd given Theresia the red buckler that had flame resistance and also tried to think of how I would explain this situation to the others while I climbed the stairs to the third floor.

The battle formation you set with your license only applied while you were in the labyrinth. It would make sense if it were necessary, but it'd be pretty surreal seeing everyone walk around town in battle formation. At the very least, you'd draw people's attention, since you didn't see any other parties walking around that way.

...But with Theresia like this...

I should have asked the property workers to prepare an appropriate change of clothes for Theresia, but I had just put her in a nightgown for now. I didn't try to put on underwear. It seemed like demi-humans only ever wore equipment on their body that was made specifically for their type. Weapons and shields didn't seem to require it, but I got the impression that the lizard-skin leather was the most preferred if it was going to touch her skin, so I was pretty hesitant to even put on the pajamas. Basically, I really didn't want any of the male Seekers in the building to see since she didn't have underwear on. Including me.

I really regretted not asking Leila for more information on the demi-humans' daily lives. What did they like? What didn't they?

"……"

Shortly after we left the bathroom, she was walking in front of me, Recovery Support activated, and Theresia's vitality went up. It healed her to full, so obviously, she hadn't taken a large amount of damage. Nevertheless, I was still worried until then.

"Theresia, sorry I didn't realize that you can't handle high temperatures." She didn't nod, which probably meant that she'd never actually been in a hot bath. Theresia must've only ever washed in cool water, so she herself wasn't aware of that weakness.

"Are you okay with only bathing in cool water from now on?"

"……"

"W-well…we could also just not have you soak in the big tub."

Theresia shook her head. She knew she'd overheat, but she wanted to come in the bath with me. I wondered what made her so stubborn… Was it bravery or sheer hardheadedness?

We'd have to find something to give her a higher resistance against heat, or maybe she'd be better with it once she got Lizard Skin 2. If we got some accessory that improved her heat resistance, she would be able to use it once she was turned back to a human, too, so that was the ideal solution.

Only in this world would I have to think of ways to let someone take a bath…

I had no idea what I was thinking, but Theresia was walking up the stairs ahead of me, and…I glanced up and would need to find some way to apologize. I could feel my cheeks burning red and decided I should ask Louisa if she had any ideas about putting underwear on Theresia.

The others returned to the room shortly after Theresia and myself. I tried to explain what happened as earnestly as possible.

"Goodness… That sounds rather difficult. Very few people have demi-humans in their parties, so I've never heard of such an incident," said Louisa.

"I-incident? Saying it like that makes me feel kinda guilty."

"If the other residents heard you'd taken a woman into the men's bath, I'm sure there'd be plenty of complaints. I think this definitely qualifies as an 'incident,'" said Igarashi.

Both of them seemed to be sobering up, and they looked like a matching set in their pajamas. I could tell they'd have each other's backs.

"……"

"Uh…Theresia, are you trying to tell us not to be mad at Atobe?" asked Igarashi.

Theresia nodded. That alone lessened my crime quite a lot and shifted the conversation of the mixed bathing incident.

"Theresia just wanted to show her gratitude to Arihito," offered Suzuna.

"Still, I think it went too far…but we also didn't notice what was happening, which is our fault," said Elitia. Suzuna was picking up what I was trying to say from the beginning. Elitia had her doubts, though that eventually seemed to go away.

"Well, this is Arihito we're talking about, so I'm sure it was a perfectly innocent bath, riiiight?" added Misaki. "Unless he gets really aggressive when it's just the two of them."

"I would've thanked you for the first half, but you just had to keep going."

"Ha-ha, actually, we were talking about you during our bath. Kyouka was wondering what you were up to while we were gone," continued Misaki.

"Rgh... You don't have to go blabbing about that. Honestly, kids these days..."

The fact that she was thinking about me while they were in the bath was going to make it hard for me to sleep...but in the end, we only had two beds. How was that going to work when we had one man and six women?

"Um, we should be heading to bed soon, so can we talk about how we're going to handle things?" I asked.

"Way to put me on the spot, staring at me when you say that...," grumbled Igarashi. "I'm fine sleeping on the couch. I feel bad for chasing you out of the bedroom last night anyway."

"Oh, no... Ms. Kyouka, there's nothing wrong with a little propriety, but Mr. Atobe is a valuable member of your party and the leader. He needs to get proper rest in a bed," said Louisa.

"Ah, uh, no, the couch works for me. Do you think you could sleep three to a bed? I think it might be pretty tight." I thought that arrangement could work, although they might fall out if they weren't used to it.

"I already used your bed, Arihito, so I'm fine with the floor or whatever," said Misaki.

"Suzuna and I are imposing as well, so we'll just take a couch," said Elitia.

"No, it's fine, I'm even used to sleeping in chairs. You guys aren't, so it'll be harder for you," I objected.

"...I-in any case...I'm gonna be up chatting with Louisa anyway, so you should take it easy in the bedroom, Atobe."

"Yes, I was hoping to do the same. Please have yourself a nice rest, Mr. Atobe."

This discussion didn't seem to be going anywhere... I was grateful that everyone was putting me first, but I wasn't too bothered about having a bed to sleep in. Back at the company, I'd line up chairs and sleep on that. The couch was a million times more comfortable than that.

"Why don't we settle this faaair and square through a lottery drawing? Great! I took that quill over there and made some tickets!" said Misaki.

"That was fast... And you are aware you're more likely to win, right?" I pointed out.

"Hee-hee, what's wrong with that? This way there'll be no hard feelings. And anyway, if I win, I'll just let Suzu take it."

"Misaki, you don't need to worry about me. Besides, I want to put Arihito first," insisted Suzuna. She was almost *too* kind. It didn't seem like she was just being considerate; she sounded genuine. Misaki couldn't do much but muster an awkward laugh.

"It doesn't matter. Even if we don't pull lots to decide, I'll still sleep on the couch. Sleeping in the same room as me is more trouble than it's worth..."

"Oh... D-don't worry about that. I was just nervous since it was our first day here...," said Igarashi.

"Awww, c'mon, I already made the tickets, so let's use them! Okay, here's how we'll decide!" Misaki had us all write our names on the slips. I looked at the last slip and decided I didn't care that Misaki, the Gambler, was likely to win no matter what and it was all the same to me and wrote my name down.

In the end, I lost the lottery and ended up sleeping on the couch like last night anyway.

"...Theresia, can you sleep there?" I asked.

"......"

I could hear everyone chatting in the bedroom for a bit, but they must have been tired since it didn't last too long. Everything soon went quiet. Theresia walked silently from the bedroom and sat on the other couch. I was lying on my side, and Theresia mimicked me and lay down. The eyes on her lizard mask started to slide closed but snapped open as soon as I thought she was about to fall asleep.

"You don't have to be my night watchman. Get some rest."

"......"

She shook her head, but in the end, she was no match for her own sleepiness. Her eyes finally closed completely, and her breathing slowed.

I was still thinking about the skills I could take that I'd been looking at earlier and finally decided I should choose one. It was good that we were able to beat Juggernaut, but I didn't want to be in a position to regret not acquiring a skill. Rear View could be useful, but it wouldn't be necessary if I took Backdraft. If I could react automatically to attacks, then I could stop surprise assaults from the rear and keep us from being defeated.

But we won't need it if Theresia improves her Lookout skill... Actually, it all depends on how strong Backdraft is, but I can't know that without testing it.

Skill points really were invaluable. I should probably first focus on what I can do that no one else can. It was obvious which skill I should take when I looked at it like that.

```
◆Acquired Skills◆
  Defense Support 1:  Reduces injury to party
                      members in front of you by
                      10 points.

   Attack Support 1:  Adds 10 injury points to
                      attacks made by party
                      members in front of you.

 Recovery Support 1:  Restores 5 vitality points
                      every 30 seconds for party
                      members in front of you.

☆ Morale Support 1:  Increases morale of party
                      members in front of you by
                      10 points.

      ☆ Hawk Eyes:  Improves ability to
                      monitor the situation when
                      in the back line.
Remaining Skill Points: 1
```

So the star meant I'd just acquired those skills, apparently. Being able to monitor what was happening would be important for when I was giving orders…though I didn't know specifically what that meant.

…Hmm, I think I can see things more clearly in the distance… and my field of vision seems wider, too. That's not too bad for…a rearguard…

I closed my eyes in the dark room and quickly started sinking into sleep. We would likely have plenty of beds when we moved to the royal suite, so this should've been the last night I had to sleep on the couch. *Oh, I forgot to ask Igarashi how she felt about moving.* Well, I could do it tomorrow; it wouldn't be too late.

I started hearing people whispering.

"…So it's the same for everyone. I woke up, too…"

"What should we do…? We won't get any sleep like this."

"Even when we're in a different room…I was just sleeping and then woke up…"

"You guys, too? What can we even do…?"

"…Um, can't we all just deal with it ourselves? Arihito's fast asleep."

"W-well… But still…"

"… He's sleeping like a baby… And he looks so cute asleep…"

Everyone was awake, but I just wanted to sleep. It should've been fine if we were in different rooms…or maybe they were having a hard time sleeping after all the excitement of the party we had.

…Just let me sleep a little more…until morning…

The room went quiet. Was that a dream, or did it really happen? I couldn't be sure... I just wanted to sleep.

I could hear birds singing. I sat up on the couch and stretched. Theresia was curled up on the other couch, using her own arm as a pillow. Her blanket had fallen off, so I gently placed it back on her, then looked around the room. It felt like everyone had been awake last night and talking about something next to me while I slept...

"...I'm feeling kinda unsatisfied for some reason."

"Ah... A-Atobe..."

"Oh, Igarashi, good morning. Sorry, I'm just standing here mumbling to myself." She must've overheard me as she came out of the bedroom. I'd have to come up with a good reason, like maybe that I had a weird dream.

"...Y-you...you got a good night of sleep yesterday, right?" she asked.

"Uh, yeah. This couch's pretty comfy so I slept like a log."

"G-good... Oh, everyone's getting up. We're gonna get changed in the bedroom, so don't come in."

"All right. Once Theresia wakes up, I'll tell her to get changed in there."

"...You really didn't wake up at all last night? You stayed asleep the entire time?"

"I think I might have woken up, but I don't really remember... It's all a bit fuzzy."

"M-must've been the alcohol… It makes your memory all hazy, y'know?"

She seemed anxious, but I didn't know why. Well, my head was ringing, and my body felt a little unsteady, so maybe there was still some alcohol in my system.

"All right, I'm going to wash my face. Maybe that'll wake me up a bit," I said.

"Okay, see you soon."

Each floor had a small room with a sink for washing your face and whatnot that was shared with the whole floor, so I went out into the hallway. I was glad Igarashi was so friendly lately, but it did seem strange. Maybe she was getting used to this world and it was making her more mellow. It seemed like a good change anyway.

CHAPTER 4
The End of the First Labyrinth

Part I: Our New Home

We ate a simple breakfast in the suite once everyone had gotten up. I was really happy they offered a light breakfast service here. We had eggs, toast, and bacon. Normally, we could only eat things that could be eaten raw, so we would have ended up with fruit and nuts without the breakfast service.

After we finished eating, I walked Louisa to the Guild. The town was quiet this morning. The other Seekers and Guild workers had already come and gone.

"Thank you for last night. It was nice to let my hair down and relax," said Louisa.

"No, thank you for coming on such short notice. We should do something together again next time we finish a big job."

"Yes, definitely. Will you be going into the labyrinth again today?"

"First, I wanted to go get that treasure chest opened. I should also be able to go see the new suite this morning, right?"

"Yes, I believe the property workers are available outside of mealtimes."

So first I'd go to the Chest Cracker that was nearby, then go look at the suite. In the afternoon, I wanted to head to the final floor of Field of Dawn. I had today's schedule planned, even if it was a bit rough.

Louisa went into an employee entrance on the back of the Guild building. She turned back and gave me a little wave right before she went in. I felt myself blushing as I waved back.

The new suite was in the middle of District Eight, about a fifteen-minute walk from the Guild. It was a great location and so much better than the middle-class Nornil Heights in every way possible: the facilities, the size of the suite, the service—everything was perfect.

"Welcome, sir, madams. Your room is this way."

The building itself was two stories and in a somewhat European style. There were only four rooms per floor. There was another building in District Eight with the same setup, but that was all of the royal suites available in the district. A number of maids lined the entrance hall to greet us and offered to take our things, but we were going to go right back out after this and instead just went to see the room. It was so overwhelmingly extravagant that even Misaki, who was normally always chatting away, was awed into silence. All the floors in the suite were laid with opulent rugs, and it even had its own bathroom and dressing room.

"…Th-this is incredible, more so than I'd expected. What do you think, Igarashi?" I asked.

"…I was told I could rent a middle-class room for myself, but…if there's space here… Are you sure I wouldn't be a bother?"

"Not at all. This place is way too massive for me to use alone, and apparently, there's a limit on the number of rooms the party can rent. I was thinking it'd be better for us to live together if possible."

"Okay then…I guess we'll continue living together."

Hearing her talk about living together made me imagine our day-to-day lives in the future. Would we come back together to this room every day? Or would we move again, keep jumping around like we were changing hotels?

"Um, yeah…and it would be nice to buy a house so we have a place to set down roots," I said.

"Uh… I-is that what you meant…?" asked Igarashi.

"If you can buy a house, then the resident limit no longer applies, so you can have multiple parties living together. If Arihito wants to keep climbing the ranks, he should start thinking about doing 'raids' with only his own companions," explained Elitia.

I had been thinking it would be nice to have one main base, so to speak, instead of having to keep moving. We wouldn't have to deal with the trouble of moving our things each time, and we could do what we wanted with the house… But like Elitia said, we'd also be able to have multiple parties—sixteen, maybe twenty-four people—all working together. I'd only made five companions so far, but if I found enough that we were able to form another party, we'd be able to swap the members around as necessary for our seeking.

If we do that, we'll have more jobs to choose from when we form a party. Right now, we're lacking someone specialized in frontline defense, plus a Pharmacist, a Wizard, or a Priest.

"We could end up getting stuck if we don't have someone with a necessary skill... It's a good idea to gather more companions, if possible. We wouldn't all have to live in one house. It'd be best if we could buy more than one house and people could live where they wanted," I said.

"You know, Arihito... If you got multiple houses and just, like, gave me one...I'd have to listen to aaanything you told me to do," suggested Misaki.

"M-Misaki, you can't just trade a house like that...," Igarashi chided.

"...As you already know, I have a certain...*problem*...so it would be best for you to find a different Swordsman until you're near my level," said Elitia. "But I still hope you'll help me, even if it's only some of the way. You don't have to go to the floor my friend is on. I can go it alone if you get me there." She must've felt like she needed to say it.

"...Elitia, you kinda changed when you got drenched in your opponent's blood. So that's why you keep your companions at a distance—because it's a danger to them as well, right?" I asked. I wasn't sure what to do in this situation, but this felt like a conversation we needed to have. Elitia looked at the sheathed blade at her side.

"This sword is called Scarlet Emperor. I found it in a treasure chest that a Named Monster dropped... When equipped, your job is changed to the weapon's 'inherent job.' I was originally a Swordswoman, but I picked up this sword...and now I can never be rid of it."

"I didn't know there was such a thing as an inherent job..."

Elitia's job of Cursed Blade was the inherent job, and the Scarlet Emperor was a cursed sword she could never get rid of. That meant she couldn't ever change her job, either. Sounded a bit like a demi-human. After they died, they were resurrected in a different form. They couldn't go back to being human, their equipment was limited, and they couldn't remove some of it.

"What happened when you first equipped Scarlet Emperor? Did you not know what it was beforehand?" I asked.

"...I used to belong to the White Night Brigade, a group that hunts Named Monsters, collects treasure chests, and uses the contents to strengthen themselves. A lot of Seekers try similar tactics to improve their battle prowess. Some say it's the easiest way for a Seeker to get stronger. But...in the White Night Brigade, you can't refuse a piece of equipment, even if you don't know what it is."

She had to equip the Scarlet Emperor even though she had no idea what it was. No matter how powerful a weapon, going into Berserk mode would become a massive problem. On the other hand, if Elitia were somehow able to counter the Berserk, she would become an incredibly powerful vanguard.

"Couldn't you take it to a shop to be appraised? Maybe there was even someone with that skill in the Brigade," I suggested.

"If you take it to a shop, then they'll find out it's cursed. The priority will become to seal the curse, so you can't use the weapon anymore. The Brigade had a policy that even if a weapon is cursed and dangerous, it's far more powerful than a normal weapon...so no, it hadn't been identified. Anyway, a failed attempt to identify is a risk to the identifier's life, so there aren't many suited to the job. The jobs that do have access to skills necessary for becoming an identifier are closely guarded by the Guild. Even the White Night Brigade wasn't able to find someone to join them who could do it."

People with rare skills were protected by the Guild. That likely also applied to this Chest Cracker we were going to see soon. Because the Guild protected these people and set up specialist shops, even the Seekers in District Eight had access to the incredible skills. Without that, it wouldn't be surprising to see those people being monopolized by high-ranked parties. It was thanks to the Guild that didn't happen.

"...I know you need to make some tough decisions in order to get stronger, and that's one way of doing it. But I personally can't get behind how the Brigade operates," I said.

"You say that, but it won't change anything. All I wanted was to become strong, but I've felt nothing but regret since I became the Cursed Blade... I can't help but feel like I'm no longer fighting as myself whenever I wield this sword..."

"Ellie... But it wasn't like that when you were fighting with Arihito, right? You were fighting to protect us," said Suzuna.

"Ngh..."

Suzuna's words made Elitia look away, tears in her eyes.

"…We would've been annihilated if Arihito hadn't been there. I let my guard down until we found Misaki because I never thought an enemy like that would appear… I may be a high level, but I'm still too inexperienced as a Seeker."

"Don't be so hard on yourself. It was a shock to me, too," I replied. "I was sure we were gonna die. We only managed to make it out because you were there. And next time, we'll do better. We can have you in the party from the beginning. We're stronger like that than if you join part way through."

"Arihito…" The sight of her bleary red eyes gutted me. I preferred not to see young girls cry if I could help it.

"Well, taking experience points into account, it might be better for you to participate as a guest for a little while," I continued. "You can join the party when you need to and use my support, and vice versa."

"…Yeah, that sounds good. I'll leave any decisions to you. Just make sure you don't get near me when I get out of control. Stay away until the fight's over."

"Yep. My support still works even if there's quite a bit of distance between us."

"Oh…"

My unattributed Attack Support was able to break through an immunity to physical attacks. Thinking back to that fight…I was completely separated from the battlefield where Elitia and Juggernaut had been fighting. If I could provide support as far as my vision extended, then that gave us a lot of flexibility in terms of battle formation. I really needed to verify the scope of my skills before we ran into an enemy that was too strong.

"Your Berserk skill might be dangerous, but I can provide support in order to minimize the risks. We should still try to break the curse somehow, though. There's gotta be a strong weapon you can use that isn't cursed."

"…You…you say that so easily. Aren't you afraid of me?"

"Nah. I mean, it'd be a shock if you started swinging at me, but I'll just make sure to keep my distance."

"Ha-haaa… I don't think 'shock' would really fit the bill there. Arihito, you're reeaaally strange. You're totally calm and relaxed even though you've just been reincarnated. You know, it's actually kind of reassuring. Don't you think, Suzu?"

"Y-yes…I feel like time flows more smoothly when Arihito's nearby."

If I seemed to be adapting faster than everyone else, that probably just meant this other world suited me. But if it made everyone feel safer, I'd do my best to keep my cool. This was the kind of world where a split-second decision could cost you your life. If the rearguard didn't keep on top of the situation and decide if they should fight or run, they could be exposing the entire party to unnecessary danger.

"Elitia, I'd understand if you said you wanted to work on your own once we help you achieve your goal, but you're an excellent Swordswoman, and I'd love to have you as a permanent member of our party."

"H-honestly… You're *way* too much of a people pleaser. Say something, Kyouka!"

"I'm fine with more members in our party, so no complaints here. Anyway, we decided that I'd follow Atobe's decisions when I first joined. Even Louisa said as much—I'm basically like his subordinate now."

"Wha...? R-really? Wow, my subordinate..."

"H-hey! What're you all smiley about? What's going through that head of yours?"

I was imagining my steadfast subordinate, Igarashi, following all of my directions. Ah, work would be so much easier then...I was starting to understand why people got corrupted by power.

"We could have problems, too, if everyone always sides with Arihito, never giving him a second opinion," said Elitia.

"Good point, Elitia. You can be strict with me, and then we should be all set."

"...All right. Just don't get angry at me for doing my job. You're the one who told me to do it. I think Kyouka's the best choice for this sort of thing, though."

"Actually, I haven't had much to scold him about since we got reincarnated. Not that I'm complaining." Everyone laughed. I had to laugh along with them.

Theresia stood there watching our entire conversation, then nodded to me. It was her way of showing she agreed.

This suite would house six people. Things were suddenly getting lively around here; I wondered if it would go well. I'd like to be in a position where I could watch over this chatty bunch.

"Right, that ends our preview of the suite. What's everyone up to next?" asked Igarashi.

"Misaki's sort of borrowed one of your beds… Would it be all right if we waited a bit until she wakes up?"

The moment Suzuna finished asking, Louisa and Igarashi came out of the room.

"Welcome home, Mr. Atobe. I'm sorry to intrude."

"We're gonna go take a bath, so you stay here and keep an eye on things. Misaki's sleeping in your bed so be quiet until she wakes up."

"A-all right. I can't believe she just helped herself to my bed…"

"…Oh, Suzuna. We won't make it home in time to take a bath even if we leave now," said Elitia.

"We can't take one any other time… Wh-what should we do? I'm all covered in sweat and dirt, if I have to adventure with Arihito and the others like this tomorrow…," said Suzuna.

I felt something big coming. No…maybe that was just my overactive imagination.

"Why don't we all go together? The bath itself is free, but you can also rent a change of clothes," Louisa suggested.

"Uh, all right…it's our only choice for these extraordinary circumstances. Is that okay with you, Suzuna?" asked Elitia.

"You're the one who really wanted to have a bath. I'm fine as long as we go together."

"Then that settles it. See you in a little bit, Mr. Atobe." With that, Louisa led everyone to the baths on the first floor. Theresia and I went into the living room, and I sank onto the couch.

"Man, I'm beat… Theresia, you can take it easy. Sit wherever you like."

"……"

"We should go back to our own place and let them know that we're moving. They'll move our things for us," said Elitia.

"They'll really bring our things here? Not that we have that much since it's only the third day...," observed Suzuna.

"Yeah. Let's decide room assignments later. For now, I'll just ask them to put our things in the living room," replied Elitia.

"Okay, once we're finished moving, let's meet back at the square in front of the Guild around noon. Atobe, we should go back to your place for a bit."

Once today's expedition was over, we'd all be spending the night together again. This royal suite had four beds between two bedrooms, so I'd finally be able to sleep in a bed.

Part II: Chest Cracker Parent and Children

After we looked around the suite, I signed the rental agreement, and Elitia and Suzuna headed back home. Igarashi, Theresia, and I returned to Nornil Heights together. Though we hadn't even stayed there an entire two days, they'd been good to us, and I was sad to have to say good-bye. Unfortunately, we'd have to keep relocating like this every once in a while, until we were able to get some permanent housing. I needed to get used to all that moving.

"You keep at it, Mr. Atobe. I'll be rooting for you," encouraged the old lady who managed the property.

"Thank you for everything. Stay well, Miss..."

"Well, since you asked, it'd do well for you to remember a lady's name. I'm Palme Arthur. I pray the Secret Gods smile upon such a bright and promising young Seeker like yourself."

So her name was Palme. She'd known my name, but I'd never asked for hers... That was really rude of me.

"Well then, where are you headed to after this, Mr. Atobe?"

"We're going to a shop to have a treasure chest opened."

"Oh, are you now? There are three Chest Crackers in the city. One is my daughter, you know."

"Really? What a small world."

Lady Palme saw us off, and we put Nornil Heights behind us.

"By the way, Atobe," Igarashi piped up out of the blue as we were walking down the hill to town, "I went up to level two and got two more skill points. Which ones do you think I should pick?"

"Congrats on leveling up. Do you mind if I took a look at your license?"

"Yeah, sure. Does yours not show other party members' skills?"

"Theresia's a special case, so I can see hers. For everyone else, I need to view their license."

The only way to do that was to gain their trust so they felt comfortable showing you. Igarashi pulled her license out of a pouch at her waist and let me look at it.

◆Acquired Skills◆
    Thunderbolt: Shoots lightning at an
                 opponent, causing damage. Has
                 a small chance of inflicting
                 SHOCK status.

```
   Mirage Step:  Adds OTHER status to self,
                 allowing you to avoid attacks
                 for a short time.
```

◆Available Skills◆

```
    Double Attack:  Increases the number of
                    attacks made with a weapon.
   Mist of Bravery: Nulls party members' FEAR
                     status.
   Freezing Thorns: Freezes opponent's legs and
                     slows their movement.
     Snow Country   Grants immunity to FROZEN status
           Skin:    and increases attractiveness.
    Bulletproof 1:  Enemy long-ranged attacks are
                    slightly less likely to hit.
          Decoy:    Skill consumes a DOLL and
                    creates a Decoy of the user.
```

Remaining Skill Points: 2

"Valkyries really do get a lot of different kinds of skills to choose from...," I commented. "There's even this thing called Snow Country Skin. I didn't realize Valkyries were related to places where it snowed a lot."

"...I wonder if it's maybe because my mom's from the north?"

"Oh, that might be it. And the reason you can use lightning is...because you always brought the thunder down on me."

"Then I guess there's something seriously wrong with me for picking Thunderbolt first..."

"Th-that's not what I meant... Thunderbolt is a good skill. Monsters are easier to hit if they're Shocked, too."

Igarashi glared at me. *I shouldn't joke so lightly about the past. I may have already put it behind me, but she might get angry with me if I didn't drop it.*

With just my first glance at her available skills, Double Attack seemed particularly strong. It would work well with my Attack Support as well. I also sort of wanted Mist of Bravery just in case, assuming the Fear status was being afraid of monsters and being unable to attack.

"...So, um... Atobe, what do you think of northern women?"

"Well, everyone talks about how Akita Prefecture is full of beauties. I picture them to have pale, alabaster skin, but I wonder if they actually do."

"Um... My mom's from Akita, actually. So I guess that's good. Let me try a different question—don't you think that'd be a good skill to have in case we run into some monsters that can inflict the Frozen status?"

"I suppose, but you could always just buy equipment with cold resistance instead... Although, I am pretty curious about what this 'increases attractiveness' means."

Igarashi was already beautiful, so what exactly would happen if she acquired Snow Country Skin? Would she get even more beautiful? I mean, she wasn't a demi-human, so I didn't think her skin would turn white like some sort of snow spirit.

"Th-that's not exactly my goal... Okay, so I should pick something else right now. I wonder if this Decoy skill is to draw monsters' attention away from us."

"I think so. It's sort of an add-on skill but could be really powerful depending on how you use it."

"Can I try it? Then I'll let you pick the next one."

I really did want her to take Snow Country Skin, but since it wasn't a skill we urgently needed, I'd have to wait and see. For now, I'd have her take Double Attack, and then she could also take the Decoy skill she wanted.

"You should prepare this 'doll' you need for the skill before we go into the labyrinth."

"Yeah, I saw a general goods store in front of the labyrinth."

"All right, we'll see if we can buy one there. I think your other skill should be Double Attack."

Any of these skills could be useful in the right situation, but if we held back on using all the points, she might not see as many opportunities to use them, except for Double Attack, which I could see being useful right away.

The other question is how much magic it takes. If it's the same as my blazeshot, then she could use it in every fight.

"…That's settled then. Ugh, I feel like I'll never have enough skill points. I keep getting new ones that I want to try out," said Igarashi.

"Me too. I want to avoid wasting them as much as possible, but given that I learn from taking them and using them, saving the skill points isn't necessarily the best move, either."

"Yeah. I think I'm going to start getting excited every time I get to acquire new skills…"

"We'll work on picking your new skills when you level up, too,

Theresia." Theresia had been walking next to and watching me and Igarashi the whole time we were discussing Igarashi's skills. It was obvious she was interested in her own skills, too. She currently had one skill point saved up, and I wanted to let her acquire a new skill soon.

I also needed to learn about Suzuna's skills. If possible, I wanted to check Elitia's skills, too, but her Cursed Blade job complicated things. It'd be best to wait for an opportunity to present itself.

We entered the Chest Cracker shop that Louisa had suggested to see a woman wearing an apron seated at a table. A little girl and boy sat nearby reading a book.

"Welcome. Are you the customers sent by the Guild?" asked the woman.

"Yes, Louisa suggested we use your services. My name is Arihito Atobe."

"Mommyyy, are you gonna open a box?" asked the boy.

"Oooh, a box, a box! Plum loves boxes!" squealed the girl.

The boy seemed to be the elder at about five years old, and the girl was maybe three years old. She looked a lot like her mother. The woman appeared to be the owner of this Chest Cracker shop and also seemed to love her children dearly. Lady Palme from Nornil Heights had said she had a daughter and grandkids in the business. I had a feeling this was them.

"I apologize. They really want to play, but the children aren't allowed in the underground rooms where I will open the chest," said the woman.

"Aww, but you let us watch when it's an easy box," whined the boy.

"I'm sorry, Eyck, but these customers have a very hard-to-open box."

"But you can open anything!" he retorted.

"'Cause Mommy's a twap master!" said the girl.

So this woman's job was Trap Master. That probably meant she'd be able to disarm any traps, no matter how complicated, and open the chest.

"Eyck, Plum, go play outside for a little bit. You could go deliver a letter to Grammy. I'm sure she'd be delighted."

"Are you coming, Mommy?" asked the girl.

"Yes, I'll come once I'm done working... You keep an eye on Eyck and Plum." That last part was directed to a corner of the room.

"Okay! We'll wait at Grammy's," said Eyck, and he and Plum went outside. They were followed by a large white dog that had been lying in the corner. He almost seemed like he was acting as a bodyguard.

Igarashi appeared to like dogs because her eyes were sparkling with excitement as she started chatting with the owner of the shop.

"Oh my gosh... He understood every word! Such a big pupper, too! What kind of dog is he?" asked Igarashi.

"...Pupper?" asked the lady.

"Uh...what's with that reaction? Doesn't everyone call dogs that?"

"Ha-ha... Sometimes I do. He's a breed called a silver hound. He was originally a guard dog working with Seekers."

So he really was a guard dog. I liked animals, too, so I was pretty happy to see a dog for the first time in a while.

"......"

Theresia looked afraid of the dog; she was standing rigidly the entire time with her hand on my shoulder. I guess everyone had their weaknesses.

"Right, sorry to make you wait. My name is Falma Arthur, a Guild-certified Trap Master. I will be opening your black chest, Mr. Atobe."

She wore an apron over her clothes that made her look like a young housewife, but in reality, she was an incredibly skilled Trap Master. Her smile contained nothing but kindness, and there was a dog pattern embroidered on the chest of her apron... Those aspects only pulled the disconnect between her appearance and skill even further in my mind.

"...Atobe, you don't want your karma to go up here, do you?"

"Huh? ...N-no, I wasn't staring!" I replied as Igarashi pinched my arm to keep me in check. Falma didn't seem to notice the meaning of our exchange. She just put her hands to her blushing cheeks and smiled as if she was seeing a cute couple.

Part III: Dimensional Barrier Lock

Igarashi noticed Falma smiling at the two of us and quickly pulled her hand away from me.

"…Oh, it's not what you think. I was just making sure he behaved himself," said Igarashi.

"The three of you are in a party together, yes? Having a good relationship is absolutely essential. Oftentimes, people are very concerned about being unable to divide the box's content up evenly," said Falma.

"That does sound like it'd be hard to deal with…," I said.

"We've made this guy, Atobe, our leader, so it should be fine. Right, Atobe?"

"It must be true if you're saying it, Igarashi."

"……"

Theresia nodded. She'd been nervous about the dog for a while, but she seemed to have finally relaxed.

"That dog's really friendly. It won't bite you," I assured her.

"It's not uncommon for demi-humans to dislike dogs. Werewolves will sometimes start fights with dogs when they transform," said Falma.

"I didn't see any werewolves on the list at the Mercenary Office," I said.

"There are different types of demi-humans for each different labyrinth. It's said the fallen Seekers take on characteristics of the last monster they fought," explained Falma.

Which meant Theresia was killed by some lizard-type monster. Thinking about it, I wouldn't be surprised if she was even worse with lizards than she was with dogs. I'd have to keep an eye on her if we came across any.

"Now then, may I please see the treasure chest?" asked Falma.

"Yes, please. This is it…" I placed the black chest on the cloth Falma had spread on the table. Upon second glance, it seemed to be made of some metallic substance. It was put together with various different parts to form a cube. I couldn't even begin to comprehend where you'd open it.

"…This chest—you found it after defeating a rare Named Monster, correct? I haven't seen one in such a long time… The magic in the labyrinths gathers into a monster's body, eventually forming a box. Black Boxes like these are almost never seen in District Eight."

"We defeated a Named orc that apparently only appears every few years. It was called Juggernaut," I explained.

"Yes, I'd heard about that. The Guild had put in place a grace period to allow the party it was after to defeat it or give them time to gather more companions to do so. If more time had passed, the higher-ranked Seekers would have been called on to vanquish it."

So that was how the Guild handled powerful monsters. That made sense. They didn't know how much damage the monster would cause, so they couldn't just leave it to its own devices forever.

"The fact that you are the ones with the Black Box and that you have brought it here will remain confidential," Falma assured us. "The Guild protects the business of the Chest Crackers, so there is no risk of the wrong people coming and attempting to steal the chest."

"That's good to hear. So this shop is guarded as well?" I asked.

"Yes, the Guild Saviors will come here if there are any issues," replied Falma.

Guild Saviors...that sounded like some sort of military force the Guild maintained to keep order. The name made them sound like allies of justice, but it was maybe a little too in your face.

Anyway, I now knew our security was guaranteed even though we'd brought such a rare box to this shop. I also felt better about having Falma handle the valuable box since I knew she wasn't going to be pulled into anything dangerous because of it.

"This chest is called a Black Box. There are a number of possible outcomes in the one-in-a-million chance that I fail to open it properly. Generally, you can assume a chest is armed with traps far more powerful than the monster that carried it."

"Far more powerful... Exactly how powerful would that be?" I inquired.

"It could destroy a section of the city, summon large amounts of powerful monsters, or other similar things. There were some cases in the past that resulted in huge amounts of damage, so a number of special steps were put in place for opening chests. That significantly reduced the number of accidents that occurred when an inexperienced person with low Sleight of Hand capabilities attempted to open one." This aproned woman was talking about things that made my blood run cold with the same nonchalance as if she were describing the weather. Though, I felt like it would be even more terrifying coming from someone who seemed overwhelmingly powerful.

"...When you say a one-in-a-million chance, do you mean literally? Or...?" I asked. If there was a high risk of something happening, then we could always choose not to open it. But Falma smiled gently and held up three graceful fingers.

"Chest Crackers are required to meet three conditions in order to avoid accidents and guarantee safety. First is that we must bring our Dimensional Barrier Lock unlocking rate to one hundred percent, using equipment for this is fine. Requirement two is to only open chests in specialized facilities. Lastly, we must maintain our skills necessary for opening chests and renew our license every year. I have Sleight of Hand 4 and use Craftsman's Earrings and Rings of Mysteries to increase my unlocking rate."

So her accessories, which I had just seen as expressions of her femininity, also had other important uses. She had two Rings of Mysteries on her pinkie.

"I get the impression that you're a pro among pros," I said.

"If it weren't for the skills I inherited from my mother, I never would have been able to open my shop at only level seven. I acquired Sleight of Hand 2 at level three and then was able to get Sleight of Hand 4 by level seven. My mother was an excellent Thief, but she told me she had only reached Sleight of Hand 3 at level ten."

I wonder about Theresia. Rogues are supposed to improve their Sleight of Hand more slowly than Thieves.

If Theresia's parents were also in Thief-type jobs...it would be nice if she could at least undo simple traps. She wouldn't have to reach Falma's ability level, obviously. It'd probably be a good idea to have her take Sleight of Hand 1. Even if a Rogue was able to acquire Sleight of Hand 2 and onward, I assumed they'd have to get Sleight of Hand 1 first.

"I'm sorry to impose. It's just, you're the first Trap Master I've met, and I have a few questions I'd like to ask," I said.

"Of course. I'll answer to the best of my abilities."

"Would someone be able to detect traps in the labyrinth if they have Sleight of Hand?"

"I believe that would fall under the Trap Detection class of skills. Even if you can detect the trap, though, you will need Sleight of Hand or Trap Destruction to disarm it. Unfortunately, there're only a few rearguard Seekers who have such skills."

So I can expect Theresia to fill our party's Thief role if she can get Trap Detection. It really was true that jobs capable of various things caused a lot of headache... I was so lost on how to solidify their role in the party.

"Do you feel more relaxed? I only have a rare chest like this about once a year, so it's been quite a while since I've given such an in-depth discussion," said Falma.

"I appreciate the detailed explanation. Now I feel I have a much better grasp on how it all works. I do, of course, hope to use your services to open this chest, though I imagine those services will be quite expensive due to the high-difficulty traps."

"Thank you for entrusting me with it. I will put my all into getting it open. I do not require payment for a chest like this. Instead, please allow me to handle any of the contents you don't require. I will make plenty profit if you allow me to do so."

I wonder what she means by things that we won't need... Maybe it'll be things that we can't equip or something that only a specific party can use? Either way, we'd know once she opened it. I signed the paperwork authorizing the job and let Falma take the box. She told us she wished us to be present when she opened it, so we followed her down the stairs that led beneath the store.

We came to a door embedded with a large blue magic stone after descending the staircase. Falma placed her hand on the stone, and some symbols appeared—they looked like the number 17.

"This is a teleportation door. I can use this to teleport to a large room the Guild has prepared in order for us to open boxes. The actual location of the room is kept secret."

"So they teleport us away from the city just in case the one in a million happens... They've got all their bases covered," I remarked.

"The largest accident to ever happen killed over one thousand of District Three's residents. Even with the risk, though, chests remain a massive source of profit for the Seekers, so there was no way the Guild could completely outlaw opening them. Ever since, the Guild has invested greatly in the Chest Crackers. Their current policy is to allow the chests to be opened but spend a large amount of money to ensure everyone's safety."

I also wanted to open the chest, so I couldn't argue with the Guild's policy. Igarashi looked nervous about the whole thing, but Falma's explanations seemed to convince her it would be all right.

"...Falma, aren't you scared?" Igarashi asked. "I'm not even the one opening it, I'm just watching, but I still feel like I have butterflies in my stomach."

"I was very scared when I first started out. But a chest can't hold a candle to experience and skill. Once I understood that, I started to find it sort of fun…perhaps a little too fun!"

…Feels kinda weird saying this about a mother of two small children, but…there's something really sexy and mature about Falma.

Falma placed her hands on her cheeks and sighed rapturously. I couldn't really claim that I wasn't jealous of any man who managed to get a wife like her.

"…You know, everyone tells me I'm like their big sister," said Igarashi.

"N-no, wait, I didn't say anything— Bwuh!"

I tried to brush off Igarashi, but she poked me in the cheek. It didn't hurt, but I couldn't stop the strange sound from leaving my mouth.

"What's with the *bwuh*? Theresia's watching you, too, so don't try anything."

"……"

It wasn't just Igarashi. Theresia's silent presence was weighing down on me. Maybe she was only just staring and it was just my own guilt making me feel like that.

"*Ahem…* Falma, it looks like that door has the number seventeen on it. Can you tell me what that means?" I asked.

"That's the room number. We're teleported to an available room, so we won't interfere with someone else opening a chest. Not to worry."

Falma opened the door, and the four of us passed through. And then we'd been teleported… I found it surprisingly immediate. When I was going down the stairs to the labyrinth, I never could tell when exactly I was teleported, but this time I knew. Perhaps there was a variety of different teleportation methods.

"Wow... This room is massive. It's really just used for opening chests?" I gaped.

"You'll understand why it's so big once I open the chest. All right, let's get started... Ooh, incredible. It's been so long since I've dealt with one so large..."

. This was the Dimensional Barrier Lock on the Black Box. You could try breaking it if you just had Sleight of Hand...but the sight of it happening went far beyond what I could have ever imagined. Falma held up her hand, and a glittering figure began to spread out from the box's center. It was like a scene you might see in a game when something's activated with magic.

The figure continued to expand—straight across at first, then vertically—until it looked like a massive three-dimensional maze.

"This...looks like those puzzles where you tilt to roll around the metal balls and get them in the goal. Don't you think, Atobe?"

"Yeah, same here. What made this thing appear anyway?"

"The chest is reacting to my skills. It's trying to resist my attempt to release the Dimensional Barrier Lock. I'll use my Sleight of Hand to delicately guide the magic and unlock it. If I flow magic down the correct route, the Dimensional Barrier Lock the chest created will vanish. It's a little dangerous then, so please move away and keep low."

"Uh... A-and that's different from a trap activating?" I asked.

"It won't explode. Ooh... Can I get it through this narrow passage, I wonder? ...Phew, I did it. This part is wider, so it'll be much easier... Take a look here, Mr. Atobe. This section is a trap. Get this wrong and...kablooey."

"K-kablooey...? Falma, that's not a good thing," I said.

"...Am I the only one who thinks we should be taking a more basic approach?" Igarashi wondered aloud. "Theresia, say something! ...Oh, right, you can't speak..."

"......"

For some reason, Theresia was sitting on the ground observing the unlocking process. The whole thing for me was just Falma saying some unsettling things, but Theresia was watching her like she was doing some sort of mystical ritual.

"No... That won't work, either... A mother knows all... And you can't cheat, either... Heh-heh, this comes next... Oh yes, that's good... Just a little more... I've almost got it... Yes, there... That's it...!"

"Uh, F-Falma, any more and—," I started.

"Atobe, get down!" Igarashi tackled me to the floor. This wasn't the time to be standing around. Falma was about to open the box.

"I, Falma Arthur, will be the one to crack this Dimensional Barrier Lock... Hang in there... Yes, you're open now...!"

The box seemed to respond to Falma's urging, though obviously that wasn't the case, but Falma's magic had flowed through the unfolded maze to create a single path. The Dimensional Barrier disappeared, and light flooded out from the grooves that ran along the surface of the box. The light filled every tiny crack in the massive room.

"S-so bright... Whoaaa!"

"Atobe!"

"……"

Theresia got down with me and Igarashi as we waited for the blinding flash to cease. I assumed the box was opened safely, but the light was so blinding that I couldn't open my eyes at all. The light finally started to fade, and we noticed the massive change around us.

"You did very well, Mr. Atobe. The box has been opened. Please feel free to peruse its contents."

Scattered on the ground were more copper, silver, and gold pieces than I could even count. There's no way all those coins would be able to fit into the Black Box, which was small enough for a woman to hold in her two hands. The contents of the box seemed to completely ignore the concept of the box's volume and were now scattered across the entire floor. Weapons, accessories, armor, I had no idea how many of each… Most of it didn't seem to be much more than junk or beginner-level equipment, but there were some things that looked like they might be high quality. We'd probably be able to upgrade the entire party's equipment with this. I suddenly started shaking from excitement when I realized that.

"This…was all in the Black Box… There's so much…," I said.

"I imagine you understand why treasure chests are so sought after by Seekers. They contain not only the items that Seekers were carrying when they were defeated by the Named Monster, they also contain many items of unknown origin. Breaking the Dimensional Barrier means breaking through the abnormal space that is housed in the chest."

"It's more than I imagined… I guess you can never know what will happen when you're in another world. Oh, that spear…can I try picking that up?" asked Igarashi.

"It's best to wait until the item has been identified before touching it. You should be able to identify everything using Novice Scrolls of Identification, as long as the item isn't a so-called colored weapon. I can provide scrolls for five gold a piece."

Colored weapons… Elitia's Scarlet Emperor was most likely one of those. Even though they may be powerful, they sounded like very ill-fated weapons if you couldn't identify it and the only way you could find out if it was cursed or not was to equip it.

It wouldn't be cheap to identify everything since we'd need a lot of Scrolls of Identification, but with the amount of money lying around, I had a feeling we'd end up making a profit anyway. We'd probably still make more than we did from the bounty on Juggernaut itself.

"Igarashi, Theresia, you should look for things you think we can use. We should have brought everyone along… Falma, could you put together as many Scrolls of Identification as you can for us?"

"Of course. Actually, I should just thank you for your continued patronage, shouldn't I?" she chirped. She was clearly in a good mood because she was going to make a serious profit from this. There was a spring in her step as she walked to where we were teleported into the room and disappeared, apparently on her way to get the scrolls.

Theresia began to search for equipment as I'd asked. I trudged around glancing at the piles to see if there was a slingshot or other long-ranged weapon, and that's when I heard something clatter to the ground by my feet.

...Huh? What's this?

It was some sort of small rod. Upon closer inspection, it appeared to be made of a mysterious material different from anything else in the vicinity.

"Hey... What's that? The end looks like a key sort of," said Igarashi.

"A key... Yeah, I guess it's the right shape. Maybe a bit big, though."

One end did look key-shaped. If that's what it really was, then I wondered if we could use it somewhere in the Field of Dawn... I had no idea what it was, but I was incredibly curious. First, we'd try identifying it, then we could decide what to do with it.

Part IV: New Equipment

I left Falma's shop for a moment and went over to Elitia and the two others, who were waiting in the square by the Guild.

"Nice work today, Arihito. We've finished things for the move. Although we'll need to separate again when you go up to the next district," said Elitia.

"Considering how amazing the building is, I imagine there's a lot of people who want to just stay in the royal suite," I replied.

"Yeah, but it's still just a rental. New reincarnates can stay in rentals for free for the first month, but they're required to pay rent after that out of pocket."

"Really? I imagine at least the barn is free, though?"

"Uh, yeah, but I don't recommend it. The door doesn't close properly and…well, it's a barn, so sanitation is an issue."

"I had some relatives who owned a farm, so I can imagine what it's like… It's amazing, though. They're living creatures, so it's perfectly natural."

I didn't have to sleep in the barn for even a single night, but it did mean I'd never have to sleep without a roof over my head even if I had absolutely nothing… Well, I should keep an eye on our remaining funds.

"All right, well nothing seems to have gone off the rails in that area. I think we have plenty of funds," I said.

"Oh, right… You got *that* thing open, didn't you? Depending on what's inside, there's always a chance you'd be all right on funds once you open one," said Elitia.

"You ought to keep that a seeecret from me. Otherwise, I'll want Arihito to take me in!"

"Wow, Misaki, you really are trying to be more independent… I also need to make sure that I'm not pampered by Arihito," said Suzuna.

When Suzuna said that, Misaki scratched her cheek in embarrassment because she felt we didn't think she was reliable. Well, she was the girl who immediately left her friend and ran off with another party.

"Right now, I don't have any skills that'd be useful in the

labyrinth, you know. I just think my good luck might come in handy in a pinch," said Misaki.

"If you think it's too dangerous, you can spend your days in the city. You'll have to do individual training, though, in order to gain levels," I suggested.

"There's that, but I reeaally want to try finding more companions, too. Besides, since we'll be getting people to join slowly, I'll end up warming the bench until you guys need me. Sooo I was thinking I could find us more friends, too, so that we can just make two whole parties from the get-go," said Misaki.

"All right. What kind of people are you going to look for?" I asked.

"I'm thinking I want to gather some people who aren't necessarily focused on battle but would be nice to have and bring along with us every once in a while. Don't you think the different roles would fit perrrfect then? We won't become like deadweight, even if we don't make too much money and need a little help sometimes."

We could have some labyrinth scouting members who were the first ones to go in. Then if they ran into something where they needed a specific skill, we could swap people out to handle it. My plans for multiple parties were still pretty vague, but a general idea seemed fine. If we could gather some members who were similar levels to form a second party, they could go to labyrinths that suited their level so they could work their way up. Right now, Misaki was the only one who was still level 1, so it would be hard for her to gain levels even though she was in my party. Elitia had officially joined our party, too, but the level difference was likely to be a stumbling block for us.

"I plan to stay as a guest in the party until everyone is up to level seven or eight. I should have gone back to a guest and let you finish off Juggernaut…," said Elitia.

"No, that wouldn't have mattered. Once the experience display on your license is full, you gain a level when you leave the labyrinth, but it resets to zero. It doesn't matter how powerful the enemy is, you can only gain one level per adventure," I said.

That meant the most efficient way to level up would be hunting monsters, which you could easily get experience from and then leave the labyrinth as soon as your experience bubbles were full. Only one bubble of Elitia's experience was filled when she defeated Juggernaut, which was probably because it was only level 5, lower than her. That did sort of mean that just because an opponent was strong, it didn't mean it would level you up easily, but really it meant that a party full of level-8 Seekers wouldn't find it a difficult battle at all.

The stronger you get, the harder it is to gain levels. It'd be good to find a monster of the same level that you can hunt easily… One level up could mean a huge increase in strength.

"Sorry about this, but I'll need you to actually join the party every once in a while when we fight a strong enemy. If we can do something about *that skill*, we won't have to keep our distance, either," I said.

"…And just what do you think could be done? If I throw this sword away, it appears back in my hand. There's no way I can just get rid of a cursed sword…," bemoaned Elitia.

"We could remove the curse or contain it. I don't mean to

sound like I'm taking this lightly, but there's gotta be *something*. You need to believe that. Otherwise, it's all just too bleak."

"…That means a lot to me. I can't seem to find anything bright about my future."

"Ellie, everything will be okay. I'm sure Arihito's right—there must be a way to break the curse," said Suzuna. It's possible a Shrine Maiden skill might someday be able to break curses. But if it were that simple, no one would be cursed in the first place."

"Suzuna, did you ever do purifications or exorcisms when you were helping out at the shrine?" I asked.

"Yes, I helped my dad with them. It was a little different from the skills I seem to have from this Shrine Maiden job, though."

"I see… Sorry, but do you mind if I take a look at your skills?"

"Oh, no, I'm the one who should apologize. You let me join your party, and I haven't even shown them to you. Here they are. I've already acquired two… Oh, I got more skill points," she said as she showed me her license.

```
◆Acquired Skills◆
    Purification:  Improves the party's
                   psychological state and
                   wards off weak spirits.
       Exorcism:   Purges spirits. Success
                   rate decreases as target's
                   level increases.

◆Available Skills◆
    Exorcism Arrow: Adds HOLY attribute to
                    arrows when using a bow.
```

```
     Auto-Hit: A number of arrows based on
               user's level are guaranteed
               to hit their target.

       Prayer: Party's success rate
               increases slightly.

  Salt Laying: Places salt around a set
               area to prevent monsters
               from approaching.

Spirit Detection: Detects spiritual matter
                  not usually visible.

Remaining Skill Points: 2
```

These are all definitely Shrine Maiden skills... Although Auto-Hit seems a little different from the rest. I wonder...?

"Suzuna, do you have archery experience?" I asked.

"Y-yes, how did you know? ...Oh, I have a new skill."

"I don't think 'Auto-Hit' is the kind of skill you'd normally get at level two. I wonder if you're able to acquire it because you already know how to use a bow."

"I would definitely like to take it if you think it will be useful."

"Yeah, I think it will. Would you mind?"

Suzuna selected Auto-Hit to acquire it. It wasn't a skill that just increased hit rate; it *guaranteed* a hit, so it'd be particularly effective against enemies that dodged attacks easily. Salt Laying seemed like it would be good for creating a safe location while in the labyrinths, and Spirit Detection would likely be necessary in any labyrinth with large amounts of ghost-type monsters. It'd be fine if we could use equipment to see them, but the thought of fighting an enemy I couldn't see made me go numb.

"Purification is constantly active, right? Whenever you're around, I feel calmer," I said.

"Oh, r-really? …I'm glad. I'm not even really sure how it works."

"It's 'cause everyone always says you're sooo soothing, Suzu," said Misaki.

"Misaki, I don't think that has to do with this…," Suzuna interjected.

I actually thought it might, however. I had the impression that most of the skills you could learn were gained from your job, but there were some skills that only came up because of each individual's personal abilities. There were probably some people with the Shrine Maiden job who didn't have Purification. The most popular skills seemed to be common across jobs, but Igarashi and even Theresia had their own particular skills. All of my skills were special, too, and given that I'd probably never run into another person with the same job, you could argue that all my skills were particular to me.

…Hang on. What would happen if someone else wrote vanguard *or* midguard? *Would they just not be accepted as that job?*

I had no idea how many people had been reincarnated so far, but I did know I was the first to write *rearguard* and be accepted in that job. The display on the license wasn't normal, either, so I have to assume that kind of thing didn't happen often.

"B-by the way, Arihito…do you have any skills that are always active?" asked Elitia.

"I think there's something like I periodically restore your

vitality if I'm behind you… I'm sorry if it makes you uncomfortable. Wish I knew how to turn it off when I didn't need it."

"Really…? Oh…my license says *vitality at max*."

"Huh? Um, mine says…"

Recovery Support 1 had been activated. Apparently, it looked different from the receiving end. Elitia showed me her license, and this was what it displayed:

```
◆Current Status◆
> ELITIA's psychological state was improved ⟶
  Currently calm
> ELITIA's vitality was restored ⟶ Vitality
  at max
```

The name of my skill doesn't show up… Neither does Suzuna's. Are different things displayed depending on if you're the user or the target? I can see the skill names when people use an attack-type skill… I guess recovery is different.

I wondered how Attack Support and Defense Support were displayed. I hadn't realized there was a difference since we didn't exactly have the time during battle for everyone to show me their licenses. If the skill names were displayed clearly, though, it'd be better if you had the option to hide them. If there were some bystander watching us fight, they'd have access to information about our skills.

"Elitia, is there a way to keep the skills you use from displaying on the license?" I asked.

"Yeah. If you have the Conceal skill you can keep others from knowing what you do. There are some types of equipment you can use in place of that skill, though."

"Is that kind of equipment fairly valuable?"

"It is… There usually aren't any free to appear on the markets, but you often get one when you open a chest."

"Thanks. It'd be great if we found one in this chest."

"What, can you use that to hide when you do bad things? Arihito, you're thinking of doing something naughty, aren't you?" said Misaki suddenly.

"Y-you think? I'm sorry, Arihito, but those items only keep your actions from appearing on licenses, your karma will still go up. You should avoid doing anything too inappropriate," said Elitia.

Should I joke around and say, Man, that's too bad? *No, both Elitia and Suzuna are too pure; I shouldn't even joke about it. I'm old enough to be their legal guardian. I should avoid doing anything to lose their trust.*

We returned to the room where the door in Falma's shop teleported us. Igarashi and Theresia had stayed behind and categorized almost everything by weapon, armor, accessory, other, or cash. The weapons, which were of the average kind floating around and being sold at shops, could be sold back without needing to identify them. Once only the items we might be able to use remained, there wasn't so much that we'd have a hard time selecting from them.

"Each one of these bags contains one thousand gold. We have just about six thousand gold in total. We removed the damaged coins and weighed them on scales. We compared the bags in weight, so we didn't have to spend the time counting outside of the first two bags," said Igarashi.

"That's exactly the kind of efficiency I'd expect from you, Igarashi. Even so, just putting a thousand gold in one pack must have been a pain," I said.

"Yeah, those bags are pretty heavy, you know. It'd be better to leave them with the bank and ask them to provide a check if we need a large sum."

That was the painful moment I realized how convenient paper money was. Actually, it'd probably be just as annoying to handle the number of bills that equaled a gold coin.

Hmm, you tend to lose any sense for the value of money when you get so much of it… Not good. I need to be able to make big purchases if necessary, but otherwise, I should stay frugal.

"The broken coins can't be used until they're reminted, so I have purchased them from you. You also have a fair amount of silver and copper coins, but since they tend to become unusable more easily, there aren't very many in good condition," said Falma.

The copper and silver tended to change color, but a mint would still probably be able to use them. That added onto the amount we sold. Those silver coins were referred to as "degraded silver coins." We had about four thousand of them, but they were worth about 30 percent of their full value. I felt lucky they were worth anything considering the effort needed to make them usable again.

"Maaan, I wish I could see it once. Gold coins going bang and scattering about like *you wooonnn!*" said Misaki.

"Don't open that bag. Igarashi and Theresia spent a lot of time counting those out. I don't know when, but we'll bring you along the next time we open a chest," I said.

"Reeeally? Wow, the power of money is so scary. At this rate, I'll have to stay away from you... Hey, are you listening?"

"You should pick out any equipment you can use as a Gambler. I wonder if there's anything I can use...," I mused.

"Atobe, how about this? It's a slingshot made from ebony." Igarashi showed me the slingshot she found. It seemed of higher quality than the one I was using. I'd lose my blazeshot, but this would improve my damage, hit rate, and range.

"Congratulations. That weapon has an open rune slot. You can make the weapon more powerful if you put a rune in it," said Falma, who had been watching us. She pointed at a hole in the slingshot. So that's what that was.

"A rune... That's not the same thing as the magic stones we used for modifying our equipment earlier, is it?" I asked.

"Runes are made from magic stones. If you gather a large number of magic stones and compress them, you get a rune, which is more powerful than the average magic stone. Even useless waste magic stones can sometimes be made valuable if formed into a rune."

"My spear has a slot, too. Unlike my lance, I can't use a shield with it, but... Atobe, can I trade for this spear?" asked Igarashi, holding the spear made of some metal alloy. It had increased damage, defense rate, and piercing power. It was actually a ranseur, a type of spear with a cross hilt at the base of the spearhead used for catching enemies' attacks. You wouldn't necessarily need a shield if you were using this type of spear.

"It's a good weapon, so I think you should switch over to it. Oh, over there is some armor... Is this for women?" I asked.

"Yes, it's 'ladies' armor.' It's light since its emphasis is on evasion, so there are many women in fighter jobs who wear this kind of armor. This also has an open rune slot," replied Falma. The armor's design seemed perfectly suited to a Valkyrie. I thought we could finally call Igarashi a true Valkyrie if she put that on. Even so, Igarashi wasn't too keen about wearing it, which was understandable because, even though it wasn't exactly a chain-mail bikini, it did leave a lot of skin exposed.

"Magical equipment has higher defensive capabilities than you might assume from looking at it. I also suggest you use this armor. It's a little weaker than my armor, but I imagine you could use this at least until you're level five," said Elitia, who was more inclined to focus on the equipment's capabilities and ignore its appearance.

Falma went around the full sets of armor and helmets and patted Igarashi's shoulder.

"If you like, I can help you try it on. It'll be all right, you're just not used to it yet, but you'll feel more comfortable once you try it on. And you can buy a cloak to wear over it," she said.

"A-all right...then, yes please. I'll be back in a bit, Atobe." Obviously, she couldn't change in front of us, so she and Falma teleported from the room so she could try on the armor.

Next, Theresia came up to me. She showed me a short sword, shield, and a pair of boots. The boots even seemed to be made of a material that Theresia could wear. The shield was a targe-type and could even be attached to the chest of her leather armor. Its defense, durability, and evasion rates were higher than her current buckler. The short sword had already been modified and had a wind-type skill available to use. Its materials were also of higher quality, so I didn't hesitate to suggest she change to them. Neither the targe nor the sword had any open rune slots, but we'd find her equipment with slots eventually. This equipment didn't give Theresia as big a power boost as Igarashi's did, but it was important to keep getting stronger by changing equipment even if it was only a little at a time.

"And your boots... Oh, you can take those off, too," I said.

These were called chameleon boots. They had the ability to change to match their surroundings. An entire suit of chameleon armor would be perfect for sneak attacks.

Theresia sat on the ground and pulled off her current boots to try on the chameleon ones. The lizard boots she'd been wearing this whole time weren't low quality, but they were well worn, and it was always a good idea to have a change of shoes so you could swap them out and reduce wear and tear...assuming these boots were like normal shoes, that is.

"......"

"Oh, the color even matches. It looks good. They really suit you, Theresia."

Theresia didn't say anything, but she did seem to like her new equipment. I just started to think that if a chameleon monster did exist, it'd attack us when it wasn't visible...and that was terrifying.

"Suzuna, how about this cape thing?" asked Elitia.

"Oh… A-are you sure? It seems so expensive…"

"We need to improve your defense, too, even if by just a bit. I think you should equip this if you can." Elitia handed the cape to Suzuna, who put it on over her white clothing. The cape was white, too, so it didn't clash with her red-and-white Shrine Maiden look.

"…Oh, Arihito, there's a Concealment Choker. It might be annoying for you to wear it around your neck, but this will let you do what you were thinking about earlier," said Elitia.

"Oh… I've never worn one of those before…"

"All riiight, I'll put it on for you! Stay still," ordered Misaki.

Meanwhile, Igarashi finished changing into her armor and teleported back.

"Uh, um…Atobe, I put on the armor, but…," she stammered.

I looked back after Misaki finished fastening the choker, and I was suddenly at a loss for words.

Part V: Ladies' Armor

I imagined that even if a Japanese person went to another world, they'd have a really hard time adjusting to the different clothing… but that didn't seem to apply to Igarashi.

"Um, uh… I tried putting on the vambraces and greaves as well. It's lighter than it looks, since it has the lightweight attribute," she said, her face beet red as she explained the equipment.

The Scroll of Identification they'd used on the armor had all that information from the beginning, though. It was called Light Steel Ladies' Armor +3, so it had an increased defense along with the lightweight attribute, making it excellent armor.

"It suits you so well I might have assumed it was custom-made for you... It looks amazing," I said.

"Y-you think...? It's got this skirt thing in the front, which is nice, but the sides are a little..."

"Whoaaa, those slits are a little risqué, aren't they? You'll have to get all prepared like before you put on a bathing suit," Misaki remarked.

"It's a...bold piece of equipment, but beautiful. I wonder if I'll be able to wear armor like that one day...," Elitia marveled.

"...I just wish I could've done something about this part here... It's armor; it should cover everything," said Igarashi.

The ladies' armor seemed to have breast support built in, but the actual armor part didn't cover her cleavage, meaning I could see the doublet she was wearing under it like underwear. It emphasized the movement of her breasts in the same manner those knit sweaters of hers did. There was no way I could ignore their existence.

Ooh man, they're huge... I almost said something I'd completely regret. I knew Louisa was above average, but Igarashi's a Japanese woman and still up there...

"...Are those shifty glances supposed to be some sort of karma countermeasure?" asked Igarashi.

"Uh, no, I wasn't thinking anything dirty. I just wanted to look at the equipment because it suits you so well. And it's rude to stare at someone for too long, isn't it?"

"Soooo cool! No way I'd be able to fill it out," said Misaki.

"Even the ladies are staring! You wear it very well," said Falma. She would have to wear armor like this if her job wasn't Trap Master, so her chest would become more of a problem, too. Though, every warrior-type job could wear armor regardless of their body type.

Elitia's equipment was tight to her chest and incredibly powerful. She wore a set of High Mithril Knightmail +4. It also had the lightweight attribute, so it didn't sacrifice speed, which was something swordsmen absolutely needed, making it ideal armor.

"I also found this crowned helm, so I'll have you equip this, too," said Falma.

"Oh, that's nice. All I need now is a surcoat for when I'm walking around outside...," said Igarashi.

"There wasn't anything like that in the chest, so you can have something of mine. You're just a little taller than me, but I think it might be just long enough," offered Falma.

"Thank you so much for everything. Hmm...once I have a surcoat..." Igarashi didn't yet seem comfortable with the clanging of her new armor as she moved. To be entirely honest, I was a little jealous of her for looking so good in equipment from another world.

"Atobe, we didn't find any other metal armor, but we did find this hard leather armor."

"Thanks. So this is stiffened, processed leather, huh...? I wonder what kind."

"It's from a Marsh Ox, a monster that appears in the Sleeping Marshes labyrinth. It's one of the labyrinths in District Eight, but as the name implies, there are many dangerous monsters that attempt to put you to sleep. Not many people venture there," said Elitia.

I took off my current armor and put on the Hardened Ox Leather Armor +2. Now that I thought about it, this piece of equipment was something that another Seeker had worn before me...though no one would be able to tell that from how it looked or felt to wear, so I decided to just forget about it.

We looked for some other things we might be able to use and found a set of Chain Gloves +1. It looked basically like a normal fabric glove just made of chain links but was also fingerless, which would make using equipment easier.

I looked at the scroll, which displayed the identification result, and almost gasped in surprise.

◆Light Steel Chain Glove +1◆
> Made of STEEL
> Manufactured with LIGHTWEIGHT attribute
> Slightly improves effectiveness of skills, which strengthen allies

Yes! If this improves skill effectiveness, then maybe it'll work on my support skills...!

The toil we'd spent putting into sorting through this equipment had reaped us plenty of reward. We finished picking out the things we thought we could use and wrapped up our equipment upgrades.

Falma got some help from the Carriers to transfer our gold to the bank, and then we rented a storage space to store any of the remaining equipment that had pluses. One storage space cost one gold per month, but that level of investment wasn't going to make a difference.

We had lunch in a restaurant in town and then headed toward the labyrinth entrance. As we passed, Leila was helping some other Seekers at the Mercenary Office but gave us a wave when she saw us. When we reached the square in front of the labyrinth entrance, we saw that Madoka's stall was open again. Business seemed to be going well. She must have had more reincarnates shopping there... She was starting to sell some things that weren't in wide distribution.

"Oh, mister! Good morning!" she called.

"Hey, morning. You're looking chipper as usual," I replied.

"You have so many companions now...and some really nice equipment. You must have had a very successful expedition."

"A few things ended up going well, partly thanks to you. I want to show our gratitude to you somehow."

"N-no, not at all. It's my job to sell equipment. Your success is thanks enough—"

"Ms. Shop Lady! ...Hey, Big Bro Ari!" Misaki suddenly called out.

"Uh, I'm not your brother, and you don't have to raise your hand. What is it, Misaki?"

Before I could have another thought, Misaki grabbed Mado-ka's hand with a sparkle of excitement in her eyes.

"Ah, uh, ummm, how can I help you?" Madoka stammered.

"Don't you think a Gambler and a weapons Merchant would make a perfect pair?" Misaki gushed.

"Hey... What's with that blunt invitation? I'm sorry she suddenly invited you. It's my fault for not keeping a better eye on her."

"N-no, it's all right... I was just surprised because it was so sudden. Actually, I was thinking I wanted to go back in the labyrinth since soon I'll drop down to level one again. I just thought she'd somehow read my mind."

"Seriously?! Seee, Arihito, inviting someone's all about the feeling! We're gonna get so many party members like this!" said Misaki.

If I understood what just happened right, Madoka wasn't going to join my party as a permanent member, but we could call on her as a Merchant when necessary and go on adventures together.

"Her drive is simply amazing. She seems so good at making friends... I'm a bit jealous," said Elitia.

"Misaki's always made friends wherever she goes. I've always thought it was incredible she could be so fearless when going up to talk to people she doesn't even know," said Suzuna.

The Merchant job wasn't a battle-focused job, but it wasn't completely incapable of fighting like some other midguard-type jobs. Madoka could probably beat a Cotton Ball at least, so it should be fine if she worked with Misaki.

Speaking of finding more party members, we really need to look for a vanguard specialized in defense... Hey, I wonder if that guy fits the bill.

There was a man carrying a large shield in Ribault's party. They also had a woman with a bow, a man with a wand, and Ribault, who seemed like the main attacker, so their party was fairly balanced.

"Ah, you finally gonna make it to the third floor today? There's different monsters on the third floor, too, so don't let your guard down," called out Ribault as we walked by.

"Yes, we'll be sure to stay alert," I replied.

As soon as we entered the first floor, we used the sparse trees as a guide and headed across the field, where we ran into five Cotton Balls. Elitia stayed out of the fight, instead letting the midguards—Igarashi and Theresia—step forward. But first, they left our line of fire clear so Suzuna and I could reduce the number of enemies. Actually, Misaki was carrying a long-range weapon as well, so she tried to support us with our attacks.

"Misaki, throw your weapon!" I commanded.

"Okay, here I go!"

◆Current Status◆
> Arihito's attack hit Cotton Ball
> Suzuna's attack hit Cotton Ball
11 support damage
> Misaki's attack hit Cotton Ball
11 support damage
> 3 Cotton Balls defeated

"A-amazing... And that was just an iron die...," said Misaki. Gamblers could equip short swords, but they could also fight with special combat-enabled dice and cards. Currently, she had ten iron dice with her.

The amount of support damage went up...that confirms the chain gloves' effect.

I could also expect it to work with defense and recovery as well. I really wanted to get more equipment like this.

"We'll take out the last ones! ...Let's go, Theresia!" shouted Igarashi.

"—!"

Igarashi darted off so fast you wouldn't have thought she was wearing armor and attacked with her spear. Theresia also swung her sword at the Cotton Balls. The two easily finished off the enemies.

"Wow...I really did beat one with my pretty dice," said Misaki.

"Your attack is more powerful when Arihito is behind you. But your aim was really good, too," complimented Suzuna.

"Nah, I'm just lucky. It hits if I tell it to."

"Arihito, I plan to try out my new skill when we're fighting orcs. Is that okay?" asked Suzuna.

"Yeah, please do. Theresia, I'd like to see your Wind Slash as well." The party returned to its battle formation as I gave my orders. Elitia was sort of acting as a mobile unit on her own, so she didn't have a set position. She did seem to have something on her mind, though, so I called her over.

"...What is it?" she asked.

"Sorry, can you keep an eye out for us? Obviously not when it comes to Cotton Balls, but I just imagine doing nothing is boring."

"N-no, not at all... Don't be silly, that's not important. What's most important is the party's growth."

"That's fine, then, but feel free to jump in if we look like we need help."

"Yeah, I plan to. I also want to try getting your 'support' again."

It wasn't just Igarashi—I could tell that everyone was in a better mood the more I supported them. That'd be the case even in a normal party, though. That's how you built trust.

"Let's try out Suzuna's new skill next. It might be a bit wasteful, but if we run into a Poison Spear Bee, I'd like you to try out Auto-Hit," I said.

"Yes, I'll give it a try."

I also tried one of the skills I'd just acquired. I activated Morale Support while we were walking, and everyone in front of me gained ten "morale" points. We'd have to do some more testing to figure out what happened as their morale points got higher.

Part VI: The Unseen Enemy

Orcs and elves; orcs and Lady Knights—Fanged Orcs were a woman's worst nightmare in most any situation, but the way ones in this labyrinth reacted upon seeing a woman was downright beastly.

"BLEHHHHHH!"

"Ewww, oh my gosh, it's drooling everywhere! It'd be curtains for me if I got caught by this thing, huh?" said Misaki.

"You're better off not even imagining it," said Elitia. "Orcs are different from Cotton Balls in that they can use weapons. They may not be as intelligent as humans, but they're still fairly smart..."

Intelligent humanoids that just follow their animalistic urges... Yeah, it's better not to think about it.

A couple of Poison Spear Bees were flying nearby as well. Suzuna had already readied her bow and prepared to use her skill, but first, I provided cover fire.

"—Strike your target!"

◆Current Status◆
> Suzuna activated Auto-Hit ⟶ Next two shots will automatically hit
> Suzuna's attack hit Poison Spear Bee
> Arihito's attack hit Poison Spear Bee
> 2 Poison Spear Bees defeated

Assuming I saw correctly, the one Poison Spear Bee moved and should have been able to evade Suzuna's arrow...but the arrow changed direction midflight and made a direct hit. Near that bee, the metal bullet I shot from my ebony slingshot struck another bee, completely piercing through its abdomen.

"BLEHHH?!"

The orcs weren't even the same species, yet they were shocked to see the Poison Spear Bees felled so easily. Igarashi and Theresia used the opportunity to close in and launch a preemptive strike.

"Give 'em hell!" I shouted.

"You got it! ...Hiiiyaaa!"

"—!"

◆Current Status◆

> Arihito activated Morale Support 1 ⟶ 3 party
  members' morale increased by 11

> Kyouka activated Double Attack

> Stage 1 hit Fanged Orc A

11 support damage

> Stage 2 hit Fanged Orc B

11 support damage

> Theresia activated Wind Slash ⟶ Hit Fanged Orc C

Slight knockback

11 support damage

> 3 Fanged Orcs defeated

Double Attack could be used to target multiple targets, and Wind Slash flung the enemy backward after the attack, making it more difficult for them to counterattack. But even though their morale went up, it didn't seem like their damage or anything increased as well. Morale was like a number for displaying a person's motivation in battle, so perhaps I should be using Morale Support to recover morale when it was low.

"Um, Arihito... The front of the party sort of looks like they're glowing...," said Suzuna.

"Huh...I can't see it at all, but you can?"

"Yes, just a bit."

Suzuna had a skill that let her see spirits or psychological substances, so maybe she was seeing the increased morale as psychological energy?

I wonder if their status changed or something...

```
◆Current Party◆
1: Arihito    ※◆$□              Level 3
2: Kyouka     Valkyrie          Level 2  Morale +22
3: Theresia   Rogue             Level 3  Morale +22
4: Suzuna     Shrine Maiden     Level 2
5: Misaki     Gambler           Level 1  Morale +22
Guest 1: Elitia
```

Suzuna was standing next to me, so her morale hadn't increased. My support really depended on position, so it would probably be best if I set a four-line battle formation with me in the back and Suzuna and Misaki in the third row.

But anyway, the morale seems to be staying high... Can they store it?

I tried to use it again but couldn't activate Morale Support. There might be a cool down period between castings, my license said 4:33 minutes until recast. So roughly five minutes.

My magic doesn't go down when it's active. I'll just keep using it as often as I can to see what happens when morale gets high.

"Atobe, that orc up ahead hasn't reacted to us yet. What should we do?"

"Okay, I'll fire from far away."

"But then you'll just take it down with your slingshot," said Misaki.

"Don't worry. Since we're working together, everyone still gets experience. See, look at your license. It might not be much, but you are getting some experience," reassured Igarashi.

"Oh, you're right. You guys really are strong. You've beaten so many things, but it's barely gone up. It's a big help for me, though!" said Misaki.

She'd only filled about two experience bubbles so far, and since you needed to fill ten before you leveled up, I was hoping we'd be able to level her up during this trip through the labyrinth.

"Elitia, do you know how strong the monsters are on the third floor?" I asked.

"No, sorry. I've only ever made it to the second floor of this labyrinth. I got reincarnated with my family. They wanted to go to a different labyrinth, so we didn't go far in this one."

"Your family... Where are they now?" asked Igarashi. Elitia smiled uncomfortably with a sort of fragility I'd not yet seen in her.

"They're doing all right. I would've heard if they'd died or anything."

"...Sounds complicated, huh? You'll feel muuuch better if you talk about it, Ellie. Big Bro Ari here's such a good listener," suggested Misaki.

"Well, as long as they're doing fine, there's nothing wrong with leaving things as is. It'd be nice to say hi if we run into them, though," I said.

"Nice to say hi, huh...? They're really competitive people, so don't feel bad if they say something weird," said Elitia. She'd been reincarnated with them, so I wondered if they'd worked together before she moved from District Five to District Eight.

"Arihito, what'll we do about these orcs and bees? They're worth money if we take them back," said Misaki.

"Yeah, that'll be tough… Oh, this bee has a magic stone on its head. A poison crystal?"

Magic stones didn't take up much capacity, and we found some ore in the pouches the orcs had tied to their waists. Those were kind of heavy, but we'd manage. We gathered the one poison crystal and two lumps of ore. Then we headed off toward the northeast where the door to the third floor was supposed to be, hunting monsters along the way.

There were two large trees growing on a grassy hill. The sights around us changed completely when we walked between them.

"…It's the same Field of Dawn, but the sky looks completely different," I mentioned.

"And there's more trees…but on the first floor, they were so scattered," said Igarashi.

There were a lot of places to take shelter, so we needed to be on guard in case something was lurking somewhere. And that's exactly when it happened.

"……"

Theresia reacted to something and readied her equipment. Out of the shadow of a nearby tree came a creature about as big as a medium-sized dog.

"GROOOOOOOAAAA!"

It let out a roar like a hacksaw on metal and came charging toward us. We'd gotten used to Cotton Balls and their speed, but this was so fast, it sent shivers down my spine.

"Yikes! ...Wh-what's that sound—?" cried Misaki.

"Let's save that for later. Igarashi, Theresia, we'll shoot first! Misaki, don't go out front! Suzuna, move ahead of me just a little more!"

"Okay! Strike your target!" cried Suzuna.

◆Current Status◆
> Suzuna activated Auto-Hit ⟶ Next two shots will automatically hit
> Suzuna's attack hit Gaze Hound
11 support damage
> Arihito's attack hit Gaze Hound

It was still alive. Igarashi stepped to close the gap in the formation as the Gaze Hound approached, and she tried to use Double Attack, but—

"GROOOOAAA!"

"Agh?!"

◆Current Status◆
> Gaze Hound activated Chilling Gaze ⟶ Kyouka was Stunned

This is bad—it can inflict status ailments...but Theresia's still there!

The Gaze Hound turned its attention to Igarashi, who was

unable to move. Theresia used Accel Dash to chase after it, then launched a Wind Slash toward it.

"*GRAAA!*"

"Igarashi, pull yourself together!" I cried.

"Ngh...my body... I can almost!" She managed to pull herself out of Stun, but I wasn't sure if the Morale Support I used had helped. This time, though, she was able to launch herself into a Double Attack.

◆Current Status◆
> Arihito activated Morale Support 1 ⟶ 4 party
  members' morale increased by 11
> Kyouka consumed Morale Support and recovered
  from Stun
> Theresia activated Wind Slash ⟶ Hit Gaze Hound
Slight knockback
11 support damage
> Kyouka activated Double Attack
> Stage 1 hit Gaze Hound
11 support damage
> Stage 2 hit Gaze Hound
11 support damage
> 1 Gaze Hound defeated

"Yes, we did it!" shouted Igarashi triumphantly.

"Kyouka, be careful! There's still something nearby!" called out Elitia.

"Huh? ...Aaahhhh!"

◆Current Status◆
> Something activated Breaking Tongue ⟶ Kyouka's Silk Clothing was damaged

Where was it hiding? Something had attacked Igarashi after she killed the Gaze Hound and let down her guard.

An enemy we can't see... Oh, right, the chameleons... I knew there was a monster like that out there somewhere. So how did Elitia notice...? ...Oh! Theresia!

"Suzuna! Aim in the direction Theresia's pointing!" I ordered.

"Y-yes!"

Auto-Hit's effect continued for two arrows in a row. Suzuna did as I instructed and released her arrow in the direction Theresia indicated... It was a gamble, but if she knew there was a monster there, it should hit. I had to believe that.

◆Current Status◆
> Suzuna's attack hit Something
11 support damage
> Something was revealed to be a Plane Eater

The arrow Suzuna shot stuck in midair, where there was nothing...and then the creature's true form appeared. Its eyes had swirls in them, and it looked like the creature you'd get if you turned a chameleon into a monster. Suzuna's arrow was sticking out the top of its head, but rather than just auto-dying, the Plane Eater was about to make a counterattack.

But before it could, Elitia made her move.

"—I'll cut you down!"

◆Current Status◆
> Elitia activated Sonic Raid
> Elitia activated Slash Ripper ⟶ Hit Plane Eater
> 1 Plane Eater defeated

It took only a single strike—she pulled her sword from its sheath as fast as some sword performer. I didn't even see it happen. The Plane Eater was split in two, purple blood spraying from its body. Elitia moved far enough away that she wasn't hit by any backsplash.

"Igarashi, are you all right?!"

"Y-yeah...I'm fine, Atobe. I'm not hurt at—"

I ran over to her, and she turned to face me. When she did, something I should never have seen appeared in front of me.

"I'm s-so sorry!"

"Huh? ...Eeeeeek?!"

Underneath her armor, she had been wearing "silk clothing," and it was torn on her chest. It was such a large tear that one of her breasts was exposed.

"Wh-why...did that monster only aim for my armor...?" Igarashi whimpered.

"It used a special attack that aims for armor... Add on the fact that it can become essentially invisible, and I'm amazed a monster like that even appears in the beginner labyrinth," said Elitia.

I wanted to believe that Ribault hadn't said anything about them because they were extremely rare.

"......"

"Thanks. There's no more enemies nearby," I reported once Theresia came back over and told me the coast was clear. Good thing Plane Eaters didn't travel in packs... If we hadn't been so lucky, we could have ended up taking a lot of damage.

"Suzu, you're good at sewing, aren't you?" asked Misaki.

"Yes, I brought a sewing kit with me. I should be able to mend it a little...but the cloth is completely destroyed, so I'll need something to replace it."

"Well, we don't really have many choices, so how about using her scarf?"

"He saw... Atobe saw..." Igarashi seemed like she was in shock. I felt really, really sorry, so hopefully, she'd forgive me. I couldn't even consider myself lucky for getting a peek, considering the conditions under which it had happened.

"......"

"...Theresia, I'm begging you. Don't stare right now," I said.

I would do everything in my power to keep another Plane Eater from using Breaking Tongue on Igarashi. That's the least I could do for her.

Part VII: What Morale's Good For

Theresia continued to monitor the area for approaching monsters. I went up to the ones we defeated to take a look, starting with the Gaze Hound.

"A one-eyed dog... Chilling Gaze, hmm. Yeah, I can imagine something like this staring at you would be pretty unsettling," I said.

"There are a lot of monsters whose gaze has awful effects, but I think this is the first time I've seen a one-eyed monster like that," said Elitia.

The Gaze Hound had damp gray fur that looked like it might be usable as materials for making a broom or some other floor cleaning tools. The suggestion might leave dog lovers speechless, though.

"I'm a dog person, but it was that hideous face that let me attack it without hesitating at all," said Igarashi.

"Y-yeah. We'll end up toast if we start to feel bad for the monsters we're fighting," I replied.

Igarashi had even fallen in love with Falma's dog, so she seemed to like all sorts of dogs. Clearly, there were dogs of this kind, though, so we'd need to be prepared to attack.

"What great teeth! Each one's as sharp as a little needle," observed Misaki.

"That'd leave a really nasty wound if it bit you...," said Suzuna.

"I feel like they could be used as materials for something," I said.

"Its fur absorbs water pretty well. It might have some anti-blaze effects. Or it could be used for a mop...," proposed Igarashi.

"Is there, like, a cleaner job or something? I mean, this is a whooole 'nother world. Anything's possible," said Misaki.

But considering the hound's size, we couldn't carry it back

with us. I tried to decide what to do, and Elitia threw out a helpful suggestion.

"Since you're renting a storage unit, why don't you send monsters like this there?"

"Send it to the storage unit? Can we do that?" I asked.

"You got a key when you rented it, right? You can use that to send any nonliving object, including defeated monsters, to your storage unit. You're limited to ten times per trip into the labyrinth, though."

The storage unit didn't have much capacity, so sending things ten times should be plenty. I also didn't really want to go into a storage unit filled with a mountain of monster corpses, so we shouldn't just send them back willy-nilly.

"Right, how about we send this Gaze Hound back, then? ...Whoa, it worked," I said.

"What about this clothes-targeting beast over here...? Isn't this a chameleon?" asked Igarashi, looking at the Plane Eater and putting into words the impression I'd had of it.

The creature was crumpled on the ground, no longer moving, mouth agape—its mouth was so large it could probably swallow a small child whole. It had rounded, bony protrusions on its forearms that were as sharp as a sword. Thank goodness we didn't get hit with those.

"Its tongue is so long...a couple yards at least. And it's wrapped around a piece of cloth...," said Suzuna.

"...Th-that thing tore my clothing... Can I chop the damn thing off?"

The Plane Eater's tongue was wrapped completely around

Igarashi's silk clothing. I guess the tongue part of Breaking Tongue was literal.

"I think the tongue can be used as materials or perhaps even food. The most valuable part, though, is probably the skin. Like Theresia's boots, it reacts to the wearer's magic to become invisible," said Elitia.

Theresia demonstrated for us and her feet—only her feet—turned invisible. So basically, you'd have to make a chameleon suit in order to do the same to your entire body.

"So could you make your whole body invisible if we made a cloak out of this? That'd be incredibly useful," I said.

"Theresia needs to wear lizard equipment, so that'd be fine, but you're not allowed to have something like that. It'd be too creepy," objected Igarashi.

"And did the chameleon have a reason for destroying Igarashi's clothing?" asked Suzuna.

"Monsters act simply out of instinct. Destroying her armor would work to its advantage... Oh. Arihito, you should check the Plane Eater's stomach later. Sometimes undigestible objects collect in the stomachs of monsters like these," said Elitia.

"Oh, uh...could I let the Dissection Center take care of that? Not that I'm afraid of doing it myself."

I'd filleted a fish before, but I obviously didn't have much experience cutting open chameleons. That made me wonder—no way I could cut up a Gaze Hound because it'd make me too squeamish, but what about chameleons?

"Oh, by the waaay…it was the party I first joined that told me some monsters' tongues are considered a delicacy," said Misaki.

"P-please, keep that to yourself. Until now, I hadn't thought about what meat I was eating, I was happier not knowing…," moaned Igarashi.

"You'll have to learn to deal with eating the monsters you kill in the labyrinth. On longer journeys, you'll need to bring along a Seeker who can cook. Lack of food is one of the top reasons people give up on seeking," said Elitia.

Igarashi glared angrily at the chameleon that'd gone after her equipment, but she seemed to pull back from the conversation of whether to eat or not to eat.

After that, we fought a number of other Gaze Hounds, but there was one particular situation where we needed to be extra cautious. There were four monsters facing us; Igarashi and Theresia handled two of them, but the two others flanked us and came running in from the left and right.

"Arihito, I'll take one—!" called Elitia.

"All right… We'll take the other!" I answered.

""Got it!""

Considering Elitia's speed, it wasn't hard at all for her to pull away from the front of the formation and immediately dash to fend off one of the hounds.

There's a good chance our attacks won't drop this one… I might have no choice but to take that.

Before I attacked, I swiped my finger on my license and pulled up the skills page. I selected the skill Rear Stance.

"GRRROOOOOOAAA!"

```
◆Current Status◆
> Arihito's attack hit Gaze Hound D
> Suzuna's attack hit Gaze Hound D
11 support damage
> Misaki's attack hit Gaze Hound D
11 support damage
```

As I'd suspected, we couldn't drop it with the three attacks. It'd get in a counterattack before we'd be able to get off our second round... I stepped ahead of Suzuna and Misaki, who had been in front of me, and shouted my order.

"Fall back, you two!" I shouted.

"Huh—?!"

"Arihito—?!"

The Gaze Hound launched itself off the ground and came flying at me, its toothy maw gaping open. That moment, I imagined myself going behind the Gaze Hound.

```
◆Current Status◆
> Arihito activated Rear Stance ⟶ Target: Gaze
                                          Hound D
> Arihito moved to Gaze Hound D's rear
```

The Gaze Hound's jaws snapped shut with a crunch in front of me. I had managed to move behind the Gaze Hound and evade its attack...and then—

Its back is wide open—this might just do it!

◆Current Status◆
> Arihito's attack hit Gaze Hound D
Blindside attack
> 1 Gaze Hound defeated

The Gaze Hound landed and was confused for a moment, but I didn't let it move before I took a shot with my ebony slingshot. The attack seemed a little different this time; it felt like the damage the hound took was more than usual.

"D-did...Arihito just disappear for a second?" asked Suzuna.

"Things were looking bad, so I used my trump card. I can't keep doing that, though..."

Just using Rear Stance once reduced my magic bar by about a third, though that seemed an appropriate amount considering its effect. It was about time I started looking for a way to reduce magic consumption.

The skill hadn't said anything about it applying only to allies, so I thought there was a chance I could use it to go behind enemies as well. It was a good thing I was right. I could have chosen instead to apply Defense Support 1 to Suzuna and Misaki, but there was still a risk of having them, both rearguard types, take the attack.

"Thank you, Arihito... But that was reckless. My new cape gives me a slight defense boost, so I can act as a shield if need be," chided Suzuna.

"Sorry…guess I was a little nervous about doing that. I had considered that our formation might split, but it was harder to deal with than I thought."

"Sorry, Atobe… We just let an enemy get past us…"

"……"

"You guys, you handled two monsters all on your own. You've got nothing to apologize for. Plus, I wanted to try out my new skill, so I got something out of it, too."

Our formation would be more stable if we had some skills that prevented attackers from getting past the vanguard, but at the moment, I could only have Elitia stand behind the vanguard and act as their backup.

"Anyway, are you two all right? You didn't get hit with a Chilling Gaze, did you?" I asked Igarashi and Theresia.

"Well, I did just once, but I was back on my feet immediately."

"……"

That seemed to be the case for both of them. Apparently, morale could be used to recover from mild status ailments. I'd used Morale Support to raise it, and it looked like it took about twenty morale points to recover from a Stun. Then there was Suzuna and Misaki who hadn't used any of their morale yet. I checked theirs and they were at morale +100. Maybe one hundred was the limit.

"Suzuna, earlier you said that everyone was glowing—what does it look like now?" I asked.

"Yes… Oh, Misaki and I are really bright!"

"Yeah? Do you feel, like, really pumped up or anything?"

"I suppose I do feel a bit energetic… Huh? Arihito, what do

you think this is?" asked Misaki as she showed me her license. It read `Morale Discharge Possible`. No matter what page you flipped to, it showed up on the top right of the display.

"Morale Discharge...don't you think it sounds sort of cool? Can I try it? Pretty please?" pleaded Misaki.

"No, hang on a second. Elitia, do you know what this Morale Discharge is?" I asked.

"Huh? ...Is that what's showing up? You should almost never see that unless you have a cheerleader in the party...," she said as she checked Misaki's license, then looked at Suzuna and Misaki. "Morale Discharge is used to activate a very powerful skill that's specific to the job. Your morale must have gone up because of Arihito's skills... I've heard it goes up faster if you have a high Trust Level, too. But I've never heard of morale reaching its max with this few battles together."

I knew perfectly well that the reason for that was I'd been constantly using Morale Support 1. Apparently, there were multiple ways of using the gathered morale, and this Morale Discharge was just one of them.

"Well, we won't know anything about it unless we try it out. Maybe they should try using it while directing it away from us all?" suggested Igarashi.

"That's a great idea, Kyouka. My daddy always said it's better to regret something you've done than something you haven't," said Misaki.

"Could I also try it, Arihito? Or should we save it?" asked Suzuna.

"Once we know what it does, then we can save it as an ace in the hole. But we don't even know if they're battle skills, so I suppose we should try it and see."

Suzuna and Misaki nodded, then faced away from the rest of the party. Then—

"Morale Discharge, Fortune Roll!"

"Morale Discharge, Moon Reading!"

Each of the Morale Discharges had completely separate effects. Or so I thought, but I looked at my license, and my eyes opened wide in surprise.

◆Current Status◆
> MISAKI activated FORTUNE ROLL ⟶ Next action will succeed automatically
> SUZUNA activated MOON READING ⟶ Success

...They worked as a combo...?!

"Suzu, what happened?! Hey, Suzu!" cried Misaki.

"H-hey... Suzuna, what's going on?!" I called.

Suzuna's body was wrapped in blue-white light. I ran in front of her and saw moons shining in her eyes. She touched my arm. I realized she was telling me to move away, so I pulled back, and she pointed... Quite far ahead where she was pointing, I saw a pillar of the same blue-white light. After a moment, it disappeared as if it had never been there.

"Ah..."

Suzuna suddenly wavered where she stood and seemed about to collapse. I rushed to support her, and she looked me in the eyes...

My breath caught in my throat. It looked like all the light and life had been leeched from her. But a moment later, the light returned to her eyes. She realized I was holding her up and flushed red.

"S-sorry... What happened to me...? I feel a little light-headed..."

"Oh, thank goooodness...! Suzu, if something had happened to you because of me, I don't know what I'd do!" moaned Misaki as she sank to the ground at her friend's side.

Suzuna's Moon Reading had succeeded because of the effect of her Fortune Roll—I wondered if Moon Reading normally had a pretty low success rate. We clearly weren't going to understand all the effects and everything from just seeing it once. The first question I had was about Fortune Roll's effect and the definition of the "next action." We needed to test that thoroughly. Basically, we would use it at very different times if the next action was open to anyone attempting an action or if it was only limited to allies.

"That was Misaki's and Suzuna's Morale Discharge... So the place with the blue light, there's something there...," said Elitia.

"What should we do, Atobe?" asked Igarashi.

"We go and check it out. I didn't think this was how it'd end up, but you can't always predict what's going to happen in the labyrinth... And besides, I'm just incredibly curious."

"Me too. I'd like to know... Um, Arihito, thank you. I think I can stand on my own now," said Suzuna as she pulled away from me and tried to rearrange her disheveled hair. It seemed that weakness she felt lasted only a moment—she hadn't lost any vitality. On the other hand, both Misaki and Suzuna were back to zero morale.

"......"

"Theresia, did you remember where the place was? That's great," I said, and Theresia led us to the location. When we got there, though, we didn't see anything. It was just a stretch of grass.

"......"

"Hey, it's too early to say for sure nothing's here. If there's nothing on the ground...we could try digging," I suggested.

"I don't know how well you can dig with a spear...but it's probably the best suited to the job," said Igarashi and then thrust her spear in the earth.

The red scarf sewn across her chest bounced around as she dug, enough that I was worried it might hurt. Next to her, Theresia began slicing the dirt with her short sword.

"Atobe, let's switch after I dig for a bit, all right? ...Ngh... I just hit something hard."

"Hang on, let me get this dirt out of the way and look... This is—"

Igarashi paused for a moment, and I brushed away the dark soil to see a slab of stone. There was something buried in the ground.

"...There's something buried here," I said.

"And it looks like it's pretty big. Let's get digging, everyone," said Igarashi.

"Whooooaaa, jackpot! Come on, guys! Dig, diiiig!" cried Misaki.

"That'll just hurt your hands. Should I go get some branches to use? I can cut them down with my spear," offered Igarashi.

A spade, long-handled pruning shears, you can use a spear for anything...but let's try not to. I decided to bring digging implements with me on future adventures into the labyrinth.

Part VIII: The Secret Buried in the Earth

While we were engaged in our excavation efforts, Theresia and Elitia had to go take care of some Gaze Hounds lurking about. Theresia would locate them, and Elitia would put them down... We'd never finish digging this thing up if we kept letting ourselves get interrupted, so I didn't join the fight with them. I did, however, continue my support for them while the rest of us kept working.

"Are you two all right?!" I called.

"No problems here!" replied Elitia.

"......"

"Okay. Not too much longer, so let's keep at it!"

◆Current Status◆

> Arihito activated Morale Support 1 ⟶ 5 party members' morale increased by 11

We continued like this, everyone chatting away and me encouraging them, which brought their morale up naturally. It was important for me to make a conscious effort to stay behind everyone. Even Elitia was in the party, just until her morale reached a hundred.

The only problem was that Misaki was wearing a skirt (apparently, there was no cute equipment she could swap it out for), and Suzuna was wearing a red skirt like Shrine Maiden clothing. If I wasn't careful, looking up from where I was behind them and low to the ground... I was feeling pretty guilty. The two trusted me, but they were crouched on the ground without any shame or feeling any need to keep their skirts down... Trust was good, but I really wished they'd care a little more right now at least.

"Hey, Igarashi, let me dig with the spear for a bit."

"Yeah, sure. You almost look like you know how to handle a spear, Atobe. I don't really know if that counts, though, since you're just digging."

"I can apparently equip any kind of weapon, so I suppose I could use a spear, too."

"Wait, you say that so casually, but isn't that pretty incredible?"

"I'm not as good with them as a specialist would be. Since I'm a rearguard, I'm just happy I can use a slingshot."

We continued digging and chatting for another ten minutes when we were finally able to see the entirety of the thing buried in the ground. Enemy attacks had also subsided for a while, so Theresia and Elitia came back over, after having collected magic stones.

"Atobe, what do you think it is? It's a slab of stone with some weird pattern drawn on it..."

"That is what it looks like. The soil gets really hard here so we can't dig any farther."

"Awww, it's not treasure? But I thought we'd find piiiiles of the stuff!" complained Misaki.

"Ellie, what do you think it is?" asked Suzuna.

"Hmm... Oh! Thinking about it, the design on the stone is similar to patterns found in other labyrinths. In those, each floor isn't connected like this one, you have to teleport to the next floor... This sort of looks like a teleportation pad I saw before."

The Field of Dawn only had three floors. That's what Ribault had said…which meant if there was something beyond this, it'd be uncharted territory.

A hidden floor…or at least a hidden teleportation pad. The enemies on this floor have given us a bit of a run for our money, so I'm sure that even if we don't continue, we'll have plenty of experience to level up…

There was no need to rush. It was perfectly fine to be overly cautious right now.

"…If there's powerful monsters ahead, if we can't escape or use a Return Scroll… Considering those possibilities, we can't make the decision to teleport lightly," cautioned Elitia. And I agreed…but—

"Atobe, should we be careful here? Or…is it a lost opportunity if we pull back now after making this discovery?"

"I suppose… I do want to keep going, but I also know we should be careful. I'm conflicted."

"Me too. I also feel both ways. It's a little scary, though…," said Suzuna.

"Well, this is a decision our brave leader should make, yeah?" added Misaki. "But if it were me, I might just go *bam* and— Eek?!"

"…Misaki!" I cried. She had stood on the edge around the pad and put her foot out like she was pretending to step on it when the now soft and crumbly dirt collapsed, and she slid down to the stone slab, landing on her rear.

"Oowwiieee…ow…huh, ah?"

"Misaki, hurry, come back… Ah!" said Suzuna.

The stone slab started to glow, and Misaki's body was surrounded by light…and then disappeared.

Of all times to screw up like this… What do I do?! I don't have time to think!

Suzuna had stretched her hand out over the teleportation pad to try and pull Misaki back, but she hadn't been dragged into the teleportation. You probably needed to have your whole body on the slab in order to teleport.

"Arihito, it won't be dangerous if I teleport there and back immediately. I'll go alone…," suggested Elitia. She seemed to completely disregard the possibility that she might not return, but I couldn't let her do something reckless just because she was a high level.

"No, I'll go. If I don't come back within one minute, you can assume we can't come and go freely. If that happens—"

"What are you talking about, Atobe? You're our leader. Nothing matters if you don't make it back alive," objected Igarashi without a moment's hesitation. She knew it was dangerous, but she was saying she'd come for me, too.

"……"

"I think Theresia would follow you, Arihito…and I would, too. So…," said Suzuna.

"I get it. But we don't know what's there. So get ready to use a Return Scroll immediately," I said, and both Suzuna and Theresia nodded. Elitia had always kept her hair down, but she put it up now while watching everyone talk. She must only do that when she was getting serious.

"If we're decided, there's no need to waste time here," she said.

"Yeah… Okay, let's go. I think we just need to go on top of it," I said, and we all stepped onto the teleportation pad.

Barely a second passed before the scenery in front of us changed completely. What we saw now was a large room made of stone. I felt like we'd come to some ancient ruins.

"A-Arihito, you came?! But you can only teleport one way—!" cried Misaki.

My shoulders slumped. I had thought that might be the case. But really, that just meant we definitely had to come for her.

"We're not just gonna abandon you. And anyone who comes here would have to bear the risk. We're the ones who discovered it anyway, so we should be the ones to go," I said.

"B-but…I was just being careless. It's my fault…"

"That's just the kind of person Atobe is. And if he weren't, I wouldn't be following him around."

"I… When Arihito said he was going alone, I knew I needed to follow him no matter what. Because we're a party," said Suzuna.

Everyone was agreed, but I was still pretty on edge. We didn't know if we'd find a way out or a strong enemy up ahead… It took real courage to take even a single step. But Theresia was already looking in one direction of the ruins. I could tell she sensed something there.

"That way, eh? …Everyone, get into battle formation, and let's go. We have no idea what's up ahead," I cautioned.

"Yeah. But it doesn't matter what we're up against. If we fight with everything we've got, we'll win. We beat Juggernaut. There shouldn't be anything in this labyrinth stronger than that," said Elitia. I prayed she was right.

I offered my hand to Misaki, who was sitting on the ground, and helped her up. She did look quite scared; she was pressing her sleeves to her eyes.

"Ugh, you guys are trying waaay too hard to look cool, seriously. I'm tough! I would've gotten back on my own!" she said.

"Just a moment ago, you looked like you thought the world was ending. Glad to see you got your spunkiness back. It's not like you to let something get you down. I'm relieved," said Igarashi.

"Urgh, even Kyouka's being nice... Stop it, you're gonna make me cryyy!" Misaki wailed as Igarashi patted her shoulder. Igarashi didn't look scared at all. She'd gotten the armor, but today I really felt like she'd become a real Valkyrie.

"Right, shall we go? ...Everyone, *be on the lookout as we move*," I said, raising their morale at the same time. Apparently, I could activate Morale Support without clearly saying *Good luck* or *You can do it*. With that last one, Igarashi and Theresia's morale reached one hundred.

"It's so pretty here. Feels a bit lonely, though...," observed Suzuna.

High up and lining the hall were bright twinkling green lights, which reflected off the white stone walls. It looked like something from a fairy tale. We got to this hidden area from a teleportation pad hidden in a beginner labyrinth... What awaited us ahead? I was curious to explore some uncharted territory, and yet I treaded as lightly as I could.

Part IX: The Gatekeeper

"Arihito, why do you think that stone slab brought us here?" asked Misaki.

"I think Suzuna's Morale Discharge lets her find things that people normally can't see. It succeeded, which led us to finding the teleportation pad in the ground. Based on what Elitia said, I think this is the actual fourth floor."

"Everyone thought there were only three floors before, riiight? So are there not many people with the Shrine Maiden job? Or maybe no one uses a Morale Discharge in a beginner labyrinth?"

"I don't know. This place might not be common knowledge these days, but I imagine we might find signs that people have been here before."

The three of us in the rear talked for a little, then went back to monitoring our surroundings as we continued forward. We saw a massive stone door and a huge statue, which almost seemed to be guarding it. It was so tall I had to crane my neck up to see its head, which looked like an eagle. It held a spear in its right hand, a shield in its left, and it was wearing armor—the whole statue was made of metal.

"I have a feeling it's a golem... Everyone, stay put for a moment," I ordered.

"Y-yeah…is that thing really going to start moving? 'Cause if it does, it looks kinda strong…"

"If it's what it looks like, its body's surface is made of metal so…like Juggernaut, blades might not easily pierce it. But with Arihito here…," said Elitia.

"…It might not move, you know. This is kinda wimpy, but let's check to see if a Return Scroll will even work. If not, we'll just have to get ready," I said.

Suzuna pulled out her Return Scroll as I directed and read it…but nothing happened. My license said Sealed. Everyone looked either disappointed or not surprised, but we quickly pulled ourselves together. If our only option was to go forward, then we'd just have to do something about that statue. I started to put together a battle strategy based on the assumption that it would move. I didn't think we'd find that silly even if it didn't. In situations like these, you could never be too careful.

"Even if I provide support, I'll bet attacks from an enemy like that would get through our defenses… Igarashi, I'll have you use Mirage Step to avoid and then use Double Attack. Theresia, don't push yourself. Watch how fast it is. If you think it's too fast for you to avoid, don't attack."

Theresia didn't nod…but she seemed to decide she should follow orders because she nodded after considering for a moment.

"Suzuna, use Auto-Hit and fire at it with your bow. Misaki, don't do anything crazy. Stay near me."

"I can at leeeast throw my dice at it!"

"If you're lucky, you'll probably even hit…but do as Atobe says and don't try anything too rash. Take a shot if you can. The more attacks the better, even if it's one, right?" said Igarashi. Even if the die bounced off, the eleven support damage wouldn't be nothing, so it could be useful.

"…The number of skills I can use drops if I don't activate Berserk. Even so, I think I could get eleven hits out of Blossom Blade," said Elitia.

"That should be plenty. Igarashi, you can avoid one attack, but you'll run out of magic if you keep using Mirage Step. Elitia, are you confident in your ability to dodge it?"

"I use Sonic Raid to also increase my evasion, so…if this thing is faster than that, then I've got a complaint to make about this labyrinth." If a monster so powerful that not even a level-8 Seeker could hold their own against it was hidden in a beginner dungeon…it wasn't completely impossible, but it'd result in a lot of damage.

"Right, next is Morale Discharge. Elitia will be at full morale shortly after the battle starts. Igarashi and Theresia should also be able to use theirs… Elitia, do you know anything about their Morale Discharges?"

"I've heard that a Valkyrie's Morale Discharge is called Soul Mirage, but…sorry, I've never seen it. Valkyries aren't part of the warrior class, so there aren't many in the Labyrinth Country."

"Soul Mirage… Atobe, what do you think that means?"

If it was a mirage of your soul, then…maybe it meant it made a copy, so it was okay if you were defeated once or something.

"Are we certain it's something that can be used during battle?" asked Suzuna.

"You'll be able to tell if it isn't when Morale Discharge Possible shows up on your license. It's not there right now," said Elitia.

Neither Igarashi nor Theresia's license displayed it, either. So that should mean they could use it in battle…but we'd just have to rely on intuition on when exactly to use it. *I'll just have to tell them to use it when I think they should.*

"A Rogue's Morale Discharge is Triple Steal. The Rogue can give each ally the ability to steal the enemy's vitality, magic, and dropped items, one time per person. The probability to steal a dropped item isn't very high, but there will be more attempts made in a short time, so it's possible to easily steal even difficult-to-obtain items," explained Elitia.

"Is the damage done recovered by the stealer? That's amazing…," I said.

"It doesn't provide support, though, so it doesn't matter if the person can't damage the enemy. In combination with you, Arihito, though, it should be quite effective," replied Elitia.

Soul Mirage, Triple Steal. If my support damage also meant the latter allowed people to recover vitality, they'd be able to recover eleven points at the very least. Theresia was level 3 and had about twenty vitality points, so she could be completely healed even if she lost half her vitality. But Igarashi had less than twenty, possibly around fifteen, but she was acting as a vanguard. We couldn't let her take a single hit. She could use Mirage Step as a way to automatically evade and draw attacks, but currently at level 2, she could probably only use it four times.

We'll have to rely on Elitia to dodge and draw the attacks… We really do need someone who can be a stationary tank. I can't wait for Defense Support 2 as well. The two combined would really improve the amount of damage they'd have to take before it got through all the defenses.

"What's your Morale Discharge, Elitia?" I asked.

"My Morale Discharge…can't be used until I've had Berserk activated for a set period of time and meet certain requirements. It's high risk, and…"

"I want to avoid you using Berserk if we can, so… Okay. Then I'll just have to wait until the curse is broken for me to see your Morale Discharge."

"…Thank you. But you should know that even my own blood can activate Berserk, so I'll try to use it if that does happen. Everyone will need to get as far away as possible, though."

More than anything, I wanted to avoid any bloodshed from my party, but whether or not that was even possible would depend on how strong the enemy was.

"Okay… Let's do this. Theresia, proceed with caution. If it moves, we engage," I said.

"……"

Theresia faced forward and treaded lightly, silently. When she got a certain distance away from the statue, its eyes began glowing mysteriously.

◆Monster Encountered◆
★Giant Eagle-Headed Warrior
Level 6
In Combat
Dropped Loot: ???

I'd thought it would move, but its presence is incredible… It's a level-6 Named Monster... That's only a one level difference from Juggernaut. They shouldn't be that different in strength!

"KRAAAAAAW!"

The metallic body started moving as though it'd suddenly been given life. It spread its giant wings and let out a deafening screech, almost like it was happy to be fighting against us.

"Don't let your guard down! Give it everything you've got!" I shouted.

"Yeah!"

Everyone yelled back in response to me, and Elitia's morale went up to one hundred. Hopefully, she wouldn't have to use her Morale Discharge and could instead put it toward other uses. I didn't yet know if it could be employed for anything other than recovering from abnormal statuses, but it didn't hurt to have the morale.

"I'm up first...!" declared Igarashi as she stepped to the front of the formation and activated Mirage Step. She launched a Double Attack at the giant statue, but I could hear a clang as the attacks bounced off. The support damage did seem to get through, though, because the statue recoiled slightly.

"KAAAAAW!"

It let out a savage eagle cry and lashed out with its spear in an attack I couldn't follow, but Igarashi was able to evade it thanks to her skill's effect. She blurred into two of herself, and the statue's spear came down on the copy of her. The fact that I could see what was happening even though they were quite far away was probably thanks to the Hawk Eyes skill I'd taken.

"Urgh—!"

"Kyouka, pull back! I'll swap with you!" shouted Elitia.

```
◆Current Status◆
> Kyouka evaded ★Giant Eagle-Headed Warrior's attack
> Elitia activated Sonic Raid
> Elitia activated Blossom Blade
```

"—I'll cut you down!"

Elitia evaded a massive swing the statue took at her and used the opening it left in its defenses to launch a whirlwind of attacks at it—

—but when Elitia got to the seventh stage, the giant warrior's eyes glowed. It shook its head violently and let out a vicious screech.

"*KRAAAAAAW!*"

```
◆Current Status◆
> Stage 7 hit ★Giant Eagle-Headed Warrior
11 support damage
> Arihito activated Defense Support 1 ⟶ Target:
                                           Elitia
> ★Giant Eagle-Headed Warrior activated Wind Burst ⟶
  Elitia's action was interrupted
```

"Tsk... Just a little more and she would have gotten it all in!" I said.

Unlike Juggernaut, who had been immune to physical damage,

Elitia's base damage was getting through this creature's defenses. However, the giant warrior unleashed a raging burst of wind, which flung Elitia aside and halted her attack. Her magic bar went down the same amount as it would have if she had finished the attack. She could probably only do another two Blossom Blades... In which case, what should we do?

We need to prepare so she can get all the stages in. If we prevent him from using magic... No, maybe we can just force it through...

"Arihito, I'm taking a shot!" said Suzuna.

"Suzuna, wait! If you shoot now—!" By the time I cried out to her, Suzuna had let loose an arrow as I'd ordered her to earlier...but right now, the giant warrior was encased in a cocoon of wind.

◆Current Status◆
> Suzuna activated Auto-Hit ⟶ Next two shots will automatically hit
> Suzuna's attack was deflected by Wind Burst

"Ah—!" Suzuna yelped.

"Theresia, it's all you!" I shouted.

◆Current Status◆
> Arihito activated Defense Support 1 ⟶ Target: Theresia
> Suzuna's attack was deflected by Theresia
No damage

"—!"

Theresia dashed from her position as midguard to guard against the arrow with her round shield. Immediately after, she activated Accel Dash and closed in on the giant warrior whose Wind Burst had just ceased. I went to provide some cover fire, aiming somewhere where I couldn't accidentally hit her instead. When I did, my vision seemed to zoom in, almost like I was using a scope, and I was able to clearly see the giant warrior.

Any weak points, how its power flows...its movements; if I keep all that in mind, I can see... There's a scar on its head—!

◆Current Status◆

> Arihito used Hawk Eyes to perceive ★Giant Eagle-Headed Warrior's weak spot

> Arihito's attack hit ★Giant Eagle-Headed Warrior

> Theresia activated Wind Slash ⟶ Hit ★Giant Eagle-Headed Warrior

Slight knockback

11 support damage

"KAAAAWWW!"

Just because it uses wind doesn't mean it has a resistance to it... and the damage from my slingshot got through. I definitely saw its weak spot... It's the scar on its head!

It couldn't send out another Wind Burst right after it stopped one; that was good. We could use that gap to get in all stages of Blossom Blade.

"Everyone, there's a crack on its head! Aim there!" I shouted.

"…All right, I'll try!" replied Igarashi.

"That high up…? No, we have to…!" said Elitia.

I pointed out the enemy's weak spot to Igarashi and Elitia. If there was any place to hit to get a one-hit KO, it'd be on the giant warrior's head—but the enemy wasn't so kind as to let us simply aim for its weak spot just because we'd noticed it.

◆Current Status◆
> ★Giant Eagle-Headed Warrior activated Survival Instincts ⟶ All abilities buffed

The giant warrior's entire body was encased in a blue light, and I felt a surge of intense rage welling up from it that made everything until now pale in comparison. Just like Redface, it became more dangerous as its vitality went down. My mind raced as we stood before this horrifying creature— How could we defeat it now? Could we safely retreat?

Part X: The Fight for Our Lives

Now that the giant warrior had used Survival Instincts, there weren't any obvious gaps in its defense. But Elitia gauged the intervals between its attacks and went in for one of her own.

"Hyaaa!"

"*KRAAAAW!*"

Sword and spear clashed. The ferocity of it made Misaki shudder every time the weapons collided.

"Eep... Ohhh..."

"This is our moment of truth... Misaki, don't pass out now!" I said.

"Arihito, if I can't use my bow, then I'm—," started Suzuna.

"Don't worry. Your time to attack will come... Look. Elitia's keeping up with it."

◆Current Status◆
> Elitia activated Sonic Raid
> ★Giant Eagle-Headed Warrior activated Triple Attack ⟶ Elitia evaded

That was a skill one level higher than Igarashi's Double Attack—three lightning-fast strikes of its spear, all of which Elitia managed to evade. The problem was that she was being held back by the enemy's energy and couldn't spend even a moment on a counterattack.

But the moment the vanguard stepped back from the enemy was our chance to attack.

"—Fire! Aim for the head, Suzuna!" I shouted.

"Got it—!"

◆Current Status◆
> Arihito's attack hit ★Giant Eagle-Headed Warrior
> Suzuna's attack hit ★Giant Eagle-Headed Warrior
11 support damage

Suzuna's arrow pierced the giant warrior's head the moment after my bullet struck it. With the added support damage, our opponent lurched forward and fell to its knees.

"KRAAAW...AAAAW!!"

But even with that, the giant warrior still refused to go down. The light in its right eye had vanished. Whatever it was using as an eyeball had been shattered.

"—You're going down!" cried Elitia as she leaped at the giant warrior. She aimed at its head, now within her reach.

Igarashi and Theresia readied their attacks, and we prepped our second round of shots. Even Misaki gripped her dice, resolved to launch it this time.

But just a fraction of a second before our combined attacks hit, I felt terrible shivers run through my body. The only word in my mind was *death*.

We stopped it—there's no way it can still... There's no way—!

◆Current Status◆
> ★Giant Eagle-Headed Warrior activated Wind Burst
> Wind Burst activated Needle Feather

Gusts of wind kicked up to wrap the giant warrior's body in wind, forcing Elitia and the others to stop. The next moment, the giant warrior spread its wings wide inside the gale and screeched loudly.

The attack would hit everyone in the party. By the time I realized as much, the enemy had launched hundreds of feathers from its wings, all of which raced toward us.

"*KAAAAAAAW!*"

"Agh—!"

I'd considered what would happen in the event of an attack like this. If it was a multi-target attack, I wouldn't be able to give myself Defense Support or reduce the damage I took. *We're still in the clear*—or so I'd thought. In the end, I'd made a serious error in judgment.

Even so, my Defense Support was nothing to sneeze at. It could keep everyone's vitality bars from dropping too much, including Suzuna, who didn't have much defense—everyone's except mine, of course.

◆Current Status◆

> Arihito activated Defense Support 1 ⟶ Target: 5 members including Kyouka

> Needle Feather hit all members of Arihito's party

> Arihito's abilities were decreased due to low vitality

"Arihito—!"

"Ari—!"

Oww... Those feathers are like needles. Man, I'm glad I changed my armor... They didn't pierce too deep. I might have a few broken bones from the impact...but I'm not done yet!

"Atobe!"

"......!"

Igarashi and Theresia cried out with worry. Elitia was bravely trying to attack the giant warrior's head on her own, but it used its spear to defend and kept her from getting close. It hadn't over-extended its attacks ever since it had activated Survival Instincts, so it wasn't putting itself in a position that we could use for a Blossom Blade hit.

"Gah..."

"Arihito, don't move! You've been pierced by the feathers!" said Suzuna.

"Let's run, Arihito! If we go now—!" started Misaki.

"I'm fine... I can still fight. Besides, we gotta beat this thing... Even if we run, there's nowhere for us to go..."

◆Current Status◆
> Arihito activated Recovery Support 1 ⟶ 5 party
  members' vitality restored

Okay... Everyone's all set with vitality.

As long as there was nothing getting in the party's way, we'd still have an ace up our sleeves.

"Rrgh... It's got such a long reach...but I need to close in somehow!" said Elitia, annoyed that she wasn't able to get in an attack. Even so, she hadn't lost her cool and was still continuing to make attack attempts. The problem was, though, that she was saving her magic to use another Blossom Blade, meaning she couldn't use Sonic Raid anymore.

Igarashi had maybe one more Mirage Step and Double Attack left. Same with Theresia's Accel Dash. We'd be destroyed if we couldn't make an opportunity to attack.

If there's a god out there, then I have faith...we even have someone with amazing luck in the party. Please!

"Ack—!"

Elitia failed to dodge one of the three attacks the giant warrior threw at her, instead guarding against it with her sword, which sent her flying backward. The giant warrior prepared to use Wind Burst—this was it; it was now or never...!

"Igarashi, Theresia! Use Morale Discharge!"

"...Got it... Soul Mirage!"

"......!"

◆Current Status◆

> Kyouka activated Soul Mirage ⟶ All party
  members gained a Mirage Warrior

> Theresia activated Triple Steal ⟶ All party
  members received Triple Steal effects

This is...a mirage? No. It's a copy that's actually here...?

Next to each of us was a copy of ourselves. The copies' bodies were surrounded in blue light. I couldn't see their faces, but they were otherwise exact replicas, down to the equipment.

"KRRAAAAAAAW!"

"Everyone, use your mirage as a shield! We can do it!" shouted Igarashi. She knew what her Morale Discharge did immediately after activating it. If my Defense Support worked on this mirage, and if I could add to its attack...

We can beat it with this if we can make an opportunity to attack!

The giant warrior used Wind Burst followed by Needle

Feathers. Each of us hid behind our mirage warrior to use them as a shield, and then—

```
◆Current Status◆
> Arihito activated Defense Support 1 ──→ Target: 6
                                                  Mirage
                                                  Warriors
> Needle Feathers hit 6 Mirage Warriors
```

They withstood it… Their vitality isn't even different from ours. That means we've doubled our number of attacks!

"—Now!!" I shouted.

We knew that it reacted quickly after finishing a Wind Burst. But if we anticipated the end of the winds and hit it with everything we had…!

"Find your mark—!"

```
◆Current Status◆
> Suzuna activated Auto-Hit ──→ Next two shots
  will automatically hit
> Suzuna's attack hit ★Giant Eagle-Headed Warrior
Additional Mirage Warrior attack
22 support damage
> Arihito's attack hit ★Giant Eagle-Headed Warrior
Additional Mirage Warrior attack
11 support damage
> Suzuna recovered vitality and magic
Failed to steal loot
> Arihito recovered vitality and magic
Failed to steal loot
```

The damage the mirage warriors did recovered vitality and magic as well... I can move normally now that it hurts less!

Invisible attacks hit the giant warrior's head at the same time as our shots. It wavered from our attacks, and Igarashi and Theresia used the opportunity to close and attack.

"Let's do this together, Theresia!" shouted Igarashi.

"—!"

◆Current Status◆
> KYOUKA activated DOUBLE ATTACK
Additional MIRAGE WARRIOR attack
> Stage 1 hit ★GIANT EAGLE-HEADED WARRIOR
22 support damage
> Stage 2 hit ★GIANT EAGLE-HEADED WARRIOR
22 support damage
> THERESIA activated WIND SLASH
Additional MIRAGE WARRIOR attack ⟶ Hit ★GIANT
    EAGLE-HEADED WARRIOR
Moderate knockback
22 support damage
> KYOUKA recovered vitality and magic
Failed to steal loot
> THERESIA recovered vitality and magic
Successfully stole loot

Our magic isn't drained even when the mirages use skills... That means that Elitia's Blossom Blade—!

Igarashi, Theresia, and their two mirages made a total of six attacks. Igarashi had the longer reach with her spear and so aimed for its head while Theresia slashed across its legs; it was beautiful teamwork.

As the giant warrior plunged forward, Elitia and her mirage leaped over its head to attack.

"—Begone!"

◆Current Status◆
> Elitia activated Blossom Blade
Additional Mirage Warrior attack
> Stage 1 hit ★Giant Eagle-Headed Warrior
22 support damage
> Stage 2 hit ★Giant Eagle-Headed Warrior
22 support damage

The attacks rained down like a maelstrom. If all stages landed, the giant warrior would take a minimum of 264 damage, and its total damage would be well over 350 by then.

"*KRAAAAWW...AAWW...!*"

But as terrifying as it was, even though we'd delivered far more damage than Juggernaut could have ever taken, this giant warrior refused to fall.

If this doesn't finish it off... No, we'll end this here!

"Rrgh... Why won't it go down...?!" cried Elitia. I understood how she felt. It hadn't fallen even though it'd just taken two Blossom Blades between Elitia and her mirage.

But that wasn't the end of our attacks. We weren't going to let it counterattack again.

"—Misaki!" I shouted.

"…Please, God…!" she said, launching a die at the Giant Eagle-Headed Warrior before Elitia had even landed again. If she just hit, then she'd get my support damage. And she was a Gambler, so it should hit even if she threw it wildly off mark.

```
◆Current Status◆
> Misaki's attack hit ★Giant Eagle-Headed Warrior
No damage
Additional Mirage Warrior attack
22 support damage
> Misaki recovered vitality and magic
No loot in target's possession to steal
```

The metal of the giant warrior's head reached its limit when Misaki's iron die backed with the support damage struck it. We heard a cracking sound, and its head split.

"Ah… Aaah…"

Even so, the giant warrior didn't fall. It brandished its spear at Misaki as if to say it was going to take her with it, but that was my moment.

```
◆Current Status◆
> Arihito activated Rear Stance ⟶ Target: ★Giant
                                           Eagle-Headed Warrior
```

It suddenly realized there was someone behind it and tried to turn around. Right after I supported Misaki, I moved to behind the giant warrior. *The damage should be increased because it's a blindside attack from behind!*

Come on!

◆Current Status◆
> Aʀɪʜɪᴛᴏ's attack hit ★Gɪᴀɴᴛ Eᴀɢʟᴇ—Hᴇᴀᴅᴇᴅ Wᴀʀʀɪᴏʀ
Additional Mɪʀᴀɢᴇ Wᴀʀʀɪᴏʀ attack
Blindside attack
11 support damage
> 1 ★Gɪᴀɴᴛ Eᴀɢʟᴇ—Hᴇᴀᴅᴇᴅ Wᴀʀʀɪᴏʀ defeated

My bullet and the one from my mirage warrior smacked into the back of the giant warrior's head.

"KAW...AWWWWW...AW..."

It stumbled a step forward and tried to thrust its spear into the ground to support itself, but in the end, it succumbed and collapsed, no longer moving.

"...Did we...win?" asked Igarashi.

I was now near Igarashi, Theresia, and Elitia after using Rear Stance, and Igarashi hadn't quite realized we'd won. She still stood there gripping her spear, and Theresia stood next to her with her sword at the ready.

"Hah, ah-ha-ha... I—I sorta...don't feel like I'm even alive... Eek!" said Misaki.

"Thank goodness... Misaki, you were so reckless...," said Suzuna.

We did have a way for Misaki to avoid the dangers of stepping in front of the giant warrior. As long as I used Defense Support and Recovery Support, she would have been able to use her mirage warrior as a shield and survive any attack. But if we didn't follow up after Elitia's attack, well, it could use Needle Feathers incredibly

quickly, twice every thirty seconds. Elitia's magic was exhausted, so we would only be able to defend while it pushed us into a corner and finished us off.

◆Current Status◆
> Soul Mirage's effects terminated
> Kyouka's abilities temporarily buffed

The mirages vanished, and what looked like the remnants of magic flowed back and collected into Igarashi. Even though the effects were over, there were still benefits. The effects of Soul Mirage appeared to last about thirty seconds, which was only appropriate considering how powerful it was. Even so, it seemed almost too powerful, but I suppose it depended on whether or not you were able to prepare for its use.

"This battle's MVP is Igarashi, hands down. She was incredibly effective," I said.

"Ah, well...I think everything just sort of fell into place. I get chills thinking about what would've happened if my ability had a really off-the-wall effect," she said.

"Now I see why not many people know what the Valkyrie's Morale Discharge does. Anyone would want to keep something that strong a secret," said Elitia admiringly. If people knew more about it, the Valkyrie job would be very popular. It was such a shame the job wasn't more popular, though, just because it wasn't specialized enough.

Theresia walked over to me and showed me a black stone she

was holding. It was semitransparent, and there was a character in the center of it.

"Is this one of those rune things? You can get them even without compressing magic stones?" I asked.

"Incredible—did you get that because of Triple Steal's effects?" asked Elitia.

Theresia nodded. She gave the rune to me, wrapping her hands around mine as she did so and giving me a squeeze.

"Hmm...? What is it?" I asked.

"She was worried about you because you got hit. I know I was... I'm sorry; it's my job to protect you," apologized Igarashi.

"Arihito, are you all right? Are you hurt—?" asked Suzuna.

"I'm fine. Thanks to Triple Steal, my wounds healed when I attacked it. It only hurts a little now..."

"I can nurse you back to health! I'll wipe your butt for you, and I'll even carry you on my back if you liiike!" offered Misaki.

"Uh... Hey, y-you don't owe me anything. You fought, too," I said, patting her on the head.

"Oh... A-Arihito..."

"We've all been through a lot. How about we continue on after you recover a bit... Wh-what's wrong?"

"...You say we did a lot, but I just feel like I failed...," said Misaki.

"I—I just...stood back and shot. If I were more useful, then you wouldn't have...," stammered Suzuna.

"You guys are ridiculous...but I actually can't say I don't understand how you feel," said Igarashi.

It wasn't just the three of them. Theresia was also staring at me, but when I looked back, she turned away in embarrassment, her lizard mask tinged red.

If I could, if there was a less embarrassing moment to do so, I wanted to show my appreciation to each of them. I had sensed they needed that, but now knowing how they all reacted to that kind of encouragement, actually putting it into action would require my generosity as a leader and as a human.

CHAPTER 5

The Secret Within the Labyrinth's Depths

Part I: The Reliquary

We approached the fallen giant warrior cautiously and searched for anything that may have fallen from it. When we did—

"Wasn't this in the giant warrior's eye?" asked Igarashi.

"Is that a gem? It hasn't been damaged at all…," I said as she showed me. Perhaps it was a magic stone? No, unlike the other magic stones we'd found so far—like the blaze stones—this wasn't rough-hewn. Instead, it was cut and polished neatly. These ruins we'd found ourselves in, the fact that we'd used a teleportation pad to get here, and this gem—they were all made by someone. There were essentially no man-made objects or structures in the Field of Dawn, but for some reason, this fourth floor was completely different.

"Its weapons are waaay too heavy. I doubt we'll be able to carry them," said Misaki.

"And we can't send something that big to the storage unit, so I guess we'll just have to leave it. It's not like there were ever any other humans who came here anyway... Actually, that might not be true...," I said.

The giant warrior wouldn't have had that old scar on its head if no Seekers had ever come here before. In that case, what became of them? Were they killed?

"...Suzuna, I know the timing's a bit weird, but could you take the Spirit Detection now?" I asked.

"Yes, I was just thinking I should do that myself. This giant eagle must have—," she started, not saying it had likely put countless Seekers into the ground. If there was a way for it to reconceal the entrance to the fourth floor after defeating any Seekers who made their way here...

Is this giant warrior some sort of test? Or just a trap to kill anyone who comes this way...? It's pretty unpleasant regardless.

Suzuna pulled out her license and acquired Spirit Detection 1. Once she did, she turned to face nothing and rang a bell she'd brought with her, then put her hands together.

"...Do you see something?" I asked.

"Yes... The Seekers who came here before us and lost their lives. Six of them fought against the giant warrior, but they were defeated and... Oh, how awful!"

The reason I'd felt the giant warrior was happy to fight us was that it was a man-eating monster. No monster in the labyrinths was about to try and resolve things peacefully with humans. We were nothing more than a source of food to them. That meant I had no reason to go easy on them in the future. There were surely some exceptions among the monsters, creatures who were in no way hostile toward us, but we didn't have room to treat them kindly in our current state.

"...It looks like it came off the enemy when we hit it. Its body is made of some metallic substance, but it looks like a portion of it turned more liquid as it moved," said Igarashi.

A liquid metallic substance had dripped from its head like blood when we broke it, but it'd now hardened. It made me think of some sort of metallic organism. That it was a living being would explain why it ate and how a wound it sustained in the past had healed to become a scar.

"I feel like it could be used as materials for something, but there's just so much we don't know. How about we just take one part back with us for now?" I proposed.

"Well, we should have some proof that we defeated it, right? Maybe I should pull off a few feathers," suggested Igarashi.

"Yeah, sure... Even if we take this gem back with us, the Guild might have no idea what it is," I replied.

"The heart is generally considered the best proof for having defeated a monster... Should I try and remove its armor?" asked Elitia.

"Urgh... I-its heart...," whimpered Misaki as she clung to me.

Well, it was a reasonable suggestion. I did cringe away from the body, though, as Elitia slid her sword under its armor and peeled it back. Buried in its chest was a round pearl-like stone.

"...Is this its heart?" Misaki asked. "It's not as...*lifelike* as I expected."

"Magic makes their metal bodies move like living creatures. This is one type of orb for that," explained Elitia.

"An orb, eh? …All right. So then this thing really was some sort of golem," I said.

This was the orb used to make the Giant Eagle-Headed Warrior's metal body operate like a living being's. Which meant someone made it. I had so many questions but decided we should at least take the orb as proof we defeated it.

"…Theresia, do those doors look like they can be opened?" I asked.

"……"

The stone doors I was talking about were so massive it looked like they'd been built to allow the giant warrior to pass through but were closed tightly. They didn't look like they would move easily. High up on the door where I couldn't reach was a small recess, straddling the crack where the doors met. What were we supposed to do, stick our fingers in there to open it?

"Arihito, would that gem you picked up fit in the hole?" suggested Misaki.

"Hmm, yeah it looks like it just might about fit. But we can't reach it even if we jump," said Elitia.

"All right. Theresia, I'll brace myself against the door. You climb up and try to put the gem in the hole," I said.

Theresia put her hand to her mouth, the one part of her face visible from under the lizard mask. She seemed uncertain about what she should do. It would be difficult for her to just climb up on my shoulders; she needed something to step on.

"Okay, it'll be just like forming a pyramid in gymnastics. I'll be on the bottom. Elitia, you're a vanguard, too, so you can also be part of the base. Then Misaki will get on top of us...," started Igarashi.

"Wooow, this takes me back. Suzu, do you have a flute or something on you? You could *tweet, tweet* on it like a whistle, and we'll all snap to attention," said Misaki.

"Heh... Argh, you're making me laugh by saying weird stuff. Stop chatting; it's dangerous," chided Igarashi

"Okeydoke. Right, I'm going up... Hup!" said Misaki, climbing up to the second layer of the human pyramid after discovering that it was actually pretty easy to make Igarashi laugh. Elitia looked a little unhappy with the arrangement but kept her hands steady on the ground as she supported Misaki's weight along with Igarashi.

Theresia removed her boots and climbed easily up the pyramid and placed her feet on my shoulders. I felt the weight less than I'd thought I would and heard a clink as the gem slid into the hole. The ground started to tremble slightly, and the doors slid open to the left and right. I was sure we made a pretty strange sight in our human pyramid as the massive doors opened, but at least it went well.

"...There's someone inside... Everyone, be careful. I'm not certain, but I sense something sinister in there," said Suzuna.

Theresia climbed down from my shoulders, and we all stood facing the open doorway. In the middle of the room was a small set of stairs, which led to a dais that was illuminated almost like there was a spotlight on it. On the dais was a large boxlike something. When Suzuna said there was something sinister, was that based on her Spirit Detection or just intuition? I suppose it didn't matter; I preferred to take a moment to put together some safety measures than go in there entirely defenseless.

"Igarashi, you acquired that Decoy skill, right?" I asked.

"Uh, yeah...now that you mention it, if I'd used that earlier, I could have drawn some of the giant warrior's attacks with it."

"No, I think that would have just given us a false sense of security. I think it's more suited to situations like this. There very well could be some traps in here. Would you try using the decoy?" I asked.

"Hmm, would you normally set a trap for after someone defeated such a powerful monster? I mean, I guess I would if I were making a labyrinth," speculated Misaki.

"Never say never in a labyrinth. We can't be certain there's nothing here. That's what you were getting at, right, Atobe?" Igarashi pulled a clay doll from her pouch. She placed it on the ground and held her hand over it while reciting an incantation.

"Human form born from the earth, imbued with my magic! Rise up and be the vanguard to draw the demon's gaze— Agh..."

"Eek! Are you all right, Kyouka?!" cried Misaki as she and Suzuna supported Igarashi, who suddenly wavered on her feet after finishing the incantation. I looked at my license and saw that Igarashi's magic was practically at zero. It was my fault. I hadn't considered the possibility that the decoy would consume all her magic.

"I'm sorry, Igarashi... I didn't think about your magic," I said.

"No, it should recover slowly if I take a rest. It's not a problem... This just happens when you run out. We'll need to be more careful in the future."

If someone ran out of magic in the middle of a battle, the

enemy would have no problem attacking them. If someone had to keep using magic over and over... Well, it'd be good if we had some way to recover magic while in battle.

The clay doll absorbed the magic that Igarashi poured into it and, after a moment, started to grow larger and larger until...it became an exact replica of Igarashi.

"Th-that's incredible... A level-two spell can do something like that...," I marveled.

"It can only follow very simple orders, though, so I could do that to use it as a decoy. Walk forward," said Igarashi, the last part a command given to the decoy, which started moving forward as directed, then... I couldn't see very clearly because it was so gloomy, but I heard a click, like it stepped on some sort of switch.

"Ah!"

Igarashi let out a sound, and the decoy suddenly started to wither and then disappeared. I looked at my license, and it said Kyouka's Decoy stepped on a Life-Sucking Trap. Thank God that was only the decoy. It would've been an utter tragedy to come this far and be taken out by a one-hit KO trap.

"I feel bad because the decoy looked exactly like you...," I said.

"Y-yeah...it wouldn't be a very good decoy if it didn't, so we'll just have to get used to it," she said.

"That's sooo cruel... Oh, what's that? I just thought I saw the box-looking thing in the middle of the room glow," said Misaki.

The decoy had been given a tiny amount of life force from Igarashi's magic. The trap sucked that out, and the boxlike object seemed to react to that... What could that mean?

...It sucks having so many things I don't understand, but we have no choice but to keep going. Cautiously. There should be some way for us to get out of the labyrinth in here.

We fixed our battle formation and started forward while being very careful of where we stepped in case there were any more traps. Thankfully, there didn't seem to be any others, so we were able to make it up the stairs to the box without any problems. It was carved from black marble. There was a circular hole in the middle of the lid.

"Don't you think...it...it's sort of less of a box and more of a sarcophagus? Like...there could totally be a vampire in here," said Misaki.

"No...I don't sense anything impure. Nor do I feel any sort of malice now...," contradicted Suzuna.

"Suzuna can even sense through the box. Wow... Atobe, what do you think this hole is?"

"Have you found anything that might fit in your time seeking through this labyrinth?" asked Elitia.

I started running through the all the seeking that'd led up to now and...

"...We have...," I said.

"Huh, you did find something?! Where, Arihito, where?!" cried Misaki in shock.

I was thinking of the rod we found in the Black Box that we got from defeating Juggernaut. One end was shaped like a key while the other was cylindrical.

"This. It came from the Black Box that Juggernaut dropped... The handle looks like it would fit in the hole," I said.

"Be careful, everyone. Even though it might not be an enemy if what Suzuna says is right," said Elitia, and everyone nodded back. I had Theresia double-check that our surroundings were safe, then readied myself and slid the rod into the hole.

"Ah!"

The moment I'd put it in, the lid of the box split down the center where the hole was, and the parts slid open to the right and left. Only the lid moved, and it did so automatically without anyone touching it. A bright light flooded out from inside the box along with cool air and a white fog like when you open a box filled with dry ice. The fog flowed down the stairs and over the sides of the dais and quickly dispersed.

"A-Atobe...there's a person inside the box...," stammered Igarashi.

"What the...?" I gasped.

There was still a pale light flooding out from the box, but inside, I could see a girl lying down. It looked manufactured, like a doll. Long aqua-colored hair flowed over her breasts. I hadn't seen this color hair since coming to the Labyrinth Country.

And these things on her ears...radio antenna? ...No. The city's no more developed than a medieval city; there's no reason why there'd be something so advanced down here in the labyrinth...

"Aaah, ummm, aaahhh...Arihito, this person, she's not breathing!" said Misaki.

"...And yet she's still alive... Her soul hasn't left her body. But should we wake her? ...She's sleeping peacefully here. There must be a reason for it," speculated Suzuna.

She wasn't wrong, but I'd already opened the box. I had a feeling the key on the end of the rod was a literal key meant to wake this girl.

"If we search this room, we'll likely find a way to leave the labyrinth. But considering the trap from before, we can assume that randomly searching will be accompanied by a certain amount of risk. If we can wake this girl, we can likely ask her what this place is and how we can leave…," said Elitia.

I didn't know what the point of killing the giant warrior was if we couldn't find a way out and instead were stuck here wasting away until we died. I wanted to take this clue that was right in front of our eyes, but the keyhole to use this "key" was in an unexpected location.

"Atobe, look…in her chest… She's definitely not a normal human if she's got a hole like that in there."

"I wonder…if I put the key part of the rod in there," I said.

"If you think about how only people who'd defeated Juggernaut and made their way here, to the fourth floor, would have what's necessary to open the box… If you consider the probability, I think it's safe to say that we, led by Arihito, are the first people to meet all the requirements and make it here," postulated Elitia.

We were standing at the end of the line where no one had ever come before, to a hidden floor in the beginner labyrinth, which almost everyone was supposed to visit first. There was that saying that the darkest place was under the candlestick… It seemed fitting here.

We found the key in the Black Box. We found a box that we

could open with the key. Anyone could have made it this far if they'd connected all the dots and followed the right order.

But that didn't happen. We're the only ones who have ever met all the requirements, and now we're here.

I was nervous. My heart was still pounding loudly in my chest, but my mind was oddly clear. I was certain that this sleeping girl would have information on how we could get out of here—and information that would change our lives.

"…I'm going to use the key. Please don't have any hard feelings if something happens, okay?" I asked.

Everyone nodded. I tried putting the key into the sleeping girl's chest. My hands were shaking, though, and I couldn't get it in even though it was the perfect size and shape.

"……"

Theresia placed a hand on my back. She left it there, and the other four also placed their hands on my shoulders to try and calm me. Even though every single one of them was as nervous as they possibly could be, I felt my fear slip away.

"…Here I go…!"

I steadied my hand as I inserted the key into the hole in the girl's chest. It felt like it clicked into place when I pushed it all the way in—and then, the girl began to tremble slightly.

◆Current Status◆
> Arihito used the Key of the Hidden God on the 117th Reliquary ⟶ Unlock successful

Part II: The Girl in the Sanctuary

"Arihito, her chest is moving…," said Suzuna.

"Yeah… Looks like the key fit. Now what…?"

The key had opened the box, so clearly is was connected to this girl in some way. As I had expected, it was a perfect match to the keyhole in her chest.

"It looks like she's started breathing… It's like some sort of cryosleep from a sci-fi movie. Her body is preserved while she sleeps for a long time, then she's woken up…," said Igarashi. It seemed she also got the impression of incredibly advanced technology. The cover-like things on the girl's ears did definitely look mechanical in nature.

"…Mm…"

"Ah…she's waking up. Arihito, everyone, be careful!" warned Elitia, seeming like her nerves had been stretched tight from caution.

I took a deep breath and watched as her eyelashes fluttered. Then her eyes opened. They were the same aqua color as her hair but seemed to lack any spark of life. She sat up in the box but then didn't move anymore. I didn't feel the urge to capture her to preempt any threat she may pose or feel any hostility from her…but there was one massive problem.

…I couldn't see before because of her hair, but…is she completely naked…?

"……"

"Uh… Wh-what is it…?" I asked as she regarded at me silently. Being looked at with those lifeless eyes made me feel uncomfortable. I tried to guess why she was staring at me, tried to figure out her intentions, but she didn't say a word and just looked behind me.

Behind me stood Theresia. She didn't turn away from the girl's gaze, the eyes on her lizard mask staring right back at the girl who had just woken.

"…A-are they communicating somehow? With telepathy or something?" asked Misaki.

"H-hey… Quit joking around!" said Igarashi.

"But…they're both calm. Neither of their souls are distressed; they're just peaceful," said Suzuna.

Her Spirit Detection was going to be really useful for determining whether or not someone was hostile toward us. All of her Shrine Maiden senses seemed reliable, so I just held my breath as I watched Theresia and the girl…until—

…*What are they doing? Can they really communicate…?*

Theresia stepped forward and extended her left hand. The girl reached out her right hand to touch Theresia's and—

"…Ngh!"

Theresia jerked her hand back in surprise. The expressionless girl seemed to gain some light back in her eyes for the first time, then she finally opened her mouth to speak.

"You are the one who has opened the Reliquary and awakened me, yes? I have obtained the necessary information from reading the fragments of your history from that demi-human girl. Your name is Arihito Atobe, correct?"

"Uh, yes… That's correct. I'm Atobe Arihito. I was reincarnated here in the Labyrinth Country from my home country of Japan."

"…The Labyrinth Country. Is that where those who have been charged with gathering the gods live? Your souls are gathered from your own worlds and reincarnated here, where you *seek* us. That must be why you are called *Seeker*."

I suddenly shivered at the unexpected words coming from the girl's mouth. Why did we have to become Seekers after we'd been reincarnated here? I'd always questioned it and hoped to learn the answer someday, but to hear it from this girl…

"What do you mean…? Charged with gathering the gods… Nobody's ever said anything like that to us before," said Igarashi.

"Wait, Kyouka. This girl knows something…something very important. Let's hear what she has to say," said Elitia, and Igarashi held her tongue. I looked at her, but she just brought her hand to her chest and nodded as if telling me not to worry about her.

"Steadfast rearguard who has been reincarnated from a far-off world—first, I would like to express my gratitude to you for coming here and unlocking the mysteries of the labyrinth," said the girl.

"…By 'unlocking the mysteries of the labyrinth,' do you mean arriving here, bringing the key, and awakening you?" I asked.

"Yes. I praise those who have unlocked the mysteries, I provide them my guardianship and offer them a reward. My name is

Ariadne, the Iron Wheel. I am the hundred and seventeenth Hidden God—a replica. I was laid to rest in the bottom of a labyrinth that was no longer explored."

"Wait... You say you're the hundred and seventeenth—isn't this is the first labyrinth? What's a Hidden God? You're a replica?"

I wasn't keeping up, either, but I glanced at my license and understood what she was saying just a tiny bit more. The key I'd used was called the Key of the Hidden God, and the box I opened was the Reliquary, or so it said. Thinking about the base meaning of *reliquary*, I had the impression of a box that held the remains or objects that belonged to a saint. And the girl inside called herself a Hidden God and a "replica of a god." A replica...so a copy, also known as a fake.

"When you say you'll give us your guardianship and rewards... does that mean you'll lend us your power?" asked Elitia, but the girl didn't answer. She suddenly stood up and showed us her body.

"Uh...what the...? The pattern on your skin...are those electrical circuits?" asked Igarashi.

Just like she said, there was a glowing pattern running along the girl's body that looked like electrical circuits. But they looked like they were broken here and there. The lines of the circuits ran out from the hole in her chest but then seemed to stop in their tracks. They were clearly visible where they started between her ample breasts but faded away and disappeared as they went. It wasn't just that they were hidden by her hair or something; they actually appeared incomplete. Perhaps the remaining circuits would disappear soon and the girl, Ariadne, would return to her previous state. She looked at me and hung her head apologetically.

"It appears it has been too long since I was disposed of. The guardianship I could offer you would be weak, and the probability that all my functionality will return is quite low. I would recommend that you awaken a more well-preserved Hidden God to control," she said.

"If we did...would that mean leaving you here like this?" I asked.

"I was originally a discarded existence. I had no kin beyond the golem, which guarded me. My creator placed me in this box as a failure, having decided that the probability of me reaching completion as a replica was too low, and hid me away deep within the labyrinth. I have never held hope that someone would find and awaken me or that I would ever amount to anything."

I hadn't thought too deeply into some of her first words: *"First, I would like to express my gratitude."* The reason she had prefaced it with *first* was that she was planning to tell us that there was nothing for us to gain from waking her, that she was a lost cause.

"A failure... That's terrible... You're a person who can talk and think and feel, stuck in a box for who knows how many years... What kind of heartless, cruel person could do that to someone?" asked Igarashi.

"...And that giant warrior, it wasn't put there to ease her loneliness... It was simply placed there to prevent Seekers from coming this far," said Suzuna, both her and Igarashi angered by what Ariadne told them, her unconcerned tone just making it worse.

One thing I could guess from Ariadne's expressionless face was that, to her, this was just a simple fact. It wasn't something that anyone needed to be upset over.

"……"

"…Theresia," I said. She was clenching the fist she held at her chest. She was furious at Ariadne's circumstances, enraged by this "creator" of hers who left her in a box. I'd never seen her that angry.

"…Arihito, what should we do about her? We do have to consider the option of leaving her here for someone else to deal with…," said Elitia.

"I can use my power to send you to the surface. The teleportation pad that leads here from the third floor moves automatically after it has been used and becomes buried in the earth again. It would be up to you whether you report my existence to the organization to which you belong, or you can leave me here," said Ariadne, making it clear that we were free to do however we saw fit; each selection was equally valid.

But that was from her perspective. There was no way I'd be able to pretend that we hadn't come all this way and met her.

"…Ariadne, you say that you weren't preserved well, but I'm not sure that's true. I have no idea how many years, how many decades even, that you've been sleeping here, but we're standing here having a conversation with you, and you have enough emotions to be concerned for us. I personally don't see anything wrong with someone like that," I said.

Her creation seemed so well done that it made me believe

she was actually modeled after some god, but to then throw her away...because she was an imperfect replica of a god. The thing was that when we thought of a god, we thought of some being with unlimited power, and throwing away even an incomplete replica of that was pretty wasteful. I might have decided that Ariadne's creator was wasteful, but we weren't. To us, there was no substitute for the guardianship she offered us and the answers she gave us to the mysteries of the labyrinth.

"When you say the probability that your functions will completely return is 'quite low,' that means it's not zero. We've just started on our journey as Seekers, well, other than Elitia, who's a veteran. What that means is I'd be happy if we could grow together. I think that would help us grow," I said.

"...If you accept my guardianship, you would have to offer your devotion to me in order to maintain my functionality. If you devote yourself to an imperfect god such as myself, you must fight with any Hidden Gods you meet who are hostile toward me. But if you still wish to accept my guardianship, show me your token," instructed Ariadne.

"Token...do you mean my license?" I asked as I showed it to her. She nodded. I looked at everyone to check how they felt. None of them were opposed; we just faced each other and forced a smile.

"I made up my mind a long time ago. I'm leaving everything up to our leader," said Igarashi.

"Arihito...I know I lack the strength, but I want to help Ariadne. It's truly sad for her to stay her alone forever," said Suzuna.

"Heyyy, if you put Arihito and Ariadne together, that makes

them Ariari! Oh, is now not the right time to joke around?" asked Misaki.

"Guess I should come to expect such a lack of a sense of danger from you, Misaki. Anyway, I agree, Arihito. We are Seekers, and I'm sure we've been gathered to search the labyrinths for beings like Ariadne. I think a partnership with her will hold a lot of weight in our future expeditions," concluded Elitia.

I thought the same as Elitia. But that meant we were acting as the being, which reincarnated us and perhaps even created the Labyrinth Country, would want us to act.

In the beginning, it's like being forced to dance in the palm of someone's hand. It's fine as long as we don't have to keep dancing forever.

I thought it was a bit early to start questioning why we were reincarnated or trying to figure out the secrets of the labyrinths since we'd only just gotten started as Seekers, but we'd found Ariadne and didn't really have a choice in the matter.

"We want to accept your guardianship. How do we offer this 'devotion' that you talked about?" I asked.

Ariadne was silent for a moment as she stared at my face. While she was standing there without answering, Theresia walked up and offered her hand. Ariadne accepted and stepped out of the box, then held her right hand out toward me. I passed my license to her. She took it in her left hand and held her right over it.

"I have added a secret function to your token, which no others will be able to detect. You can use this to contact me. You can make me an 'offering' to receive my guardianship. If you have provided me sufficient offerings, I will be able to bring you back here if you are defeated while seeking in the labyrinth. When that happens, however, you will lose any equipment and items on you at the time," said Ariadne.

"…Sounds like we can't go wrong there, right?" I said.

"Even with this, my functionality is limited. I am the weakest of the Hidden Gods, and there are many who wish me harm. I do truly suggest—"

"You don't have to put yourself down so much. I haven't heard of a single Seeker yet who's received the guardianship of a Hidden God. But if we have your guardianship and you could save us if we end up in a really horrible situation…just knowing that we can rely on that is really helpful," said Igarashi.

We didn't even know how many people were aware of the Hidden Gods' existence. Louisa and Palme had mentioned Secret Gods, but even if we assumed that was referring to the Hidden Gods, it didn't seem like they knew the Hidden Gods actually existed. Were we the only ones to have ever discovered them? Or maybe there were a lot of people in the upper Seeker ranks who knew about them. I wasn't sure, but I would be able to conceal Ariadne's existence from the Guild or other Seekers unless I wanted to show them, since she'd made the additional functions undetectable by others.

"…Ariadne, are you not able to leave this place?" I inquired.

"In my current condition, I am unable to leave the Sanctuary. If you are able to gather the parts necessary to restore my lost functionality, then I would be able to assist you outside for a certain period of time. Until then, I can only offer temporary support on a strictly limited basis."

Did she mean we'd be able to borrow her power in some form? Well anyway, I could only see positives to the arrangement, but she was so hesitant to do it that I was certain there'd be some risks depending on the situation. It didn't matter, though; the new function was already added to my license. There was a new page for Hidden Gods, and Ariadne's name was listed in the Faith column.

"…If we leave here, can we return by using the teleportation pad on the third floor or some other method?" I asked.

"If you can find it. Depending on the offering you provide, I can use it to refill the Sanctuary's power in order to place another teleportation pad outside."

"Right. First then, this offering thing…," I started.

"…I will contact you later regarding that. I am just delighted at the moment that you have selected me. I can ask no more of you."

She didn't seem to want to tell us any more. She was still naked; the only thing covering her was her aqua-colored hair. Now what looked like glowing characters of some kind appeared on her skin, and she held her hand up toward us. The moment she did, we were suddenly transported to the middle of an expansive field. What we saw around us was the first floor of the Field of Dawn. Everyone's face looked like they were questioning whether or not we'd dreamed the whole thing.

"…Don't worry, it wasn't a dream," I assured them. We still

had the proof that we defeated the giant warrior as well as the additional function on my license.

"We really did make it baaack... Ugh, I feel like I'm gonna collapse...," said Misaki as she sank to the ground where she stood. Everyone else was the same, seemingly losing their strength out of sheer relief.

We had managed to make it back, but how would I report this to Louisa? So much of what had happened would cause her to faint, but I decided to worry about that later. Right now, I just wanted to forget everything and enjoy the fact that I was still alive.

"Ahh...I'm so glad we made it back. There was a point where I wasn't sure we would...," I admitted.

"You did great, Atobe. How about we take a short rest before going home?"

"I agree. You've been so tensed up this entire time, Arihito," said Suzuna.

"...Meeting you has probably been the most incredible discovery of all. I have a feeling there's a lot more in store for us...," said Elitia.

Her words made me feel awkward, but I pretended I didn't hear and flopped down on the grass. Theresia then came over and knelt right next to me.

"Uh... T-Theresia, what are you—?" started Igarashi. I could tell she was flustered, but Theresia took my head and guided it into her lap.

"Th-thanks, but...what's gotten into you all of a sudden?" I asked.

"……"

She didn't reply. I did see, though, that her mouth—the only thing visible under her lizard mask—was curled up in a tiny smile. I could feel the rest of the party staring at me. But all I wanted was to lie there for a little while, my head on her soft lap, basking in the joy of having survived this adventure.

The Rearguard at Night and the Party's Troubles

It was the night that Louisa stayed in Arihito's suite with the party.

He had assumed the effects of his Recovery Support wouldn't reach the other room, but he was wrong. Sleeping on the couch in their room put him in a rearguard position behind Kyouka and the others. That was the reason why he had been concerned about his friends sleeping in the bedroom.

The first to wake up was Theresia, who was sleeping on the other couch in the living room.

"……"

She watched him in the dimly lit living room after he'd fallen asleep. She pulled her hands to her chest, and the face of her lizard mask blushed a deep red. She curled herself up in frustration. She rolled over so her back was toward Arihito, so she wasn't looking at him, and tried to get some rest, but the next moment, she couldn't keep herself from staring and so rolled back to watch him.

She had no idea that when her back was to Arihito, Recovery Support was being activated even if her vitality was maxed out.

Theresia pressed her hands over her mouth to hold her breath, perhaps worried that Arihito would hear her. She became conscious of the strange beating of her heart. She was at a loss for what to do and coming close to fainting from lack of oxygen, then—

The door to the bedroom opened with a soft click and out came Kyouka, her face flushed as red or redder than Theresia's, breathing heavily and seemingly concerned about her pajamas that were damp from sweat.

"...You, too, Kyouka?" came a quiet voice.

"Hmm... H-huh? You're awake, too, Misaki?" whispered back Kyouka.

Theresia lay perfectly still on her couch, staring in their direction. It was partially because she was surprised by their sudden appearance but also because she instinctually decided this was one of those times when she shouldn't move.

And it wasn't just the two other girls; everyone who should have been asleep in the bedroom came out. Louisa, Elitia, Suzuna...all five of them, flushed and bleary-eyed, exchanged glances.

"...So it's the same for everyone. I woke up, too..."

"What should we do...? We won't get any sleep like this."

Suzuna and Louisa were generally very modest girls, but they now looked at Arihito with their blushing faces and teary eyes.

"...Um, can't we all just deal with it ourselves? Arihito's fast asleep," said Misaki.

"W-well... But still...," stammered Kyouka, uncertain of what to do.

"... He's sleeping like a baby... And he looks so cute asleep...," Louisa said, taking a step forward.

"H-hey, don't get so close! …Honestly, Louisa…," sighed Kyouka.

Louisa herself was aware that she was being too brash, but seeing him sleeping and looking so unguarded really made her want to touch him.

"Mm…"

"…Mr. Atobe… M-my, how bold…"

Arihito rolled over in his sleep on the narrow couch. Now he lay on his back with his arm up on the arm of the couch, the front of the button-up shirt he was wearing as pajamas undone most of the way. The five girls' eyes were glued to his chest. It was the first time any of them had seen a man's bare chest so close up. The next person to step forward wasn't Louisa but Misaki.

"So this is what men are like… All toned and firm. It's kinda unfair…," she said.

"S-stop it, Misaki… If you wake him up…," rebuked Kyouka as she half-heartedly tugged at Misaki's sleeve. There was no stopping her—Misaki's Trust Level toward Arihito had gone up a lot while they slept, and so she was free to undo the buttons on his shirt.

Kyouka was frozen, her eyes opened wide when most of his top half was uncovered. She knew she should stop this, but she couldn't get the words out of her throat. Elitia was the most collected of the five girls, but even she couldn't tear her eyes from Arihito. She pressed her hand to her mouth as she tried to suppress the emotions she was feeling for the first time.

"…It's not like it's wrong. It's just physical bonding, like when a mom cuddles her baby," said Misaki.

Even Kyouka, who always had her guard up, was speechless. Misaki pulled Suzuna from where she was sitting on the floor, and the two of them sat next to Arihito. His hand was hanging listlessly to the side. Misaki gently took it (who knew what she was thinking) and squeezed it between hers.

"So big and strong... You guys might like his hands," she said, enjoying herself yet passing Arihito's hand to the next in line, Suzuna. Even her ears were bright red at seeing Arihito's torso so close, but she did as Misaki suggested and took Arihito's hand.

"...Mm..."

He let out a groan—it would be no surprise if he woke up at any time during this; they all knew that. Every time he moved the slightest amount, each of their hearts went off racing, but none of them tried to back out part way through.

None of them had ever spent the night in the same room as a man who wasn't a family member, each one of them knowing the others were the same even without having to say a word.

"...Arihito's sleeping so soundly. He'll never know if we don't tell him," suggested Misaki.

"I—I...really don't think that's a good idea. It's better to tell him in case he starts to catch on," said Elitia.

"Hee-hee... You say that, but I can tell that even you want to touch Mr. Atobe. I feel the same way," Louisa confessed.

"...Misaki and Suzuna seem so happy...b-but I feel so embarrassed. I can't calm down," said Elitia. She thought what they were doing was strange, but she was so incredibly jealous of Suzuna as she sat there holding Arihito's hand.

She suddenly sat down and took her turn after Suzuna, taking his hand in hers. It was big and warm, the hand of a grown man. She desperately tried to rein herself in from the rapturous sensation it brought her.

"Ms. Kyouka, what should we do? What can we do that won't wake Mr. Atobe...?" wondered Louisa.

It went against her conscience to approach him while he was sleeping. On top of that, she owed him so much, but she couldn't help herself. She just really wanted to touch him.

"Th-that...doesn't seem like my place...," she murmured.

"...It's fine as long as we keep it our little secret. I think everyone here can do that... I will, of course...," said Louisa.

...*Ah! N-no, Louisa! You can't—!*

Kyouka was alarmed when Louisa went around to the back of the couch, climbed on top of it and stared down at Arihito. She brushed the hair from her cheek, putting it behind her ear, and she gazed at Arihito's face. Kyouka watched, thinking that she might kiss him, and almost couldn't stop herself from saying something.

"...Mm..."

"Ooh... He might wake up if I do that... This is tough," said Louisa.

"...Were you just trying to kiss Arihito's cheek? You can't do something like that when he's sleeping...," objected Elitia.

"I think it's fine as long as it's just on the cheek or forehead. Obviously, kissing his chest would be wrong," said Misaki, and everyone exchanged glances. Suzuna and Elitia were adamant they'd never go that far, but Louisa was a different story.

"I am the oldest here…and Mr. Atobe has done a lot for me. So I—" Her voice tapered off.

"W-well that applies to me, too, even more so…," said Kyouka.

"Well then, I defer to you, Ms. Kyouka. I'm fine with this anyway," replied Louisa.

"Huh…?" She had been so desperately trying to stop Louisa. It came as a surprise that she wouldn't back down so easily. Instead, she just stroked his arm while being very careful not to wake him.

How did things get to this point? Kyouka wondered if kissing Arihito on the cheek would calm the burning she felt inside her, but really, she just thought it'd make it worse. She was also starting to feel annoyed by Arihito, who looked like he was just sleeping more and more pleasantly. She had decided she needed to stop everyone, but he was the reason she had been woken up yesterday as well. She couldn't really say she was sleep deprived, though—she still felt energetic enough that there wasn't much she really could complain about.

And when it came to this warmth she felt—now that she'd joined Arihito's party, she'd just have to figure out a way to deal with it on her own. They all would.

But if Atobe knew about our problem…what would happen to us if he tried to help get rid of this…frustration…?

"Ms. Kyouka, you don't have to push yourself…"

"…I'm j-just gonna do what everyone else did… Hopefully that'll calm me down a bit."

"Next, if we could get him to sleep in a different position, we could try ooother things," suggested Misaki.

"D-don't be ridiculous… What if it made him not want to stay with us anymore…?" Elitia objected.

"When that happens, he could come stay at my place like I originally suggested to him…," said Louisa.

Kyouka couldn't stand Louisa's competitiveness or the warmth in her body pushing her to the breaking point and finally took Arihito's hand like the others.

…Wh-what…is this…? I'm only touching his hand, and yet…

She had just meant to touch his hand, but she shocked even herself when she took it and hugged it to herself, pressing it between her breasts.

"Whoaaa… Th-that was gutsy…"

"…Gosh, I'm not nearly bold enough to try that… Oh, but—," said Suzuna.

"…I—I just wanted to show him I appreciate him… See, Suzuna?"

"…Arihito looks so happy… I just know I'm not…," said Suzuna a little sadly, but Kyouka was focused entirely on hugging Arihito's hand. Suzuna could see how much it calmed Kyouka, how much she'd needed it.

These past few days of being in Arihito's party made it impossible for Kyouka to imagine a life without him. She started thinking things that surprised even her. She wanted to show him sometime when he was awake, not asleep like this, how much it meant to her that he was here with her.

After the five girls took turns touching Arihito's hand, they rebuttoned his shirt and reluctantly returned to the bedroom.

"......"

Theresia had been watching them the entire time but now stood up quietly. She walked silently over to where Arihito slept and stared at his face, a tiny smile on her lips. She didn't say anything to her sleeping owner. She simply watched over him quietly until the sky faded into dawn.

AFTERWORD

Hello everyone, my name is Tôwa. Thank you so very much for picking up *The World's Strongest Rearguard*. This book was originally published online, like many other works of the same nature, on the website Shousetsuka ni Narou. Again, I really can't thank you enough for reading this official print version.

This book is actually a revised version of the web novel, so some parts have been changed quite significantly. The following will likely be spoilers for anyone who hasn't read this book yet, so please only continue if you don't think that will be an issue for you. I'll put a line break between this paragraph and the spoilers just to be safe. I personally think the changes were quite shocking.

What I'm referring to is the beautiful twenty-five-year-old demon manager Ms. Igarashi (that was kind of long), who is four years younger than the main character. I ended up reducing the tyrannical acts of her previous life by 50—or actually closer to 80—percent.

I received a lot of feedback from readers of the online edition regarding how Igarashi would act as a manager. I also used my own experiences as a reference. I wouldn't say the company I worked for treated their employees like complete dirt, but it was the kind of place where you'd have to either use overtime for any tasks that didn't directly benefit your department or the company as a whole, or come into the office on your days off. When I wrote Igarashi based on that period of my life, I got a lot of feedback from readers saying she was horrible or that they had a hard time believing she and Arihito could even form a party together.

I read those comments and just thought, *Yep, I get it.* I didn't even have a good rebuttal; I just completely acquiesced. I knew that as the author but still plowed forward. I knew it would make it hard to read for many people, but I just decided that was the way Igarashi was and went with it. I had no intention of upsetting my readers by writing her like that. Even though she had high expectations for the protagonist, she couldn't be upfront with him and instead ran hot and cold. But even taking that into consideration, Igarashi said and did a lot of awful things to Arihito. The web novel readers were experiencing the hardships and absurdity of corporate life day in and day out, and they went to this website as an escape. But then, for some reason, even the novel had a realistically demonic boss. They questioned why it needed to be that way. And I realized that they were absolutely right.

I had an earnest discussion with my editor about the "Igarashi Problem," and we came to the conclusion that I should make her more sympathetic so readers could forgive her even if she did join the party. That ended up giving me slightly more hope for the book.

I am really quite curious to hear my readers' impressions if they decide to read the web version after finishing this edited and revised one. Regardless, any manager who cuts up someone's time card and makes them work extra hours is out of line. My hope is that the managers of the world can be consistently kinder to their employees. In the web novel, Igarashi did slowly become kinder, so I don't think you'll hate her too much if you decide to read beyond the first volume.

I've come this far writing about Igarashi, but when I asked the wonderful Huuka Kazabana for illustrations, I had in my mind, as the author, a beauty in a knit sweater who could knock the main character's socks off—and there she was. Neither do I have any qualms about her Valkyrie equipment. However, I imagine I might get some comments about whether it'd really be suitable for a serious battle or how the protagonist is able to keep his cool even though he's stuck staring at her rear all day like that. Thank you, Kazabana, for your wonderful designs.

Speaking of design, there's also Theresia the lizardman. I get the impression she's been the most popular heroine among readers ever since it was first published online. I had a lot of really complicated requirements for her design, like she needed to be wearing a "lizard mask" that only showed her mouth, but you still needed to be able to tell she was beautiful. When I saw Kazabana's first sketch of her, it felt like I'd been hit with an electric shock. Was that what Theresia looked like? True, a person like that would be a strange sight, but she was supposed to inspire affection in the protagonist, like he could understand her intentions. This kind of equipment made that all seem just a little more natural. If she had been a lizardman wearing a mask that actually looked like a lizard, it wouldn't matter how much you trusted her; you'd get a nasty shock running into a face like that in the middle of the night. This kind of mask, however, you could really get used to in almost any situation.

I also gave a detailed description of Theresia—for instance, the slit in her armor that extended from her chest to her navel and how some of her black hair was visibly peeking out from under her mask. Every single one of those details was included in the illustration. The result is something really cute with parts that still catch your eye, in my opinion.

The last person on the cover is Elitia. She was perfect from my very first draft; no one brought up any issues about her. I am very grateful to my editor for helping to refine each character. They combed through every detail of the manuscript and pointed out any areas that needed fleshing out, which really helped me make the story a much smoother read. If the readers are also able to feel that, then as a writer, I will never be able to express the true scope of my gratitude to my editor.

As the story continues, Arihito and the others will meet new friends with a variety of different jobs, different people who live in the Labyrinth Country, and more powerful monsters, so the battles will get more intense. The series will continue as they each accomplish their various goals and Arihito eventually becomes *The World's Strongest Rearguard.*

I expressed my gratitude earlier, but I am actually cutting it very close to the deadline as I write this afterword. I would like to offer my sincerest apologies for all the trouble I've caused my editor. I plan to submit all future work as far ahead of schedule as possible.

I would like to extend my thanks once again to Huuka Kazabana for capturing the spirit of the Labyrinth Country and for portraying the characters in such a beautiful and fresh way. The illustrations gave the characters shape and breathed a new life into them, which makes me feel like I need to get them out and going again.

Thanks to the proofreaders who painstakingly combed through the entire text, I was able to identify various inconsistencies, particularly when it came to how the license displayed things. That allowed me to publish something that I wouldn't be ashamed of. Moving forward, I would like to maintain that consistency even in the serialization so that everything reads more easily.

I can never express the depth of my gratitude for the support from all of my readers, from the people who have only just picked up this book to those who have been with me since I first began posting the web novel.

Good-bye for now. I hope we meet again in the next installment.

Tôwa

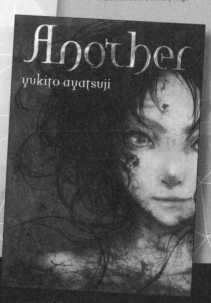